Gabrielle Kimm teaches English and Drama.
This is her first novel.

His Last Duchess

GABRIELLE KIMM

SPHERE

First published in Great Britain in 2010 by Sphere

A CIP catalogue record for this book
is available from the British Library.

ISBN 978-0-7515-4450-3

Typeset in Fournier by M Rules
Printed and bound in Great Britain by
Clays Ltd, St Ives plc

Papers used by Sphere are natural, renewable and
recyclable products sourced from well-managed forests and certified
in accordance with the rules of the Forest Stewardship Council.

Mixed Sources
Product group from well-managed
forests and other controlled sources
www.fsc.org Cert no. SGS-COC-004081
© 1996 Forest Stewardship Council

FSC

Sphere
An imprint of
Little, Brown Book Group
100 Victoria Embankment
London EC4Y 0DY

An Hachette UK Company
www.hachette.co.uk

www.littlebrown.co.uk

For my mother and father — Colette and Peter Kimm —
who inspired me to write in the first place,
and who have provided
unconditional support and encouragement
ever since.

'Desire does not so much transcend its object, as ignore it completely in favour of a fantastic recreation of it.'

Angela Carter

Prologue

He can see no breath. No movement. No life.

It is done.

Pushing his hand beneath the rucked linen of her shift, his fingers touch one small breast: already chill, veined a delicate blue like malleable marble. She is no more than a soft statue. Her cold curves slide comfortably under the warmth of his cupped palm as he runs his hand over her skin, and he wonders at its exquisite unresponsiveness.

Looking down at her, he sees at last the image for which he has longed for so many months. She is beautiful. In this breathless silence she is truly beautiful. The perfect reflection has finally been restored and the glass is again quite flawless.

He imagines his warm flesh contained within her chill stillness and his skin crawls.

He knows he has to do it.

Part One

Villa Cafaggiolo,
Barberino di Mugello, Tuscany
July 1559
Two years earlier

1

A heavy heat had draped itself across the afternoon, pinioning the landscape into shimmering immobility. The great house stood tall, bulky and square, the fortress-like appearance of the walls softened by the ochre of the stone and the bleached red of the pantiled roofs; in the bright light, the deeply arched crenellations of the roofs cast dark blue scoops of shadow all along the length of each wall. Cicadas chirred rhythmically, ceaselessly, falling into and out of time with each other, and a soporific feeling of warm lethargy hung above the castle like a sun-baked blanket.

A door banged open at the back of the house and, with a scream, a young woman burst out into the heat at a scrambling run, her skirts clutched in her fists, her breathing audibly ragged. She threw a glance behind her, gasped and increased her speed.

Another figure ran through the same door in pursuit, his shadow an untidy ink-blot below his thudding feet.

For a moment it seemed as though the cicadas held their breath: the only sounds in the torpid stillness were the panicked footsteps of the girl and the heavier tread of the young man who was fast closing in upon her. She ran along a path between formal beds of flowers and herbs, kicking a frantic way right through one of them, as, with a wordless whimper, she headed for the longer grass by the gates that led to the walled vegetable garden.

He caught up with her and threw himself at her. Locking his arms around her knees, he brought her down. She flung her hands up to protect her face and, as she landed, the wind was knocked out of her with a grunt. Before she had had time even to draw breath, the boy let go of her legs and rolled her onto her back, his fingers gripping her wrists, pressing them into the grass on either side of her head. She struggled, but his hold was too firm. His knees held her hips, his face was no more than a foot above hers. For a wild fraction of a second they held each other's gaze.

'You bastard, Giovanni!' said the girl, coughing out a laugh. 'Get off me!'

'You're just –' said Giovanni, his chest heaving '– just too slow, that's all there is to it. Go on – admit it!'

His fingers still encircled the thin wrists and he leaned his weight more heavily on them as he spoke; despite her continued struggles, the girl could not sit up. She worked spit into her mouth and lifted her head.

Giovanni grinned. 'You wouldn't dare!' he said, but she drew in a long breath through her nose. Giovanni rolled backwards out of her range. 'God, you're disgusting, Lucrezia!' he said.

Lucrezia sat up, spat her mouthful into the grass, then poked her tongue out at him. Giovanni lay flat on his back, his face half-hidden by tangled grass blades; he raised an eyebrow and smirked at her. She kicked out towards him, but he grabbed her foot and, lifting it, tipped her back into the grass, where they both lay sprawled, laughing at nothing.

A distant voice startled them.

'Lucrezia!'

They looked at each other.

'Lucrezia, *cara*, where are you?'

Sighing heavily, Lucrezia said, 'I must go – I should have been back hours ago. Come with me, Vanni.'

The boy jumped up, all long limbs like an eager puppy, and reached out to pull his cousin to her feet. She took his hand and stood, smiling, but, to her surprise, Giovanni did not smile in return. Instead a crooked little frown creased between his brows – he seemed suddenly awkward and ill at ease – and as she watched, he rubbed at his eyes with the heel of his hand, and flushed.

The voice called again.

Lucrezia ran her fingers into her hair and found crusts of earth on her forehead; scratching at it, she examined the dirt now lodged under her nails. She turned her hands over. Her palms were grazed and grass-stained and she had badly torn yet another dress: the great three-cornered rent that hung down across one hip was not the sort of tear anyone would be able to mend. Flapping the ripped corner back and forth, she began walking back towards the house with her cousin.

'Giulietta is going to be angry with me again, Vanni,' she said. 'She thinks I should . . .' Lucrezia's voice deepened and her features pinched into a parody of her nurse's beaky dignity, '. . . behave as befits a Medici heiress, of the *impressive* age of sixteen.' She jutted her chin forward in a scowl and Giovanni's face brightened again.

He grinned at her. 'Poor Giulietta,' he said. 'You're such a disappointment to her.'

Lucrezia gasped. 'Me?' she said. 'You bastard, Giovanni – she thinks *you* are a very bad influence on me, if you must know. It's all your fault.'

'What is?'

Lucrezia thought, then said, 'Everything.'

'You're not wrong,' Giovanni said. He scuffed at the path with one heel.

Lucrezia leaned across and kissed his cheek. 'Come on,' she said, 'run with me.' She began to run; Giovanni caught up easily and together they jogged back through the knot gardens. A strong smell of sun-warmed lavender rose up as Lucrezia's skirts brushed the bushes.

'You've completely destroyed that bed,' Giovanni said, nodding towards a sad mess of trampled plants.

'Your fault.' Lucrezia shrugged. 'Told you everything's your fault.'

Giovanni pushed her and she stumbled into another bed. More crushed herbs. A pungent scent of thyme. Regaining her footing, Lucrezia stretched out her arm to shove back at her cousin, but he dodged out of her reach, running faster now, and disappeared around a corner. The hard-packed stones of the path scrunched under Lucrezia's feet as she followed, passing the wide, castellated archway to the courtyard.

Giulietta stood on the stone steps, dwarfed by the great oak doors. Her lined old features crumpled with disapproval as the two figures ran up to her, barely out of breath. Glancing at Giovanni, Lucrezia saw the corners of his mouth twitch, before he bowed with an ostentatious flourish to Giulietta. The old woman clicked her tongue in annoyance and glared at him. He straightened up and, without a word, ran off towards the stables at a steady lope.

Lucrezia watched him go, then turned to Giulietta, her face stinging with the heat now that she had stopped running. The old woman was grumbling under her breath, though Lucrezia felt sure she was meant to hear every word. Giulietta held out an arm behind the girl's back to shepherd her into the cool gloom of the entrance hall.

'That boy will be the death of me,' she clucked. 'Oh, he is a—' She broke off. 'Every day something else, and you never seem to learn, either of you – and now look at the state of you, and there's the banquet being prepared as we speak, and—'

'Banquet?'

'Yes, *cara*, the banquet. How many times have I told you that it will be tonight? *He*'ll be here by sunset – and just look at you! What sort of a fright are you?'

'Him?' Lucrezia stopped, her eyes wide. 'I had forgotten it was tonight.'

Giulietta swung her round by the shoulders and bent so that their faces were on a level, her eyes bright with concern. With her prominent nose and her close-set eyes, she reminded Lucrezia – as she so often did – of an anxious eagle. Giulietta stroked the tangled hair back from Lucrezia's face. 'Yes, *cara*, him. The duke. It will not be long now, will it, before you are his wife?'

'I must put on clean clothes,' Lucrezia said, and Giulietta held out one of her gnarled hands. Lucrezia took it and then gasped as the hard old fingers squeezed the fresh graze on her palm. She pulled away.

'What is the matter?'

'Nothing.'

But Giulietta had turned the hand upwards and seen for herself. Clicking her tongue again in grumpy disbelief, she nonetheless planted a swift, dry kiss on the graze, turned Lucrezia's hand back over again and patted the knuckles with her other knobbly hand. Together they walked down the vaulted corridor and out into the central courtyard, entering the house again at the far end and climbing the wide staircase that led to the bedchambers.

Inside Lucrezia's chamber, where the shutters were closed against the fierceness of the sun, the light was cool and dim. At the centre of each shutter was a small round hole; a blade of light from each hole sliced diagonally downwards across the room, as slim and straight as a pair of jouster's lances. Lucrezia bent to peer through one of the holes, her hands cupped around her eyes, but the sun was too bright for her to see anything and after a second she screwed her eyes shut and drew back.

'Come here, *cara*, and I'll undo your laces,' Giulietta said.

Blinking, Lucrezia stood with her back to her nurse, and Giulietta started to pick at the knotted fastenings. She began to hum.

'I love that song,' Lucrezia said.

'I've been singing that to you since you were a baby.'

'I wonder if *he* will sing to me when he unfastens my laces,' Lucrezia said, more to herself than to Giulietta. She imagined unfamiliar fingers working unseen at her back, and as she pressed her hands flat onto the stiffened front of her bodice, the skin on the nape of her neck prickled. Would he sing? Would he speak? Would he laugh with her – or would he perhaps prefer to undress his new wife in expectant silence? She pictured in her mind the duke's shadowed eyes and his slow smile and, with a whisper, the dress slid from her and fell to the floor around her feet.

Giulietta paused, but made no comment.

'He's very handsome, isn't he, the duke?' Lucrezia said, stepping out of her skirts. She crossed the room to the small table near the window and picked up a miniature portrait in an elaborate gilt frame.

'He is.'

'And very clever, so Papa says. That's so important, don't you think, Giulietta? I shouldn't want to be married to anyone who wasn't clever.' She put down the little picture, dropped her voice and said with conviction, 'I would never say so to Papa or Mamma, but I really think I should rather be married to somebody poor but clever than to a noble idiot.'

'Well, you are a very fortunate young woman, then,' Giulietta said, 'as your parents seem to have found you an intelligent aristocrat.'

'Who is handsome as well,' Lucrezia said.

'As you say.'

Lucrezia stood in her shift. What would it be like to stand like this in her chemise in front of him? What would he think of her? She imagined his eyes on her and felt a catch behind her nipples. Breathing slowly, she watched the light paint a bright stripe up and across Giulietta's back as the old woman bent over a long, carved chest at the foot of the bed.

'What would you like to wear, *cara*?'

'I think the russet,' Lucrezia said, and Giulietta knelt, pushed her arms under layers of folded fabric and tugged out a richly embroidered, bright brown damask skirt and bodice. Lucrezia crouched down to help her unfold it. She stood then in front of Giulietta, sucking in her breath as the old woman pulled the new dress down over her head and laced it tight.

'Plum sleeves?'

Lucrezia smiled assent. Giulietta opened a smaller oak chest and found two deep reddish-purple silk sleeves. Long laces dangled from the shoulder ends.

'Arm,' Giulietta said absently and Lucrezia stretched out an arm, pale and thin in the gloom. The lawn of the shift showed creamy-white through the slashes in the silk.

'When I'm ready,' Lucrezia said, 'I'll run to the stables and see if Vanni has finished.'

'You will do no such thing, my love.' Giulietta's voice lost its customary warmth. 'He will be in presently and if you go down there you will only get yourself dirty and we will have to change your clothes again.'

'Who will be at the meal tonight?' A deliberate change of subject.

Giulietta considered. 'Well,' she said, 'the duke will bring his party, of course – there will probably be about a dozen of them – and then there's your father and mother and—'

'And Vanni . . .'

'Of course – and I believe your father has asked several dignitaries from Firenze. Other arm, my love.'

'And you – you'll be coming, Giulietta, won't you?'

'No, *cara*, not tonight. I have asked your mother if I might eat quietly up here.'

'Oh, Giulietta, are you unwell?' Lucrezia took the old woman's hands in hers. The second sleeve, still unfastened, drooped from her shoulder.

'No, *cara*, not at all, just a little tired.'

'I'm so sorry.'

'Why do you say that, child?'

Lucrezia pointed at the crumpled dress on the floor at the far side of the chamber. 'I always seem to cause you so much work. I'll pick that up and put it away and—'

Giulietta rubbed the side of her thumb back and forth along the girl's forehead like an episcopal blessing, then patted her cheek. 'You just enjoy this most important occasion, *cara*. I am very happy to be up here quietly on my own. That poor dress is no longer fit for anything but throwing away. Give me your arm, now, and let me finish lacing that sleeve.'

Lucrezia paused, gazing intently at the old woman. Then, a

wrinkle of concern still creased between her brows, she lifted her hand out sideways and said, 'Shall you mind the move very much, Giulietta?'

'The move?'

'To Ferrara. I hope you won't find it too dreadfully tiring.'

Giulietta did not answer. She shifted position and unwittingly moved into the stripe of light from the shutter. It ran down the centre of her face and body, cutting her in two. 'I . . . I will not be coming,' she said.

Lucrezia stared at her.

'Your mother thinks it best you start afresh, with a younger woman to care for you.'

Giulietta's voice was flat, and the finality of the decision was immediately obvious to Lucrezia. 'But—' She felt hot tears behind her eyes, nipped the end of her tongue between her teeth and swallowed a few times before she spoke. 'But . . . I want you to come with me.'

'I know, *cara*.'

'Is it quite certain that—?'

Giulietta nodded.

'But why? And why did nobody tell me until now?'

No reply.

Lucrezia held her breath, unsure whether she wanted to cry or to rage at her nurse. The enormity of the changes that were about to happen to her loomed up, unstoppable and inexorable as a battalion of soldiers on the march, real to her suddenly as they had not been before this moment. She had not even considered the possibility that Giulietta might not come with her to Ferrara. Lucrezia looked at the old woman and saw – perhaps for the first time ever – the infirmity of age. With a pinprick of shock, she imagined the skull beneath the lined skin, the bones within the meagre flesh, and then – as though it was her own pain – felt Giulietta's anticipation of loss as keenly as her own.

She put her arms around her nurse, aware of the old woman's bony stiffness as she held her, and they embraced for a long moment.

Breaking away, and making herself smile at Giulietta, Lucrezia said, with deliberate lightness, 'Where would you like me to put the poor ruined dress?'

Giulietta wiped her eyes with a small square of linen. 'In that old chest by the door. Don't bother to try to fold it, *cara*. It can't be mended.'

Lucrezia gathered the wrecked dress into her arms, went to the big carved box by the door and lifted the lid. Something unexpected caught her eye. 'Oh!' she said. 'Oh, Giulietta, see what I've found in here! I've been wondering where that was – I haven't seen it for months!'

Giovanni scratched his mare's neck and grinned as she puckered her muzzle in pleasure, stretching forward and half-closing her eyes in lazy abandon. He glanced up as a stocky young man of about twenty-five walked into the stableyard, grinning at the pony's expression. 'Likes that, doesn't she?' he said.

'Pietro.' Giovanni nodded a greeting.

Pietro reached out a hand, cupped it beneath the mare's nose and tilted her head towards his face. 'Just like women, mares are – all you have to do is scratch them in the right place and they'll do anything for you,' he said, with an air of authority. Checking to either side to make sure they were alone, he added, 'Spent a fair bit of last night scratching young Maria Fabbro in all the right places.'

'Paolo's daughter?'

Pietro nodded, a smug grin on his face. Giovanni swallowed. An image of the saddler's ripe peach of a daughter pushed into his mind. He caught his breath. He often saw Maria around the stables and each time he did, he found himself thinking rather too much about breasts. His face felt hot.

'Hope her father doesn't find out,' he said. 'I wouldn't give much for your chances if he does.'

Pietro grinned again, hoisted a net of hay over his shoulder and strolled the length of the yard, whistling as he ducked under the low lintel into the feed store.

Giovanni gave his pony a final pat. He began to walk slowly back towards the great house, kicking a single pebble along in front of him, scuffing dust up from the track as he went.

He might well be nearly fifteen, but today everything was conspiring to make him feel like a child. When he had pulled Crezzi to her feet this afternoon, out by the vegetable garden, she had suddenly seemed quite different. So grown-up, even if she was so small and thin, and so *beautiful* – it had made him feel clumsy and stupid. As if his hands and feet were too big and didn't fit him any longer. Normally, the year and a half's difference in their ages was not so noticeable. Then, though, she had pulled that face at him, and she had looked like herself again, and it had been all right. And now Pietro – so confident, telling him about his conquests. Not that last night was much to boast about though – Maria would go with anyone.

As he reached Lucrezia's bedchamber window, he stopped.

'*It's all your fault.*' He heard her voice from this afternoon.

'*What is?*'

'*Everything.*'

He snorted, and called up to her. Waited. Called again.

There was a moment's noisy fumbling with the fastenings, then the two shutters were banged back against the wall. Lucrezia leaned out of the window, face screwed up against the light.

'I'm almost ready,' she said. 'Don't go away.'

Giovanni flicked his head in acknowledgement.

Lucrezia said, 'Is something wrong?'

He shrugged.

'Wait!' She moved back inside. Giovanni stood with his weight on one foot, looking up at the window. After several moments, Lucrezia reappeared with a small straw basket in one hand; a long, rather hairy length of twine was looped over the other. She leaned out, bottom lip caught between her teeth, and began to lower the basket. Giovanni raised his arms as it reached him; he peered inside and, despite his unease, grinned to see a knot of flame-coloured ribbon, twisted into curls like a small orange lily. He picked it out and began to fiddle with it.

'Don't spoil it!' Lucrezia said. She jerked the basket back up, hand over hand. 'It's supposed to be a *favour*. As if you were a knight. I'm . . . I'm practising being a duchess.'

Giovanni gave an exaggerated bow in apology and, head near his knees, heard a soft laugh from above him. He straightened.

'I found my basket again just now in an old chest. Do you remember it?' Lucrezia called.

'Of course.' He tilted his head back to see her better and the sun caught his eyes. He raised a horizontal hand to shade them.

'After Papa was so angry that time – about the roof.'

'I didn't know you still had it.'

'Neither did I. It was a good game, though, wasn't it?'

Giovanni looked back down and fingered the ribbon, remembering how fiercely his buttocks had been stinging, the last time he had taken this basket in his hands. Lucrezia might have been confined to her chamber, but he had been beaten, the day they had both climbed out onto the roof of the castle, stupidly reckless in their search for adventure. It had been her suggestion – she had admitted as much to Uncle Cosimo – but it was *he*, Giovanni, who had been the more soundly punished for it. The injustice still rankled after two years.

Crezzi was right, though: it had been a good game – the only one available to them for the three days of her confinement. He had searched for little treasures, he remembered, and had stolen food from the kitchens, and put it into Crezzi's basket for her to pull back up to her room, and she had sent back silly scribbled messages for him. It all seemed a very long time ago.

'Don't go away,' Lucrezia said. 'I'll be down in a moment.' Her voice sounded thick, as though she had been crying, Giovanni thought, or perhaps more as though she was trying not to cry now. He wondered why.

The shutters were pulled together once more and the noise of the cicadas was loud again as Giovanni sat down with his back against the wall, knees bent, hands hanging loosely over them, turning the knot of orange ribbon over and over in his fingers.

2

The two cousins stood just inside the door of the vaulted kitchen, unnoticed in the steamy chaos of the banquet preparations. Lucrezia's mouth was dry: watching this bustling activity, a fizzing feeling of anticipation was starting to disperse the gloom that Giulietta's news had cast over her. She ran her tongue over her lips, then nudged Giovanni and pointed to a long table. 'Go on, Vanni – take one!' she whispered.

'Why me?'

'Because Angelo likes you more than me, and if he sees you taking it, he won't be as cross as if he sees me.'

'You do know that *this* is why everything is always my fault – because you make me do everything for you.' He sounded cross, but stepped across to the table and took one of a dozen or so large pomegranates from a wooden bowl. He handed it to his cousin. Lucrezia traced around its spiked crown with the tip of her middle finger, lifted it to her nose, then pushed a thumbnail down into the skin, making a small crescent-shaped hole. Picking with one finger, she chipped away at it, revealing a round patch of gleaming, pinky-red seeds, then she hooked a few out and dropped them into Giovanni's outstretched hand. He grinned at her and lifted his palm to his mouth. She scraped out a few more for herself.

They stood for a while, eating their pomegranate seeds, watching and listening.

The great grey stone hood of the furnace stood scorched and glistening above the flames. Smoke wisped and curled out around the jut of the stone, as if, Lucrezia thought, from the mouth of a drowsy dragon; it glowed blue as it tendrilled up into a shaft of light from a high window. The fire was fierce and the three men tending it seemed blurred at the edges, sketched in bold slashes of orange and darkest blue. One of them leaned back from the heat and wiped sweat from his face, grimacing. Up in the eaves, linen-wrapped joints of meat hung from racks, kippering in the billows; an unsettling suggestion of the gallows hung about them as they dangled from their wicked iron hooks. And, at the far end of the room, two squat oak barrels stood open under a window. Lucrezia shuddered. The surface of the liquid within them was seething. She tugged at Giovanni's sleeve and pointed. 'Eels,' she said, pulling a face.

'What about the swans, then?' Giovanni said. He gestured towards another long table. Plates, dishes and tall pots were stacked at one end, huge bowls of fruit and piles of peeled vegetables stood ranked in the middle, then came mounds of artichokes, orange and pink squashes and a colourful majolica bowl full of green beans. At the end, near to where the two cousins stood, lay the limp bodies of a pair of enormous swans. They lay sadly side by side, their slender necks crumpled and lifeless. One head hung heavily, blank eyes staring at the floor.

Lucrezia crossed to them and touched one with the tip of a finger. The flesh felt chill, like unbaked clay, beneath the velvet feathers. Swans mate for life, she thought. Had these two died together, their lifelong partnership continuing into death, or was their proximity here coincidental? Did two other swans now mourn the loss of their mates as they swam alone on unknown waters?

She turned from the swans and saw on yet another table a startling array of sculptures, carved from what she knew from other occasions was sugar. Poking Giovanni in the ribs, she pointed at the display.

'Aren't those—' he began.

She interrupted him. 'Copies of Papa's favourites? Yes. The ones from the back courtyard. Aren't they lovely?'

Giovanni rubbed at one of the sculptures with two fingers, then put the fingers into his mouth. 'Mmn. You're right. They're lovely,' he said.

'Don't, Vanni! If Angelo sees you, he'll kill you!'

Giovanni snorted, then rubbed the damp fingers back over the carved backside of the simpering sugar nymph. Sucked them again. Smiled.

'You're disgusting!'

Giovanni opened his mouth to retort, but before he could say anything, a scream startled them both. They swung round.

Lucrezia gasped.

The moment hung frozen.

The chaos of the kitchen was a painted tableau, a silent second, hanging suspended and motionless.

A kitchen girl, one hand wrapped in sacking, was grimacing with pain as boiling water from the huge pan she had been struggling to move out of the embers slopped out in a glittering lump across her wrist. The sacking she had shaken from that hand had fallen into the flames beneath the pan and caught alight, flaring brightly, underlighting her distorted face. Though few in the kitchen seemed to have noticed what had happened, the three cooks had turned from the furnace as one, and were gaping at the girl, identical shock on each face. One of them held a dripping ladle; soft gobbets of soup fell to the floor around his feet.

Lucrezia was transfixed.

And then noise surged back through the room and the scream became a panting whimper; the girl stumbled backwards, burned hand held out and back, her other hand snatching her heavy skirts away from the flaming sacking. In a sudden panic at the inactivity, Lucrezia ran forward and stopped in front of the girl. 'Quick! Hurry! You must put it into cold water!' She reached for and held the unharmed hand, but the girl gasped, trying to snatch it back out of Lucrezia's grasp. Lucrezia, however, held fast. 'No! Come with me – you have to – Vanni, where is the nearest water?'

Giovanni was hovering anxiously near the door. She said again, 'Where? Where should we go, Vanni?'

'The well in the outer courtyard?'

'No – too far.'

And then an idea occurred to her, though her insides shrivelled at the thought. She held the kitchen girl's good arm and pulled her through the bustle of the kitchen into the shadows at the furthest end. 'Come *on*,' she said. 'This way.'

They stopped in front of the two squat oak barrels. A nauseous lump rose in Lucrezia's throat as she watched the slimy tangle twisting and writhing below the surface.

'Put your arm in here. They won't hurt you and the water is cold.'

With a whimper, the girl shrank back, twisting her arm to try to free her hand from Lucrezia's grasp. The scalded arm she held up against her chest.

'I'll put mine in with yours,' Lucrezia said and, gritting her teeth, she took the girl's red, angry arm by the fingers, shut her eyes and plunged both their arms down into the barrel before the girl had a chance to fight against her.

The water was thick, opaque and slimy, and the eels slid around each other in silky knots. Lucrezia's sleeve covered most of her arm, but they slithered horribly around her hand; she felt the occasional graze of unspeakable sharp teeth, though nothing that really hurt. The girl's fingers were tense and stiff and she was pulling hard against Lucrezia's grip, breathing in shallow gasps through an open mouth, her eyes huge and dark as she stared into the seething barrel.

'How does it feel now?' Lucrezia said. They were pressed together, so close she could feel the girl's hair against her neck. She smiled, but the girl did not smile in return.

After a few more moments, Lucrezia said, 'Perhaps it has been in the water long enough now. My hand's frozen. Let's see.'

She pulled her arm out of the barrel, letting go of the girl's fingers. The plum-coloured silk sleeve was a sodden dark brown to a line above her elbow and clung to her like a second skin, glistening with the eels' slime. Thick droplets fell from it, staining the russet skirt, so Lucrezia bent forward and held her arm out to the side. With her other hand, she picked at the laces on her shoulder, then, lips squared with disgust, she peeled the soaked sleeve over her hand and off. Holding it away from her in both hands, she squeezed it out, and more viscous drops splattered onto the dusty floor.

The kitchen girl began to examine her scald. The red stain was less vivid, and beads of glistening water clung to the hairs that stood up through the red on her thin wrist. She gingerly touched the place with a trembling finger, then raised her eyes to Lucrezia. 'It is a little better,' she said. 'Thank you, Signorina. You did not have to do that for me.'

Lucrezia saw the girl eyeing the russet dress, jewelled and beautiful – now stained with eel-slime. She watched her take in her bare arm, and the crushed and sodden sleeve in her hand, and wondered what she was thinking. How did she see her? As a benevolent, compassionate young noblewoman, prepared to sacrifice part of her sumptuous wardrobe to aid a stricken castle drudge? As a silly girl, dressed like a duchess but reckless and babyish, spoiling her fine clothes on a whim? Or, worse still, as nothing more than an interfering busybody?

She opened her mouth, trying to think of something to say that might reassure both the girl – who looked frightened – and herself, but before she could utter a word, an angry yell cut through the buffeting background noise of the kitchen, making her jump.

'What are you playing at, Catelina, you lazy trollop? Get back here! That accursed pan will have boiled dry by the time you've finished your pointless prattling!' The enormous and corpulent Signor Angelo, hands on hips, mouth like a rectangular hole in his unbaked loaf of a face, was glaring at them from the far side of the kitchen. 'And you – you two children!' He flapped a hand. 'Get out of here – before I call for the Signora!'

'Come on!' muttered Giovanni. He jerked his head towards the door. Lucrezia began to move with him, but saw as she did so that the part-eaten pomegranate still sat on the long table where she had dropped it. She picked it up, smiled at Catelina and threw her the fruit. Then she and Giovanni slipped out through the narrow kitchen door. Catelina caught the pomegranate one-handed and waved it at Lucrezia in shy farewell.

'Oh, for heaven's *sake*!' Giulietta stared in disbelief. 'Not much more than half an *hour*! Can you not stay clean and tidy for more than five *minutes*? What is *wrong* with you?' She paused, her pulse thudding uncomfortably in her ears. 'Come here!'

Lucrezia began to cross the room.

'And you can give me *that* for a start!' Giulietta added crossly, snatching the sodden lump of silk from Lucrezia's hand. She flapped it out and held it up, clicking her tongue.

'I'm sorry, Giulietta, I truly am, but if you had seen—'

Giulietta raised her hands, palms forward, to silence her. 'Don't tell me! Don't speak! I don't want to hear it. Is it any wonder I am not coming with you to Ferrara? Much more of this and you really will be the death of me.'

She unfastened the strings of the clean sleeve and pulled it from Lucrezia's arm with one sharp tug. 'You can find another pair for yourself, my girl. I am *not* getting down on my knees a third time for you today. Any new waiting-woman you choose to come to Ferrara with you had better be warned that she should expect to lead a *very* difficult life.'

Lucrezia said nothing, but Giulietta watched her go to the smaller of the two chests, and kneel in front of it. Lifting the lid, she rummaged inside, then sat back on her heels, a pair of ember-orange sleeves in one hand. Wordlessly, she handed them to her nurse.

Lucrezia clicked a handful of walnuts in her pocket, rolling them over each other between her fingers. 'I wouldn't have been surprised if she had slapped me, Vanni – she was *so* angry.'

Giovanni shrugged.

'She simply wouldn't listen to a word I had to say – I tried to explain that I—'

'Do you want an apricot?' Giovanni said. 'My pockets are too full.'

Irritation tightened like a band around Lucrezia's head. After her scolding from her nurse, she badly wanted to pour out her frustration at the injustice of Giulietta's anger; she wanted Giovanni to champion her, to agree that what she had done this afternoon had been entirely selfless, and not the 'rash action of a thoughtless baby', as Giulietta had so vehemently assured her it was. The distress she had felt at the thought of losing her nurse was now coupled with relief that she would be escaping the old woman's relentless iron grip for the first time in her life.

She took the apricot Giovanni held out, but, rather than eat it, she put it into her pocket.

The two cousins stood in the shadows of a corridor, peering around the open door of a long, wooden-ceilinged hall, down the middle of which stood a great pathway of a table. Its polished surface was now hidden by draped and layered linen, plates and glasses, flowers, fruit, candles and ribbons – enough for at least thirty diners.

At the far end of the room, her mother and father were giving final orders to the servants who would be welcoming in the party from Ferrara. She imagined the bustling arrival of the duke and his retinue, and her irritation faded.

'Aunt Eleanora looks beautiful,' Giovanni said. Lucrezia's mother was dressed in deep blue damask; the sleeves, slashed many times, showed little puffs of gold, and, as she raised an arm to point across to one of the windows, a glitter of tiny pearls caught the light from the torches blazing in their brackets on the walls. Even from her vantage-point in the corridor, Lucrezia could hear the soft whisper of the blue silk skirts as Eleanora de' Medici moved.

She watched her mother's gaze wandering over the flowers, which tumbled down the walls like many-hued waterfalls, over the four huge bay trees, standing sentinel at each corner of the hall, over the deep red, white and green silk hangings that trembled in the breeze where they hung between the windows. Those, Lucrezia knew, were the Este colours – her mother must have chosen them to please her prestigious guest. She, Lucrezia, was the ultimate prize that awaited the duke, she supposed, but her mother was making sure that the gift was well wrapped.

She watched as her mother spoke to her father, gazing up into his face as though seeking reassurance. He put big hands on his wife's shoulders and smiled down at her, then laid a palm against her cheek. Lucrezia swallowed, sure they were discussing her, anxious suddenly at what appeared to be her mother's unease.

'Come on, let's go before they see us,' Giovanni said. He took Lucrezia's hand. She turned away, lip caught between her teeth, and they walked the length of the corridor and out onto an open balcony, which overlooked the central courtyard.

'They'll have to come through here, won't they?' Giovanni said. He sat down on the tiled floor between two large terracotta pots of clipped box. He fished in his pocket, brought out a couple of walnuts and cracked them together in his hands.

Lucrezia nodded and sat down next to him.

'So if we just wait here, we'll see them.'

Another nod. Giovanni held the crushed walnuts in one palm; he picked out the kernels and threw the shells over his shoulder. Lucrezia, meanwhile, retrieved the apricot and held its velvety skin to her closed lips. Fragments of images and nonsensical broken sentences danced through her mind as she smelt the warm, summer-sweet fruit; her eyes slid out of focus and, as she pressed her forehead against the iron bars of the balustrade, she could feel her body moving infinitesimally with her pulse-beat.

A sudden clatter of hoofs and wheels, and sharp voices calling for immediate action made her start. Giovanni scrambled to his knees, walnut shells scattering untidily around him.

'They're here, Crezzi,' he said.

They folded their arms on the balustrade, chins resting on their hands, looking, Lucrezia imagined, like a pair of eager gargoyles. She still held the apricot, now hot and damp, in one hand.

The heavy doors from the entrance hall slammed open. Some half-dozen Cafaggiolo servants backed out into the sunshine. Lucrezia saw her mother and father, walking arm in arm; both were smiling at a tall man dressed in black, who strode beside them.

'That's him, isn't it?' Giovanni whispered.

The duke was looking around the courtyard. He took off his feathered cap and coat as he walked and handed them to a young man just behind him. Beneath the coat, his clothes were very plain, and simple in their cut. His presence was impressive enough, Lucrezia thought; he did not need to resort to ribbons and slashes to make an impact. He was taller than she remembered, but she had not in the least degree forgotten the dark, slow-blinking eyes.

A black-brindled dog loped at his side – a tall, rough-coated creature with a long, thin tail. Lucrezia's eyes widened at its height. The duke's hand was resting on the dog's head as they walked – and his elbow was bent.

Lucrezia watched the newcomer as he crossed the courtyard with the rest of the party. He was taking in every detail of his surroundings, it seemed, until suddenly he raised his eyes to the balcony and his gaze met hers. He stopped speaking. Lucrezia dropped the apricot she was holding. It rolled through the balustrade and fell to the ground, landing on the flags with a soft splat not six feet from where the little party was standing. The dog growled softly, but the ghost of a smile flickered across the duke's face. Lucrezia's cheeks burned. The duke made no other sign that he had seen either her or the apricot, but resumed his conversation with her father and mother.

As the party reached the far side of the courtyard, her father turned back and glared at her.

'You do promise you'll come straight down, now, Signorina?' Her mother's youngest waiting-woman shifted her weight from one foot to the other. Awkward and embarrassed, the girl added, with ill-thought-out honesty, 'Only my lady said I was not to go until I had seen you actually start moving.' She hesitated. 'They are all waiting for you.'

Giulietta opened her mouth, but Giovanni said quickly, 'Don't worry – I'll make her hurry.'

The girl bobbed a curtsy, flushed as Giovanni smiled at her, then disappeared.

'How do I look?' Lucrezia said.

'Quite lovely, *cara*,' Giulietta said, giving her a kiss on the cheek.

'Vanni?'

Giovanni considered. The rude, unthinking response he would usually have offered seemed inappropriate in the face of his cousin's startlingly unfamiliar appearance: she was like a beautiful stranger. He decided upon the truth. 'You do look lovely,' he said, feeling foolish.

Lucrezia smiled, bottom lip caught between her teeth. She kissed Giulietta and left the bedchamber, and went along the corridor that led to the main staircase. Giovanni followed, caught up with her quickly and walked by her side. His arms seemed to belong to someone else – he felt irritated by their swinging.

A new and uncomfortable image had pushed its way into his mind earlier that afternoon. He could not get rid of it, although it embarrassed him very much that it was there. Somehow it was acceptable when it was Pietro, with Fabbro's whore of a daughter; it was positively entertaining when it was himself with – well, he did not know who it might be, in the end – but to think of Crezzi and – and that man! Giovanni shuddered. He felt a hot buzz of shame in his belly to be thinking such things, but the image was insistent.

He did not really understand why it was that he felt so uncomfortable about it. It was not simply what Crezzi said – that he seemed to think about, well, the activities of the bedchamber more than anything else, these days. No. There was just something about *him* that made Giovanni feel like a dog, nose to nose with an enemy – hackles up, ears back, growling, shoulders hunched. In fact, when they had been introduced a few hours before, the hair on his arms had actually prickled. He could not explain it, but he just knew that he did not like the duke.

'Do you remember that day we put cloaks and hats on all the statues in the *loggia*, Vanni?' Lucrezia interrupted his reverie.

'How could I forget? I had another whacking for that, didn't I?'

Suddenly Lucrezia stopped. They had reached the doorway to the courtyard. 'Oh, *cielo*! There they all are,' she whispered.

Aunt Eleanora, Uncle Cosimo and a few of their friends, whom

Giovanni vaguely knew, were standing out in the *loggia*. With them were some ten or so men he had never seen before and several of Aunt Eleanora's waiting-women. And, there, deep in conversation with Uncle Cosimo, was the tall man in black. Curled at his feet, tail thumping occasionally on the stone flags, lay the great brindled dog.

Lucrezia walked outside and the sun gleamed on her hair so that it shone like copper. Like one of the statues come to life, Giovanni thought. Conversation died. She stopped in front of the duke and sank into a deep curtsy, head bowed, dress crumpled around her on the floor, and then she turned her face up to his, still sunk in the curtsy. He held out a hand, which Lucrezia took in hers.

From where he was standing, Giovanni could not see whether his cousin was smiling, but the tall figure in the black doublet certainly was.

Giovanni's hands tensed into fists. With one disgusted glance, he turned away and walked back into the darkness of the corridor.

3

The wolfhound scrabbled up to standing, its claws scraping on the stone flags; it shook itself and a shudder ran from nose-tip to tail. It crossed the *loggia* to where its master sat deep in conversation and pushed its muzzle up and under his hand. Without breaking off from what he was saying, the duke began to fondle the dog's great head, stroking around its muzzle and up behind its ears. The dog leaned heavily against the side of the chair and the long tail swung.

'No, you're right,' the duke said. 'It has been – what? just over three months – since Cateau-Cambrésis, has it not? And despite all the dire warnings that followed the signing of that appalling treaty, I have to admit that I haven't noticed any overt French interference.'

Cosimo de' Medici nodded. 'But I think you have been lucky in Ferrara, Este. Here in Tuscany we are fast becoming almost entirely hidebound by objectionable "interference" at every turn.'

'Who knows what will happen, though, now Henri is dead?' said Este.

De' Medici sighed. 'I have to admit that I'm relieved he's gone:

his influence in Spain and England was rather too . . . *colourful* for my liking – but to die like that! What a pointless way to go!' He grimaced.

Este said nothing. His skin crawled as he pictured the scene: the late French king, pierced through the eye by a shard from a jouster's shattered lance. In through an eye and out through an ear, they had said. 'Yes. Quite horrible,' he said quietly.

Then de' Medici's frown cleared – so quickly it was almost comical, Este thought.

'But to happier things,' his host said, now positively beaming. 'How *entirely* satisfactory to think that by our forthcoming alliance we will be thwarting – even in the smallest degree – this infernal imposition of bloody French hegemony!'

'It is certainly an unadulterated pleasure to be taking such a step, sir.' Este inclined his head. This was not an exaggeration. He saw in his mind the slight figure of his future duchess, gazing up shining-eyed from the depths of her graceful curtsy, earlier that afternoon. The sun had flamed in her hair, her skirts had billowed around her as though she was bathing in them, and a small spot of colour had risen on each cheek. It had been an arresting sight. Lucrezia's was not a traditional beauty, he thought: her figure was unformed and boyish, but she had a certain naïve, elfin, freckled sweetness about her, which – though of course quite unlike Francesca's sybaritic voluptuousness – was nonetheless charming.

Lucrezia's inexperience was obvious.

Este felt a moment's unease at this thought, remembering the exuberance of his most recent wild coupling with Francesca. His hedonistic whore, he thought, positively encouraged him in his more abandoned pursuits, but until now, he realized, he had never lain with a virgin – had never been given the opportunity to discover the pleasures of cracking through unblemished perfection, making his mark upon untouched territory. He imagined the sensation and, feeling himself stiffen, shifted position in his chair.

'Lost in thought, eh, Este?' Cosimo de' Medici's voice punched into his mind like a fist. 'Contemplating the future delights of marriage, perhaps? Why don't we walk before we go in to eat? The women will be down soon and no doubt we shall be bidden to the table before long.'

Alfonso d'Este stood up. The dog stretched and wagged its tail as it, too, got to its feet. Cosimo de' Medici held out an arm, gesturing away from the statue-filled *loggia* towards the knot gardens. The two men walked slowly along the narrow paths, and the smells of the sun-baked lavender, basil and thyme were heavy in Alfonso's nostrils. One of the beds was crushed and its clipped-box edging flattened and broken. The wolfhound dropped an inquisitive nose to the wreckage, but Alfonso snapped his fingers. 'Folletto!' he hissed. 'Here! Leave it!'

'Oh, let him explore!' Cosimo de' Medici said cheerfully. 'No idea what happened to that poor bed, but the dog cannot make it worse than it is already. I'll tell the gardener tomorrow. It will certainly need fixing before – oh, we have been summoned!'

Lucrezia shifted her weight a little onto one buttock, and ran a flattened palm under her thigh, easing out a crease in her skirts. The noise from the thirty or so diners was considerable: the insistent clatter of conversation punctuated by the sharp scraping of cutlery and the clinking of glass.

She glanced down the length of the table. Right in the centre lay the two great roasted swans, re-feathered, stiffened necks twined together in what now seemed to Lucrezia little more than a miserable parody of courtship. Plate after plate was pyramid-piled with fruit, vegetables, sweetmeats and oysters, and drooping sprays of flowers fell on, over, behind and around the displays.

A quartet of musicians stopped playing, and a cackling troupe of dancing dwarfs bowed to the assembly and ran from the room. Lucrezia watched them leave, without enthusiasm. She had never liked them, though she knew they were favourites with her parents. They unnerved her: their oddly proportioned legs were comical, their steps too quick and short for an adult, but too heavy for a child.

'Your father has gone to a great deal of trouble and expense, Signorina,' the duke said.

'He has simply made sure that the banquet is fit for the occasion, sir.'

The duke inclined his head.

'You must attend so many feasts and banquets,' Lucrezia went on, 'that it must be difficult to remember one from another after a while.'

'Some remain in the memory longer than others.'

Her face hot, Lucrezia looked down at her plate. Eels. She flicked a glance at Giovanni and smothered a laugh. The duke looked at her curiously. 'The eels amuse you?'

'It's nothing, Signore – something that happened this morning. Nothing of any importance.' Her cheeks were flaming now. The duke drew a short breath, as though about to speak, but before he had uttered a word, a booming voice to his right said: 'These eels are from your marshes in Comacchio, Este – absolutely the best in Italy.'

Cosimo de' Medici's face was split in a broad smile; as he caught Lucrezia's eye, he winked. Loud and cheerful as ever, he continued: 'You are indeed fortunate to have the lands around the Po in the Duchy of Ferrara – an exceptionally productive part of the country, Este, exceptionally productive!'

'I have excellent men managing the area.'

'And it has been a good summer so far, too.'

Servants in bright livery appeared through several doors; they bustled around the table, took away the eels and cleared the used glass and silver, creating space along the length of the table. Guests turned towards the end of the hall expectantly, as the musicians began again. This time, their music was haunting and plaintive, and filled the room with a sweetness that Lucrezia felt sure was supposed to reflect the grace of the swans 'swimming' along the flower-strewn table. Poor things, she thought.

The guests applauded and the head carver set to work.

'His name is Girolamo Tagliente,' Lucrezia said to the duke. 'He was only promoted to head carver last year, but he's been with us since I was little, both here and back in Firenze.'

The duke was watching Tagliente and seemed, Lucrezia was pleased to see, at least a little impressed.

'He was always someone with whom we felt safe begging for titbits when we were small,' she said, and the duke smiled.

'Our head carver in Ferrara has a ferocious reputation,' he said, 'though I am not entirely sure from where it sprang, originally. His temper, so I have been told repeatedly, is legendary – but I have never actually known him to lose it. As is so often the case with legend, it seems, the facts rarely live up to the fiction.'

Lucrezia said, 'You would have to treat someone with great respect, though, wouldn't you, if they had both a reputation for ferocity and an impressive skill with a knife?'

The duke laughed. 'You would indeed!' he said, and his gaze slid from her eyes to her mouth and back. Her words and his appreciative laughter sounded again in her head; she caught her lip between her teeth to stop her smile becoming too broad.

'Thinking of our head carver,' the duke went on, 'we entertain frequently in Ferrara. At this time of year, we often eat outside in the central courtyard. Torchlit, it can be most attractive, and if we are lucky enough to dine at a full moon, it can be quite enchanting.'

'I look forward very much to seeing the castle and its grounds, Signore.'

'And the household holds its collective breath, awaiting your arrival,' the duke said with a slow smile. Lucrezia held his gaze. He blinked slowly at her, almost lazily, and Lucrezia looked down at her hands.

There was a long pause. The silence, Lucrezia thought, bulged between them, threatening to burst like an overfilled wineskin.

After a moment the duke said, 'I must thank you for my tour of the house – you have a most refreshing set of opinions on your father's collection, Signorina.'

'Papa loves his paintings, and – I think particularly – his sculptures, Signore,' Lucrezia said. 'Perhaps his enthusiasm is infectious – I've always enjoyed them too.' She glanced towards her father, who was engrossed now in conversation with a tiny woman to his left; although reassured that he was not listening, Lucrezia nonetheless dropped her voice. The duke bent towards her, his eyebrows raised, and Lucrezia felt her heart race at his closeness. She said, in little more than a whisper, 'He has told all of us about each piece so often that I would be a poor student indeed if, after such frequent repetition, I did not remember at least *some* of the details.'

She expected a smile, but to her dismay, the duke's eyes were suddenly cold. Unsure of what she had done to offend him, she began to fiddle her food with her fork, but her throat seemed to have swollen and her appetite had quite disappeared. The duke turned away from her and began to speak again to her father.

Lucrezia ate little of the meats that followed the eels and only

34

picked at the salads – the broad beans and Parmesan cheese, which she liked very much, but somehow no longer felt like eating. ('Damned peasant food that the nobility like to think illustrates their *broad-mindedness*!' she remembered Angelo the cook sneering, last time her mother had requested the dish.)

The duke – and his dog – seemed happy with their meal: the great wolfhound sat pressed against its master, their heads almost level. From time to time, it would rest its muzzle upon the linen table covering, and stare at its master's plate, the fringes of hair over each eye twitching as it watched the progress of each mouthful of food. The duke seemed to enjoy passing titbits to his pet, and they both appeared pleased by what they ate.

Lucrezia picked up a piece of bread and began to shred it. The soft crumbs scattered across the table and onto her lap. What could it have been in her remarks that had so quickly discomposed him? Perhaps what she had intended as no more than an affectionate mockery of her much-loved parent had been interpreted by Signor d'Este as disrespect. Glancing sideways at the duke, she saw that he was still talking earnestly to her father, both hands held up before him in emphasis.

'. . . and to my mind it is unaccountable that such a reaction should even have been *tolerated*, let alone encouraged,' he was saying.

'Oh, I could not agree more, Este!' she heard her father say in reply. 'In fifty-six, if you remember, just after the abdication, it was just the same when Charles's opponents attempted to interfere.'

'Indeed it was.'

Lucrezia listened to the political discussion with little understanding, her eyes upon the duke's mouth. Within weeks, she thought, running the tip of her tongue over her teeth, she would know the feel and taste of that mouth, would have been caressed by those hands. How easy would this man be to please? Or perhaps, given his reaction to her just now, perhaps the question would best be phrased: how easy would he be to *displease*?

Most of the guests had left: the insistent blare of voices that had so vividly filled the evening had died to a rumble, and now only a few sporadic conversations still held sway in the statuary-filled *loggia* behind the great house of Cafaggiolo. The scratching buzz of the late-evening crickets zigzagged up and over the dome of the star-filled sky.

Alfonso d'Este raised Lucrezia's hand to his lips and kissed her knuckles. 'Thank you for your company at dinner,' he said, still holding her fingers. 'I shall look forward very much to seeing you in the morning.'

He watched a faint flush bring colour to her cheeks as she smiled at him, her eyes shining. Gold lights flickered in her hair in the lamplight. She was very pretty, he thought. He wanted to look at her breasts – he could see the square neck of the rust-coloured dress rising and falling as she breathed, and it pulled like a kite-string at his concentration – but he would not let himself do it. To be seen so doing would be shamefully undignified.

'Perhaps you would care to see something of the land around the castle tomorrow, Signore,' Lucrezia said.

Alfonso felt the smallest of pulse beats in her fingertips. He said, smiling, 'I should be more than delighted to explore the country-side that has been your home for so many years.' Then, giving her fingers a brief squeeze, he released her hand.

To his left, he saw Eleanora de' Medici watching their conversation. Her eyes were wide and black in the lamplight; she seemed, more than anything else, he thought in surprise, *wary*. Suspicious.

Catching his eye, she started, and smiled, though the smile seemed uncomfortable and lasted barely a second.

Her husband, arm draped across her shoulder, patted her on the back and said, in a carrying voice, 'Well, Eleanora, *carissima,* it is time our honoured guests were offered the respite of a bed.' Snapping his fingers a few times, he summoned a number of servants from shadowed corners. Striding ahead of them, he stopped before Alfonso and nodded briefly. 'Sir, it has been a great pleasure to have your company this evening. I do hope you have enjoyed yourself. I trust that your sleeping arrangements will suit you, and that you will have a restful night.'

'I have been charmed by the experience,' Alfonso said. He glanced at Lucrezia, who dropped her gaze to the floor, then looked up at him through her lashes. Alfonso arched an eyebrow at her. She twitched down a smile.

A few moments later, accompanied by a bright-liveried manservant, Alfonso climbed the three flights of stairs which led to his allotted suite. Assuring the anxious servant several times that he was more than adequately provided for, and finally bidding him good night, he closed the door of the chamber, crossed the room in a few long-legged strides, pulled back the bed-hangings and sat down on the edge of the mattress.

The shutters were still open; a thin moon like a wide smile hung low and yellow in the night sky.

Alfonso lay back and closed his eyes. Apart from the increasingly sporadic chirrups from the crickets outside, all was silent. He ran both palms up and over his face, pressing the heels of his hands onto his eyes; flickering patterns of light and dark erupted beneath the pressure and his thoughts, surprisingly calm for most of the day, exploded into their usual clamouring confusion.

In through an eye and out through an ear . . . like a child unable to resist picking at a scab, he returned to this horrible image yet again: the moment at which, a fortnight before, the resisting firmness of King Henri's eye had given way and the wooden shard had pushed inexorably through into the softness within. He imagined, with a nauseous squirm of the guts, the white-hot, panicked agony of it. The speed and the sharpness. Sharp. *You would have to respect someone, wouldn't you, with a reputation for ferocity and an impressive skill with a knife?* She seemed, he thought, to have a modicum of a sense of humour, which was to be encouraged, though somewhat to his disquiet, this appeared to be allied with an unsettling and disrespectful tendency towards independence. That must be contained. How best to do it, though? The image he was beginning to build of his perfect duchess had to be maintained. How would this child compare with his whore? Would she – could she – be happy to accept from him what Francesca so energetically enjoyed? Would she be as accommodating as his pleasure-loving wanton with her ripe-peach breasts and that backside that would make Aphrodite weep? What was it Francesca had said? *Shall I be redundant now, after your marriage? Will you still need me?* Would he? Would he need Francesca once he had this girl in his bed? Once the resisting firmness of Lucrezia's maidenhood had given way and he had pushed inexorably through into the softness within? Inexorable. Exceptionally inexorable. *Exceptionally productive, Este, exceptionally productive.* Would Lucrezia be so? An heir was imperative, after all. Imperative.

Alfonso's thoughts climbed over each other, frantic to reach the top of the pile; the images that accompanied them danced ever more frenetically, and snatches of music from the evening's meal wove their way in and around it all. Alfonso gripped his skull with his fingers. 'Stop it!' he said aloud.

The wolfhound shifted in its sleep at the sound of its master's voice.

He made himself breathe slowly. He would walk through the maze again. Taking himself on the familiar journey through the ill-lit, tortuous passages in his mind, he would concentrate on counting his footsteps as he moved slowly through the darkness towards the inevitable final door. He would not go through, though. Could not. He would wait outside it, looking at it, leaning against it, knowing what lay on the other side, both entranced and repelled by his awareness of what he wanted, but needing the respite from the chaos.

'Will you stop this, Eleanora – I simply cannot understand why you are making such a fuss.' Cosimo de' Medici pulled the sheets up to his chest and jerked the bed-hangings shut. 'The man is obviously cultured and intelligent – his opinions on the Ghiberti bronze panel—'

'Oh, Cosimo! I simply couldn't care a *fig* if he knows everything there is to know about every artist in Italy,' Eleanora snapped. She glared at her husband. 'You've been refusing to listen to my worries ever since you first suggested this alliance, and now that it has gone too far to retract—'

'Why on earth would I want to retract?'

Eleanora felt a shout of frustrated anxiety fist itself in her throat. 'Because I don't think this marriage is going to make her happy. That's why.' She flung back the bedcovers, flapped aside the hangings on her side of the bed, swung her legs out and stood up.

Her husband's normally cheerful face, now creased with incomprehension, peered through the hangings after her. 'What in heaven's name do you mean?'

'She's too young.' A heavy stress on each of the three syllables.

Cosimo was angry now. He climbed out of bed. 'Nonsense! Sixteen is a perfectly acceptable age to—'

'I don't *care* about acceptability! Quite apart from the fact that I've told you a dozen times or more that the average age for a bride – even in *Firenze* – is now seventeen or eighteen, I'm not talking about acceptability or averages! I'm talking about our daughter.'

'And so am I! What else is this about?'

'What else? I'll tell you what else it's about! It's about your blinkered determination to maintain the "continuance of the Medici superiority" at whatever cost . . . and your desperation to make your personal mark upon the annals of history and—'

'Oh, no, no, no! You go too far!'

A sudden pause.

'Do I?' Eleanora deliberately dropped her voice to just above a whisper. As she had intended, it wrongfooted her husband: he gulped back the shouted retort he had obviously been on the point of hurling at her, breathing heavily, as if he had been running for some time.

After another pause, Cosimo said, clearly making an effort to sound calm and concerned, 'Very well. Tell me then, *cara*, what is troubling you?'

Feeling tears behind her eyes now, Eleanora struggled to keep her voice from trembling. 'I don't know, Cosimo. I don't know. If I tell you it is a mother's instinct, you will tell me I am being foolish.'

'You are being foolish.'

'I know that I have no reason to feel like this. But . . .'

'Come here,' Cosimo said. He held out his arms to her, but she remained where she was, her gaze fixed upon his. He walked over to her and hugged her, pinning her unresponsive arms inside his embrace. He spoke into her hair, and she felt his words buzz against her scalp. 'Of course you are anxious. She's your baby, your little girl, the little lark you have kept safe in a comfortable cage for sixteen years. And you are just about to open its door and tell her to fly free. Of course you feel anxious. You have been a good mother – but, Eleanora, he is a good man. He will take care of her. Trust him.'

Eleanora imagined her lark flying from one cage straight into another, and said nothing.

Lucrezia rolled over to the edge of her bed, tangling herself in her sheet, and turned onto her back across the width of the mattress. The muffled sound of raised voices she had heard from her parents' room had stopped. She stretched her arms above her head and leaned backwards so that she could see her room upside-down; her hands hung down and she touched the wooden floor. Her hair lay tangled around her fingers. She watched the sky through the inverted window for a moment, enjoying the sensation of pressure in her face, then rolled back onto her stomach. The sheet became even more tangled until, after a brief struggle, she kicked it to the end of the bed.

She pulled off her shift and walked to the window. A welcome breeze blew cool on her sweat-damp skin; she shook her hair off her face, leaned against the sill and stared up at the stars, shivering as the bricks pressed chill on her hot body and legs. The hair on her neck and arms lifted.

He had smiled at her again, just before they retired for the night. A slow smile as though he desired her. His earlier coldness – which had perturbed her – had gone. Perhaps she had imagined it. She felt almost sure that he had wanted to kiss her. And, she thought, with a tight little smile, she would quite like to have kissed him, too.

She had never kissed anyone. A soft laugh puffed in her nose as she thought of the few occasions in the past that she and Giovanni had – as children do – made brief, giggling forays into each other's privacy: damp little moments of probing fingers and explosive snorts of laughter. She had no doubt that what awaited her in October would be as different from this as silk from sacking.

The handsome Signor d'Este would have much to teach her, she felt sure. The raising of his eyebrow as he had kissed her fingers just now had been knowing, playful – even teasing. Lucrezia felt a warm, prickling sensation in her belly. She sat back down on her bed and with searching fingers that suddenly seemed as detached from her as though they were no longer her own, she explored her skin. Her hands were lover's hands – *his* hands: the right traced up and over her left wrist, forearm, elbow, shoulder; the left moved back down the right arm. She put a hand over each breast and held them, and then, flat-palmed, stroked one hand down her belly, searching and curious. She lay back across the bed. Her breath caught in her throat as raw, inexplicable sensations ignited and burned, fierce and sweet inside her expectant body.

An owl called in the still night air and a fox barked twice. The castle was silent; Lucrezia wondered if she were now the only person awake in the entire building.

Part Two

Castello Estense, Ferrara
October 1559
Three months later

4

The candle guttered and its bobbing flame sent shivering shadows across the room. The red bed-hangings seemed to flutter and points of candlelight flickered in every one of the diamond panes of the two windows.

Lucrezia watched her new husband close the chamber door. He leaned with his back against it, facing her, his eyes fixed upon hers. Lucrezia's skin tingled, as though she had been running, though she had only climbed a flight of shallow steps – and that, slowly. She realized she was trembling. She tried to smile, but the smile died before it could reach her lips. Until a moment ago she had been sure that she felt elated and happy – as she knew she should today, her wedding day – but at the same time everything seemed insubstantial and unreal, as though she were playing an exciting, but clearly fictitious, part in a play. She felt detached from reality, an observer of her own emotions, aware of herself as though she were a separate third person hidden somewhere in the room, eavesdropping on what was about to unfold.

Alfonso said nothing. Leaning lazily against the bedroom door, weight on one leg, the other crooked up with the sole of his foot flat against the wood, he just stared at her with his head tilted to one side. As though, she thought, he were observing a painting or admiring a piece of sculpture. The corners of his mouth lifted as his eyes left hers and wandered from her face, down to her feet and back, slowly, slowly; appraising – approving, she imagined, for his smile broadened as he looked back into her eyes.

'You're beautiful,' he said at last.

Lucrezia tried to swallow. A burst of music from downstairs, and the sound of voices still celebrating, pushed its way through the open casement making her start.

'If you remember, I told you that my household was awaiting your arrival with great anticipation,' Alfonso said softly. 'They are merely demonstrating their pleasure at your presence in the Castello. Come here.'

She knew this to be a command.

She walked a few steps and stopped in front of him. Alfonso looked at her mouth. Lucrezia realised it was slightly open: her lips were dry and she could feel her breath on them – cold in, warm out. Alfonso put his hands on her shoulders, then turned her so that she faced away from him. He ran the fingers of one hand up into her hair, and a shiver ran down her spine. She tipped her head back, pushing against his touch. Then, slowly and deliberately, much as she had imagined in her other life, back in her old chamber with Giulietta that summer, Alfonso began to unfasten her laces. In the event, he did not sing, but his breathing deepened and quickened as he worked.

First came the sleeves, which he slid from her arms like a caress. Then the more complicated laces of the bodice. He was taking his time, Lucrezia thought, apparently unaware of her trembling, seeming to enjoy flipping the long, thin cords through their stitched eyelet holes. She closed her eyes as Alfonso – still stand-ing behind her – reached around her. With his head next to hers, his cheek against her ear so that he could see what he did, he eased her shift from her shoulders and let it drop. Her clothes fell from her, piece by piece, until everything – skirt, overskirt, bodice and shift – lay in jewel-bright folds around her feet, and she was naked in the mass of material, like Venus in her floating shell.

She stood quite still, watching the points of light dance in the windows, aware of Alfonso's warm bulk behind her, afraid to move, afraid to breathe.

She felt his hands on her shoulders again; he turned her back to face him. Exquisitely and entirely exposed now, she held his gaze, wide-eyed, fearing that if she should so much as blink, he would look away from her eyes, and – would look at her body. At the thought, her nipples contracted and a hot thread from her throat hooked itself deep in her belly, where it jerked like a fish on a line.

But without taking his eyes from hers, Alfonso reached behind him and blindly picked from a small table a carved rosewood box. He held it in one hand, unlocked it and opened it with the other. Lucrezia drew in a sharp breath, and the hot thread tugged again as Alfonso pulled from the box a long, long rope of dark red, glit-tering stones. He stepped forward and began to wind it around and around Lucrezia's throat, sliding it each time underneath the mass of her hair. Each time he slid his hand across her neck, his face drew near to hers and the stuff of his doublet brushed against her breasts but, still, he did not speak.

Once fastened, the rope hung heavily around the base of Lucrezia's throat. Alfonso stood back and gazed at her, apparently entranced. The stones were cold and heavy against her skin, and she shivered.

Seeing this, Alfonso picked her off her feet and into his arms.

47

Startled, she smothered a gasp. He walked swiftly across the room, pausing to blow out the candles as he passed them. As the flames went out, Lucrezia saw the wood-panelled walls and the gilt-framed pictures all but disappear; only the thinnest lines gleamed along the pictures' edges as the moonlight caught them. In the candlelight just now, the colours of the room had glowed as warm as late-evening embers, but now the moonlight turned this, in an instant, to silver.

The bedcovers had been folded back in readiness. Alfonso placed Lucrezia carefully on the linen sheet and, without comment, stepped back into the shadows. She pulled the covers over her, watching him in the dark, feeling the linen chill against her skin.

A moment later, Alfonso sat down on the edge of the bed, pushed back the blankets so that Lucrezia was once more quite uncovered, and then, slowly and deliberately, began to explore her body with his hands and his mouth. At the first touch she stiffened, her whole body prickling with shamed embarrassment, and with what in her confusion she hoped might be desire. She wondered what she should do. The silence seemed to be growing more and more robustly elastic between them, increasingly hard to break. The only sounds in the room were those of her new husband's breathing and the paper-smooth whisper of his hands on her skin.

She reached towards him, wanting to touch him, but he grasped her wrists and pressed them back onto the bed without comment, returning straight away to his own searching, insistent caresses. She tried again, twice, with the same result. Alfonso did not speak or look at her face and, to Lucrezia's bewilderment, seemed determined that she should take no active part at all in what was transpiring.

She began to feel increasingly unconnected with her body.

Alfonso's touch excited her, but it was like trying to hold an image from a dream: as fast as she acknowledged the sensation she was feeling, so it retreated from her, disappeared into nothingness, leaving her bemused, confused and hungry.

It was not long, though, before Alfonso's hands became more insistent; her heartbeat began to quicken, and anxiety pushed thick fingers up into her throat, as she realized that the loss of her maidenhood must be fast approaching. She had been longing for this moment for months, but now, as she faced its immediate arrival, a suffocating feeling of panic began to tighten around her chest.

Even as she thought this, Alfonso lifted his mouth from her breast and, eyes black in the almost-dark, ran the tip of his tongue over wet lips. He did not smile, and Lucrezia shivered.

Alfonso shifted himself up her body and pushed one knee in between her thighs. At first she tried to hold her legs together, resisting him, her face cold and hollow at this unprecedented sense of exposure, but Alfonso edged his leg more firmly into place, crooking her knees upwards with his hands. Lucrezia closed her eyes and held her breath, expecting the stabbing soreness she had once been warned might come. Alfonso pressed down against her hips, but although she could feel a blunt nuzzling, as though of some hot-nosed animal, she was surprised that, in the event, it seemed quite soft and made little impression.

Alfonso swore quietly and pushed his hand down between Lucrezia's body and his own. His arm jerked awkwardly against her stomach, and then he tried again. She felt the hot nudging once more, then Alfonso's hands pulling and probing – she was startled as his fingers slid inside her, and let out a sharp mew of surprise. She was unsure what he was doing and did not dare to ask him, for her husband now seemed quite oblivious of her, other than as an obstruction to his achieving fulfilment.

He tried a third time, muttering angrily to himself and, as he failed yet again, Lucrezia's eyes filled with tears that ran, scalding, down the sides of her face and into her ears. After all the months of expectation, it seemed now that her new husband did not truly want her after all. He had seemed to at first – her body had appeared to please him – and she had thought him so assured, so grown-up, so experienced as he had begun to make love to her. It had to be her own failing, something she was or had done, that had debilitated him like this.

Despair draped itself around her like a wet sheet.

Alfonso rolled away from her to lie on his back on the far side of the mattress. Lucrezia sat up, dragging the covers up and over herself. With the untidy linen clutched in white-knuckled fists, she could just make out his profile, staring up at the ceiling. The whites of his eyes caught the light from the window. A sob swelled in Lucrezia's chest and she tugged the sheet nearer to her chin. Say something to me – please! she willed Alfonso. Tell me you are not angry with me. Hold me!

And then, after a few long seconds he turned, but he did not hold her, and still he said nothing. He reached forward and unfastened the rope of red stones, unwinding them slowly from Lucrezia's throat. Then, with the jumble of crimson clasped in one fist, he sat up, swung his legs over the side of the bed and stood.

Stiff with misery, Lucrezia watched him. It was now so dark in the room that she could not properly see what he was doing, but she heard the click of a tiny lock and the muted rattle of what sounded like glass. A rustle of material followed.

With a pinprick of shock, she realized he was dressing. 'Are – are you leaving?' she said.

The words sounded horribly loud, whispered into the silence. There was no reply. Lucrezia watched her new husband cross the dark chamber. The lower edge of the door caught on the floor as it opened, then again as it closed. There was a scraping of claws as the waiting wolfhound scrabbled up to standing in the corridor outside the bedchamber, and then Alfonso was gone.

Left in the dark, Lucrezia sat up and hugged her knees, feeling those first tears itch in the creases of her ears as they began to dry. Her eyes stung. She blinked and bit her lip, feeling it tremble under her teeth, and then she began to weep again, unrestrainedly, over-whelmed with a bitter sense of failure.

She became aware of feeling cold, as she wept, and, rubbing her eyes, she climbed out of the bed. She knelt on the floor in the dark and ran her hands over the boards, searching for her chemise. Finding it, she pulled it on, then scrambled back under her bed-covers, curling up tightly with the blankets tucked close around her.

Her thoughts raced. She had, she realised miserably, pictured many versions of her first encounter with her new husband. In the teeming, childish images that had filled her mind as she had con-templated her first night in her marriage bed, she had seen the then unknown Alfonso as being perhaps gentle and tender, maybe forceful – even brutal – perhaps wild, and funny and unpre-dictable. Her imaginings had been vivid and entertaining, and she had thought she had touched upon every possibility.

But there was one thing she realised she had not envisaged: in none of her dreams had he ever been absent.

Lucrezia awoke after a short, unsatisfying sleep, just after dawn, with eyes so dry and puffed from crying that they would not easily open, but, unable to sleep further, she rolled onto her back and gazed through stiffened eyelids up at the canopy of the bed.

She felt quite numb. For months her focus had been almost

entirely upon this first night. She had spared almost no thought for the weeks, months, years before her, so entirely had her mind been trained upon this exciting realization of her newly emerging womanhood. There came to her now the prospect of a whole life unfolding ahead of her in the company of a husband who seemed unable to love her – an image quite terrifying to her in the potential of its bleak loneliness.

Tears leaked again from her still-swollen eyes. She wanted to go home, for everything to be as it had been. She wanted her mother. She wanted Giovanni, and the uncomplicated warmth of their undemanding friendship. She wanted to be a child again, having so manifestly failed in her first attempt at becoming a woman.

And then a noise startled her; she stifled a sob.

The door to the bedchamber opened.

Alfonso was carrying a candle, one hand cupped around the flame, which glowed crimson through his fingers. He was wearing a long robe and an intense expression Lucrezia could not determine. She watched him, unblinking, as he placed the candle down on the table. He took off the robe, and draped it over the end of the bed.

Lucrezia's eyes widened. It had been dark before, and she had been unable to see what the candlelight now revealed. As she saw the indisputable proof of Alfonso's new readiness to attempt the consummation of their marriage, an alarming image of herself as a pig impaled on a spit pushed its way into her mind. She put her hand over her mouth. The child she had been wanted to laugh. The woman she hoped to become felt a wash of relief that she appeared to be – at least a little – desirable.

Alfonso saw Lucrezia cover her mouth with her fingers as she flicked a covert glance at his prick. Her eyes were coin-round; her hair had fuzzed and tangled around the white, freckled triangle of her face. She had put her shift back on, he saw – the linen was sleep-rucked, and one small shoulder protruded from the gaping neckline. The bedclothes she held gathered up in both hands at chest height. She looked wary and frightened and terribly young, and he realised that he wanted her very much – his groin ached with the wanting – but as much as he intended to try again, so a pinching feeling of unprecedented anxiety held him back.

It had never happened before.

Never with any woman he had bedded in the past – not with the castle servants he had once 'persuaded' to indulge him as a boy, not with the harlots he had paid for more adventurous activities as he grew up, not with the libidinous countess with whom he had tumbled for several years under the nose of her unintelligent husband, and certainly never with Francesca. Never.

The thought of his failure this evening frightened him. Accusations and misgivings whined in his head. What if it happened again? Now? Another time? Every time? Why had it happened earlier? What if— Alfonso swallowed uncomfortably and then spoke aloud to drown the doubts. 'Take off your chemise, Lucrezia.'

He would not give it a chance to happen again.

Lucrezia said nothing, but knelt up on the mattress, crossed her arms in front of her and grasped the hem of her shift. In one fluid movement she pulled it over her head, and then sat back on her heels, her arms folded across her breasts, her eyes on his. His cock twitched.

Alfonso climbed onto the bed; he held her shoulders. She unfolded her legs and lay back. Compliant. He liked the word. Searched for another: obedient. He ran a hand up over her belly and onto her breast. She stiffened again as she had before. He felt as though he had a fever: his skin was burning but the flesh below it was chilled and shivering. He looked at Lucrezia's body. The perfect image. His to possess. His to enjoy. He slid one knee up and over her legs. The swollen heaviness in his groin tightened again. He moved her breast under his palm, then pushed his other hand downwards, between their two bodies.

Lucrezia sucked in a shuddering breath. 'I'm sorry,' she said. 'I'm so sorry if I . . .' Her voice cracked and died away.

At the sound of her voice, the softening began and, as it did so, a knot of anxiety tightened around his throat like a noose. Determined not to fail again, he closed his fingers more firmly on Lucrezia's breast. Too firmly: she made a small noise of distress and squirmed away from his grip.

It was like trying to stop water trickling away into sand. The tightness in his cock subsided. Retreated. Faded. Shrivelled. He closed his eyes, almost suffocated by a black drench of defeat and swore under his breath. He turned away and sat on the edge of the bed with his back to her.

There was a long pause.

Lucrezia whispered, 'Please – don't leave.'

'No,' he said, still facing away from her. 'The servants would talk, should I not be here when they arrive in the morning.'

He felt her flinch, as though he had made to hit her.

Alfonso wanted to leave the room – as desperate for the silent safety of his own chamber as is a drowning man for air. With the humiliation of this second failure sneering at him from one side, and the thought of his servants' shocked reactions if he were to abscond taunting him from the other, he forced himself to remain in the room. He walked slowly to the window.

He stood motionless for what seemed like hours, sightlessly staring at nothing, his mind numb. Then, too tired to stand any longer, he returned to the bed and lay on his back next to Lucrezia. She made no move to touch him, and so they remained, side by side – like two stone effigies from the great cathedral – until the grey light of morning filled the room.

5

Waiting-woman to a duchess? Catelina stroked the corn-coloured woollen skirts of her newest dress and stifled a disbelieving grin. She picked up an ivory comb and began trying to work it through the Signora's hair. It felt strange to be standing so close to someone so grand, someone dressed in such beautiful clothes, actually being asked to touch her lovely hair. Catelina looked at her own hands. They were red, and the skin on her fingers was scratchy and rough, despite the oils she had been given to soften them. There was no avoiding the fact that they were still kitchen hands and they still looked bad – particularly the burned one. Even if it no longer hurt, there was a big crimson patch, right across her wrist and the back of her hand, where the skin was softly puckered, like a turkey-cock's wattle. It looked horrible, but Catelina knew it might well have been much worse if the Signora had not done what she did that day in the kitchen, with the eel-barrel.

Catelina breathed in. She smelled nice, the Signora – of roses, and some other, sharper flower Catelina could not name – not like most of the people she had lived among so far. Until a week ago she had shared her life with people who were far more likely to smell of mutton fat, sweat and stale woodsmoke than of flowers. Catelina thought she had probably washed more often in the week and a half she had been in Ferrara than she had done in five years at Cafaggiolo.

'Will it be long before you've finished? Is it dreadfully tangled?' The Signora's voice interrupted her musings.

Catelina started. 'Oh – I'm sorry, my lady – have I hurt you?'

'No, no – not at all.' The Signora turned round. She was smiling. 'I was just thinking it seemed to be taking rather a long time. Shall I have a try?' She took the comb from Catelina and began to work with it, her head on one side, a hank of hair clutched in her fist. 'Ouch! We should have done this last night, Lina,' she said, grimacing.

Lina. No one had ever thought to shorten her name before. Catelina sat down on a carved chest.

The Signora continued her struggle with her hair, and then laughed, saying, 'What on earth do you think Giulietta would say to see you sitting there and me fighting with my own hair?'

Catelina bit her lip.

'Oh, don't look like that! I didn't mean to make you feel guilty . . .'

That morning in the kitchens at Cafaggiolo . . . Catelina could still hardly believe it had happened: there she had been, sitting in her usual corner, peeling vegetables, one hand all prune-wrinkled and chilled from being too long in the water and the other still sore and stiff and wrapped in bandages, when the big door to the upper floors had slammed back on its hinges and the Signora had burst in, followed by that gangly cousin of hers.

'Angelo, where is she? Where's that girl who burned her arm a few days ago? Catelina, I think her name is.' She had been all out of breath from running. Catelina remembered how her name had cut right through the noise of the kitchen. She had looked up at once and seen Signor Angelo jerk his head towards her corner. The Signora had pushed her way across the room, through all the bustle and noise, and had stopped in front of her. Then she had just come out with it – asked her to come with her to Ferrara. Catelina hadn't understood. It hadn't made sense at all.

But, sense or not, here she was, with little or no idea of how to be a waiting-woman, working for a girl who (though Catelina felt guilty even thinking it) seemed to have not much more idea of how to be a duchess. A week they had been here, now, and to Catelina's way of thinking, the Signora seemed as ill at ease and out of place in this great castle as she did herself.

There had been all the bubbling excitement of the wedding – well, that had been quite an event, and Catelina had been proud to play even a small part in it – but then, the day after the celebrations, she had seen her mistress deflated and miserable, moping about her chamber like a sad little ghost, refusing her food and so pale she was almost transparent. Homesick, probably, Catelina told herself. She had cheered up a little in the week since that day, it was true, but there was a – she searched for the right word – a *breakableness* about her now that had not been there back in Cafaggiolo.

'Lina,' the Signora said, 'I have finished the tangles. Could you try to braid it for me?'

'Of course, my lady,' Catelina said politely, hoping very much that she was telling the truth.

'You don't feel guilty, do you?' the Signora asked, as Catelina separated the copper hair into sections.

'What do you mean, my lady?'

'About what I said just now. About what Giulietta would think of us.'

Catelina did not reply. She continued working.

'Because you simply mustn't. It's my fault, isn't it? I asked you to come here with me—'

'But why did you, Signora?' The impertinent question slid out before she could stop it. Catelina dropped the hair and put her hands over her mouth as though to stop any more ill-advised words following in its wake.

'Oh, Lina.' The Signora laid a small hand on Catelina's arm. 'It's precisely because you could say something like that that I wanted you here.'

Catelina's fingers were still pressed to her mouth.

'I haven't told you, have I, about the people my mother suggested I might bring with me before I thought of you? After it was decided that Giulietta was too old to come to Ferrara, Mamma suggested seven or eight replacements. Oh, Lina! They were all horrible!'

'Like what?'

'Oh . . .' The Signora frowned, remembering. 'One who was very grand – I felt like a naughty little girl. Then there was one who was terribly shy, wouldn't speak – she made me feel I had to talk all the time. Even after a few moments, I had bored myself most dreadfully. The one my mother liked best was plump and dumpy and so fussingly motherly – oh, Lina, each one was so wrong. And then I remembered you, the expression on your face when you caught the pomegranate I threw to you, and I knew you would be just what I needed.'

Catelina smiled shyly at her mistress. 'I hope I shall live up to your expectations, Signora,' she said.

The Signora took her hand and squeezed it. Catelina felt the rough skin of her fingers catch on her mistress's soft palm.

'Come on, Lina, finish these braids, and we can go down to the little room we found yesterday. Alfonso will be back soon – we can watch for him.'

A few moments later, mistress and maid left the bedchamber and walked together through endless rooms and down a couple of flights of stairs. After one or two wrong turns, they arrived at a small room which overlooked the central courtyard. The walls were lined in silk; there was a mirror in a fancy gold frame on the wall opposite the window, and what must have been dozens of pictures lined the other two walls. It seemed quite unbelievable to Catelina that anyone would spend so much time and money decorating a little room like this that was obviously hardly ever used.

She waited awkwardly just inside the door, and watched as her mistress crossed to the open window and climbed up onto the broad recess in front of it. She leaned out to peer down into the noisy bustle of the courtyard.

'Do you want me to stay, Signora?' Catelina asked.

'Oh, yes, Lina, please stay. Come here – there's so much happening.'

Catelina looked at her face and saw, as if in a mirror, all the anxiety and excited curiosity that was churning in her own head. Perhaps there wasn't so much difference between someone like the Signora and a girl like her after all.

She stood next to her mistress and together they gazed down into the courtyard. All was motion and haste. At least a dozen horses were being made ready; busy men scurried around collecting equipment and then, into the midst of this, a plain carriage drew up and a shabby, brown-clad figure climbed out. Short, stout, grey hair with a circle of sunburned skin on the top of his head. A Franciscan, probably. He was followed by a dark young man carrying several long rolls of heavy paper.

'Maybe he is making a map of the duchy.' The Signora pointed at the young man. 'Alfonso said he wanted a proper one drawn up.'

Several people spilled out of the front doors to meet the new arrivals, who were quickly shown inside. The brown drab of the friar's robes stood out, Catelina thought, against the bright colours of the castle servants.

'Alfonso will be home soon, I expect. I'm not sure where he has been, but I imagine he has had important things to do. What do you think, Lina?'

Catelina did not know what to say. She had a good idea of what sort of 'things' the Signore might have been doing that morning but thought it inappropriate to share her ideas with his wife. The Castello was full of interesting sources of information, for people who were prepared to listen.

Francesca Felizzi was on her hands and knees, her head and shoulders beneath the bed and her bare backside facing towards where Alfonso sat on the big elmwood chair under the window. It was, no doubt, a deliberate move, he thought, enjoying the sight, for she was certainly taking her time in finding her lost belonging.

After a moment, however, she stood up, pushed her hair back from her face and sat on the edge of the bed. Stretching one leg out and flexing her toes, she bent her knee up and put on her newly recovered stocking. 'So, are you going to tell me or not? What's she like?' she said.

Alfonso watched her for a moment before he replied. 'The new Signora?' he said. 'Lucrezia is beautiful, of impeccable stock and is quite charming.'

His words sounded cool and confident, but Alfonso could hear the deliberate omissions screaming their accusations into the silence that followed his pronouncement. A hot wave of shame washed over him as he contemplated the pitiful fiasco that constituted his experience of the marriage bed so far. It would have been a relief, he thought, to pour out to Francesca his bewilderment at his humiliation. His uninhibited whore, after all, knew his capabilities better than anyone, and this morning, thank God, he had proved them again to her with a vigour that had at last silenced the mocking voices that had infiltrated his dreams since his unexpected incapacity of a few nights previously. But he knew he would not do it. Could not.

He said, hoping he sounded unconcerned, 'Yes – it seems that I have married a beautiful child. Her lineage and nobility are faultless and her family have clearly understood the importance of the alliance we have forged with this union. Particularly since Cateau-Cambrésis—'

'Oh, for God's sake, don't start talking politics!'

As usual when Francesca spoke with so little regard for propriety, Alfonso felt a shudder of shock at being spoken to in a manner none other of his acquaintance would dare to adopt. 'You are impolite,' he said coolly.

'I know,' she said, tying her garter, 'and you are far too fond of the sound of your own voice. But you make up for it in other ways, Alfonso, as do I, which is, after all, why we put up with each other.' She crossed the room and bent to kiss his mouth.

'Perhaps, though,' she said, her smile fading, 'you will tire of me now, with such competition in your legitimate bed.'

She spoke flippantly, but there was an edge to her voice. Alfonso stood up, slid his hands down her back and held her by the buttocks. Her head tilted back and her arms went up and around his neck.

'She's beautiful, Francesca,' he said, 'but she's a child. She has little sophistication, and I doubt very much she will be able to compete with so . . . experienced a rival. You are very necessary to me.'

And you have no idea quite how true that is just now, he thought.

Francesca said nothing, but seemed reassured. Pulling away from Alfonso, she took a blue damask cloak from the back of another chair and swung it around her shoulders, then kissed him again. The kiss was brief, but arousing: had he not been sorely pressed for time, Alfonso thought, it might well have resulted in his detaining her at the cottage some while longer. Her lips lingered against his for a moment, and then she was gone.

He looked around the room as he finished dressing. The largest room in the little *villetta*, it was simply furnished: a wide, canopied bed dominated, but several other charming pieces of furniture gave it an old-fashioned appeal. Alfonso ran his fingers over the carving on a small wooden chest at the foot of the bed. This in particular gave him great pleasure, worked as it was by none other than Filippo di Quercia.

Alfonso recalled the women with whom he had coupled in this room – over a period of more than ten years, he realized. Some he remembered more clearly than others. Lisabeta, sweet-faced paragon of all the virtues of the bedchamber; the appalling Agnese and now Francesca, his— He stopped himself. He had been about to say 'courtesan' but in fact the only word that would serve adequately to describe the redoubtable Signorina Felizzi was 'whore'. A seemingly limitless lack of inhibition. A sharp mind, though, to accompany the exquisite body, and a refreshing – though at times disarming – honesty, which Alfonso always found reassuring in a world where sycophancy and flattery were almost universal.

He shrugged on his coat, gathered up the rest of his things and left the *villetta*. Collecting his mare from where she had been stabled, he quickly readied her for riding. Folletto yawned, stretched long legs and got lazily to his feet from where he had been curled in the hay, as Alfonso swung up into the saddle. He turned the mare towards the Castello and the wolfhound loped beside the horse, keeping pace with ease.

The hours he spent with Francesca, Alfonso reflected, were perhaps the most honest he passed anywhere. Her enthusiastic response to his preferences was pleasing: few women seemed genuinely to derive the enjoyment she did from an appetite as demanding as his own. He knew, though, that he had just been considerably less than truthful with her about his new duchess. Hot shame broke over him again, and he saw in his mind an image of Lucrezia back in Mugello in August. He had been enchanted by her naïve charm at the start of that visit, and had begun, he knew, to believe that he was acquiring a truly admirable consort. Despite the worrying evidence of that potentially troublesome streak of inappropriate independence, he had thought his new wife to be someone who might not only bestow prestige upon the House of Este by virtue of the nobility of her own family, but who would – Alfonso searched for the right word – become another *conduit* for his not inconsiderable energies. Energies he had never before questioned.

When he lay with Francesca, he was always utterly and completely overwhelmed by a soaring sense of physical abandonment, and for those moments his normally chaotic mind was subsumed by the sensations that invaded his body. He had never expected his whore to meet any but his baser needs, and he knew that Francesca was aware of how effectively she fulfilled those demands. But – he could hardly bear to articulate it, even to himself – something about his new wife had . . . *unmanned* him. Alfonso clenched his fists, and the mare snatched at the tightening reins, tossing her head irritably.

Images of Lucrezia jostled in his mind. He had found her captivating in Mugello. The vivid smile. The boyish figure and the obvious innocence. Her unformed and instinctive responses to the artistic treasures that had surrounded her since childhood – surprisingly impressive. All charming. All adding to the sum of the various elements he had hoped to combine in the creation of an admirable duchess, even if something indistinct and unfathomable about her had been needling him since the banquet.

But none of this explained that first night – God! How could it have happened? Yet again, he tried to think back through the events, to unpick the impossible knot. He had entered Lucrezia's bedchamber, candescent with anticipation. Having undressed her, he had been entranced by what he had seen – he had congratulated himself on his luck at his acquisition. And then it had all begun to slip away from him. Unexpectedly, he had found himself unable to conjure the words with which to woo her. The aggressively bawdy phrases with which he regaled Francesca had elbowed their way into his mind, pushing and catcalling like a bunch of drunken delinquents into a church, making it impossible to find the words he sought. So he had remained silent.

He had brought out the garnets then. The red of the stones against the skin of her throat – vivid as a knife-cut – had been quite exquisite, but even as he had marvelled at the sight, he had felt some essential vitality continue to ebb from him. Something about Lucrezia – he did not understand what it was – had screamed at him that he would be ill-advised to impose upon her his usual vigorous preferences; but he had realized with dismay that if he were to be forced to stifle his instincts each time he lay with her, he had no idea how he would ever achieve a satisfying union with a woman whose charm had nevertheless entirely seduced him.

Alfonso was deep in the mire of these unpleasant thoughts when, with a scrabble of paws, Folletto barked and broke away.

Startled, the mare bunched her quarters under him and sidestepped as the dog wheeled off to one side and disappeared into a gap between two houses. Alfonso reined her in and patted her neck, murmuring soothing nonsense to calm her. He could hear scuffling and snarling, but before he could make any move to follow his dog, Folletto reappeared, head high, tail wagging, a dark shape squirming between his jaws.

Dismounting, Alfonso called him and he came at once, proudly displaying his catch. An enormous grey rat writhed in his mouth; black eyes bulged beneath a gaping gash in its head. Folletto dropped his prize. It landed at Alfonso's feet and convulsed in the dust, squealing. Sickened by its obvious distress, he picked it up, gripped the body with one hand, grasped its bitten head in the other and, with a sharp twist, wrung its neck. There was a soft, gristly crack and the sleek body hung limp across his hand.

Alfonso was surprised, and unexpectedly moved, to see how the stillness of death lent to this pitiful, broken thing an unwonted dignity. His own hands had brought an end to an agony. With ease he had released a creature from pain. He ran a thumb along the grey fur of its side. Clumps of hair were matted and wet from where the dog's jaws had held it; Alfonso gently raked them straight with the tips of his fingers. It was, he thought, as though he were ordering the body, laying it out for burial.

The mare snorted softly. Folletto sat on his haunches on the cobbles, the fringes over his eyes twitching as he watched his master expectantly.

Alfonso's skin crawled. With disgust, or a tingle of excitement? To his shame, he realized he was not sure he could tell the difference. The little animal seemed in death to embody a transition that he loved to contemplate, a transmutation he frequently yearned to understand: that of chaos to tranquillity.

On many occasions, when his thoughts became too tumultuous, Alfonso knew he could often steer himself from the one to the other from within the labyrinth, walking though the ill-lit corridors of the maze in his mind, counting his steps, striding into shadow, confronting and subduing each image as he moved towards the centre.

The labyrinth, unsurprisingly perhaps, resembled for Alfonso the subterranean passages in the Castello, dank corridors that led, ever narrower, ever darker, below the level of the moat to the dungeons. The time he spent down there now was oddly restorative, though as a boy, he had thought the actual dungeons the very lair of the Minotaur itself. His father had forbidden him to go near them, but he had on several occasions defied the injunction. He remembered the first time he had decided to disobey this most vehemently issued order. He must have been about ten years old.

He is creeping along a low-ceilinged corridor towards a heavy iron door. There is a sharp smell of damp, of mould, of decay. He is surprised to see that the door is not much taller than he is himself, though it looks impossibly heavy. It has a tiny window in its centre, with a little hinged shutter lying closed over it. The door is fastened with two great bolts, each as long and thick as his forearm; they gleam with grease. He reaches out and touches the grease, looks at the black smear on his fingertips, puts his hand to his nose and grimaces at the smell of it.

The silence of the place seems to wrap itself around his head as he stands there, muffling and smothering him, and he can feel his pulse still twitching in his ears. The only sound is that of his own tentative footsteps, but then he hears a soft shuffling and a long, indrawn breath from the other side of the door. Someone is behind the door, inside the cell. And whoever it is, is moving, back and forth, a few steps at a time. Alfonso's skin crawls; he is intrigued and frightened at the same time, at the thought that a person as real as himself, someone he cannot see, is only feet from him on the far side of that door. He has never seen inside any of the dungeons, cannot imagine what it could be like to be locked away down here in this lightless world below the moat. He reaches out towards the tiny window, wanting to lift the little shutter, wanting to see the inmate of the cell.

And then a noise slices out like a blade into the silence – a horrible, howling cry of despair.

Alfonso snatches his arm back and puts his hands over his ears, but the sound pushes in through his fingers, on and on, wordless, incoherent, desolate. Too frightened to run, he stands facing the door, his hands still clutching his head, eyes screwed shut, legs trembling, until the terrible cry falters and fades. Then his paralysis lifts and, retching and whimpering, he runs.

That sound had stayed with him for months, he remembered. It had woken him, sweating and terrified, night after night, from nightmares he had endured alone, never able to describe or exorcise them – to do so would have forced confession of his disobedience and incurred his father's anger.

Looking down at the rat now, he wondered whether that moment in the dungeon had ever truly left him. He heard the echo of that cry often, in and amongst the jumble of fragmented conversations in his head, the remembered expletives, imagined narratives, snatches of music – and now the squeals of Folletto's mangled victim. A confusion of cries, from those in the throes of what might be ecstasy or despair. Alfonso pondered the similarities. The sounds a woman makes from the depths of passion, he thought, do not change noticeably when you beat her. That slide up the scale from moan to howl always quickened his pulse, however he induced it. In fact, he thought, the more energetic the induction, the wilder the resultant intoxication.

There were times when the inside of his head was little more than a cacophony.

But the labyrinth always led to the same end: through Babel to chill perfection. As though behind a locked door, lay the chill perfection of death. For a long time now, Alfonso knew he had been strangely enamoured of the notion of finality – he craved relief from the tumult of his imagination. He stroked the rat's damp fur. The silence of the dungeons was perhaps the only place he knew that brought him close to quiescence, but perhaps, he thought, the deeper peace he found himself seeking from the heart of the labyrinth might come not from his own death – as he had so often imagined it would – but from the taking of another life. A heavy heat slid down through his guts and the hair rose on his arms. Shame or excitement? Which was it? Were the two distinguishable? Until that moment it had always been his own death he had contemplated from within the maze. But now the occasioning of it in another creature had happened in his hands – and the sensation was, he realized, not unpleasant.

With a toss of her head, the mare jerked Alfonso's arm and he dropped the rat. Putting the toe of his boot underneath the body, he flipped it to the side of the road and remounted. Man, horse and dog walked slowly through the streets of Ferrara, unobserved by passers-by, and arrived at the castle just before noon, clattering across the bridge that spanned the moat.

'There he is! Quick, Lina, I don't want him to see me.'

The Signora slid off the window recess. Catelina saw the Signore, with his big black wolfhound, striding away from his horse. He turned his gaze upwards and she stepped back quickly from the glass.

'Why not, my lady?' she asked.

The Signora was fiddling with her hair, and biting colour into her lower lip. 'I don't want him to think I have nothing better to do than to sit and wait for him,' she said. 'I want it to seem as though I just happened to be passing downstairs. Do you think——?'

'Just go!' Catelina flapped her hands towards the door, as she had so often shooed the chickens out of the Cafaggiolo kitchens, and then stopped, mid-flap, horrified again by the way she had spoken to her mistress. But the Signora smiled a tight, anxious smile and scurried away towards the stairs.

Catelina followed more slowly. She was not sure she wanted to see the Signore. If he caught her eye, she was afraid she might betray her suspicions about his morning's activities. If her face were to redden, he would be sure to guess that she knew. She descended the staircase, deliberately taking her time, pausing by the great bronze statue that stood on a ledge at the corner. A big bearded figure with a muscled chest and a fish's tail rose out of angry metal ripples, pointing a three-pronged fork at a strange sea creature, his free hand raised above his head. Catelina ran the tip of one finger along the edge of a wave. She was not sure she liked the stern expression on the figure's face and decided, as she moved on, that she felt rather sorry for the little fish, which seemed to be entirely at the bearded man's mercy.

At the foot of the stairs, Catelina found she could see quite clearly into the entrance hall without, she hoped, being noticed. She leaned against the edge of the archway and peered round.

Her mistress had dropped into a curtsy and was looking up at the Signore, her eyes bright, a smudge of colour in her cheeks. He proffered a hand and smiled as she straightened, though there was something uneasy about his expression, Catelina thought, something forced. Perhaps it was embarrassment. Well, if he had just been in some other woman's bed, that would be more than well deserved.

'I was not expecting you till later, Alfonso,' her mistress said.

'Nothing but the most urgent business could have kept me from you, madam.'

Urgent business? Catelina almost snorted.

Footsteps sounded on the stairs above. Standing away from the wall, and hoping that whoever it was had not noticed her eavesdropping, she took a step back. One of the Signore's men appeared and strode past her at speed. With his shock of white hair and his close-set black eyes, he reminded Catelina fleetingly of a fretful egret. He pecked a perfunctory nod in her direction, then walked out into the entrance hall towards her mistress and the Signore.

'Er . . . my lord? Signora?' he said.

They turned to him.

'Franco?'

'Fra Pandolf is here, with the initial sketches, sir, when you have a moment.'

6

Alfonso said, 'Excellent. When did he arrive, Franco?'

'A few moments before you did, Signore. I have shown him into the small chamber by the North Hall.'

'Good.'

Alfonso reached for Lucrezia's hand, and together they followed Franco Guarniero, the chief steward, back towards the stairs. Both men walked fast, Lucrezia taking two steps to every one of Alfonso's long strides.

'Who is Fra Pandalf?' she asked.

'Pandolf,' Alfonso said. 'He's a painter. A Franciscan friar, from Assisi itself. The man is a genius – very popular in court. He has works in several royal palaces and—'

'Why is he here?'

Lucrezia saw what she thought might be irritation on Alfonso's face, and the familiar clutch of anxiety tightened across her scalp. She bit her lip. Not again. Was it because she had interrupted? Was it her ignorance? Since the disastrous wedding night, and the repeated failures since, she had begun to dread displeasing Alfonso, and an uncomfortably heavy consciousness of every word she said hung over her now, each time she spoke to him. She had determined to try to make up for whatever was so wrong in their bed by attempting to smile, be attentive and engage him whenever they were together during the day, but so often, as now, she seemed only to manage to annoy him.

She saw his gaze move to her mouth, and then he said, 'I have been talking for some time about commissioning a fresco to be painted along the wall of the gallery in the hall on the north side of the castle. Pandolf is here with his first drawings.'

'What is the painting to be about?'

'Wait until you see the drawings.'

The aforesaid Fra Pandolf, Lucrezia discovered, was a grey-haired, plump little friar, whose unremarkable appearance and expressionless eyes gave no indication at all of the extraordinary artistic talent Alfonso had described to her. He seemed, she thought, particularly dull and colourless. As she and Alfonso entered the room, Fra Pandolf stopped the muttered conversation he had been having with a tall, black-haired young man of some twenty years and bowed to them.

The smile was audible in Alfonso's voice as he spoke to his visitor. 'Fra Pandolf, what a pleasure to see you in Ferrara again.'

'Signore, I am honoured,' Fra Pandolf replied, in a flat, reedy tone. Turning to the dark boy, he said, 'Jacomo, find the drawings for the Signore . . .'

The young man called Jacomo nodded and unrolled a length of heavy oiled cloth, which was protecting several large sheets of ivory-coloured paper. It must have been rolled for some time – it kept springing back on itself, and curling itself up again and the young man struggled to flatten it.

'Can I help?' Lucrezia asked, stepping forward.

'Th-thank you,' he stammered, too involved with what he was doing to look at her. But Alfonso snapped his fingers and Franco Guarniero stepped out of the shadows at the edge of the room with a heavy candlestick in one hand and a large book in the other. Bowing, he edged in front of Lucrezia and, between the two of them, he and the boy called Jacomo managed to tame the unruly papers.

Fra Pandolf held out a pudgy hand and Alfonso stepped forward. He stared intently at the drawings for some minutes, brows puckered in a frown, breathing audibly. Lucrezia craned her neck to see around his shoulder. He appeared to have forgotten she was there: he did not move, and offered no opinion on the drawings in front of him for several long seconds, but then he began to nod, almost imperceptibly.

'Mmmn,' he said, at last, in little more than a whisper. 'Brilliant. It is a conception of pure genius, Pandolf.'

Lucrezia felt rather than heard the room give a barely audible sigh of relief and she saw Fra Pandolf close his eyes for a second, as though offering up a brief prayer.

Alfonso turned to her. 'Lucrezia, come and see the drawings,' he said. 'Tell me what you think of them.'

She slid between him and the edge of the table, and Alfonso placed a hand on each of her shoulders.

The image she saw was astonishing.

It was the story of Jason and his quest for the Golden Fleece. The sketches were vivid and powerful, simply drawn in fine charcoal but, Lucrezia thought, showing a passion and animation unlike any drawing she had ever seen. She looked up from the paper to the face of Fra Pandolf and struggled to imagine such a dull, doughy man creating this extraordinary epic tale. She tried to picture him, charcoal stick gripped in his plump fingers, drawing vigorously – feverishly, even – flushed with pleasure at having captured the inspiration that had just sparked into life in his mind, but found herself only able to see the friar gazing into space before a blank sheet of paper, the charcoal lying unused on the table before him, his eyes unfocused.

Fra Pandolf did not meet her gaze; he was smiling anxiously, eyes fixed upon Alfonso. Lucrezia returned to the drawing.

The story was broken up into several stages. The image on the far left of the picture, Lucrezia saw now, was of the *Argo* setting sail. A noble Jason stood up in the prow, arm companionably draped around the neck of the figurehead, apparently unaware of the mutinous expressions on the faces of his crew. The waves had been depicted with little more than a few free strokes of the charcoal, yet their motion and power had great energy. She marvelled at the artist's skill.

Further on, the *Argo* was anchored off Talos's island. The great metal giant was stirring, and the Argonauts were running for their lives across a rock-strewn beach. Jason was in the lead, racing out of that scene and into the next, towards the figure of Medea, who pointed behind her at the gleaming fleece with its golden, curving ram's horns, hanging in the sinuous branches of a leafless tree. She was slim as a wraith, with wild hair and graceful limbs, and she was watching Jason with unmistakable desire.

Lucrezia smiled as she imagined the finished painting, in full colour, running the length of the North Hall gallery, from where it would be seen by anyone entering from the main entrance hall. 'Oh, it's wonderful! It's going to be a *beautiful* fresco,' she said, briefly forgetting her preoccupied anxiety.

Alfonso gripped her upper arms more tightly and the corners of his mouth crooked upwards as his gaze met hers. 'You like the idea, then, Lucrezia?' he said. 'I hoped you would.'

'I can't wait to see it take shape. I love it!' Lucrezia turned back round to smile her appreciation at Fra Pandolf and, as she did so, she caught sight of the dark young man, Jacomo. She had only seen him in profile until that moment; but now he was facing her and she noticed, with a jolt of surprise, a crimson stain splashed untidily down the side of his nose and across one cheek – like blood spots, she thought, but perhaps more the colour of crushed berries than of blood. Her skin prickled with aversion – she had never seen such a blemish up close before – but then she looked at his eyes and forgot the crimson mark. Jacomo was staring at the friar from the far end of the table. His expression was difficult to read, but in it she saw what seemed to be anger, frustration, long- ing and a fierceness that surprised her. A muscle twitched in his cheek and his eyes blazed. When he caught her eye, he started and flushed. The tension in his face relaxed – by design, it seemed to Lucrezia; he held her gaze for a long moment, then looked away.

She continued watching him, and wondered what he had meant by that stare. It had not been the usual deferential glance of the hireling, she thought – it had been steady and searching, and it had raised the hairs on her arms.

7

A few miles south of Ferrara, some way off to one side of the long road from Bologna, a stone house stood before a large, walled yard. It was in poor repair – half a dozen tiles had fallen from one end of the roof, exposing the rafters below, and the long front wall was significantly cracked in several places, but the yard itself was pristine. A dozen or so large barrels were neatly double-ranked along one side, with a couple of long-handled, flat-bladed wooden paddles lying across them. A pyramidal pile of filled sacks rose against the back wall of the house under a projecting wooden roof, and a long row of gleaming spades leaned against the yard wall like off-duty soldiers.

In the centre of the yard a stone well was covered with a heavy wooden lid.

At the far side, on the ground near the gate, four flat, rect-angular mounds had been covered with damp hessian. If these looked – as they did – like impromptu graves, then the five sweat-gleaming men who stood in front of them appeared to be the grave-diggers. They were all peering at a new hole in the ground and at the large pile of earth they had removed from it. Leaning on the handles of their spades, they ran filthy hands through damp hair, stretched aching backs and grinned at each other in tired camaraderie.

'That was a grand job, lads,' said the oldest of the five, nodding at the hole. The skin around his eyes and across his forehead was pitted with small scars; more covered his hands and forearms. 'Just the cloth lining to do, and then I reckon we've earned ourselves a little sustenance before we set to with the barrel.'

His companions murmured agreement. They shook out several lengths of tightly woven sacking, dipped each into a bucket of water, then lined the hole with it, first one way, then the next, neatly overlapping the strips so that no raw earth showed. After checking the pit carefully, they all moved in a pack, towards the back of the house, leaning their spades up next to the rest of the regiment as they passed.

The interior of the house was as dingy as the outside. The windows of the main chamber were small and, being covered with thick squares of waxed parchment instead of glass, admitted little light. Everything in the large, low-ceilinged kitchen seemed thus sketched in sepia: the table, laden with pots, pans, plates and jugs; the dilapidated *credenza*, the stone fireplace, across which hung an iron spit, festooned with dangling pots and implements, and the sulky-looking girl of around fifteen, who was seated on a low stool under one of the windows.

The fire was little more than red embers and white ash as the men trooped indoors.

'Stir yourself and stoke that up, Chiara,' said the oldest of the guildsmen. 'We could all do with ale and some of that lamb from yesterday before we begin the slaking. And we'll need to wash.'

At his words, Chiara stood, and bent to pick up a pair of leather bellows. She crouched in front of the fire and, pushing the nose of the bellows into the embers, began gently puffing until a few bright little flags of flame broke from the glowing lumps of charred wood. She laid a few more split logs on top of this, and then went back to the bellows. Soon the fire was crackling confidently beneath a large iron pot of water. 'Will you be starting straight after you eat, Papa?' she said to the oldest guildsman.

Eduardo Rossi shook his head. 'No. I reckon we need a bit of a rest before we get going on the next batch.'

At her father's words, Chiara looked across at one of the workers, a stocky boy of about her age and she flicked her head towards the door. He raised an eyebrow and nodded once; Chiara's mouth tightened in a smile, as she busied herself carving slices from a leg of lamb, which she laid neatly on a plate. She lifted a couple of flat, round loaves down from a shelf and passed them, with the lamb, to her father and the others, who had seated themselves around the table. She then left the room, making as though to go upstairs, but remained instead crouched beside the door, watching her father tear the loaves into large pieces and hand them around. The men helped themselves to slices of the lamb.

The stocky boy, she was pleased to see, finished eating first. Pushing back his chair, he crossed to the fire. On the floor nearby there was a big wooden bowl, made like a half-barrel, in slats. Wrapping one hand in sacking, the boy tilted the pot allowing some of the hot water to run into the bowl.

'Make sure those hands are properly clean, Niccolò,' said Chiara's father. 'I know we'll have gloves but I don't want dirt in the lime.'

Niccolò nodded. Kneeling, he washed his hands carefully in the hot water, picking the earth out from under his nails, then rubbing vigorously up past his wrists. He checked the palms and backs of both hands, then scooped up a double handful of water to splash over his face. He pushed his hair out of his eyes, rubbed a fold of his shirt across his cheeks and wiped his hands on his breeches. With a nod to the others, he left the room by the yard door.

'I didn't think I'd get to talk to you on your own today. You all seemed so busy earlier,' Chiara said. Niccolò said nothing, but leaned towards her, his mouth seeking hers. She tipped her face up towards his and he kissed her. One hand slid up her bodice to press itself against her breast, at which Chiara arched her back and pushed against him, nudging him with her hips. Niccolò's free hand sought the hem of her dress; he fumbled with the fabric and reached upwards into the folds of linen. Chiara moved her knees apart.

But, after no more than seconds, they heard the house door being banged and voices loud in the yard. Niccolò and Chiara froze.

'*Cazzo!*' Niccolò hissed. He pulled his hand out from under Chiara's skirts and she raised her fingers to her hair, tucking back the wisps that had curled out around her face.

'Your bloody father!' Niccolò mouthed. 'I thought we might have at least half an hour.'

Chiara was on her feet. Her mouth felt wet and swollen – she wiped it with the back of her hand. 'Niccolò – quick! Go out through that door.' She pointed to the far end of the barn. 'I'll stay here until you're with them and they're busy again.'

Niccolò bent to kiss where the tops of her breasts pushed against the neck of her dress. 'We'll find a moment soon – I promise,' he said.

'Please be careful,' Chiara said. 'I hate when you do the slaking. Are you mixer today?'

'No.'

'Well, thank God for that, at least.'

'Barnabeo and Niccolò, bring a barrel over here!' Chiara's father called.

The two men rolled one to within a few feet of the newly dug hole. It was stoutly built, thickly banded with iron and wide at the rim.

'Right. Water! Chiara, *cara*, come and work the handle.'

Chiara appeared from behind the barn and took her place at the well.

All five men lined up between the barrel and the well, wooden buckets in hand, and within a few moments they had filled the barrel about a quarter full.

'Now,' said Chiara's father, 'cover up, all of you!'

He and the other four men wrapped long leather aprons around themselves, tied broad strips of doubled linen over the lower parts of their faces, and finally pulled on heavy leather gloves.

'Barnabeo, you and Antonio bring over a sack.'

Chiara held her breath. No matter how many times she had seen this done, as the daughter of the head of the city's plasterers' guild, she had never watched the start of the slaking without her heart quickening. She had seen too many accidents – she had a horror of burning.

Barnabeo and Antonio hoisted the big sack onto the rim of the barrel. Eduardo pulled out a knife. 'Ready?' he asked them.

They nodded.

'Niccolò, is the cover ready?'

Another nod.

'Good and damp?'

Nod.

'Right then. Off we go.'

Eduardo paused, like a man preparing to dive from a great height. Then, after a deep breath, he pushed the blade of the knife into the bulging hessian and jerked it across the length of the sack. White powder fell fast, with a lisping hiss, down into the water in the barrel. Barnabeo and Antonio shook out the last of it and Niccolò moved in quickly to drape a length of damp cloth across the open top as steam billowed up angrily below him.

Everyone but Eduardo stood back; Barnabeo passed him one of the long-handled paddles.

There was a long moment of silence. As he did each time he slaked, Eduardo strained his ears to hear the first sound.

A rhythmical thumping. The liquid hissed and rumbled and the barrel shifted a fraction along the ground. The thumping intensified and the barrel began to shake, as though some furious, captured creature within it was trying to break its way out. A corner of the hessian cover lifted, a gush of steam poured out and the sacking began to flap frantically. Eduardo lifted the wooden paddle and laid it on top of the hessian, trying to flatten it, but steam continued to stream out in several directions. A fat splatter of hot lime spat out and he jumped back, sucking in a hiss of pain as a speck landed on the inch of arm visible between the leather glove and his rolled sleeve. His skin flamed red instantly where the lime had touched him. That would be yet another scar to join the hundreds already pocking his arms and face.

He waited until the roiling and bubbling had begun to subside, then lifted the paddle, grasped the hessian cover in one hand and lifted it slowly, face screwed up in anticipation, leaning back as far as he could. The still-steaming lime shrieked its displeasure at the exposure, and spat out another half-dozen white-hot gobbets towards him, but this time they all missed and fell to the ground. Eduardo pushed the paddle down into the volcanic contents of the barrel, eyes reduced to crumpled slits, mouth distorted into a shape like a shout. For a moment, both fists tight on the handle, he figure-of-eighted the paddle, moving the lime back and forth, then pulled it back out, banged it on the rim of the barrel, to knock off any clinging mixture, and replaced the hessian.

The frantic activity in the barrel began to die down. Eduardo mixed again. Waited. Mixed again.

'Right, lads. Into the pit now.'

All the guildsmen crowded close around the barrel to shift it the few feet to the pit. Carefully, inch by inch, they manoeuvred it into position, then tilted it. The porridge-like slush splattered into the linen-lined hole.

Eduardo and the others stood back, breathing heavily.

'There you are, boys. One down, three to go. This will be,' he said, with more than a touch of pride in his voice, 'a lime plaster truly fit for the new fresco at the Castello Estense. We should, my boys, be very proud to be of such service to our duke.'

Chiara looked at Niccolò. He smiled at her – a smile that held much promise – and she ran the tip of her tongue along her upper lip, which suddenly felt rather dry.

8

The main drawbridge was down. The sky was the colour of old pewter and a fine drizzle was dimpling the surface of the water in the moat. The four great red towers of the Castello Estense glowered down at the rain-slicked city like scowling sentries, the aggressively military precision of their dimensions somehow softened and blurred by the waterlogged air. Diamond droplets hung along the length of all the white stone balustrades.

A sodden group turned into the main piazza in front of the Castello as the cathedral bell chimed the midday: four riders, one small cart, laden with luggage and, tethered behind it, a bedraggled white mule, ears drooping, small hoofs scraping across the cobbles, as though too exhausted even to pick its feet up from the ground. The group crossed the piazza and clattered up on to the drawbridge.

As they reached the central courtyard, Giovanni de' Medici ran a hand down his pony's neck. He kicked his feet from the stirrups, swung his leg up and over the horse's rump and jumped down. Hunching and rolling his shoulders, he stretched his back to ease out the stiffness of hours in the saddle, as several Estense horse-men emerged to greet the new arrivals. One, tall, round-faced and cheerful, took Giovanni's pony's reins.

'Thank you,' said Giovanni. 'She's absolutely soaked – they all are. Can you give her a good rub down and throw a blanket over her?'

'Of course, Signore. All the horses will be dried and stabled straight away.'

'Her name's Brezza,' Giovanni began, 'and she—'

'Vanni!' He was interrupted by a shriek. 'Vanni!'

Lucrezia was running across the courtyard, her skirts bunched inelegantly in her fists. He grinned and began to walk towards her. She let go of her dress and threw her arms around him; hugging her back, he lifted her right off her feet.

'Oh, Vanni, you're here at last! But you're *soaking*! How was your journey? Was it horrible? How are Mamma and – oh!' She broke off and stood back from him, her mouth a shocked circle. 'Oh, *cielo*! Violetta!'

She had seen the mule. Pleased with the impact of his surprise, Giovanni watched his cousin scramble across the courtyard to where the disgruntled donkey stood behind the cart. She wrapped her arms around its dirty white neck and it tossed its head, stamp-ing a hoof irritably. One of the stablemen unhitched it from the tailboard of the cart. Lucrezia cradled the creature's muzzle in both hands, kissed it, then turned back to Giovanni, her eyes shining. The bodice and sleeves of her dress were now blotched and stained with rain and mud, and her face was dirty. Giovanni rubbed the heel of his hand across his eyes and laughed. 'Look at you,' he said. 'Nothing changes . . .'

'You brought her,' Lucrezia said, through a wide, muddy smile, ignoring him.

'I take it you're pleased.'

'Did she complain *all* the way?'

'She certainly did. God, Crezzi, I can't imagine why you're so fond of her. She has the filthiest temper and the—'

'Don't! Don't be horrible! She's my darling mule and I love her – and I love *you* for bringing her.' Lucrezia hugged him again. 'Come on, let's get out of the rain.'

Then, raising her voice, she said, 'Please, everybody, do come inside. The servants will show you to your rooms, where you can change out of your wet things. There will be hot broth and wine, and I believe a fire has been lit in the East Hall.'

Giovanni proffered an arm, feeling suddenly pleased with himself, and rather older than his fifteen years. Lucrezia took it with both hands and squeezed, smiling up at him again. More servants in bright livery were appearing at the doors now; they seemed, Giovanni thought, out of place in the open air, like a group of pet cats in a field. Their shoulders hunched against the rain, they hastened to welcome the new arrivals inside out of the wet and, in a damp huddle, the party from Cafaggiolo finally entered the Castello.

Alfonso heard a commotion in the courtyard as he strode up from the falconry.

He slowed his pace.

Pausing in the shadows of the tunnel from the back drawbridge, he ran a hand through wet hair as he looked from one figure to another. A trickle of rainwater ran down the back of his neck. One of his horsemen was leading a muddy cob – still harnessed to the shafts of a covered tilt-cart – while another held the reins of a handsome little chestnut mare. Three other horses were being led towards the stables, with an obviously elderly, and mud-soaked white mule. A cluster of servants were collecting the luggage from the cart – and then he saw her.

Lucrezia.

She had mud on her face and hands, and her dress was unaccountably filthy, but her face was alight with pleasure. Her eyes were shining as she laughed up at a lanky, dark-skinned boy, and Alfonso's heart clenched tight for a moment until he recognized the newcomer. His mind on his hawks, he had forgotten that his wife's cousin was due to arrive today.

Lucrezia's hands were wrapped around the boy's arm and she was walking, pressed close to him, towards the main entrance. The boy threw back his head and laughed at something Lucrezia had said. She let go of his sleeve and shoved hard at his side, throwing him off balance. He straightened, jabbed at her ribs with a finger and Alfonso heard her squeal, gasp and laugh.

A hot blade of disapproval turned in his belly. His jaw tensed and something vertiginous shifted and fell in his guts. As in those moments when his horse startled and shied beneath him, Alfonso was rocked by a sense of the bunched precariousness of a potentially uncontrollable force.

Breathing quickly, his hands balled into fists, he stepped back into the shadows of the tunnel and waited for his wife and her cousin to pass into the castle. Once he was certain they had gone, he went in through a side entrance, descended a narrow staircase and walked along the corridor that led to the dungeons.

'Alfonso's not here,' Lucrezia said, as she walked with Giovanni up a wide spiral staircase. He felt a guilty stab of relief, which was, however, short-lived, as she added, 'He's out hawking – he'll be back soon. I thought he'd be here before you arrived.'

Giovanni's sodden boots squelched at each step, oozing bubbles of water along the seams. Looking back, he saw a trail of glistening footprints. His feet were frozen. He was aching to ask Lucrezia about her new life. All the questions he had been thinking through over the three days it had taken them to ride up from Cafaggiolo were clamouring to be heard. He had repeated them in his head, over and over again as he had pictured the two of them sitting alone, he asking his questions, she dissolving into tears, admitting to a life of brutal subjugation with a man who had distorted in Giovanni's head from someone he had simply disliked to a fully fledged monster, capable of anything. But now, here in Ferrara, he found himself faced with a Lucrezia who in the event just seemed delighted to see him; she appeared to be at home in her new life, more grown-up than ever. He felt stupid and childish, and his questions now sounded ridiculous.

He knew he would not ask them.

'Here we are. You can change your clothes – and I'll need to change mine. How are Mamma and Papa?' Lucrezia asked again. 'I'm so sorry they didn't feel they could come. Is Papa truly getting better? And Giulietta, is she well?'

Giovanni followed her into a large room. A tapestry covered one wall, depicting the climax of a successful hunt, with the tops of the towers of the Castello visible in the background above a line of trees. There was a curtained bed, two highly polished cross-frame chairs and a low table. Not unlike his room at Cafaggiolo, he thought, only tidier.

Lucrezia sat on the end of the bed.

'They are all well,' he said. 'Uncle Cosimo's still resting, but Aunt Eleanora says that, having been a meek and biddable patient for weeks, he is becoming exasperating again, so she feels much happier about him than she has been since he had his fit.'

Lucrezia laughed.

'They send their love – and a cartload of presents and letters,' Giovanni said, sitting down and trying to pull off one of his boots. Being so wet, it stuck. He struggled with it, swearing softly, then thrust out his leg towards Lucrezia. She smiled, bent and took hold of his ankle. Bracing one of her feet on the seat of the chair, she tugged and jerked. With a sucking gasp, the boot came off, and she staggered backwards, laughing.

'Can you do the other one now?' Giovanni asked.

Lucrezia tried hard to listen to Giovanni's news from Cafaggiolo as he put on clean, dry clothes, but now that the first euphoric rush of delight at seeing him had subsided, she found herself confused and oddly detached, unable to focus on what he had to say. Watching him now, she was torn in two. First, a sharp pinch of homesickness caught her in the throat as he described the long litany of advice that Giulietta had exhorted him to pass on to her. It was an instantly recognizable imitation of Giulietta's voice – *is she making sure she brushes her hair out thoroughly every night, and is that* kitchen girl *quite certain that Lucrezia's shifts are properly dry and aired before she gives them to her to put on?* At the same time, though, an uncomfortable lump of resentment towards her parents, which had been growing ever since the wedding night, sat heavy in her belly like too much meat.

With the way things were between her and Alfonso, she knew she was not fulfilling her role as her parents must have envisaged it. She was the vessel that would carry the heir to the Este dynasty – but she was increasingly aware of being, in the end, little more than a commodity, raised for the purpose like a prize heifer and traded last October between her parents and her husband. Her mother and father of course knew nothing of the awful, dragging tension that now sucked the spontaneity out of her every encounter with Alfonso. How could they? But somehow, Lucrezia thought angrily, they *ought* to know. Ought to have guessed.

'Are you listening, Crezzi?' she heard Giovanni say.

'What?'

'Are you listening? You look half asleep.'

'No – I mean yes, I am listening. And no, I'm not asleep. Of course I'm not.'

Giovanni frowned at her. She wanted to tell him – oh, God, she wanted to tell him! The words were crowding into her mouth, demanding to be given their freedom. To begin to tell him, though, would mean wading out into the treacherous waters of an intimacy she knew she could not share. She had confided in her cousin for so long, about so many things – they had been the closest of companions for years – but this new situation stood between them like a brick wall. Lucrezia knew she could not describe the shameful failure of her marriage to anyone. Even to imagine the words leaving her mouth made her insides squirm and her face flame.

Giovanni said, 'Crezzi – is something wrong?'

She knew he thought there was. She breathed in slowly, hesitated, then knowing she couldn't say it, smiled and said, 'No. There isn't. Really.'

For several long seconds they gazed at each other. Lucrezia's smile felt as though it had been pinned in place. Then Giovanni said, 'Well, if there ever is, you tell me, do you understand? I want you to tell me.'

Lucrezia nodded.

It was the week before Christmas and a hopeful morning sun was doing its best to break through patchy cloud. Outside the Castello, in the great open space that fronted the castle, half a dozen men were constructing a wooden gallery big enough to hold some twenty or thirty guests. Cartloads of sand were being dumped and spread thickly across the entire square, along the centre of which was a balustrade of waist-high wooden poles, spiral-striped in the Este colours of red, white and green; the railing effectively split the space into two.

'There'll be jousting tomorrow before the banquet,' Lucrezia said. 'Alfonso said it depended on the weather, but now that the rain has eased off, I expect it will take place as planned. I hope so.'

Giovanni watched the new tiltyard taking shape. 'I quite like the idea of attempting to joust,' he said.

Lucrezia snorted her contempt. 'Just because you think you ride well?' she asked scornfully. 'Don't forget what happened to the poor King of France.' She grimaced. 'Come on – we can watch the final banquet preparations.'

They crossed the drawbridge and entered the castle through the enormous front doors. Arm in arm, they crossed the entrance hall, walked down a corridor and into the North Hall where the meal was to take place.

The room was almost literally covered with men. Men on ladders, stringing hundreds of little red, white and green flags; men hanging glittering chandeliers from which dangled gold-paper decorations; men constructing an enormous striped awning and festooning every available surface – horizontal and vertical – with great swags of flowers. The three tables were decorated too, with more flowers, fruit, candles, ribbons and a number of small naked figurines, very lifelike and made from some sort of dark brown material.

'What *is* this?' Giovanni asked, reaching out and picking one up.

'Some sort of biscuit,' Lucrezia said.

Giovanni snorted. 'Hmm. Fairly impressive proportions for a

biscuit . . .' He raised his eyebrows at her.

Lucrezia laughed. 'Oh, I'm so glad you're here, Vanni!'

He put the figurine back on the table and, with deliberate care, draped a spray of flowers across its front to preserve its modesty. He squeezed his cousin's hand and said, 'And I'm pleased you're not busier. I thought you'd be run off your feet overseeing all this – Aunt Eleanora is always frantic on the day of a banquet and they've never done anything on *this* scale at Cafaggiolo.'

There was a moment's uncomfortable silence.

'Well, Alfonso prefers to organise these events himself,' Lucrezia said awkwardly. She did not add the thought, which was loud in her head, that she was longing – *longing* – to be given a role to play in the castle beyond that of 'newly acquired artistic treasure', but that Alfonso seemed determined to prevent her taking any active part in the running of the household.

'Do you mind that?' Giovanni asked, frowning.

'A little, I suppose.' Lucrezia's smile was tight and rather apologetic. 'Perhaps it's just that he thinks I shouldn't wish to do it myself.'

'Have you asked him?'

Lucrezia shrugged. It had only been a week since Alfonso had made his opinions on the matter quite plain enough for her not to think of questioning him any further.

The Castello kitchens are bigger, better equipped and far more efficient than the old and well-worn rooms at Cafaggiolo but, to Lucrezia's mind, the rows of stark new red-brick ovens and the almost window-less walls have a great deal less charm. She stands in the doorway, watching the cooks, the vintners, the sweat-soaked scullions, intent upon their myriad tasks. For several moments, in all the noise and the acrid blue smoke-haze, no one notices her. Then a young boy – no more than twelve, Lucrezia thinks – nudges his neighbour and jerks his head in her direction. One by one, like deer at a watering-place newly aware of a possible danger, they look up from what they are doing and stare at her. The activity of the kitchen hangs suspended.

Lucrezia's face flames. 'Please,' she says, 'please don't stop what you are doing on my account. I only wished to acquaint myself with my new surroundings. Please, carry on.'

They return to their abandoned tasks, backs bend once more over pots and spits, but one bulky man steps forward, smiles and bows, and Lucrezia smiles too.

'My lady,' he says, 'we are honoured to see you down here. Welcome to Ferrara. Is there anything in particular you wanted to see?'

Lucrezia shakes her head. 'No – I had just hoped to explore the castle a little further today. And . . .' She hesitates.

'My lady?'

Biting her thumbnail, Lucrezia says, 'I am a little hungry . . .'

The heavy figure stands with his big fingers spread across his hips and laughs. 'Well, if my lady is hungry, we must do something about it straight away.' He indicates with an arm that she should accompany him across the kitchen. They cross the big, crowded room together.

'Now, what would you like, Signora?' he says, reaching into a bowl. 'A peach, perhaps?' He throws the peach up in the air, catches it – one-handed and surprisingly deft – then holds it out to her with a bow and a swirling flourish, like a conjuror completing an illusion. 'Or why not have a small bowl of ricotta and honey? We have some lovely sweet ricotta fresh in from the dairy this morning.'

Lucrezia has just begun to decide which of the profferred foods might be the most tempting, when she senses a sudden rigidity in her companion. She turns and sees Alfonso in the doorway she has just left. The disapproval in her husband's face is naked.

'Madam, a word, if I may,' Alfonso says. It is hardly louder than

a whisper, but it carries across the noise of the kitchens with ease. Lucrezia excuses herself, then joins Alfonso, who takes her by the arm – his grip is painful – and shepherds her away. 'I am more than a little surprised to have found you in there, Lucrezia,' he says.

'I've been exploring the Castello.'

'I thought I made it quite plain that any meal requests, any menu planning, should be relayed to the kitchens by way of Guarniero . . .'

'Indeed you did, sir. I was not—'

'It matters little what you were not *doing. What concerns me is what you* were *doing.'*

Lucrezia's throat tightens. Alfonso's eyes are glittering. She senses a cataclysmic rage hovering behind his closed expression – the air between them almost crackles with it, like unheard thunder on a heavy evening – but his voice, when he speaks again, is quiet, and only the faintest tremor betrays his discomposure.

'Perhaps,' he says, 'it would be best if you continued to leave the minutiae of domestic organization to me. Familiarity such as I have just seen displayed will inevitably lead to inefficiency, and to liberties being taken by the staff. You need not concern yourself with the running of the kitchens.'

The look he gives her is frightening: blank and unreadable. His gaze flicks to her mouth, rests for a moment upon her breasts, then returns to her face. He says coldly, 'I do not expect to see you in the lower regions of the castle again, Lucrezia.'

She turned back to Giovanni, her thoughts in fragments, as a gust of wind rattled the leaded lights of the bedchamber window.

The crowds cheered as the armour-clad figure pushed up his visor and smiled at Lucrezia. He tilted his lance upwards and held it out towards where she sat in the gallery. Lucrezia reached forward, a long green ribbon in her hand, and tied her favour in a bow around the end of the lance. To her surprise, this felt embarrassingly intimate, and a flush dragged colour into her cheeks. Seeing this, the knight's smile broadened, but then Lucrezia saw him glance towards Alfonso. The slow-blinking gaze was fixed impassively upon the knight's face; his smile faded and he reined back, the lance now horizontal, the handle end tucked in against his hip.

'Why did you choose him?' Alfonso asked quietly, as the knight neck-reined the big grey horse round to the left and jogged noisily back towards the far end of the tiltyard to a ripple of applause, the little green ribbon fluttering cheerfully at the tip of his lance. 'Why him, and not any of the others?'

Lucrezia was unsure how to answer. Still hurt by Alfonso's continued dismissal of her attempts to establish herself in the castle, she now found herself fighting not to let her resentment show in her voice. 'I liked the look of him,' she said. Would her answer anger him? She lifted her chin a fraction of an inch and added, 'And I liked his horse better than the others.'

Alfonso's mouth twitched. 'As good a reason as any, I suppose. What say you, Signore?' He turned to Giovanni.

'Crezzi has a good eye for a horse, sir. That Percheron is quite something.'

'It certainly is. And Zudio is a spectacular tiltsman – I've seen him on several occasions. You chose well,' Alfonso said to Lucrezia. She managed a smile.

The combatants edged their horses into position, one on either side of the striped railing at the two furthest ends of the tiltyard. The great animals sidestepped and snorted; one pawed the sand like an angry bull, tossed its head and snatched irritably at its reins. Their riders shifted position and edged their weapons into place.

To one side of the yard, halfway between the two combatants, a small podium had been draped with the Este colours. On this stood a boy. In his hand was a flag – the Este arms – raised up as high as he could reach.

The crowd's murmur died to silence. Each combatant lowered his visor.

Lucrezia's fingers were so tightly interlaced they were aching.

The boy's face puckered into a grimace of determination as he swept the flag downwards.

Both horses began to move. Picked up speed. Their hoofs thudded into the sand, both lances now lowered to the horizontal. As they neared the centre, Lucrezia found herself hunching her shoulders and screwing her eyes into slits, pushing her body back into the seat as though to protect herself from the collision.

She gasped as Zudio's lance found its target, shattering upon impact; his opponent lurched backwards, but found and held his balance. A surge of noise mushroomed upwards from the crowd. Lucrezia clapped. Giovanni whooped. Alfonso said nothing, but leaned forward and rested folded arms along the edge of the gallery.

The riders jogged back to their positions and readied themselves once more. Someone reached up and tied Lucrezia's green favour to the end of Zudio's new lance and he shifted the weight of the weapon, edging the handle back against his hip. The big Percheron's front feet left the ground and hung in the air for a second. Lucrezia held her breath. Seeing the great arched neck and the muscled legs as the hoofs thudded down, she was suddenly awed by the horse's power, sensing the vigour and energy and raw *maleness* in the scene before her, that maleness that was still so tangled and confused and distressing in her bedchamber. As Zudio and his opponent charged again, it seemed to Lucrezia that their outstretched lances were mocking her and Alfonso. Was her husband thinking the same as she was? His eyes were bright, his gaze riveted on the two combatants. The hot, hooking thread slithered down through her belly as she wondered if this exhilarating exhibition of such uninhibited, thrusting power might finally break through her husband's inexplicable barrier. Perhaps this would be enough to—

Giovanni whistled and whooped again.

The crowd burst into applause.

Lucrezia turned her attention back to the tilt.

Zudio was pushing his visor up. His right hand, in which he held a second shattered lance, was held high. The Percheron was once more on its hind legs, and, sprawled on the sand on the far side of the spiral-striped balustrade was the other knight, already pushing himself awkwardly up onto his elbows. His horse, reins flapping loose, was trotting away towards the furthest corner of the tiltyard, where several young men were poised to recapture it.

'A resounding success for the chosen combatant, Lucrezia,' Alfonso said, clapping enthusiastically. He looked sideways at her, his gaze moving from her eyes to her mouth and back. Lucrezia smiled at him.

'She's quite a find, Este. In the event, the Medici have done you proud.'

Agnese de Rovigo said nothing as her husband leaned towards Alfonso and thus offered his delighted approval of the new Duchess of Ferrara. Alfonso could see, however, that Agnese's black eyes were fixed upon Lucrezia, who was at that moment happily engaged in conversation with one of the courtiers.

'Not your usual type, Alfonso,' she whispered, as her husband then turned to speak to another guest. 'What was it you called her family just before your betrothal? *"Nothing but a long line of mercantile upstarts"*, was it not?'

Alfonso raised an eyebrow. There was, he thought, more than a touch of venom in the remark, and he was forcibly reminded of the relief he had felt some years before, when the unexpected arrival of Francesca had put an end to his liaison with this woman, the admittedly beautiful, but rapaciously demanding Contessa de Rovigo. He did not believe she had ever fully accepted the cessation of the affair – certainly, to look at her now, one would have thought her the wronged wife rather than the discarded mistress she actually was. But, he supposed, as he glanced across at Lucrezia, Agnese was quite right. This boyish, copper-haired, unsophisticated girl – coming from a line of upstarts or not – was indeed unlike any woman he had ever bedded.

Or had at least attempted to bed.

A tangle of images patchworked in his mind: the pounding hoofs of those two horses this afternoon; Lucrezia's small fingers tying the favour around Zudio's lance tip – and her charming confusion upon realizing the symbolism of what she was doing; the admiration on the faces of his guests tonight at the sight of his new duchess; the silky skin of Lucrezia's breasts under his fingers; the great curved neck of Zudio's Percheron . . . the pictures pushed in one after the other. He resolutely refused to let himself think of his discovery of his duchess in the kitchens the other day: she had been smiling up at that great lump of a cook as though she admired him . . . and at least two of the menials had been eyeing her breasts. It was not to be condoned. But a shameful, childish part of him secretly rejoiced at the thought of bedding a woman he knew was desired by his underlings. Alfonso began to feel a creeping certainty that tonight, at last, in the face of this almost universal approbation of his choice of bride, he would finally be able to overcome the incomprehensible obstacles to consummation that had so far so horribly hindered their union.

Almost universal approbation.

Agnese de Rovigo's naked jealousy was obvious – but this merely fuelled his certainty. He compared Lucrezia to the debauched sybarite who was now positively scowling at him; though he had thoroughly enjoyed the many energetic hours he had once spent coupling with the *contessa*, he had come to understand, as did every man who took Agnese into his bed (and there were many), that despite her beauty, she was at heart little more than an unthinking trollop. Alfonso felt as suddenly proud of his own aesthetic sensitivities as he felt sorry for Agnese's ignorant cuckold of a husband. He turned to the *contessa* and laid a hand on her arm. He felt her flinch but kept hold of her sleeve. Stroking her wrist with his thumb, he said quietly, 'You are quite right, Agnese. Not at all my usual type. But, then, one's taste improves with age, so I've been told.'

She said nothing, but stared at his hand on her wrist. Her breathing deepened and for a moment he watched the upper swell of her breasts rise and fall, pushing at the constraining neckline of her bodice. And then, knowing well how little she would enjoy the encounter, he gripped her arm more firmly and said, 'But, Agnese, you must meet the duchess – Lucrezia!'

Lucrezia turned.

'Come here!' he said. 'There is someone I should like you to meet.'

Lucrezia laid a small hand on the arm of the courtier. She smiled at him as she excused herself. Alfonso saw the boy smile in return and – entirely unexpectedly – a flash of raw, screaming, black jealousy suddenly obliterated the banqueting hall, the guests and the whore of a countess who still stood unwittingly beside him. For an instant he saw and heard nothing. Then he felt Lucrezia at his side and looked down at her. The corners of her mouth crooked again as she met his gaze, desire drove rage before it, and in its wake, the noise and colour of the banqueting hall surged back into vivid life.

'Lucrezia,' Alfonso said, more calmly than he felt, 'this is Agnese, the Contessa de Rovigo. Agnese, my duchess.'

'It is a great pleasure to meet you,' Lucrezia said sweetly. Agnese de Rovigo did not smile. Her face twisted into a parody of polite interest, though Alfonso could sense a tremor in the arm he still held, and knew at once that he was not the only person in the room experiencing the torments of frustrated lust. Her discomfiture pleased him, however. Agnese's self-centred hedonism had long since become so boring that Alfonso found himself now thoroughly enjoying seeing it thwarted by his diminutive duchess, despite his own frustration with Lucrezia.

The desire to provoke Agnese gripped him, like the urge to prod a sleeping dog. 'I have known Agnese for many years, Lucrezia,' he said. 'I really feel that you two should make an effort to spend some time becoming acquainted. You would find her an excellent source of information about the duchy and its traditions, and . . .' Alfonso paused '. . . she probably has a fair amount to tell you about me, too.'

Agnese's face stiffened with shock at the impropriety and Lucrezia's mouth opened. Alfonso watched them for a moment, amused by the spectacle, until Ricardo de Rovigo – the 'ignorant cuckold' – turned back from his conversation and exclaimed delightedly to see Lucrezia at such close quarters. 'Why, Signora,' he said, bowing extravagantly, 'what a privilege!'

Agnese rolled her eyes and snatched her wrist from Alfonso's grasp.

'I trust,' Rovigo said, 'that you are finding ways of making yourself comfortably at home in this great sarcophagus of a castle?' He beamed at her.

'The Castello is indeed very big,' Lucrezia agreed, 'but each day I find myself a little more familiar with it.'

'Well said, my lady, well said! A diplomatic answer! But what you actually mean is, you agree with me that it is a vast, old-fashioned, comfortless fortress. A couple of generations of the Estes have attempted – unsuccessfully, I might add – to convince the Ferrarese that it has been transformed into a palace, but in the end a comfortless fortress it remains. And you are far too well bred to admit it.'

'I should not dream of speaking so ill of my new home, Signore,' Lucrezia said. She smiled as she spoke and Alfonso found himself watching her mouth. He wanted to speak to Rovigo, and turned to his friend, but felt his head move for at least a second before he was able to drag his gaze from Lucrezia's slightly parted lips.

He said, attempting an amicable tone, 'You take considerable liberties, sir, from your necessarily humble position as guest in my oversized and underheated sarcophagus.'

'Indeed I do, Este, indeed I do – safe in the knowledge that a host as magnanimous as yourself will take such pleasantries in the spirit in which they were uttered. Merely in jest, sir, merely in jest.'

'Of course.'

Agnese took Ricardo's arm and, with naked antagonism, stared haughtily at Alfonso and Lucrezia, before steering her unfortunate husband away across the hall.

'Did I say something to offend the *contessa*?' Lucrezia asked.

'I shouldn't worry. I don't think it was what you said, rather what you are.'

Lucrezia was clearly distressed. Her eyes were round and anxious. Alfonso looked at her for several long seconds, with what he hoped was a clear declaration of his intentions.

*

After eleven courses, almost every guest at the great Christmas banquet at the Castello Estense was wondering if they had room enough for even another mouthful – but according to the servants, yet one more course still remained. Even Giovanni, Lucrezia noticed, had slowed the pace of his eating.

It had certainly been a spectacular occasion. Not only had the food been extravagant beyond anything Lucrezia had yet seen, but the music that had accompanied each course had been exquisite: blaring trumpets with the venison, flutes with the fish and a singer with a lute when oysters and fruit had been served. Pasta dishes and salads had been brought in by dozens of men in bright Ferrarese peasant costume, with flowers in their hair, and the candied fruit, sweets and cakes had been accompanied by a team of jugglers. Lucrezia had watched, speechless, as they had astounded the company by juggling not just balls, but fruit, knives, spoons and – most breathtaking of all – glassware. Not one thing had broken, and when they had finished juggling, they had tumbled round all three long tables and out of the hall to resounding cheers and applause.

Lucrezia finished the wine in her glass. A servant appeared at her side and refilled it immediately, and she turned back to continue the conversation she had been having with the man on her left. Slight, curly-haired, with a thin-bridged, beaky nose, Francesco Panizato was one of Alfonso's few close friends.

'I think so,' she said, in answer to his previous question. 'My father is considering asking him to come and work as court sculptor at Cafaggiolo.'

'He's very young, isn't he?' said Panizato.

'He *looks* young, yes – I don't know exactly how old he is. He was very friendly – I liked him.'

'You've *met* him?'

'Yes. Last Easter. He—'

Panizato cut across her. Leaning forward, he raised his voice a little and said, 'Alfonso, did you know your wife has *met* Giambologna?'

Alfonso broke off the discussion he had been having with an elderly woman, whose name Lucrezia had forgotten. He looked at Panizato, and then at her. 'Have you?'

'Yes, last Easter,' Lucrezia said again.

'You never told me.'

'I didn't know you'd be interested.'

'I have been wanting to acquire one of his sculptures for some time. Or perhaps to commission a new one. What do you think of his work?'

Lucrezia held her breath. Held breath was safe. If she let it go, the wrong words might slip out before she could stop them. Alfonso was watching her intently, Panizato was smiling, Giovanni had paused with his fork halfway to his mouth and several other guests had stopped their conversations, and seemed suddenly riveted upon what the new duchess might have to say.

Alfonso did not repeat his question, but his raised eyebrow and the enquiring tilt of his head made it plain that he expected an answer.

Lucrezia made herself breathe out. For weeks now she had been aware of how frequently – and easily – she incurred her husband's unpredictable displeasure. After the awful, shameful failure of the wedding night, they had lurched from one humiliating attempt to the next. The attempts had becoming increasingly rare – in fact, Alfonso had not come to her bedchamber at all for at least three weeks. She had been wondering if he would ever try again, but today, for some reason, something had changed. Since he had sat in the tilt-gallery, watching her tie that ribbon onto

Zudio's lance-tip, the hunger had been back in Alfonso's eyes: a hunger for her that had not been there since the wedding. Since before the first failure.

That hunger was glittering visibly now as he awaited his answer. What should she say? Would her thoughts on Giambologna's work please him – fan the flames – or would she extinguish his appetite entirely with her unwitting ignorance?

'Papa says—'

'No, don't tell me what your father says. The least intelligent of his servants could report upon their master's pronouncements. I want to know *your* thoughts.'

Lucrezia's face became so hot that her eyes stung. She drank another few mouthfuls of wine, feeling increasingly light-headed. She imagined it must feel like this to be on trial, falsely accused of some unspecified crime; so much might hang on something as simple as her choice of phrase. She could almost sense the held breath of the watching guests, as they waited for her to speak, as though they held taut-pulled longbows, aimed at her, ready to loose.

'Well . . .' she said, and her voice sounded in the stillness like a stranger's. She gripped the first two fingers of her left hand in her right fist and twisted them. 'I like the way he seems to be trying to create a feeling of – of weightlessness. Airiness. Out of something as solid and heavy as marble.' She paused. 'Papa has two of his pieces and . . . and that was what I thought when I saw them.'

Panizato grinned. The watching guests looked from him to Alfonso to Lucrezia, waiting, Lucrezia presumed, for the duke's reaction to her opinion. The bowstrings tautened still further. Alfonso held her gaze, the corners of his mouth lifting a fraction. 'Weightless marble?' he said.

Several of the guests laughed, loosed their arrows. Lucrezia flinched.

'Very clever, madam, very clever. *Contradictio in terminis*, no less.'

More laughter.

Lucrezia, not understanding Alfonso's words, but hearing his mocking tone and realizing that she had now become the butt of the guests' sycophantic mirth, felt tears in the corners of her eyes. Determined not to let Alfonso see her distress, though, she caught the tip of her tongue between her teeth and for nearly a full minute they held each other's gaze. Lucrezia imagined two fighters, fists raised, circling warily as a blood-lustful audience pressed in around them, waiting for the first punch to be thrown. The hunger in Alfonso's eyes was now unmistakable.

'I see that I shall indeed have to acquire one of his works for the Castello,' he said, his eyes on her mouth. 'A commission, I think. Something substantial.' He smirked at her. 'Weightless, of course, but substantial.'

There was another ripple of appreciative laughter – another handful of arrows found their target – and then the guests seemed to understand that the spectacle was at an end, for the bee-swarm hum of the banquet's many conversations began to buzz again.

Alfonso leaned back in his chair and spoke to Panizato behind Lucrezia's back. 'Make my excuses, Francesco, will you?' Then, squeezing her fingers, he said to Lucrezia, 'Come with me. I have something I want you to see.'

They pushed back their chairs and Alfonso led the way past dozens of curious diners. Lucrezia saw openly lascivious expressions on several faces as the guests saw their clasped hands and, presumably, drew their own conclusions. She was surprised not to be feeling acutely embarrassed but, increasingly fuzzy and disconnected with the wine she had drunk, she found she did not much care. She battled to maintain a reasonably dignified expression until they had left the hall, her face quite stiff with the effort.

Giovanni watched Lucrezia and the duke leave the banqueting hall, their fingers linked. His cousin's cheeks were flushed, as though she had had too much to drink. A dull anger pulsed behind his eyes and, looking down at the table, he picked up a piece of bread and crushed it inside his fist. That bastard – how dare he make fun of Crezzi like that in front of their guests? It was a cheap trick. Unforgivable. Giovanni was certain the duke would not have dared to behave like that in front of Uncle Cosimo.

At first, he had been pleased that his uncle and aunt had not travelled to Ferrara with him, fond as he was of them: over the past couple of weeks at the Castello, he had much enjoyed the independence and the lack of supervision that their absence had allowed him. But now, watching *Il Duca* leading his cousin out of the hall, with a smug smile on his face and a bulge in his breeches – like a man in a brothel who knows he has picked the prize *puttana* – Giovanni wished fiercely that Uncle Cosimo could have been here tonight to witness how shamefully his adored son-in-law had just treated his beloved daughter.

Giovanni had only a few days left in Ferrara; perhaps, he thought, he should just leave in the morning, race home to Cafaggiolo and pour out to his aunt and uncle his suspicions, his observations and his re-established fears that, despite her protestations to the contrary, Lucrezia was fundamentally unhappy.

But then he remembered why his aunt and uncle were not here.

He pictured again the morning of Uncle Cosimo's collapse. The day his uncle had returned from a ride and dismounted, then clutched at his chest and sunk to his knees, sucking at the air with a sound like a pair of punctured bellows. Oh, he had recovered soon enough, but Aunt Eleanora had made it abundantly clear to the entire household (not in his uncle's hearing, of course) on numerous occasions since, that her husband should not be unnecessarily alarmed or agitated, that he should not have to travel any further than he must, and that everyone should make a strenuous effort to keep him calm at all times.

What Giovanni wanted to say would probably kill him.

He would have to keep his fears to himself.

But he would return to Cafaggiolo the following day.

He pushed his chair back from the table and left the banquet by the door at the opposite end of the room.

'Where are we going? Your apartment?' Lucrezia asked.

'No.'

Alfonso, with her hand still tightly clasped in his own, led her to a small hall just beyond the great entrance doors.

'I want to see if you can offer me another inspiring opinion on a work of art.'

Lucrezia felt sick.

'Here, Lucrezia, tell me what you think,' he said. He stopped in front of a small painting in a simple gold frame. It depicted a languid, bare-breasted woman, leaning on one hand. She had one leg stretched out before her, the other was bent up under her crumpled white dress, which seemed to Lucrezia to be little more than a draped sheet. Leaning over her was a man in Roman clothing, a coronet of leaves around his head. The painting seemed oddly unfinished: the brushstrokes were broad and free and there was little detail.

A gauntlet had clearly been flung at her feet.

'It reminds me of another painting,' she said slowly. 'One I think I've seen here in the Castello. But this looks like a sketch –

it's not finished properly.' That last remark slipped out before she could stop it, and for a frozen moment she thought she had said the wrong thing – criticized a new acquisition and thus proved her ignorance. She looked up at Alfonso, her scalp prickling with anxiety, expecting the dark eyes to be flashing with anger.

But he said, 'I'm impressed. It is a study for the *Feast of the Gods* that Bellini did for my father nearly forty years ago. You're right – you have seen it here, up in the Long Gallery. Do you like the study? I found it and bought it only last week.'

'I like it better than the big painting.'

'Why?'

'It's . . .' Lucrezia tried to speak sensibly through the wine-muddled jumble of her thoughts. 'It's like a brief second of reality, somehow captured by a brush. The finished painting is more . . . more static. Artificial.'

Alfonso did not speak again but took Lucrezia's hand and led her out of the room. As they went back past the banquet, the buffeting concoction of voices, clattering silverware and joyous music gave their covert passage past the great doors an unexpected frisson of illicit naughtiness. A tingling sense of anticipation began to creep over Lucrezia, and by the time they reached Alfonso's apartments, she was vividly nervous and excited.

Folletto the wolfhound scrambled to his feet as Alfonso and Lucrezia entered the largest of the three chambers. He uttered a few deep barks of pleasure at the sight of his master, but tonight, it seemed, his master's attention was elsewhere.

'Get out!' Alfonso hissed. He raised a booted foot and shoved roughly at the dog's side. Folletto yelped. Alfonso held open the door to the apartment and said again, 'Go on, get out!' The dog's tail drooped and, with a reproachful look, he loped from the room.

Alfonso closed the door, turned to Lucrezia and walked her backwards to his bedchamber, unfastening laces as he went. He began to kiss her as they reached the bed. His mouth upon hers, he pulled open her now laceless bodice and, as she lay back, he pushed up her skirts, exposing her legs, bunching the cloth untidily around her waist. For some moments it was the experience Lucrezia had longed for and she revelled in sensing and seeing Alfonso's hands on her body – dark against her pale skin.

But then, poised on the brink of consummation, with, on this occasion, every expectation of success, her gaze met his. Earlier that evening, she had seen a naked hunger in his eyes – a hunger that had indeed fired her own longing for physical satisfaction – but his expression now was different. No longer hunger, but greed: a greedy, dissolute stare, devoid of warmth or affection. She had never seen such a look on his face before and it frightened her. There was no love in it. This was how a man might look at a whore. Her eyes wide with fear, she shrank away from him towards the pillows, crossing her arms over her breasts and pulling her knees up towards her chest.

Alfonso's expression changed. For a second, what appeared to be panic distorted his face, but then this was followed by a hard, shadowed anger. '*Cazzo!*' he hissed. Then, almost under his breath, in a voice somewhere between a mutter and a moan, he said, '*Merda!* Not again – not now!' And then louder, more guttural, 'No, no, no – by the rancid piss of Beelzebub, you will *not* fuck it up *again*!'

He clenched his right hand into a fist.

Lucrezia gasped. For a cold empty second, already shocked by the venom of his oaths, she felt sure he was going to hit her; she shut her eyes tight and turned away from him, shoulders hunched, palms over her face.

But the blow did not come.

Lucrezia opened her eyes again and saw him get up off the bed. He bent and reached for his discarded doublet. Suddenly aware of her exposed legs and breasts, Lucrezia sat up, pulled the front edges of her bodice together with fingers that trembled, and then pushed her skirts back down over her knees.

Alfonso said, 'Go to your chambers, Lucrezia – I do not think we should see each other again tonight. I . . . I will return to the banquet.' He stared fixedly down at the laces of his doublet as he spoke.

Without a word, Lucrezia crossed the room and opened the door. Folletto lay across the threshold, blocking her way out. As she made to step over him, he growled and stood up. His head was almost level with her shoulder.

'Oh, God, please move!' she muttered.

Alfonso swore again. 'Folletto!' he snapped. The great dog pushed past Lucrezia, into the apartment. Turning back into the room, Lucrezia saw that her husband was facing away from her, staring silently out of the window. The dog seated itself at his feet and he laid a hand on its head.

For a long moment, nobody moved. Then, with hot tears on her cheeks, Lucrezia walked unseeingly along the two corridors and up the spiral staircase to her own apartment, barefoot, with her arms folded over her chest to hold her bodice closed.

Catelina stood up as the door to the Signora's apartment opened. At the sight of her mistress she dropped the shift she had been mending. The Signora's hair was dishevelled, her bodice was unlaced, her feet were bare – and her face was slick and swollen with tears.

'Oh, my lady – oh, dear God – whatever is the matter?'

The Signora shook her head, either unwilling or unable to speak. Catelina crossed the room and put her arms around her mistress. The Signora stood stiffly within the embrace; she felt small and thin, and that chicken-bone breakableness now quite tore at Catelina's heart. And then the stiffness dissolved and the Signora was weeping: great shuddering sobs that shook her whole body. It was, Catelina thought, a sound of utter despair. The thin arms crept around Catelina and the small fingers gripped the stuff of her dress. They stood clasped together for several moments, and Catelina stroked the Signora's hair, muttering soothing nonsense until the weeping subsided.

Part Three

Ferrara, April 1561
Fifteen months later

9

A fresco is a truly monumental form of art, Alfonso thought, as he lay on his back with his fingers interlaced behind his head. How long was it since he had seen those first sketches? Well over a year. Admittedly, Pandolf had been obliged to finish another commission and had not been able to turn his full attention to the Castello's fresco design until some ten months ago, but still, it had not been until that very morning that the letter had arrived, announcing his readiness to begin work on site. The sketching, drawing and cartooning had taken him the best part of a year. The enormity of the task pleased Alfonso very much; he ran a hand over and around Francesca's bottom, and admitted to himself that he was almost childishly excited at the prospect of the painters' imminent arrival.

'Get off!' Francesca murmured sleepily.

Smiling, he closed his fingers more tightly on one buttock. Francesca, eyes still closed, moved away from him and shifted position to lie on her back. The exquisite body was still damp with the sweat of their coupling and her hair had tumbled around her face and shoulders. He lifted a lock of it and wound it around his finger. He was thankful she had not attempted to bleach it, as so many women seemed to be doing now; it was still raven-black and lustrous. The lock of hair slipped from his finger and lay curled over her breast and around one brown nipple. Like a dark comma, Alfonso thought, punctuating the intoxicating statement of the perfect body.

Francesca sighed and ran a hand over her breast, pushing away the hair; her nipple slid into and out of the space between her first two fingers.

Alfonso watched her for a moment, but, rather than arouse him again, the languid voluptuousness of his whore made him think, unwillingly, of the contrast between her and the diminutive creature whose understated, boyish allure continued to obsess him. Francesca had always been pliant, enthusiastic, uninhibited: a willing vessel into which he knew he could pour himself whenever he needed to sate his restless energy. But even after so many long months, access to Lucrezia's more intimate charms was still denied him.

Although a persistent longing for his wife now tugged almost continually at his consciousness, his attempts at consummation had become increasingly rare; the scorching humiliation he felt at each failure had become so intensely painful that he knew he was now avoiding the issue as often as he could. But he had to continue trying. He had to produce an heir. Without an heir, the future of the duchy was dangerously unstable.

A wave of anger thrust up into his throat like bile: a black, bleak anger that Alfonso knew was directed as much towards himself as Lucrezia. Here they were, locked into a lifelong contract that was impossible to rescind on pain of damnation. Was this some game of God's? Was the Almighty punishing him for some unwitting misdeed? The injustice seemed catastrophic: his wife –

the potential mother of the heir to the duchy – reduced him to the status of a eunuch each time he attempted to bed her. What did it signify that he could fuck Francesca like a lust-crazed satyr as often as he chose and that he had fathered upon his whore a pair of beautiful bastard children? Nothing whatsoever – for as far as the fate of the duchy was concerned, the only fact that mattered was that his wife . . . castrated him. Hobbled him. Rendered him impotent. The words sneered their way into his mind and Alfonso clenched his jaw, balling both hands into fists in an attempt to stem a rising tide of what felt perilously near panic.

He pushed back the bedcovers and walked across the chill brick floor to the window. The *villetta* overlooked flat fields, ditch-edged, fringed with regiments of rushes. Regiments, Alfonso thought sourly. An apt image. It seemed to him now that inside his embattled head, his thoughts were continually pushing their relentless way forward like massed legions. Knock one down, defeat another and infinite numbers of replacements would mobilize and continue the onslaught.

'What's the matter?' Francesca said.

Alfonso did not reply.

'What is it? Did I not please you today?'

He turned back into the room.

'You seemed content enough just now,' Francesca said. She rubbed her still chafed and reddened wrists somewhat ruefully.

'It is nothing you have done.'

Alfonso knew that Francesca would not question him, but he could see that she was stifling her curiosity. The great mass of unspoken truths lay heavy in his chest and the need to unburden himself swelled up into his throat like rising nausea.

'Lucrezia,' he said at last.

The four syllables hung in the air. Alfonso sensed Francesca stiffening. She said nothing, but sat up and raised both arms to her hair, which she piled on top of her head. Alfonso watched, holding his breath, as her breasts quivered with the movements of her fingers. Holding her hair with one hand, she reached out to the table next to her pillow and picked up a long ivory pin, which she pushed through the pile. She lowered her arms, her eyes fixed upon Alfonso's face. He breathed out slowly, trying to decide which of the myriad unpalatable truths he could bear to reveal.

'She is . . . indiscriminate,' he said at last.

'Other men?' Francesca said, sounding astonished.

He shook his head. 'You misunderstand me. She is – is a gracious consort, and many of my guests continue to congratulate me on my good fortune in obtaining a wife as beautiful and charming as Lucrezia. But . . .'

The horrible truths were jostling for release, like flotsam building up behind a dam. For it was, Alfonso thought, not only in his bed that Lucrezia humiliated him so effectively. No, it was far more than that – her eviscerating influence upon him had become increasingly insidious and wide-ranging. She still seemed to have no sense of the signal eminence of the position he had bestowed upon her with their marriage. No, that was not right, it was not that she was unaware . . .

'Do you know what she said to me the other day?' he said.

Lucrezia looks at him, perplexed, and irritation tightens around his throat like a garrotte.

'It can hardly be difficult to understand,' he says. 'You have married into a family considerably older and more prestigious even than that into which you were born.'

'I know.' She sounds suspicious.

'Do you not think,' he says, 'that, given the position in society into

*which you have now been placed, a certain sobriety of disposition might
be seen as appropriate?'*

She frowns. 'I don't know what you mean.'

*'It is . . .' Alfonso searches for the apposite word '. . . it is – to say
the least – unfortunate for the Duchess of Ferrara to be seen about the
Castello by all and sundry, behaving little better than a street urchin.'*

*'I still don't know what you mean.' Her voice is a little louder this
time.*

*'You were begging food from the head cook in the kitchens again the
other day, were you not? And this morning I find you doubled over with
laughter in the central courtyard in the company of one of the stewards.'*

'He's very funny.'

'He is a servant, Lucrezia!'

'Do you know what she said? Hear this, Francesca, this is my
duchess! The most prestigious woman in the House of Este!
"Surely," she says to me, "surely, if a person is funny, or clever, or
in any other way talented, they should be valued as such, whatever
place in society God has chosen for them?"'

Francesca said nothing.

Alfonso continued. 'She is *pleased* by *everything*! And everyone.'

Francesca frowned. 'What's wrong with that? I don't understand. Is that not good?'

'It could be seen to be so, I suppose, but my duchess seems as
pleased by the simplest and least worthy gift she is offered by a
transient guest, by a smile from a kitchen drudge, by her elderly
and foul-smelling mule as she is by the honour of my lasting gift
of a place in the ancient Este lineage. It's – it's—' He stuttered in
frustration. 'It's . . . humiliating.'

'Have you told her how you feel?'

'As best I can,' he said.

'Perhaps the situation will improve when . . .' Francesca hesitated '. . . when she produces an heir. Perhaps she will rethink her position then.'

Alfonso winced. 'Yes. Well. She has not managed to fulfil that task as yet,' he said sourly. Inwardly he cringed at his words, knowing how unjust he was being in reapportioning the blame, merely to ease his own sense of shameful culpability.

Francesca said nothing. She sighed and Alfonso wondered if she was thinking of her daughters. The two bastard children he never could, or would, acknowledge. They were beautiful, though, he thought. Beautiful, wilful, clever little sluts – just like their mother.

'What will you do?' Francesca said, at last.

'Nothing. As I say, I do not care to *make* her change her ways. I need her to understand and appreciate her position without my intervention. If I have *told* her what she should think, there can be no merit in her thoughts.'

Alfonso was surprised to see a scowl on Francesca's normally passive face, but he realized almost at once that it was a reflection of what she saw on his own countenance, for when he deliberately relaxed and softened his own expression, he saw the sulky lines vanish from her brow.

Crossing to the untidy pile of his clothes, Alfonso picked up his shirt and pulled it over his head.

Francesca sat up. 'Don't go yet, Alfonso,' she said. 'Perhaps before you leave – if you have time – I can . . .' The triangular tip of a pink tongue moistened her lips. 'I can . . . raise your spirits a little.'

Alfonso checked to see how high the sun had climbed, and decided he might linger another hour before his presence would be required back at the Castello. Francesca came to where he stood and crouched on her heels in front of him, her hands on his hips. Alfonso closed his eyes and pushed his fingers into her hair as she bent forward.

A little later, Francesca knelt up on the bed and watched through the window as Alfonso swung his mare round and clattered away on the road to the city, then she lay back down and ran her palms over her face. She screwed her eyes shut and gently kneaded her jaw with her fingers, easing out the stiffness, then ran her tongue over her lips, which felt swollen and hot. She lay quite still for several moments, the faint draught from the window raising the hairs on her arms, legs and belly.

At least he had left in a better mood.

'One quick suck and he's smiling again,' she muttered aloud, remembering the first time she had ever been asked to perform *that* particular trick. On her first evening as a whore.

She is seventeen years old, newly arrived from Crespino, standing outside a tavern near the cathedral: penniless, hungry, warily anxious, but nonetheless happy to have escaped the prospect of replacing her late mother as the preferred target for the undisciplined fists of her frequently drink-sodden father.

'God, you're beautiful, mignotta! What a mouth! How much would you want . . . just for a . . .?' the man says, pushing his tongue into his cheek and waggling it back and forth. He glances meaningfully at his breeches, then strokes her hair, cupping her chin in his hand. He is young, fair-haired, slack-jawed and smells strongly of grappa.

She has been expecting something like this for days. The idea frightens her, but from the moment of her arrival in Ferrara, she has presumed that whoring will be her probable source of income. Feeling sick, she suggests a price, trying to sound unconcerned, experienced. He puffs out his cheeks in surprise, but then he nods, jerks his head away from the tavern and mutters, 'Well, come on, then . . .' Taking her wrist, he leads her to a dark alcove beside the furthest of the little covered shops that nestle in under the long protective side wall of the great cathedral.

And then she is on her knees in the mud and his iron fingers are gripping her shoulders; she grabs fistfuls of his doublet to steady herself. He puts a hand behind her head, beginning to enjoy himself, and in the next few blind moments of gagging panic, she is afraid he will choke her.

Francesca rolled onto her stomach on the big bed in the *villetta*, the never-forgotten nausea of it thick in her throat again. She remembered the fair-haired man finally groaning, releasing his grip and jerking away from her; remembered falling onto all fours, retching into the dirt, remembered the final humiliation.

'Well,' he says, 'you certainly rate yourself a lot more highly than you deliver, stronza. I wouldn't suggest you ask for a fee like that again.'

Flipping a couple of small silver coins onto the ground in front of her, he walks away, whistling and refastening his laces as he goes.

Shaking with relief, burning with anger, she watches him go. 'Never again,' she says, spitting the last of him into the dirt. 'Never again will I do anything like that – without making damned sure I have my money in advance.'

'Come on, then, *puttana*,' Francesca muttered to herself. 'Stop all this. It's time to get up.'

Sighing, she padded across the room and picked up her lawn shift from the floor; she pulled it on and ran her hands down her front, smoothing out the creases. Her bodice and skirt she put on with practised ease, tightening laces, wriggling her shoulders and shifting each breast into a more comfortable position within the stiff damask with her fingers.

She closed the window, raked the embers, straightened the bed-covers, pushed her feet into her shoes.

A bag of coins lay on the low table near the door. This Francesca picked up and weighed in the palm of her hand. 'At least I command a better price today,' she said. Throwing the little bag up and catching it, then closing and locking the door, she set off for the city. It was a good half-hour's walk, but Francesca was used to travelling on foot and, in today's mild sunshine, she was happy to be out. Snatches of Alfonso's conversation repeated themselves insistently in her head, and, as she walked, a small seed of curiosity put out a little green shoot.

She is indiscriminate, he had said, and *pleased by everything.* That either implied a particularly sweet and generous disposition, Francesca thought, or nothing more than a lack of judgement. *If I have told her what she should think, there can be no merit in her thoughts* . . . Not for the first time, Francesca wondered what this girl was actually like. She rather approved of someone who had to be 'told what to think': it suggested a certain waywardness with which she could easily identify, and she was quite impressed with those sentiments Alfonso had found so disturbing. '"Whatever place in society God has chosen for them . . ."' she said to herself. God had not, she thought, chosen a very comfortable place in society for the duchess: it could not be easy to be married to the complex and controlling Alfonso.

She rubbed her reddened wrists, which still felt hot and sore, and wondered for a moment if he imposed upon his wife the same demands in his bed as he did upon her, and if he did, whether or not she was . . . *pleased* by them. He had told her several times that the duchess was *beautiful and charming*. Well, Francesca thought now, the girl's beauty and charm certainly did not seem to be *pleasing* her husband: Alfonso appeared to be increasingly at odds with her as the months went on. And the girl had not yet conceived. That had to be saying something.

'Do you know, after all this time, I think I'd very much like to see this woman for myself,' Francesca said aloud, suddenly aware of the singularity of the fact that she had not done so before.

An old man, dozing on a stone bench at the side of the road with a scrawny dog curled at his feet, started at the sound of her voice as she walked past him. Francesca smiled at them both; the dog thumped its tail in the dust but the old man made no response.

Seated on the floor in Francesca's front room were two small girls, some six years old, black-haired, huge-eyed, identical to the last hair. They were picking glass beads out of a bowl and carefully threading them onto lengths of thin twine.

'Girls, I want to go up to the Castello again,' Francesca said.

'Again?'

Francesca smiled. 'Yes. Again. Of course, if you don't want to come too, you can go to Signora del Sarto's house.'

Both girls shook their heads, and so, for the fourth day running, they and Francesca walked up from their little house in the Via Vecchie, round the façade of the cathedral and on up to the wide piazza in front of the Castello.

'We'll do what we did yesterday and the day before, and walk right the way around the whole building,' Francesca said. 'We might see her today.' She saw the twins glance at each other, but they made no comment.

They walked around three sides of the big red fortress, stopping every now and again for the girls to plip pebbles into the black water of the moat and count the ripples, and then, as they approached the gateway to the main drawbridge, they stopped, hearing the clatter of hoofs on the wooden bridge.

'Hold hands, and stand back,' Francesca said. They stepped backwards, away from the gateway, their fingers tightly laced.

Two horses appeared: a heavy black cob with a long fringe hiding its eyes, and a smaller bay pony. A grey-haired man rode the cob, but the pony was carrying a thin girl. She was finely dressed in beautifully cut, dark-green velvet, though Francesca could see that, despite her finery, the girl sat the pony with little confidence. The grey-haired man pointed across to the girl's hands and, gesturing with his own, said something Francesca could not catch, though she heard the words 'my lady'. The girl shortened her reins and, somewhat gingerly, shifted her position in the saddle. The bay pony tossed its head; the girl caught her lip between her teeth.

Francesca stared. This had to be her – the elaborate, jewelled clothes, her companion's air of deference. The tawny hair and freckles matched Alfonso's descriptions of her. Surely this was the duchess.

Her idle wish to see Alfonso's wife for herself had fed upon itself for nearly a week now, and much to her daughters' annoyance, had had all three of them pacing the outskirts of the Castello for days. Now, somewhat to her surprise, Francesca found that her pulse rate was quickening at the sight of the duchess. Alfonso's description of his wife as 'beautiful' was perhaps a little inaccurate, Francesca thought, but there was something arresting about the small, freckled face, while the slightness of the velvet-clad shoulders made her seem touchingly vulnerable.

Despite herself, Francesca began imagining this girl in Alfonso's bed and realized, with an unexpected jolt in her guts, that the emotion which hit her as the images played out in her mind was not jealousy but concern. Solicitude. He would be able to break this creature into pieces with ease. She drew in a sharp breath.

'What is it, Mamma?' Beata was holding her hand and looking up into her face.

'Nothing.'

But it was not nothing: it was the sudden cold dawning of a creeping disaffection.

Beata's fingers gripped her own more tightly. Francesca saw that the duchess was staring at the twins, a wondering smile tilting the corners of her mouth. Then she turned to Francesca, the smile widened and a bright look of unaffected sweetness broke across her face.

'Signor Bracciante,' she said to her companion, her eyes still on Francesca, 'could you wait a moment, please?'

The grey-haired man reined in his mount.

'Forgive me, I did not mean to stare,' the duchess said to Francesca, 'but I thought for a moment that my eyes were playing tricks upon me . . .'

'My girls are indeed very similar,' Francesca said.

'It's quite extraordinary.' The duchess turned to the girls. 'And – not only are you so very much alike, you are both so very pretty!'

Beata and Isabella smiled shyly at her, wriggling with bashful self-consciousness.

Francesca was startled to see longing behind the duchess's smile and heard again the coldness in Alfonso's voice from a few days before: '*Yes. Well. She has not managed to fulfil that task as yet.*' She had sometimes wondered if Alfonso's frustrations might stem from his wife's wilful withholding of her favours, but now, seeing that hunger in her face, it was, Francesca thought, quite clearly no fault of this girl's that she had not yet conceived.

The duchess was speaking again to the twins. 'Wait a moment, don't move – I have something for you both . . .'

The little girls held hands and stared up at her. Francesca watched as she turned to her companion. 'Signor Bracciante, can you hold his reins a moment?'

The man leaned across and took the bay pony's reins. The duchess tugged at one of the pearl-centred knots of grass-green ribbon on her left sleeve. After a moment it came loose, leaving a pulled thread and a tiny hole in the velvet. 'There's one . . .' She leaned down and held it out to Beata. The little girl looked at Francesca, who smiled and nodded. Beata took the ribbon from the outstretched hand, and then the duchess jerked another free and handed it to Isabella.

'Thank you, my lady,' Francesca said. 'Say thank you, girls!' She nudged Beata with her hip, and both children looked up from their awed contemplation of their new treasures to murmur their gratitude.

The duchess's smile widened. 'Take care of them, won't you?'

Francesca fancied that this appeal was addressed as much to her as a mother, as to the new owners of the little green favours.

The duchess gathered up her reins, clicked her tongue and the pony began to walk, some two paces behind the cob. A moment later, both riders broke into a trot and were soon out of sight.

Alfonso, watching from a window in his apartment in the Torre dei Leoni, saw Lucrezia and the riding master turn south out of the piazza, heading no doubt for the open ground beyond the city walls.

He pulled on a doublet, snatched a couple of candles from a low table and left his chamber. Walking quickly, he made his way down through the Castello. At the entrance to the long, sloping corridor that led to the dungeons, he flicked a glance to left and right. Reassured that he was unobserved, he lit one of his two candles from a burning torch in a nearby wall bracket, and descended towards the Stygian gloom of the underground cells.

Ducking his head, he turned left into a short passage, whose ceiling was no higher than his shoulder. He walked awkwardly, bent-backed, some half-dozen paces and stepped down into a low, vaulted room. Had he chosen to reach upwards, his fingers would have touched the stone ceiling with ease. The door to this room, made of heavily banded iron, stood wide open. There were no windows, instead, a single square aperture, into which Alfonso might have been able to squeeze himself, had it not been cross-barred, led steeply upwards, narrowing like a funnel, up beyond the level of the moat to allow the access of air. No light penetrated.

Alfonso sat on the floor with his back against one of the walls, and, holding the lit candle sideways, allowed a few drops of wax to fall onto the stone flag. He placed the candle upright in the soft blob, and laid the second nearby. Crossing back to the door, he pushed it, two-handed, until it was barely an inch from closure, then returned to the candle and sat back down.

Tipping his head back, he closed his eyes and rested his arms across his bent knees, fingers loosely touching.

The silence in the cell was thick and soft and it pressed in around him, blocking his ears and filling his throat. Here, in this smothering quiet – for a matter of minutes, at least – his mind was still.

10

Lucrezia was surprised at the lack of ceremony when the painters arrived. Infected by Alfonso's growing excitement over the previous week, she had expected drama, an impressive number of people, something significant to indicate the eminence of Fra Pandolf's reputation. But when the group from Assisi reached the central courtyard of the Castello in the second week of April, she was a little disappointed to find that the entire party consisted of the friar, his apprentice and another lad, who seemed to be there solely to take charge of the three horses and the shabby little tilt-cart. It did not seem appropriate for the creators of what she understood was to be a significant new work of art.

Alfonso, however, was smiling broadly as he stepped forward to greet the new arrivals. Fra Pandolf climbed wearily from the cart, the apprentice and the boy dismounted from their horses and they all stretched cramped limbs and looked about them.

'Fra Pandolf, all of you, welcome to the Castello,' Alfonso said.

The friar beamed, holding out his arms as though in benediction. The tall apprentice with the crimson-splashed cheek sketched a brief bow, and the boy bobbed his head embarrassed at thus being acknowledged.

Pandolf took one of Alfonso's hands in his own, bowed to Lucrezia, and then said over his shoulder to his companions, 'Tomaso, can you take charge of the horses? Jacomo, bring the box of pigments and the brushes, will you? I want to get them in and put away as quickly as possible.'

Tomaso began to do as he had been asked, and Jacomo reached into the tilt-cart and hitched a large wooden box into his arms, leaning a little backwards to accommodate its considerable weight. Lucrezia smiled at him, as he followed the friar and his hosts into the Castello, but Jacomo was looking at the ground around the side of the box as he picked his way across the uneven cobbles and did not see her. She quickly straightened her face, and made a play of tucking a wisp of hair behind an ear, feeling foolish and hoping that no one else had noticed.

Of the new arrivals, only Fra Pandolf attended the evening meal on that first night. Lucrezia wondered briefly why Alfonso had not invited the apprentice or the boy, but presumed that some incomprehensible castle protocol lay behind his decision. Fearing his displeasure, she had decided not to ask him.

She looked around the room, seeing it now with Pandolf's eyes, wondering what his artist's mind would make of his surroundings. The Long Room: Alfonso usually called it the Room of Mirrors, for a dozen great Venetian looking-glasses – four on each long wall, two at each end – created a sensation of endless repetition as they reflected upon themselves over and over. Though only four sat at the table that evening, around the walls a crowd appeared to be enjoying their meal: a dozen friars, as many black-clad dukes; a flock of shimmering, silk-gowned duchesses, and a clutch of brightly dressed noblemen. Lucrezia blew softly at one of the candles, and watched the dipping flame multiply and replicate itself a hundredfold in the glittering glass, like evening sunlight on water.

'Father Guardian at Assisi is indeed generous in allowing his most gifted son to bestow his extraordinary talents upon the Castello Estense,' said Francesco Panizato, inclining his head towards the friar.

The friar blushed deeply at this unctuous comment – to Lucrezia's delight, even the patch of pink scalp inside his tonsure had reddened. 'Gracious Signore, you misunderstand,' he replied, in his flat, Genovese accent. 'Do not forget, we Franciscans are mendicants – beggars. We wander where we choose and we praise God with whichever talents He has seen fit to bestow upon us.' He bowed towards Alfonso. 'Signor d'Este is merely allowing me a more than welcome opportunity to praise my Lord with brush and with plaster . . .'

A picture pushed its way into Lucrezia's mind of a jostling crowd of cheerful winged seraphs, ineptly wielding paint and plaster-laden brushes, sending splashes and wet lumps flying around the gates of Heaven. A furious St Peter stood, hands on hips, keys clinking, glaring at them, a splash of vivid blue across his nose, chin and down the front of his gleaming white robes. She smothered a laugh. Then, glancing up into one of the mirrors, she saw the imagined anger of the guardian of the gates reproduced on the face of her husband. Alfonso's eyes were blazing and his mouth was no more than a thin line. Lucrezia dropped her gaze to the table, her cheeks flaming and tears threatening.

Picking up her fork, she began to push her food around her plate. Orange-poached sardines. One of her mother's favourites. Her own choice, this evening. She sighed. For once she had actually been given the task of choosing the food, as Alfonso had been preoccupied with the arrival of the painters and had unexpectedly delegated the responsibility. She and Catelina had constructed the evening's menu earlier that week.

'I had thought,' she says to Catelina, in an unguarded moment, quill in hand as they list possible dishes, 'when I left Cafaggiolo, that this would have been one of the tasks for which I would be responsible as the new duchess.' Her voice sounds – even to her – stilted and unnatural as she fights not to betray her anger. 'Mamma always chooses the food for the more important meals at home. She often showed me what to do. How to construct an interesting range of dishes. I think I could probably do it quite well. She and I talked about it several times when I went home to see them a few months ago, and she was very surprised that I hadn't really begun to make an impression upon life in the castle yet. She was quite unhappy about it.'

Catelina looks anxiously at her.

Lucrezia says, and there is a sharp note of bitterness in her voice, 'I didn't like to tell her that Alfonso is not confident in my abilities to do very much at all.'

'Oh, I'm sure it's not that, my lady.'

And then it bursts from her. 'But it is, Lina! He has told me quite clearly! And he continually makes sure I don't go behind his back and accidentally display any unexpected ability that he has not personally sanctioned. What – of any note – have you ever seen me do in this place?' She glares at her maid, then answers her own question. 'Nothing! I do nothing! What point is there in my being here at all? Why does he want me here?'

The tip of her quill cracks as she presses it too hard into the paper, and ink spatters across the list of dishes she has already written down. The obvious answer to her question screams itself into the silence. The obvious, horrible answer. She has been traded between families like a brood mare — but is it not the case, she thinks bitterly, that a brood mare which continually fails to excite the stallion is of little use to anyone as anything other than dog meat? Perhaps it is because she is so signally unsuccessful in this most fundamental role that Alfonso has no wish to trust her with any other tasks.

She and Catelina stare at each other, not speaking.

Lucrezia remembers being so curious on her arrival at the Castello that simply absorbing her new surroundings had seemed stimulating enough. For weeks she had been happy to be little more than a fascinated bystander. But as the months have passed, she increasingly wishes to take a more active part in her new life. Try as she might, though, she finds her ideas crushed almost before she utters them, her opinions ridiculed or ignored, and her interactions with the servants continually controlled and limited by her husband.

It is all so very different from the life she knew before her marriage.

Alfonso seldom speaks to Lucrezia of his own childhood, or of his parents and his upbringing in the Castello, but from the fragments of memory he occasionally allows her to grasp during their rare conversations, she imagines a boyhood almost unbearably bleak in comparison with her own experiences. She feels a surprising lurch of sympathy for him, as she pictures a lonely little boy, friendless in this great rambling, city-bound fortress. His father, by Alfonso's own admission, was a distant, unloving man, and Lucrezia discovers that Alfonso had spent much of his early youth without his mother.

His formality and lack of warmth is, she supposes, understandable, though to her it seems both alien and horribly restricting. Only with Catelina does she truly feel unconstrained, but the intimacy and informality she cannot suppress with her maid, she keeps well hidden from Alfonso.

'He makes me feel so powerless, Lina,' she says, pressing the cracked nib against the ball of her thumb. 'What sort of woman am

I growing into? I am given no opportunity to manage my house, I am forbidden to communicate with my servants – and at the merest glimpse of my naked body, my husband's prick wilts like yesterday's picked daisy.'

Catelina blushes scarlet at the intimacy.

Lucrezia's voice sounds hard. 'To be still a virgin after a year and a half as a wife – how shameful is that? I can only imagine that it must hurt Alfonso as much as it hurts me – but how will I ever know? He never talks to me.'

She falls silent, recalling the embarrassing attempts at consummation that she and Alfonso still sometimes endure. Inevitably, she thinks, these moments are ever more awkward, silent, loveless. On each occasion she has begun to feel as though the as yet unconceived heir squats, like an incubus, in a corner of the room, watching, accusing, demanding to be given the opportunity to exist, pouring angry scorn on their repeated failures.

Fra Pandolf scraped the last fragment of sardine from his plate, and turned to Lucrezia, a gilded Murano glass in his hand.

'What think you, my lady, of the idea of having a fresco painted here at the Castello Estense?'

Lucrezia pulled her thoughts back to the present. 'If the promise of the drawings I saw before is borne out in the fresco itself, it will be a truly magnificent achievement, sir,' she said, smiling at the doughy figure, and longing to remove the tiny fragment of fish that clung to his lower lip. She thought back to the day she had seen the extraordinary preliminary sketches, and said, 'Shall you be working together on the fresco, you and your apprentice?'

For a moment, Lucrezia thought she detected a tightening in the friar's face, but then he smiled, and said, 'Oh, yes, Signora, Jacomo is indispensable. I have not had such a capable apprentice in years.'

'Where did you find him?' Alfonso asked.

'His father approached me several years ago now – and asked if I might take him on. Said he thought the lad had talent. I admit now that I was not expecting much – you would be surprised, Signore, at the number of doting fathers who are quite convinced their children are budding Buonarottis . . .'

Alfonso and Francesco Panizato smiled.

'But,' Fra Pandolf continued, 'in the event, he proved to be quite a remarkable artist. Quite remarkable. In fact, I have – oh, yes, thank you . . .'

The friar broke off as he was offered a plate, laid with grilled bream. Lucrezia's plate was placed before her. She knew she should eat. The wine she had drunk was fuzzing her thoughts and her head felt woolly. She was losing the thread of the conversations that flashed across the table like contestants in a fencing competition. She picked at the fish and watched Alfonso and Francesco vying happily with each other to prove to Fra Pandolf that each was the greater connoisseur of the arts.

They were both bright-eyed and flushed, though Lucrezia could see that Alfonso was striving to maintain his dignity, despite the energy of the conversation. However passionately he felt about something, Lucrezia reflected, she knew he preferred not to show it; even now he was probably struggling to contain his animation. He would want to appear deeply knowledgeable, she thought, but he would be constantly checking to make sure he was not revealing too much of the emotion behind the enthusiasm.

Panizato made a strong contrast with his black-clad host – his red and gold doublet and breeches sparkled in the candlelight and gave him an impish air. He was slight and thin, and had soft, curly hair that wisped into tendrils around his rather elfin face. His eyes, which were set close to his nose, were alight with pleasure in the conversation and a boyish, excitable grin crossed his face each time he felt he had scored a point.

Lucrezia turned then to Fra Pandolf, who was regarding the two men with mild interest, answering all the questions put to him with detachment and an unworldly calm. His robes were shabby and a drab earth brown, his small plump hands protruded from the frayed cuffs, and lay clasped on the white linen table covering. Though fleshy, they were hard and brown, and flecks of different-coloured paints clung around the nails, which were short and tidy. These, Lucrezia thought, were hands that had spent a lifetime praising God – in prayer and in paint. The next day they would start work on the great fresco.

11

Chiara Rossi opened the door that led to the yard and called to her father. He did not appear to hear her at first, being deep in conversation with a tall young man in a scuffed deerskin doublet. The two men were standing by one of the lime-pits. Her father had peeled back the hessian covering and was squatting on his heels. The young man said something Chiara could not hear; he made a wide, measuring gesture with both arms, then indicated a height with one hand crooked horizontally above his head. Her father nodded, calculated something on his fingers, then both men smiled. They shook hands.

'Papa!' Chiara called again.

This time her father turned to her and raised his eyebrows in response. The dark young man turned too; Chiara wondered if the crimson stain on his cheek was a lime-burn.

'Will you be wanting dinner, Papa, or have I enough time to take the bread up to Anna's?'

'Go, if you want to, *cara*. Signor Pennetti and I need a few moments to discuss quantities and dates for delivery. We'll probably be . . .' he looked at Signor Pennetti '. . . about half an hour?'

The young man nodded.

'Thank you, Papa. I will be back as soon as I can.'

Chiara shut the door, crossed the kitchen to the little entrance hall, pulled a coarse linen wrap from a hook on the wall and shrugged it around her shoulders. Picking up a basket in which were several small loaves and a block of cheese, she left the house.

It took her no more than a few moments to reach Anna's little cottage – so shabby it might well have been described as a hovel. She did not bother to knock, but pushed open the door and walked into the main downstairs room. A small fire was burning in the furthest corner. An iron pot stood on a trivet over the flames, steam puffing gently from under the loosely fitting lid, and an elderly woman was hunched in front of it on one of two stools, a clay pipe wedged between her teeth, her hands clasped between splayed knees.

'Anna?' Chiara said quietly. She put the basket on a table near the door.

'Come and sit down, child,' Anna said. She unclasped her hands and patted the second stool, still staring into the flames.

Rather awkwardly, Chiara lowered herself onto it.

'Well? Have you told him yet?' Anna said.

'No.'

'Do you not think he has noticed?'

'I'm quite sure he hasn't.'

'The man must be blind. Or stupid. How are you feeling?'

'Better, in the last couple of weeks. At last.'

'And that Niccolò?' Anna said, somewhat sharply.

Even the sound of his name gave Chiara a sharp little pain in her chest. 'I haven't seen him. I still don't know where he's working now.'

'What are you going to do?'

Chiara stroked her rounded belly with both hands, as if to soothe the child within. 'I don't know.'

'Now, listen. Stupid or not, your father will know soon enough, child. You have no more than a matter of weeks now. It's only because your belly has stayed so small that you have been able to hide it so long. You must tell him.'

'But I don't know how. I don't know what to say.'

'Do you want me to do it for you?'

Chiara stared at the old woman, round-eyed. She did not know how to answer. She was lethargic with chronic anxiety, drowsy, detached.

Anna clicked her tongue irritably. She patted Chiara's cheek. 'Wake up now, Chiara! One of us has to do it. We have to make arrangements for the birth, *cara*. Time is running out. A lime-pit is no place to bring a child into the world, and a group of ignorant slakers cannot be given the responsibility of attending your confinement. I am not well enough to do it – we must to arrange for you to go to the city.'

'He will not forgive me.'

'He will have to.'

'You don't know Papa.'

'Oh, I think I do, child.'

Chiara pressed her hands onto her belly. A small rounded lump pushed back against her palm, then slid to one side and disappeared.

'I'll tell him when I get back,' she said.

Eduardo Rossi stared at his daughter. As she finished speaking, his gaze moved from her face to her belly, over which her small hands were now spread protectively. He saw the neat swell of it beneath the linen dress, as though she held an upturned pudding bowl beneath her fingers. He saw the new heaviness of her breasts, and realized there was a fullness in her cheeks: unmistakable, unmissable. How could he not have noticed it? For a brief moment, the accusing face of his long-dead wife glared at him. *How could you, Eduardo? Just look at her! How could you have been so stupid? How could you have left Chiara to face this alone?* A flood of guilt at his lack of awareness pulsed cold behind his face; but then hot shame and an anger such as he had never felt before, broke over him and swamped everything else in his mind.

'When? When did this happen?' His voice was shaking. He could feel his jaw trembling.

'The beginning of November.'

Eduardo calculated quickly. 'My God! You are nearly seven months gone?' he said, utterly astonished. 'Chiara, who is . . .?'

His daughter flushed a dull, dark red. She stared at the floor and said nothing.

'Who is the father of this child?' he said, his voice rising.

A long pause.

'Tell me, Chiara!'

Still she said nothing. And then a thought struck him. Young Contadino's departure at Christmas had been a disappointing surprise: a talented lad, with a good future ahead of him.

'Was it Niccolò?'

The tears that glistened straight away in Chiara's eyes gave him his answer. He saw her lip tremble, saw her bite it to steady the tremor. An unfamiliar sense of fatherly compassion moved deep within him, frail as an invalid unused to light and fresh air, but almost as fast as he acknowledged the emotion, it crumbled beneath the torrent of imagined accusations and the smug self-righteousness of friends and family. He knew he had never taken the time to care for his motherless Chiara, beyond providing basic material comforts. She had been an unpaid servant – cook, yard assistant, laundress – throughout the years since her mother's death, provided for and sheltered, but not, he realized now, truly loved or cherished. He had always had something else to do. No wonder, he thought, through another sickening, slippery skin of guilt, that she had turned in her loneliness to a feckless young man in search of amusement.

But he would not raise a bastard under his roof. He could not endure the shame. The child would have to be found somewhere else to live. He could forgive Chiara her mistake – of course he could – but he would not live with the evidence. She would have to be taken to Bologna to have the baby, not Ferrara – too many of his best customers were from Ferrara – and then perhaps the Dominican sisters would take it.

'We will have to find a home for the child.'

'No!'

Eduardo was surprised at the vehemence in Chiara's voice. He said, 'I have no intention of keeping your bastard under this roof.'

'I won't let you do it!'

'You do not, I'm afraid, have any choice.'

Chiara's expression was unreadable. Then, squaring her narrow shoulders and lifting her chin in a gesture of defiance that reminded Eduardo forcibly of his late wife, his daughter left the room through the door that led to the stairs.

12

The sun was already high by the time Lucrezia opened her eyes. There would, she thought happily, blinking at the open window, be light flooding into the North Hall and along the long gallery all morning, just what the artists would need as they prepared the wall for the fresco.

She was pushing back the bedcovers when Catelina knocked vigorously on the door.

'Oh, Signora, you must come and see – they are up there already,' she said. 'There's a boy chipping away at the old plaster – right down to the brickwork, he's taking it.'

Lucrezia dressed hurriedly and went with Catelina through the Castello and into the hall. In the carved wooden gallery three people were busily working. Fra Pandolf had the sleeves of his habit rolled up above his elbows and secured with twine. He was seated on a low stool, poring over an enormous sheet of paper. The skinny boy who had taken charge of the horses in the court-yard the day before, was balanced on a ladder, chipping at the plaster. He had already stripped bare a section some seven feet across, and from floor to ceiling, Lucrezia saw, so she imagined he had been at work for some time: his short black hair was grey with plaster dust.

And the tall, dark-eyed young man whose name was Jacomo was standing at the top of the spiral staircase, pulling off a shabby deerskin doublet. Lucrezia watched him covertly as he hung it over the balustrade, ran the fingers of one hand through tangled hair and then pushed his rucked shirt back down inside his breeches. He rolled up his sleeves. His hands and arms, she saw, were strong and brown. A hot little shiver moved down through her insides as she watched him walk the length of the gallery and squat on his heels next to Fra Pandolf. The friar laid a hand on his shoulder. They spoke together for a moment, though Lucrezia was unable to distinguish what they were saying. Jacomo handed a folded sheet of paper to the friar, who flapped it open, read it, nodded approval and pointed up at the wall. Jacomo reached into a big tool box and brought out a wooden hammer and a wide, flat chisel.

Lucrezia's eyes seemed to have taken on a strange determination of their own: if she tried to look away from Jacomo, she could feel a tugging at her vision, pulling her gaze back to his face, to his hands, to the crescent-shaped creases around the corners of his mouth, like iron to a lodestone.

She wanted him to notice her.

She did not want him to notice her.

She sat on one of the wide window recesses, wriggled herself into a comfortable position and watched as Jacomo placed the chisel against the old plaster.

Tomaso had done well, Jacomo thought, during the time that he, Jacomo, had been at the plasterman's that morning. It had been a worthwhile trip: it was good-quality lime, which boded well for the success of the fresco. He had been happy with what he had seen, and the plasterman had seemed to know his business well.

'It's coming off fairly easily, Jacomo,' Tomaso said, patting the wall affectionately. Jutting his bottom lip outwards and closing his eyes, he puffed a breath up and over his nose to clear the dust.

Jacomo ran one hand across the newly exposed brickwork, picking over the rough surface with his fingertips. 'This is good,' he said. 'It's completely dry, and the whole wall seems to be brick from end to end, thank God. We can get the coarse scratch coat up as soon as the whole site's cleared.'

'Not always so straightforward, eh?' said Tomaso.

'No. Certainly isn't.' Jacomo studied the remaining length of wall. 'Come on, let's get it finished. I'll start from the far end and meet you in the middle.' He stepped over a pile of rubble, went to the other end of the gallery and set the edge of the chisel into the plaster.

He always enjoyed this time spent preparing a wall. Though he knew many patrons were surprised that an artist of Fra Pandolf's reputation did not have a team of plasterers, it had been Jacomo's own suggestion that they manage the work between them. He had always found that the early hours spent close to the wall on which the fresco would be created were invaluable. Fresco was unlike any other form of painting: you had to establish a relationship with the wall, with the plaster, with the pigments. They were all unpredictable elements. You had to understand their demands, and at the same time impose your own restrictions and obligations: preparing the brickwork was, Jacomo thought, not unlike the tentative, introductory conversation you might have with a new acquaintance, forming the foundations of a friendship, a love affair, even. And, as well as getting to know his materials, Jacomo liked to spend time with the space he had been given, planning the task ahead, thinking through the shape of the overall design, deciding how he would divide it all into the separate *giornate* – the sections that could be completed in a single session.

He and Tomaso chipped away at the wall together for some time, prising off the layers of plaster, pulling it back to the original pink-red brickwork right along the length of the gallery. Tomaso chiselled away, frowning, stolidly mute, but Jacomo whistled softly as he worked, adapting his tunes to the rhythm of the blows of his hammer. Rubble and grit piled up around both men.

A short while later, Jacomo turned from the wall, needing to cough, to rid his nose and mouth of the dust and dirt. Looking down into the hall over the balustrade, he saw a small figure sitting on one of the window-ledges: a thin girl in a pretty green dress. The duchess.

He remembered the expression on her face that time a year or so ago, when she had caught him glaring at Pandolf over the early sketches they had brought to show the duke. He wondered if she had understood the cause of his anger. There was no earthly reason she should have done, but, seeing her now, Jacomo had an unnerving feeling that she might have indeed understood quite well.

He held her gaze briefly and then smiled. The duchess blushed and smiled back. The sweetness and warmth of her expression took Jacomo by surprise.

'Do you mind if I come up and see what you are doing?' she called.

Jacomo raised an eyebrow at Fra Pandolf, who nodded amicably. Turning back to the duchess, he beckoned to her to come up the stairs. She seemed pleased; she slid off the ledge, picked up her skirts and ran like a little girl towards the spiral steps.

At the top of the stairs, she peered along the length of the partially stripped wall, then, dropping her gaze to the rubble-strewn floor, began to pick her way onto the gallery. Jacomo walked towards her and reached out to help her across the largest pile of plaster. Her hand was small and smooth. She did not meet his eye at first; gripping his fingers, she was watching her feet and holding her skirts bunched out of the way. But as she stepped into a clear space, she let her skirts fall back down and looked up at him. She was very close to him and their two clasped hands seemed an inappropriate intimacy, as though he was holding her fingers up to kiss them. They both let go very quickly. The duchess's eyes widened for a second – just a brief second – and then she stood back and looked down at the floor again.

'As you see, Signora, we have begun,' Fra Pandolf said, beaming.

'I see you have begun to demolish the Castello Estense . . .' she said, and the corners of her mouth twitched.

It took Pandolf a moment to laugh. Jacomo, however, straightaway puffed a soft laugh in his nose, and the duchess's gaze immediately moved to his face. His stomach lurched as he saw her glance at his cheek, but her eyes were alight with interest.

'Can you explain what you've been doing?' she said. 'I've been watching you for some time.'

'We have to strip the whole wall right back to the brick, Signora,' Jacomo said. 'Any plaster already in place has to go. After that, we'll put on what's called the rough scratch coat – half lime-plaster, half sand – and then that has to dry out.'

'And you paint into that, do you?'

Jacomo smiled. 'No – it's rather more complicated than that.'

Pandolf bustled up. 'Indeed it is, my lady, indeed it is,' he said. 'Several coats of plaster have to go up before the wall is ready for painting. As I heard Jacomo tell you, we start with the rough scratch coat, and then—'

A voice interrupted him. 'My lady?'

A black-haired girl, in a corn-yellow dress, had appeared. The duchess laid an apologetic hand on the friar's sleeve and turned from him to lean over the balustrade. 'What is it, Lina?'

'My lord says he would like to see you before he leaves for Firenze.'

'Oh.' The duchess paused, and then said, more to herself than to anyone else, 'Yes, I had forgotten he was going.' She called, 'Yes, Lina, I'll come now. Wait for me.'

She looked briefly at Fra Pandolf and then at Jacomo. 'Thank you,' she said. 'Thank you so much for showing me what you're doing. I should very much like to come and see the wall taking shape tomorrow, if I won't be in your way . . .'

'It'll be dirty work, Signora,' Jacomo said.

'Oh, I don't mind that at all.' The duchess began to walk back across the plaster-strewn floor, skirts bunched again in one fist.

'My lady?' Jacomo said, offering a hand.

'Oh – thank you.'

He helped her to the top of the spiral staircase.

'I shall see you in the morning, then,' the duchess said. Her eyes lingered fleetingly on his mouth, then she let go of his hand and began to descend the steps. Jacomo leaned on folded arms against the balustrade, weight on one foot, and watched as she drew her maid close, as though to share a secret.

She turned briefly, glanced up at him, then left the hall.

Something hot turned over itself in her belly at the sight of his smile, a tangled knot of excitement, guilt, wonder and wanting. She saw the little crescent-shaped crease on each cheek crook more deeply around the corners of his mouth and the knot tightened.

Catelina was shocked. She had never seen her mistress's face lit up like that. As the Signora came down the stairs from the gallery, she had looked quite different from the sad little creature she had been over the past months. Ever since the day when she had seen her in that terrible state – oh, *cielo*! Catelina had been so distressed by the sight of her on the day of that banquet, dishevelled and frightened and so dreadfully unhappy. As for the revelations her mistress had sobbed out that night . . . Catelina had been struck dumb. She had always had her reservations about the Signore, she admitted as much to herself, but had never imagined he would have the problems the Signora had described. Quite the opposite! She had always presumed he had at least one other woman somewhere in the city – she had seen that gleam in his eye on so many occasions when he left the Castello on that fancy ginger horse of his, the gleam she had so often seen on her father's face when he used to disappear off to the wrong end of Mugello, right under the nose of her poor mother. She knew it well. She was sure she was not wrong – so how could it be that things were as they were between him and the Signora, if what her mistress had said was true?

'I've been learning how to prepare a wall for a fresco, Lina,' the Signora said. Catelina saw her turn briefly and look back up at the dark lad with the big eyes, who was leaning on the balustrade and watching them leave. Well, Catelina supposed she should say he was watching the *Signora* leave: she did not think he had spared a glance for herself. The fat little monk and the skinny boy had gone back to work on the wall.

Catelina felt suddenly sick.

She hoped to God that the Signora was not planning on doing anything foolish while the Signore was away.

If she did, and he found out, Catelina thought that he might well kill them both. And probably her too, simply for being the maidservant.

13

The papal nuncio held up thin hands in what appeared to Alfonso to be something between a placatory conciliation and a blessing.

'. . . and that is about the sum of it,' the nuncio said. 'I realize, of course, that I have but restated the information already presented to you by His Holiness in the document you hold here, but should there be any—'

'No,' Alfonso said. 'There is no need to expand any further, Your Grace. I understand the facts perfectly. That those facts are deeply unpalatable is obvious, and I would ask you to relay to His Holiness that my cousin and I will want to arrange to see him in person, should he be willing to grant us an audience, as soon as Cesare returns from France.'

'I will do my best to arrange it, Signore. Of course, we hope that this situation will resolve itself naturally to your satisfaction. I suppose it is fair to say that, after less than two years of marriage, the lack of issue is not yet a catastrophe, but His Holiness felt you should be made aware of the gravity of the situation.'

'I should be grateful if you would inform *His Holiness* that I am now acutely aware of the "gravity of the situation" and that I have absolutely no intention of letting the matter rest without investigating every possibility of an alternative resolution.'

Alfonso was finding it hard to contain his rising temper. He said, 'I have made my will known quite clearly, and find it hard to understand why His Holiness is refusing to accept the legality of the arrangements I have already finalized with my cousin. I will take the matter up with His Holiness, as I said, upon Cesare's return from France.'

Archbishop Ercole Verdi, *legatus a latere* to His Holiness, Pope Pius IV, shook his head anxiously. As papal nuncio – a permanent representative of the Holy See – he stood as intermediary between the Holy Father and those sovereigns, governments or other potentially disgruntled parties with whom the Vatican intended to negotiate. Archbishop Verdi, Alfonso mused, was a skilled intermediary: his diminutive stature rendered him immediately unthreatening and his skill in speech was softly disarming. But, Alfonso thought angrily, he had no intention of allowing this unforeseen and disconcerting news to slip past him and become irrevocable fact without fighting bitterly, whatever his companion's prowess as a diplomat.

He took his leave of the little nuncio and left the building. Striding across the sun-soaked square and down past the long side façade of the vast Brunelleschi cathedral, he dimly registered the relief of the shade as he walked towards the Palazzo Vecchio, where he had left Panizato.

Panizato was waiting, as he had said he would be, in the cool of their borrowed apartment. Alfonso opened the door with rather more force than he had intended; it banged against a chair and knocked it over, but, leaving it where it had fallen, he crossed the room to stare out of the window, unable to find words to express his agitation. His frequently chaotic thoughts were now fragmenting past the point at which he could make any sense of them.

Panizato moved from where he had been standing and, still facing the street outside, Alfonso heard his friend set the chair upright again without comment.

After a pause, Panizato said, 'What did he say?'

Alfonso struggled to find the words to explain, feeling as though he were standing in a fast-flowing river: everything was rushing past him at such speed, and so inexorably that all at once he felt utterly unable to reach out and stop any one part of it. All the miserable mortification of his marriage, his increasingly unhappy awareness of Lucrezia's wanton profligacy of affection – everything now whirled past him like speeding flotsam, all thrown into sharp relief by this new and frightening revelation.

'If I die without legitimate issue, Francesco,' Alfonso said to the street beyond the window, 'His Holiness intends to reclaim the rights to the entire Duchy of Ferrara. Any bastards I may have spawned across the years are, of course, not even worthy of contemplation, and my intention to will the titles and land to my cousin, Cesare d'Este, should there still be no heir at my death, is, it seems, not even to be taken into account. His Holiness is graciously suggesting that Cesare be allowed to retain rights to Modena and Reggio, but without Ferrara, the might of the Estes will be virtually annihilated, as well he knows. Here I have been worrying myself sick for months that the encroaching French influence in Italy has been set to destabilize the future of the duchy – and now I am given to understand that if I am unable to produce a legitimate heir, everything I hold dear is to be snatched from me by force, not by a foreigner but by my own country-men.'

In the stillness that followed this pronouncement, Alfonso

watched a young woman walk awkwardly along the street below. She was simply dressed and barefoot, leaning away from the weight of a young child who sat astride her hip, his fat legs wrapped around her slight waist. A larger child held her other hand and a skinny boy of about ten scuffed the cobbles with ill-fitting shoes as he trailed crossly behind them. The irony of this sight's presenting itself to him as he contemplated the devastating consequences of childlessness seemed to Alfonso to be bitter indeed, and his fragmented, confused anger began to crystallize into a louring resentment towards Lucrezia. Not only, he thought, was she continuing to rob him of his manhood, she was now, it seemed, potentially to become the sole agent of the destruction of the entire House of Este.

And yet, something in him that he could not quite suppress still yearned to possess her. Despite himself, he continued to long for the unattainable.

'But, Alfonso,' Panizato said, 'you have only been married two years – not even that. Surely your lack of children so far is not a serious problem. Why is the Vatican acting as though your decease without issue is a foregone conclusion?'

Alfonso was still facing towards the open window. He said, 'They merely, I understand, wish me to know of their intentions. Unless they have some gift of divine clairvoyance, I imagine it to be merely His Holiness indulging in a little emotional blackmail at my expense.'

'I am appalled, Alfonso. What will you do now?'

Alfonso turned to him, grateful for his support. 'Cesare is back from France in August. I have told His Grace Verdi that Cesare and I wish to speak directly to the Holy Father, and we will put our case to him once more.'

'And in the meantime,' Francesco grinned, 'you will just have to keep trying to prove them wrong. At least you will enjoy the attempt, eh, Alfonso?'

Without comment, Alfonso turned away from his friend, fighting to quell the nausea that rose in his throat as he contemplated his marriage bed. Panizato could not have said anything worse, he thought. If Lucrezia were to continue so to castrate him, thus rendering him incapable of fathering an heir and securing the future of the duchy, Alfonso began to wonder how he could continue to co-exist with her.

He ached to possess her and longed to be rid of her.

Neither option seemed possible.

But, he thought, if he were to retain his sanity, he knew he had to try to achieve one or the other.

14

The Castello, Lucrezia thought, was certainly more relaxed with Alfonso away. Over the months, she had felt increasingly detached from him, and ever more nervous of incurring his hovering disapprobation. Being in his company was always tiring. But, as the days – and nights – since his departure passed, she realized that she was beginning to feel more spontaneous, more like herself again; her spirits lifted and the mask-like smile, behind which she so often hid her instinctive responses, could be safely unhitched and packed away for a while.

Although, thanks to Alfonso's rigid domestic strictures, Lucrezia was never as busy as she had imagined a duchess should be, she was now untroubled by the many hours in which she was nominally unoccupied. She had found something to do. She had learned the names of at least twenty-five different pigments and their various properties; she now knew how to mix plaster – in theory: she had not attempted it herself – and yesterday she had been given to understand that once mixed, lime-plaster had something of a life of its own.

*

'It's like a living creature: it has changeable moods. The way it absorbs colour changes at different times of day,' Jacomo says, laying his hand flat on a newly firm section of the wall and rubbing it softly with his fingertips.

Lucrezia frowns, watching his hand. 'So, are you saying that if you paint into it in the morning, it will behave in a different way from if you paint into it last thing at night?'

Jacomo smiles at her. 'Its appetite changes all the time – a bit like a baby: you have to feed it what it wants when it wants it.'

'But how do you know what it wants?'

'You remember what you have been taught,' Jacomo says, glancing over to where Fra Pandolf is cleaning his big square plaster-pallet, 'and you experiment, and record the results.'

'Tell me something you discovered for yourself.'

'That it's important to wash brushes in lime-water. If you use rain-water, or river water, it might not be completely clean, and you can end up with rust spots in the finished painting.'

'Has that happened to you?'

Jacomo nods. 'I collected my brush-washing water from a well in Milano – last year, it was – and a crop of rust spots in just the wrong place on a fresco we did there has given poor San Sebastiano a faceful of freckles.'

His gaze moves over her face as he speaks; his lips are slightly parted, and Lucrezia feels herself blush. He looks at her for longer than she expects. Embarrassed, she changes the subject. 'Is there any one painter you particularly admire?'

Jacomo answers immediately. 'Tiziano Vecellio. He's a genius.'

'Oh – I saw a portrait of his, in Firenze, once. A man in black, holding a glove.'

'Did you like it?'

'I loved it – I felt as if I knew the man, straight away.'

Jacomo smiles, but Lucrezia corrects herself. 'No,' she says. 'That's not right. It wasn't that I felt I knew him, it was more that I felt he knew me.'

Jacomo's smile fades. He seems to be trying to see inside her head, and then he nods slowly, not taking his eyes from hers.

Lucrezia was well aware, though, that Catelina was not entirely happy about her mistress's new-found interest in the development of the fresco. She had a niggling suspicion that her waiting-woman knew exactly what drew her to the gallery so frequently, and she was determined to avoid any confrontation on the subject. Even the thought of Jacomo now raised the hairs on her arms and her neck; she doubted she would be able to speak of him without blushing scarlet.

'Are you going to the North Hall again, Signora?' Catelina said, a couple of weeks into Alfonso's absence, as Lucrezia brushed her hair and began to wind it into a knot.

'Oh, yes, Lina. They are putting on the *arricio* this afternoon.' A deliberately bright tone.

Catelina was silent.

'What?' Lucrezia said, lowering her hands from her hair. 'What is it, Lina?'

After a moment or two, Catelina said, 'Forgive me, Signora, but . . . but . . .'

'But what?'

'I hope you don't think I am being forward, Signora, but might it perhaps be seen as . . . well . . . unusual, for a noblewoman like yourself to be taking such an interest in – in the work of an artisan?'

'Oh, Lina, Fra Pandolf is an artist, not an artisan!' Lucrezia said, determining to steer the conversation away from Jacomo. 'I am most privileged to be able to watch him creating a work that might be talked about across Italy for years to come and . . .' She tailed off, seeing Catelina's doubt. 'What can you be worrying about? I am just watching them working.'

Catelina did not have to answer. Her expression was eloquent. Lucrezia said, examining her fingernails, and twisting a thin gold band around one finger, 'I shall be back in time to change my dress for the evening meal. Could you make sure you are here to help?'

'Of course, my lady. I'll lay everything out ready.'

Catelina's unspoken suspicions hung in the air around her like a cloud of mosquitoes.

They were all hard at work. Tomaso was bent double, stirring a huge pot of plaster with a stick, while Fra Pandolf and Jacomo each had a square wooden pallet in one hand. They were standing at some distance from each other, working towards the middle. Using a long, narrow trowel, each was scooping the plaster from the pallet onto the wall with sweeping, seamless movements.

Looking at the mounds of plaster on the two pallets, Lucrezia could see that this was a smoother, finer-grained substance than the other layers she had seen go up; this was like thick, whipped cream. With each sweep of an arm, the shining wet mass left the blade of the trowel and was flattened into a glistening arc on the wall. The two men were working steadily, and the *arricio* was already spread some distance across the length of the gallery.

Fra Pandolf's habit and his gleaming pate were dappled with splashes of plaster. Jacomo was similarly freckled with the stuff, which stood out clearly against the crimson stain on his cheek. It clung in droplets to his black hair and had, Lucrezia saw, whitened his hands until he looked as though he was wearing thin, white, ragged-cuffed gloves. His arms were dark brown by contrast.

Both men were engrossed in their work, Jacomo whistling softly again.

Fascinated, Lucrezia watched them for some time, the iron drawn irresistibly to the lodestone. The suspicion on Catelina's face came into her mind, and she could not banish it. She knew that as a dutiful wife – as the Duchess of Ferrara – she should go from here now and make a point of avoiding the North Hall until the painters had left the castle. She should keep away from temptation. The Castello Estense, she thought, was quite big enough to avoid any persons you would rather not meet or . . . ought not to meet. But—

'My lady!' Fra Pandolf raised a hand in greeting. Lucrezia hoped that she was not blushing too obviously as Jacomo stopped what he was doing, ran his hand through his hair and smiled at her. He spoke quietly to Fra Pandolf, his eyes fixed upon Lucrezia's, and then the reverend brother called down to her. 'Come up to the gallery, my lady. Jacomo wants to show you something.'

Lucrezia walked across the hall, forcing herself to move with dignity. It would, she thought, be unseemly to rush.

As she reached the top of the stairs, Jacomo gestured to a section of the wall they had finished some time before. 'Do you remember my telling you how the plaster heats up as it dries?'

Lucrezia nodded.

'Feel this.' He took her hand and placed it, flat-palmed, against the newly firm surface, leaving his hand covering hers. He laughed at her gasp of astonishment.

'I told you,' he said.

'Yes – but I thought it would be *warm*. This is like a furnace. How long does it last?'

'Not long. You were lucky to catch it.'

They were both standing close to the wall, Lucrezia's hand

pressed flat against the plaster with Jacomo's lying warm over hers – almost as warm above as the plaster was below. His body was very close behind her. She could feel his breath on the back of her neck. Then, lifting her hand from the surface of the wall and squeezing her fingers for the briefest moment, he said, 'I must get back to work – Tomaso won't thank me if everything he has prepared goes off before I can get it onto the wall.'

'You're not wrong, Jacomo,' Tomaso said grumpily. Lucrezia smiled at his scowl, and Jacomo grinned as he bent over the bucket and scooped another great mound onto his pallet. He began trowelling the plaster onto the wall again. Lucrezia sat on the lid of the wooden tool box, with her back against the balustrade. Tomaso, who, she presumed, was not experienced enough to work on the wall himself, busied himself with keeping the big pot filled with fresh plaster, while Pandolf and Jacomo worked steadily across the gallery.

Some time later, they were almost at the point where their two sections would meet. Jacomo, Lucrezia saw, had been working more quickly than his master; he had covered more of the wall, so the meeting-point was not in the middle.

'I'll let you finish off, then, Jacomo,' said the reverend brother, standing back to admire their work. Jacomo nodded and scraped up another quivering trowelful of wet plaster, which made a satisfyingly gritty, slicing sound as it hit the wall. Within minutes, the narrow gap between the two sections was filled with no mark remaining to show where they had joined. Both men stood back, reviewing the results of their labours.

'Well done, lad, a fine job,' Fra Pandolf said, patting Jacomo on the back.

Jacomo scraped his pallet clean and wiped the last few lumps of thickening plaster off the trowel onto a rag, dropping the trowel neatly into a bucket of clean water. He took Fra Pandolf's pallet and trowel from him, scraped them clean, then crouched in front of the bucket. He washed and dried both trowels carefully.

While he was doing this, Fra Pandolf turned to Lucrezia. 'Once this has fully cured, Signora,' he said, 'we can brush on the *sinopia*.'

Lucrezia had no idea what he meant.

'The *arricio*, as you know, is the second-to-last layer of plaster – rather like a fine-grained underskin,' Pandolf explained. 'Then comes the *sinopia*, my lady: a sketch of the final composition of the fresco, which will cover the entire area of the *arricio*, giving us a guide so that we can plan which sections to paint in which order. Then, each day, we plaster up the section we are going to work on. That's called the *giornata*. Jacomo will do the *sinopia*, working from the cartoons.' He pointed to several large rolls of paper at the far end of the gallery, propped against the walls.

'Are those the drawings I saw before?'

'The design is the same, but the drawings are now full-sized, Signora.'

'Can I see?'

'Of course. Jacomo, can you show the Signora? Take them down into the hall – there is too much mess on the floor up here. I'll be back shortly. I just want to attend to one or two little mat- ters before we begin the next stage . . .' He looked suddenly vague and trotted off towards the staircase, humming to himself as he went.

Jacomo was rinsing his hands in a bucket of water. He shook them, then dried them by running them, palms first then backs, down the front of his paint-stained breeches. 'Go back down into the hall, my lady,' he said. 'I'll bring the drawings.'

Lucrezia made her way to the top of the stairs. 'I do hope I am not being a nuisance,' she said.

161

'Not much,' Jacomo said, hoisting one of the rolls of paper up to lean against his shoulder, then crouching straight-backed to pick up another.

Lucrezia's insides jumped uncomfortably. She stood on the first step, irresolute, very much afraid of having somehow upset him. But then she saw that his face was full of laughter, though his mouth barely twitched. It was the sort of thing, Lucrezia thought, that Giovanni would have said, and she very nearly responded as she would have done to her cousin. Just in time, though, she decided that 'You bastard!' was probably not the most appropriate way for a duchess to address a painter in her husband's employ. She squared her shoulders, lifted her chin, and tried to appear disapproving, but Jacomo's smile only stretched wider, as he nodded towards the steps, encouraging her to go before him down to the floor of the hall.

Some people look best when they laugh, Lucrezia thought, as she reached the bottom step and turned back to Jacomo, while others – like Alfonso – are at their most handsome with quite other expressions on their faces. Her husband, she thought, was probably at his best when wearing his customary scowl of moody superiority; a laugh seemed like a guest on his countenance, not necessarily unwelcome but a guest with whom Alfonso was usually ill at ease. With Jacomo, however, Lucrezia could see that laughter was a frequent and welcome visitor.

'Here, come and see,' Jacomo said. He was on hands and knees, holding the far edge of the paper at arm's length, his body arched over the drawing. His shirt was untucked; it had rucked up, and Lucrezia was stilled by the stripe of olive-brown skin between his shirt and the top of his breeches. She ran the tip of her tongue over her lip and swallowed.

'This is the *Argo*,' Jacomo said.

Lucrezia knelt down next to him, sat back on her heels and examined once more the wonderful image of the ship cutting proudly through the water. Compared to the sketches she had seen, these drawings were detailed, complex, beautiful – and obviously the result of many, many hours' work. Jason was noble, she thought, standing next to the arrogant figurehead, his arm draped companionably about her shoulders. Her wisdom and superior knowledge were obvious and Jason seemed hopeful that he would acquire some of her eminence merely by association. His crew, however, were clearly unimpressed. They bent to their oars with resentment and a lack of enthusiasm, and obviously had little appreciation of their captain's prestige.

'I love their expressions,' Lucrezia said, pointing at one of the oarsmen. 'They don't seem to think very highly of Jason, do they?'

'With reason. I think he must've been a bloody nuisance. Convinced he was in the right all the time, and always dragging everyone into danger,' Jacomo said. 'Would you like to see more?'

'Please.'

Lucrezia was expecting to see the next scene – Talos, the great bronze warrior – but when Jacomo leaned across the new drawing, the muscles in his brown arm taut as he stretched to hold down the far edge of the paper, she saw the wild, wraith-like Medea, waiting and watching for the arrival of Jason as he ran across the beach and into her scene.

Lucrezia felt suddenly breathless.

The picture of Medea was – quite clearly – a portrait of herself.

Her mouth opened, but no words came and she closed it again.

She stared at the picture. She had never worn wisps of silk like these, and her hair, though often unruly, had never wound itself around her like marsh mist, as Medea's did here, but there was no mistaking the features or the expression on her face. Lucrezia did not know what to say.

'Fra Pandolf likes to have portraits of patrons in his frescos,' Jacomo said quietly, and Lucrezia realized that he must have been watching her reaction.

'But I didn't sit for this portrait. How did the reverend brother know my features so well?'

'If the sitter's face is striking, it can be done from memory.'

Lucrezia's heart began to beat a little faster. Had Fra Pandolf made this decision, or had Jacomo asked him to include her? Or had Jacomo sketched her himself, and then given the picture to the reverend brother? If he had, did that mean he might be feeling something of the confusion into which she herself had become so inextricably tangled?

Her heart thudding now, she turned back to the drawing, and said, 'What happens next?'

In the silent seconds that followed, it seemed to Lucrezia that there were actually several potential answers. A terrifyingly huge possibility stretched itself like a waking giant and sat up, blinking.

Jacomo paused. Then he said, in a voice that sounded strangely detached, as though he was thinking something quite different from the words he was uttering, 'I have to transfer the design onto the *arricio*. I can show you with one of the drawings now, if you want.'

Lucrezia sat back on her heels and folded her hands in her lap; the giant sat quietly behind her, trying not to draw attention to itself.

Jacomo climbed back up the spiral staircase, and returned a moment later with a wooden box in his arms. He sat down, pulled off his boots and threw them unceremoniously to one side.

Opening the box, he took out of it several round lead weights, each about the size of his fist. Then he unrolled the first drawing and crawled across it, weighting down three of the corners with the lead. He took a long needle from where it had been pinned through the linen of his shirt and, almost lying across the drawing, he tucked one arm under the paper near the free corner, to hold it slightly off the floor, and began to follow the drawing, puncturing the paper with the needle along the drawn lines. After a time, there were little holes all over one corner. He sat up and stared intently at what he had done. 'There's a fair bit more to do – I'll finish it later. Before I put it away, though, would you like to try?' he said.

'Me?' Lucrezia saw the crimson stain on his cheek crinkle, and the crescent-shaped creases crooked round his mouth, as though his face wished to emphasize his smile by enclosing it in brackets.

'It's not difficult – I'll show you.'

He moved back from the paper, so that Lucrezia could kneel at its edge. Crouching behind her, he gave her the needle, then pointed out the section he was suggesting she could prick out. A wisp of his hair brushed against her cheek as he reached past her. She smelt warm skin and plaster, and a little jolt of wanting pushed down into her belly.

'Hold your other arm up under there, like I did just now – to keep it off the floor – then poke the needle through.'

Lucrezia leaned forward and slid her left arm under the paper. She held the needle above the drawing, then peered over her shoulder at Jacomo. 'Is this right?'

A nod and a smile.

She pushed the needle through, pulled it out, pushed it again. Enjoying the process, she finished the few lines she had been given to perforate with ease.

'That's perfect. Now, if we were ready to use the cartoon – which we're not yet – we would need a pounce pad,' he said.

'What's a—' she began, but Jacomo was already rummaging in his wooden box. From it he took a small ball of muslin filled with something dark and soft. He held it up and tapped it, and grey dust puffed through the cloth. 'Charcoal,' he said.

And Lucrezia understood. 'So, you hold the picture up to the wall, and tap that little bag onto where the holes are, and it will leave marks on the plaster?'

Another smile. 'Well done. We pounce the whole design up onto the *arricio* from the cartoons, then paint over the marks free-hand so we have a complete line drawing on the wall. Then, day by day, we plaster up the area for the *giornata*, and paint directly into that – that layer of plaster is called the *intonaco* – section by section.'

'It seems so complicated.'

Smiling, Jacomo shrugged.

Tomaso shambled back into the North Hall with a loaf of bread and a large lump of cheese. He walked past them, stumped up the staircase, then leaned over the balustrade and said indistinctly, his mouth full, 'You hungry, Jacomo?'

'What do you think? I won't be a moment.' Jacomo rolled up the cartoons, and hoisted them back onto his shoulder. 'What about you, Signora? Are you hungry?'

It occurred to Lucrezia that she was – but for other things than bread. The giant possibility clambered to its feet behind her. She held Jacomo's gaze, suddenly tongue-tied, but managed to nod. He held out his free arm to the staircase, and Lucrezia walked ahead of him.

They climbed together to the gallery and Jacomo propped the cartoons once more against the wall at the far end, like dislodged pillars in a ruined temple. Tomaso was sitting on the floor. He had torn the loaf into two; one piece he now held out to Jacomo, who nodded his thanks.

Lucrezia made to sit down, but Jacomo started and said, 'No, wait! You can't sit on the floor, Signora.' He put down his food, ran back down the staircase and returned seconds later with the box in his arms. He put it on the floor, took his doublet from where it was draped over the balustrade, folded it into a semblance of a cushion and placed it on the lid. He took Lucrezia's hand and helped her to sit on the makeshift stool.

'Now,' he said, 'bread.' He handed her the half-loaf Tomaso had given him. Lucrezia tore off a corner and handed the larger part back to him.

'Cheese?' he said, taking it from Tomaso.

Lucrezia shook her head.

'Not that hungry, then. I can't have given you enough work to do on that cartoon.' Jacomo began to eat.

Lucrezia had just taken a bite of her bread, when she heard footsteps and Fra Pandolf appeared at the far end of the gallery. He seemed startled at the sight of her seated on a tool box, eating a torn hunk of bread with his two assistants. She stood up and shook the creases out of her skirts.

'Thank you for showing me the designs,' she said stiffly. 'I am very grateful for your time, Signore.'

'A pleasure, Signora,' Jacomo said. He spoke gravely, and inclined his head in a formal little bow, but Lucrezia saw that his eyes were shining.

'You saw the cartoons, then?' Fra Pandolf said.

Lucrezia said, her voice wobbling a little, 'Oh, yes, thank you. They were quite lovely. I'm so looking forward to seeing the painting take shape.'

'Well, not long until we are ready now, my lady,' Fra Pandolf said, with a broad smile. 'Eh, Jacomo?'

'No. I think everything is just about ready to begin,' Jacomo said, looking at Lucrezia.

The road that led out of Firenze was pitted, uneven and crowded: with people on foot, people on horseback, and carts of all sizes and conditions. Alfonso and Francesco Panizato slowed their horses to a walk. Alfonso slackened the reins; holding them in one hand, he wiped the sweat from his forehead with the other. Despite the early hour, it was already very warm. 'Can you wait a moment, Francesco? I'm going to take my doublet off,' he said.

Panizato reined in his horse. As both animals dropped their heads to graze at the side of the road, the two men shrugged off their coats and secured them behind their saddles.

'How long do you think it will take us to get back to Ferrara?' Panizato asked.

'I have no wish to hurry. Four days, perhaps, five? I would not wish to ask Farfalla to do more than, say, twenty or twenty-five miles in a day. Much further than that would risk her legs.'

He thought for a moment. 'If we aim to get to Mugello tonight, I am sure that Lucrezia's parents will be happy to offer us hospitality. In fact, now that I think of it, I should be delighted to have the opportunity of discussing the nuncio's news with my father-in-law.'

They rode on. Alfonso tried to keep Lucrezia from his mind, tried to concentrate on the undulating movements of the horse beneath him, tried to sustain conversation with Panizato. But with the prospect of seeing Cosimo and Eleanora de' Medici that evening, however hard he tried to shut Lucrezia out, he could not suppress her, and a number of turbulent images threatened to overwhelm him.

15

'I've tried, Lina – I've tried. It's been three days since I've been to the North Hall. I really have tried, but I can't bear it. I am going down there this morning – I have to see him.'

Catelina said nothing. She saw her mistress's wild eyes and the pale face, on which the tawny freckles now stood out quite black, and felt sick with worry.

'Please – don't look at me like that.'

She seemed on the point of tears, Catelina thought. 'What if anyone finds out, my lady?' she said.

'Finds what out? We haven't done anything!'

'But, Signora—'

'Listen, Lina.' The Signora glanced at the door of her bed-chamber, ran to it, opened it and peered out into the corridor. Closed it again. 'Come through into the studio,' she said.

Catelina followed her mistress into the little anteroom, only accessible through the bedchamber, the most private space they had in which to talk without fear of being overheard.

The Signora pushed the door shut behind her, leaned against

it and burst out, 'I think I am going mad! You are the only person I can talk to who I know will not rush off and tell Alfonso.' She paused, her eyes wide. 'Oh, God, you won't do that – will you?'

The Signora clutched at her hand so tightly that Catelina gasped. 'Oh, my lady, of course I wouldn't!' she said, hurt. 'How could you even think it? But what . . .?'

The Signora's voice was little more than a whisper, and she stood very still as she spoke. 'You know that our marriage has yet to be consummated, Lina. After all this time. What sort of a shameful admission is that? My husband hardly speaks to me any more – probably because the very sight of me reminds him of his failures. Sometimes I see such bleak emptiness in his eyes it quite frightens me.'

'But . . .' Catelina did not know what to say.

The Signora carried on speaking in a voice that was low and fast, and trembling with what might have been anger, or perhaps it was fear. 'They sold me, Lina. That's what my life amounts to. My mother and father – I loved them and I trusted them, and I thought they wanted my happiness. But they traded me for a stake in the eminence of the Duchy of Ferrara, and now I am trapped in this life for good, on pain of eternal damnation. I am nothing! I have nothing! I have less than you! Far less! If I were to make you unhappy, you could just leave and go elsewhere, but me? I can go nowhere. Between them, God and the damned nobility have trapped me in this castle like a rabbit in a noose. I am a failure – I cannot be called a true duchess – how can I? My duke will not bed me, and because he will not, or cannot, bed me, I have no child, nor any prospect of ever becoming a mother – and I want to so very much. I can't talk to Alfonso. I can't share my unhappiness with him, or try to comfort him in his, because he won't ever let me anywhere near him.

'And will you still tell me it is so wrong of me to want to spend a little time with someone who makes me smile, Lina? Someone who seems to enjoy my company for what it is? Who doesn't look at me as though I am some rare and expensive piece of sculpture, and then raise a fist to me when I somehow prove to him my unwitting inadequacy? There are times when I think Alfonso would prefer it if I were *dead*!'

Catelina stared at her mistress, aghast at this outburst.

'I'm going to the North Hall now. Don't try to stop me.'

And Catelina could only watch as the Signora tucked a stray wisp of hair behind her ear, pinched colour into her cheeks and left the room.

She put her hands over her mouth. 'Oh, dear God,' she said aloud, through her fingers, 'what in Heaven's name is she planning to do?'

Jacomo was exhausted. He had been pounding the lime-mixed body-colour – the *verdaccio* – into the plaster for hours. The colours were singing from the wall at last, true and bold, and clearly worth every ounce of the effort, but his heart was loud in his ears, his arms ached, and he was breathing as heavily as though he had been running for miles. He thanked God for the effort it always took to put on the *verdaccio*, though: for the past three days he had been able to take out his frustration on the wall without the reverend brother suspecting a thing.

He had not seen her for three whole days. Three *giornate* had gone up and been completed with no sign of her. He was shocked by how much he minded her absence. This, he kept telling himself, was insane. Ridiculous. She was a duchess – a married woman – and entirely unobtainable. What did it matter that she was young and pretty, and had a smile that made him feel weak with wanting?

He could not have her – there was no question of it. He was a painter, the son and grandson of fishermen, and she was an aristocrat. She was married to the Duke of Ferrara. One of the most powerful men in Italy. His patron. Not a man to suffer any sort of humiliation without exacting retribution, either, Jacomo was quite sure.

But the duchess felt the same way he did. He knew it. God, even to say it to himself sounded stupid! How arrogant was he? Just because she had spent a few hours up here in the North Hall over the past couple of weeks, showing an interest in his painting, this meant she had fallen for him as comprehensively as he had fallen for her, did it? He was losing his reason.

He looked down the length of the gallery to where the reverend brother was hard at work and began painting again.

Lucrezia climbed the steps to the gallery. Her heart was hammering as though she had run the length of the Castello. Neither Fra Pandolf nor Jacomo heard her arrival. Both men were intent upon their task: Fra Pandolf standing on a low wooden trestle, Jacomo a few steps up a taller ladder. The painters were, she saw now, finally waking the wall to jubilant life with their vivid, beautiful colours. Lucrezia sat for some moments on the lid of the wooden toolbox, rapt and unnoticed, until Jacomo turned from the wall to replenish his paintpot. His face and clothes, Lucrezia saw, were covered in blotches and freckles of blue and purple, and both his hands were deeply stained with paint.

He saw her and froze, mouth slightly open, eyes huge and unblinking.

Fra Pandolf turned too. He, however, waved cheerily and scrambled down from his trestle to refill his own paintpot.

'Signora!' he said. 'A pleasure to see you, my lady. It has been some days since we last . . .' He tailed off, frowning at the jars of paint. 'Jacomo, have we no more sienna?'

Jacomo shook his head, his eyes fixed upon Lucrezia's. Lucrezia heard Fra Pandolf make a small noise of irritation with his tongue against his teeth. He crossed the gallery, wiping his hands on his already much-stained habit. 'I shall not be long then, Jacomo – I must go to Brother Alessandro for some more. We need it quite urgently. I will go myself – I shall enjoy the walk. I hope to see you when I return, my lady. I'll not be long.' Humming cheerfully, suspecting nothing, Fra Pandolf pattered down the spiral staircase and left the hall.

Jacomo climbed down from his ladder. The sight of her had sent such a jolt through him that he had come close to falling. She was pale; her eyes seemed bigger than usual, and the freckles across the bridge of her nose stood out dark against her pallor. He had to be right. She *did* feel the same as he did. What else could be causing her to look at him like this, her eyes brimming with an eloquent echo of the longing that was now utterly consuming him?

He heard a soft sound and glanced down to see paint dripping steadily from the end of his brush onto the floor.

He had to talk to her. What, though? What was there to be said? He came down off the ladder and took a step towards her. She stood up.

'Signora – I . . . I . . .' He stopped. What was there to say? *I want you so badly that I can no longer think properly, I cannot paint any more and I've not eaten sensibly in three days?* No. Jacomo struggled with himself. He knew he had no choice – she had to stay away. Anything else would be madness. He had to tell her. He said,

'Signora, you must – oh, God, you must—' but then stopped as she stepped forward, put a hand on either side of his face and kissed his mouth.

For a wild moment he kissed her, and the wave of desire that struck him was almost more than he could control, but he knew that if he laid even a hand on her, the paint stains on her clothes would condemn them both, so he held his arms out and back, away from her body, while she kissed his mouth and then lipped up and over the crimson stain on his cheek. Tenderly her lips moved across the uneven skin while her fingers pushed up into his hair and round onto the back of his head.

Then she let go of him and stood back.

Even in the midst of this turbulence, Jacomo smiled: purple and blue was smudged around her mouth and across one cheek, like a child caught gorging on stolen berries. But enchanting as it seemed to him, it would, he knew, be a death sentence for them both, if seen. He knelt down, picked up a linen cloth and soaked it in the bucket of fresh water that stood near his ladder. Still saying nothing, he cleaned his own hands, then stood before her and washed the paint from her mouth and her cheek and her hands.

He was tender as a mother, Lucrezia thought, as he pulled a fold of his linen shirt out from inside his breeches and she stood quite still while he dried her face and hands with the skin-warm cloth, then smoothed her hair back away from her forehead.

She could find no words.

She stared and stared at him, searching his face, *learning* him. Jacomo's eyes were fixed upon hers, shining bright brown in his paint-smudged face.

Then he said in a whisper, 'This is madness. We should not be doing this.'

'I know.'

'You should go – stay away from here, and from me, until we've finished the fresco and left the Castello.'

'I know.'

'If this were discovered, we'd probably both end up dead.'

'I know.'

'But . . . oh, God, Signora! I've not been able to stop thinking about you.'

'I know.' Lucrezia paused. 'But listen – we can't talk now, not here – it's too public. Someone might see us. Come to my chambers tonight, Jacomo.'

'Are you mad? How can I?'

Lucrezia smiled. Perhaps she was mad. Perhaps madness was the result of enduring such longing for so many days. But suddenly the danger she knew she was courting seemed inconsequential. She had kissed Jacomo. She had been aching to kiss Jacomo for days – and now she had done it. His mouth had been as warm and giving as she had imagined, and her whole body was yearning to touch him again. She felt taut as a bowstring with wanting, and the possibility of discovery seemed now entirely unimportant.

'There is a way you can do it without anyone knowing.' And Lucrezia explained her idea. Jacomo looked sceptical as he listened to her detailed instructions, but he nodded. 'Are you certain it'll be unlocked?' he said.

'No, not absolutely certain, but I've been down there a couple of times and it wasn't locked on either occasion.'

'I'll be there. I . . .'

'What? What is it?'

'I might have something to give you. If I can get it in time. How can I . . .'

'I know just the way! Be there — wait until it is properly dark, though. Bring whatever it is with you and I'll show you then.' Lucrezia smiled, kissed the tips of her fingers and pressed them for a moment against Jacomo's lips. She examined the smudge of blue paint, then folded her hand into a fist, which she clasped inside her other hand and pressed back against her mouth.

'I'll be watching for you as soon as it's dark,' she said.

16

Eduardo Rossi stood at a fork in the road. Both the stony tracks ahead of him, he knew, led eventually to Ferrara and he was certain that the city was where Chiara must have gone. 'Which way, Barnabeo?' he said to his companion. 'If we pick the wrong one, we'll miss her.'

The other man – tall, bald, with the pocked and scarred skin of the limesman – said, 'You're quite certain she'll have gone to Ferrara?'

'Where else could she have gone?' Eduardo said. 'I've been with Matteo – she's not there – and she's not at Anna's. She doesn't really know anyone else.'

Barnabeo frowned, and looked down each of the two roads. 'Which way's longer?' he said.

Eduardo pointed.

'The other one, then,' said Barnabeo.

'But what if she expects us to make that choice, and she's deliberately picked the longer road, hoping to avoid us?

Barnabeo said, 'You take one road, and I'll take the other.'

Eduardo hesitated. 'I have no idea what time she left the lime-works. She might already have reached the city.'

Barnabeo pushed his mouth out in a *moue* of scepticism. He said, 'You found she was missing when you got back in from fixing that hinge . . .'

Eduardo nodded. Mending his old neighbour's door had taken hours, he thought, trying to justify his long absence to himself – the whole thing had proved to be rotten and he had had to take it off completely and remake most of it.

It had been dark when he had arrived back at the house.

There had been no fire, no food cooking; the place had been – unexpectedly – damp, cold and deserted. A prickle of guilt-stained fear crept down the back of his neck. She could have been gone for hours. He heard his own voice, from that morning, filling the downstairs room with an untidy, painful anger: 'Don't you look at me like that – you've brought this on yourself, Chiara – and you've brought shame on this house. Shame on the Rossis. You've behaved like a whore and I'm not prepared to live with the conse-quences. I won't have your bastard child living here, forever reminding me of your waywardness. No, Chiara. No! Don't try to persuade me – there's no point.'

Eduardo's eyes stung as these echoes of his unloving implac-ability filled his head. With a sharp pang, he saw Chiara's face, angry and frightened as she had tried to plead with him. Then he imagined her scrambling in his absence that morning to fill a bag with her few belongings, and leaving the house, bound for – oh, God! Bound for where?

'Eduardo, come on! The quicker we are, the more likely we are to catch up with her,' Barnabeo said, clapping a heavy hand onto Eduardo's shoulder. 'And there's not much more than a couple of hours' light left.'

Eduardo closed his eyes for a moment, then he said, 'You're quite right. You take that road and I'll try this one. We meet up outside the cathedral. Agreed?'

The early sun was already bright, and bluish shadows lay thick and dark along the foot of the great wall that encircled the city of Ferrara, darkest beneath the great jutting ramparts. The most southerly gate, the Porta Paula, was open, and the usual morning traffic was streaming through in both directions. There were market traders going in, some pushing hand-barrows, some driving carts; peasant farmers with grain or vegetables or animals to sell; a couple of well-dressed young noblemen were leaving the city astride impressive horses, setting off for a day's hawking with their hooded peregrines gripping their sleeves; a clutch of chattering children scampered ahead of a small group of women.

And in the midst of all this, unnoticed by the crowd, one lone traveller was moving very slowly, heading into the heart of the city. Each step was costing Chiara Rossi more energy than she had to spare. The poorly wrapped bundle she held in her arms was not heavy, but the burden she carried within her belly was weighing her down. Her clothes were damp from the night she had spent wrapped in her cloak on a makeshift mattress of hay in an outbuilding about a mile outside the city, and her back ached dully.

She stopped and wiped her forehead with the back of her hand, pressing the sweat up and into her already damp hair. She had reached the city. She was still as fearful of discovery as she had been since leaving the house the previous morning, but she saw no familiar faces among the anonymous figures coming and going through the great gate, so after a moment, she began to walk again.

No more than a few paces further on, though, she stopped and held her breath, head bent, hands splayed around the swell of her belly, as a griping cramp stiffened and hardened it for a long moment. Her face felt as if it were swelling, and her eyes watered; then the cramp loosened its grip and she could breathe again. She sank down to sit on the grass at the side of the road, dropping her bundle beside her and stroking her belly in slow circles; beneath her fingers, the child stretched and pushed, rubbing uncomfortably under her ribs. The lump of some indeterminate limb pressed up beneath her palm.

'Go to sleep,' she said softly. 'We've a fair way to go yet.'

17

'I'm sorry, it was stupid of me. I should have asked you before you went down to Alessandro's – you could have collected all the pigments together. I'm sorry, Brother. I'll go straight away. I won't be long.'

Jacomo managed a brief smile at a startled Fra Pandolf as he snatched up his doublet from the floor of the gallery and put it on. Not bothering to lace it, he ran down the spiral staircase and out of the North Hall. Forcing his pace down to a swift walk, he made his way through the castle to the door that led to the back draw-bridge and crossed it, out into the piazza beyond.

The light outside was a bright, flat, shadowless white. Jacomo began to run again, away from the Castello, past the great façade of the cathedral and off towards the centre of town. He turned down the long, narrow Via delle Volte, running towards the river until his sides heaved and his breath rasped raw in his throat. Hands on knees, head bowed, he waited for his wildly jumping heart to settle.

Around him thronged the bustling activity of the wharves

that lined the banks of the Po, where itinerant hawkers and tradesmen pushed and jostled among bales of cloth, barrels, stacks of wood; bargemen shouted in unfamiliar dialects and over-laden porters delivered their goods. The air smelt sharply of sodden wood, decay and a multitude of spices, with a soft underlying scent of sweat. Jacomo straightened, and watched the milling crowds. He began chewing the side of his thumbnail, the fingers of that hand softly stroking the raised skin of the crimson stain on his cheek.

This was insane. Completely insane. He was quite certain that what he planned to do – what he was about to arrange now with Alessandro – was courting not only his own death but hers as well. He could not do it. It was impossible. Even if they managed to avoid discovery, it would only make leaving the Castello – and her – that much more painful in the end. That one kiss had been almost more than he could resist –he could hardly contemplate what anything more intimate would do to him. Jacomo began to argue with himself as he started walking again. He did not have to do this, he could just ask Alessandro for the pigments he needed and not mention his . . . other request. Then he could go back to the Castello and keep away from her. He did not need to go to her chamber tonight. They had risked enough already.

But.

The aching yearning that had been ignited by that kiss was not going to be easily ignored; he had been shaken into pieces that no longer quite fitted together. He felt again her mouth on his cheek, her fingers in his hair, smelt the sweet rose scent of her, and a wave of wanting her flooded through him. He stood still, letting the sensation pulse through his body.

He knew her name – Lucrezia – but he had never used it. God – this was madness! He was contemplating risking everything –

career, reputation, both their lives – so that he could make love to a married woman he had so far only ever addressed as 'Signora'.

Jacomo walked past the end of the wharf and down another narrow street. This opened out into a bright little square, facing onto which was a small, wide-windowed shop, lined with blue and white pottery jars, bunches of herbs and glass bottles full of brightly coloured spices. He paused outside the door, the two sides of the argument still raging in his head, then went in.

The apothecary looked up as he entered the shop, a small, bent figure with a head almost bald, save for the few wisps of white hair that clung to it like down on a speckled egg. Jacomo's heart lifted as the egg cracked in a wide smile. The apothecary stepped forward and patted his sleeve.

'What's the matter, Jacomino?' Alessandro Giglio said. 'Been running?'

'Yes. We're out of ultramarine.'

'But the reverend brother was in here not half an hour ago. Why did he not—'

'I didn't tell him in time.'

Alessandro reached for a large earthenware jar, which he unstoppered carefully. 'How much, lad?'

'As much as you can spare – the piece we're tackling tomorrow has a large section of sea and sky in it, and Medea's dress will need ultramarine shadows, too.' Jacomo cleared his throat as he tried to work out a way of phrasing his more delicate request.

The apothecary frowned at him, holding a horn scoop piled high with bright blue powder. 'Something's troubling you, lad. What is it?'

Jacomo took a long, slow breath, held it for a moment, and then made his decision. He said, 'Can I ask you a favour, Alessandro?'

'Of course, lad. What is it?'

And Jacomo told him.

He phrased it carefully, trying to give away as little as possible, but even so, Alessandro was clearly surprised. The white tufts of his eyebrows rose high onto his forehead, but then he gave a twisted little smile and agreed. He tipped the ultramarine into a jar and stoppered it, then rummaged in a capacious leather bag which was hanging on a hook on the wall. 'There you are, lad,' he said. 'It's a spare. Keep it until you see me again.'

Catelina reached into her basket and brought out a small waxed-linen bag. 'Gingered bread,' she said, holding it up and shaking it so that the contents rustled.

The tall, round-faced horseman's eyebrows lifted. 'For me?' he said.

'You told me you liked it, Giorgio,' Catelina said. 'They were making a big batch in the kitchens this morning, and . . . well, I asked nicely. I've brought you some pears too.' She lifted the basket.

Giorgio grinned at her and took the bag. He opened it, and, holding it in one broad palm, peered into it. Dipping thumb and forefinger in, he picked out a golden, sugar-dusted cube. 'Here,' he said, holding it towards her. 'You have some.'

Catelina reached out a hand, but Giorgio ignored it and held the bread to her lips. Her eyes fixed upon his, Catelina allowed him to put it directly into her mouth. His fingertips touched her lip. Giorgio took out another two cubes for himself. 'Mmm!' he said. 'That's good. Thank you.'

'Are you busy this afternoon?' Catelina asked, her heart beating a little faster. Was she being too forward?

Giorgio rolled his eyes and clicked his tongue. 'Forget this afternoon. I've been busy all day and it's not finished yet. That big brute over there needs strapping – he's completely filthy after a carriage trip yesterday – then I need to make up a poultice for the old mare. Her hock's still swollen. I have to take the Percheron – the one His Lordship sold last month – over to its new owner later on. I'll ride him over there – about ten miles, I think it is – and I'll take the grey Murgese mare with me to ride back on. Why d'you ask?' He picked more gingered bread out of the little bag.

Catelina hoped her disappointment did not show. 'I wondered, that's all.'

Giorgio held up another piece of the bread, eyebrows raised quizzically. Catelina nodded and he once more put it gently into her mouth. 'I won't be back until late, but perhaps . . . we can share a bite of lunch tomorrow?'

'I'd like that.' She smiled at him.

A scurry of footsteps startled her, and she turned from Giorgio to see who had arrived. With a jolt of surprise, she saw the Signora, her hair fuzzy and untidy, her face pink from having – Catelina presumed – run all the way from the castle. The Signora's chest was heaving as she caught her breath.

'My lady?' Catelina said.

'Oh!' The Signora stopped abruptly. 'Lina!' She looked from Catelina to Giorgio, hardly seeming to register their presence; she seemed quite distracted.

'My lady, is there anything wrong?'

'What? Oh – no, there isn't. I'm – I'm just looking for something. I—' She stopped, and then said, 'Lina, could I borrow your basket?'

Catelina raised her eyebrows in surprise, but nodded. 'Of course, my lady.' She bit back her curiosity, saying no more, then she took out the three pears and gave them to Giorgio, who was watching the Signora as if quite fascinated. He put two of the pears, with the rest of the bread, into a large pocket in his breeches; the third he began to eat.

'Was this what you were after, my lady?' Catelina asked, handing over the now empty basket.

'What? Erm . . . no. No, it wasn't.'

'What was it? What is it you need?'

Lucrezia told her. More puzzled than ever, Catelina turned to Giorgio, who smiled broadly, swallowed the last mouthful of pear and said cheerfully, wiping his chin on his sleeve, 'Easy, my lady. I'll fetch you one straight away.' He threw the only remaining part of the pear – the stalk – over his shoulder as he walked towards the saddlery.

Lucrezia had tried hard to ignore Catelina's obviously burning curiosity ever since they had returned from the stables, but the truth was bulging up inside her, desperate for release.

They had walked back to the Castello in silence. Lucrezia's agitation was now almost painful – her insides were fermenting, expanding, churning. Her longing to see Jacomo again was becoming quite overwhelming. She decided as they walked along, side by side, that she would have to tell Catelina. Her skin felt thin and stretched, as the enormity of what she was planning swelled inside her. If she did not tell *someone*, she thought, it began to seem possible that she might, quite literally, *burst* – split open like an overripe plum.

More to break the silence than because she really wanted to know, she said, 'What were you doing down at the stables, Lina?' She was surprised to see Catelina flush and bite her lip.

'I – I went to see Giorgio, my lady. That's the horseman I was talking to down there. I'd taken him a bit of food.'

Momentarily distracted from her own thoughts, Lucrezia said, 'Giorgio? Who is he? How do you know him?'

The flush deepened. 'Well . . . he's one of my lord's horsemen. I'd already seen him with the horses a few times, I suppose, but I first spoke to him properly about two weeks ago when I went down into the town that time for that length of lace you wanted.'

Lucrezia nodded, remembering.

'Giorgio had to go into the city himself that day, to pick up some piece of metal harness that had had to be mended at the armourer's. We met by chance at the drawbridge and walked together. He collected the metal thing and then waited to take me back with him.'

'And you like him, do you?' Lucrezia said, with a smile.

Catelina did not need to answer; the shine in her eyes betrayed the truth most eloquently. Lucrezia knew a moment's searing jealousy. How simple to be in Catelina's position, she thought, unmarried, anonymous, ignoble and free to choose her own future, a simple, flat pathway ahead of her, compared to the mountain of impossible obstacles that loomed between her and Jacomo.

Her feelings must have shown in her face, for Catelina took her hand and squeezed her fingers. 'Oh, my lady,' she said, 'please, what's troubling you? Something is wrong, isn't it? What did you want this for?' She held up the basket, now filled with something quite other than pears.

Lucrezia knew she would have to tell her.

'Let's go up to the Roof Garden when we get in,' she said. 'I'll tell you there.'

They climbed up through the castle, out into the little *belvedere*, with its terracotta-potted orange trees and bay bushes, and onto the sunlit Roof Garden. Some thirty feet square, it was surrounded by head-high castellated brick walls, in which were several tiny peep-hole windows. Lucrezia crossed the red-tiled floor and gazed through one of these to the bustling street below.

After a moment, she sat down on a stone bench. Catelina sat beside her.

Lucrezia hesitated, then began.

When she had finished, Catelina's mouth was open and her eyes were quite round. She stared at Lucrezia for a moment, evidently struggling to find a response, but then she took Lucrezia's hand and held it between both her own. '*Pazza!*' she whispered. '*Che pazza!* Oh, dear God, I thought this might happen. If you are discovered, Signora, you know you are both dead.'

She said this without emotion, but the hair on Lucrezia's neck and arms stood on end. She knew Catelina was right. And she knew, too, that it would not stop her. The fizzing excitement began to bubble up again.

'He will be there after dark. Come with me to my apartment, Lina. I'll try to work on that stupid tapestry for a bit to make the time pass, and then perhaps you could find us something to eat.'

'You look tired,' Fra Pandolf said. 'Still, we're almost done, now, and the light's going, so let's just finish this last little corner and then we can tidy up.' He smiled at Jacomo. 'After that you can go and rest, lad.'

Jacomo smiled back at him. He looked over his shoulder. Out of the window, the sun was low in the sky and had darkened to a thick, egg-yolk orange. Not long till dark. It was a miracle, he thought, that in his distracted state he had managed to complete this *giornata* without ruining it: *mezzo fresco* is an unforgiving medium, and even a single blunder might have meant that the whole day's work would have had to be chipped away and redone on a new coat of plaster. There can be no overpainting in a fresco.

Jacomo and the friar finished painting and spent a few moments cleaning brushes and tidying, ready for the following day's *giornata*, and then Jacomo left the gallery. He crossed the castle, unseeing, his thoughts in confusion, back to the two rooms he and Tomaso had been given to share.

He pulled some things out of a large bag next to Tomaso's bed, hoping Tomaso would not mind the liberty he intended to take with his friend's belongings. He held them up, assessing their suitability. 'A bit big, but they'll do,' he muttered. He wrapped the items tightly in a length of linen, and tied the bundle securely with twine. Pulling a sheet of paper from an untidy pile on the small table under the window, he wrote a short note and tucked it carefully into the rolled cloth.

Glancing out of the window, Jacomo reckoned that some two hours remained until it would be dark enough to risk setting out on his venture. Agitated to the point that he was now physically incapable of sitting still, he left the room, the cloth bundle in his arms, and began to walk. Through room after room, down staircase after staircase he went, until he found himself at the foot of the Torre San Paolo. He had been told that of the four towers, this one had been unused for years, and as he stood there now, he smelt the deserted, musty odour of long neglect. A wooden staircase led up out of sight. Jacomo began to climb. He had no candle and the tower was almost windowless; after a couple of dozen steps, he found himself climbing in total darkness, one hand on the stone wall. So many steps. It seemed to him he might climb for ever.

Perhaps, though, that was what he deserved for even contemplating such a thing as bedding the wife of the Duke of Ferrara.

The steps led to a small lobby. As Jacomo stood in the little room, his heartbeat thick in his throat from the long climb, he could see, by the light that fell from a single window, that another half-dozen roughly made steps led upwards again to a heavy wooden door. He opened it.

The room at the top of the tower was large and airy; wooden-floored, with a great beamed ceiling through which a long ladder rose into an indistinct space high above his head. An unlatched door proved to lead out onto a balustraded balcony. Jacomo leaned over the balustrade: far below him was the black water of the moat. A few stars pricked the darkening sky, and at these Jacomo stared, unblinking, his eyes stinging, searching for the different constellations, trying to order his thoughts.

Some time later, he heard the tower clock chime and went back into the beamed room. From there he ran down the stairs, on and on in the darkness, hearing nothing but the thudding of his feet on the wooden treads. At the bottom, he leaned for a second against a wall, then made his way towards the door that he knew led to the lower regions of the Castello.

The sky had deepened to a rich inky blue, and Catelina leaned out of the bedchamber window. She looked intently in both directions, then straight out below her; turning back into the room, she shook her head. 'Nothing, my lady.'

Lucrezia's heartbeat was now so frantic she was feeling quite sick. 'He'll be here soon,' she whispered, more to herself than to Catelina. A round embroidery frame lay across her lap. She stared at it blankly, and picked at the skin of one fingertip with her needle. An untouched plate of fruit, cheese, bread and meat lay beside her; she stared at it for a moment, then turning once more to Catelina, said, 'Say an *Ave* and then try again.'

They began to mouth the prayer together.

A few candles were burning in brackets on the walls as Jacomo passed. He prised one out and carried on round another corner, shuddering as he passed the door that he knew led to the dungeons, then, free hand cupped around the flame, he ran down another narrow staircase and along to a small, metal-studded wooden door.

It was locked and bolted.

He put his candle down, then held the bolt in both hands and tried to pull it backwards. It screeched its protestations out into the choking stillness and Jacomo's heart began to beat so fast he could feel it shaking his whole body. He stood still, breath held, listening for any sounds of investigative footsteps, but none came and, after a few terrifying moments, he tentatively tried the huge key. It turned unexpectedly smoothly, cushioned, Jacomo discovered in the flickering flamelight, by thick, black grease. He wiped his hand down his already paint-filthy breeches.

The moat water smelt stagnant.

Three little boats thunked softly against each other and against the wooden bulk of the jetty. Jacomo stepped into and across two of the three, taking his time to balance as they wobbled beneath his feet, the cloth bundle jammed under one arm. Sitting down in the third, outermost boat, he stowed the bundle by his feet, undid the rope that secured the boat to the jetty and pulled out one of the two oars, which he laid across his knees.

The huge, dark mass of the Castello reared above him as he hand-over-handed around the edge of the overhang. The brick was rough and scratchy beneath its slimy coating of weed, and the dank smell of the water was strong in his nostrils. Once out into the moat itself, Jacomo began sculling with the single oar over the back of the boat, keeping as close as he could to the wall. He hugged the deepest shadows and the single oar was almost silent.

A dove clattered out from a hole in the brickwork, making him jump – so close to his head that he felt the draught from its wingflaps.

He sculled around the last corner and lifted the oar back into the boat as he reached the window Lucrezia had described to him, pulling himself to a halt by gripping the bricks with his fingertips.

'*Ora pro nobis peccatoribus, nunc, et in hora mortis nostrae,*' Lucrezia muttered. 'Now try again, Lina.'

Catelina went to the window once more, and this time she gasped. Lucrezia stood up. The embroidery frame fell to the floor with a clatter.

Catelina said, 'He's here, Signora – quick!'

Lucrezia scrambled past her and leaned out of the window. The shadow at the base of the wall was thick and clotted, and the reflection of the parapet of the tower above her shifted and wobbled in the almost black water, but she could just make out a darker shape that had not been there before.

'Jacomo?'

Lucrezia could hardly hear his hissed reply, but there was no doubt that it was him.

'I've found the things I wanted to give you. How can I get them to you?' Jacomo said softly.

'Stay there.'

Jacomo stared up towards the open casement. And then he jumped, as a woven straw basket, inexpertly tied to a long dirty rope, came whispering down the wall towards him, scratching as it caught against the roughness of the brick. If he had not felt almost strangled with anxiety, he thought he might have laughed. Pulling the basket into the boat, Jacomo placed the linen bundle into it and then twitched down on the rope, which smelled of horses. The basket rose back up to the window and Lucrezia pulled it in, then leaned out again. 'Thank you,' she said.

'There's a note with the things. Read it first and tell me what you think.'

'I will. I'll do it now. Don't go away!'

Jacomo pictured her scrabbling to pull the paper out from where it had been tucked inside the knotted twine, imagined her thoughts as she read the words he had written. '*Put on the things you will find in the bundle. I hope they fit you. Come down into the city with me – now. I'll be waiting by the clump of poplars near the gateway to the city. Bring some of your own clothes in a bag – J* '.

The basket reappeared and was lowered once more. Jacomo took it again as it fell near his hands, and felt inside. For a moment, he thought it was empty, but then his fingers touched a velvety softness: a tightly furled rosebud. He picked it up, held it to his nose, breathed in its sweetness. The basket rose out of sight.

Jacomo waited. Long seconds snailed past and then the window above him banged open, and she leaned out so far and so fast that for a second he thought she might fall right out.

'Jacomo! Are you still there?' A barely audible whisper.

'Yes.'

'I'll be there. I promise. I'll be a few moments. Wait for me where you said.'

Jacomo tucked the little rose into a hole in his doublet, and then sculled back round to the jetty, negotiating his way under the louring black archway and into the low tunnel. He moored the boat, clambered out and made for the door, which he prayed would not have been refastened in his absence.

It was still open.

Jacomo closed his eyes and stood motionless. Letting out the breath he only now realised he had been holding in, he locked the door again and retraced his steps through the castle.

The smallest side drawbridge was still down. He crossed it,

walked round two sides of the Castello and down to a group of six poplar trees. He sat down on a tussock of grass and wrapped his arms around his knees. With his back against one of the tree-trunks, he stared up into the star-spattered sky.

18

Jacomo had tied the twine too tightly, Lucrezia thought, as her trembling fingers fought to loosen the knots. Catelina stood at her shoulder, hands clasped, not speaking. Lucrezia could feel Catelina's breath on the side of her face.

The covering linen finally fell away to reveal . . . a paint-stained pair of brown breeches, grey hose and a linen shirt. There was a brownish-grey woollen doublet, and a scarlet cap.

Catelina's eyes were wide with curiosity.

'He means you to wear this, Signora?' she said.

'So the letter says.' Lucrezia fingered the clothes, which were worn and soft with use. Flecks of paint and plaster clung to each garment; they were certainly artist's clothes, Lucrezia thought, but they seemed far too small to belong to the tall, long-limbed Jacomo.

Catelina said, 'Well, come here, my lady. You'd better hurry. He's waiting.'

Lucrezia gasped. 'Oh, *cielo*! Quick! I must—' She stopped as Catelina swung her round and busied herself with laces and fastenings, then, wriggling out of her stiff bodice, Lucrezia ducked down and picked up the two separate legs of the hose, turning them this way and that, smiling at the thought of herself clad in such grubby, unappealing articles. Catelina started to laugh, covering her mouth with her hand.

Lucrezia stepped out of her skirts, pulled off her shift, and then sat naked on the floor, pushing her legs into the hose. They fitted quite well, though when she stood up, she felt certain that, within seconds, they would be round her knees. Frowning, and fingering the top edges, she saw a dozen little lace holes.

'Look, Lina! We tie these to something to keep them up!'

'Here,' Catelina said. 'There are holes here, in the doublet. I'll get some laces.'

Lucrezia pulled the shirt over her head and pushed her hands into the doublet sleeves.

'Arms up!' Catelina said briskly.

Lucrezia raised them and Catelina knelt in front of her, a bunch of laces between her teeth, one in her fingers.

'I feel like a parcel, Lina. This is worse than women's clothing!' Lucrezia said, as Catelina wordlessly pulled and knotted her into her new garments.

At last, hose, breeches and doublet all neatly fastened, Lucrezia stood back to examine herself in her glass. 'Oh!' she said. 'My hair. What shall I do with it?'

'Let me, my lady.' Catelina plaited it quickly, then between them they rolled the braid up against the back of her head, and pulled the scarlet cap over it, hiding all but a few stray wisps. Lucrezia looked at her feet. 'Jacomo hasn't given me any shoes.'

'The brown kid slippers will do well,' Catelina said, crossing to the chest at the foot of the bed.

Lucrezia hooked a finger into the heels of the proffered shoes and pulled them on. 'What do you think?'

A wide smile and a hug were her only answers.

Catelina pulled a dress and a shift from the chest, and rolled them into a tight bundle, using Jacomo's twine to secure them. She pushed them into the straw basket.

'Well, come on, my lady,' she said. 'We have to get you out of the castle now.'

Lucrezia thought her heart might burst right out of her as they crept through the Castello and out to the back drawbridge, which, thank God, was still down. Every sound she heard struck like a chill blade in her chest and the faces in the portraits along the many walls seemed to her to accuse at every step. She felt, though, strangely liberated and unlike herself in the unfamiliar clothing, stronger, braver, in these men's garments. They were an effective disguise, she thought.

Catelina had been carrying the basket. Now she pushed it into Lucrezia's arms and said, 'Go on, Signora. He's waiting for you. Oh . . . God keep you safe.'

Lucrezia hugged her, then crossed the drawbridge and ran along the shadowed path that led around the dark castle walls – only one or two yellow-lit windows now punctuated the heavy black mass of it – until she could see the clump of poplars, which stood a few feet from the main gateway into the city.

She saw no one, heard nothing but the pinking of the toads as she crept the last few steps to the trees. Eyes stretched wide in the darkness, she looked for him, but saw only shadow, thickest between the straight poplar trunks.

And then an arm reached out, a hand caught her wrist, and he pulled her into the denser darkness. Her gasp of surprise was cut short. She dropped the basket. There was no bitter paint taste this time – Jacomo's mouth was warm and sweet. His hands were clean of paint now, and this time he did not hold them away from her, but pulled her in close to him, one arm around her back, gripping her shoulder, the other hand reaching down around her buttocks. She clung to him, pressed up against him, ran her hands over every inch of him she could reach, finally uttering the soft little noises of longing she could no longer suppress. Her mouth on his, it was as though the feel and taste and smell of him were seeping into her, expanding within her.

Eventually, Jacomo cupped her face in his hands and drew back. 'Will you come down into the city with me, then?' he said, stroking her cheek.

Lucrezia nodded.

'Give me your dress – we can leave it here. It'll be quite safe, and we'll pick it up on the way back so you can change.'

She nodded again, unable to speak, light-headed with kissing, and handed him the basket, which he tucked into a deep patch of shadow below the poplars.

Lucrezia had no idea where Jacomo was leading her – despite her year and a half's residence in Ferrara, she realised now how little she knew of the city beyond the castle walls. She reached for Jacomo's hand; he caught her fingers, but quickly let go.

'Put them in your pockets. We can't hold hands in the street,' he said, smiling at her, 'not with you dressed like that. Two lads, hand in hand? They'd arrest us soon as look at us!'

Lucrezia wanted his hand in hers so badly it made her feel dizzy. She twisted around, searching for the pockets in the unfamiliar breeches, found them and pushed her hands deep into the dusty linen, where she balled them into trembling fists.

A maze of narrow, twisting streets led away from the looming bulk of the Castello; vividly painted houses and shops jostled each other like an excitable crowd of brightly dressed peasants. Stripes and patterns crawled over walls and around doorways; painted fruit and flowers twined above windows. Lucrezia saw by the light of a flaring torch over the doorway of a cheerful second-hand clothes shop that here, at least, the Este colours of red, white and green loudly proclaimed their allegiance. And everywhere there were people: busy, working people.

'Do they not sleep?' she said.

'Not this close to the river, not for hours yet,' Jacomo said.

The river. The Po. She smelt it long before they arrived at the wharf, a drifting concoction of sodden wood, fish and spices. They crossed a wide piazza, where merchants' and artisans' stalls crowded under the arcades. Some, Lucrezia saw, were darkened now and closed for the night, but others still plied their trade. Chickens clucked crossly in cramped coops, a rainbow of silks and damasks gleamed in the flickering torchlight, while nearby an armourer's furnace glowed a vivid red-gold and sparks showered as hammer was brought to blade with a ringing clang.

There were shouts, cries, laughter all around. Lucrezia started as a woman shrieked – a woman in wild, mismatched clothes – but the shriek was one of mirth. Her painted face was cracked in broken-toothed lasciviousness, as she grinned up into the laughing face of an elegant man who, Lucrezia thought, should probably have known better. The woman was lost from view then, as a noisy crowd of rowdy young men swaggered past in front of her. Lucrezia's eyes widened as a knife-blade caught the torchlight and flashed for an instant in one waving hand.

'Come on, this way,' Jacomo said, pointing down another street.

In sight of the river now, they stopped outside a shop, whose wide window was lined with blue and white jars, labelled, Lucrezia saw, with whispering names that made her think of adventurous ships in faraway seas: anise and cardamom, cinnamon and saffron.

Jacomo stood in front of her and held both her hands in his. He looked at her for a long moment and then said, 'We're here. Are you quite sure you want to do this?'

Lucrezia nodded. She felt as though she were melting. She and Jacomo looked at each other, not speaking, cocooned in a conjoined separateness around which the jostle and madness of the riverside nightlife milled and thronged, entirely unaware of the two anonymous strangers on the brink of an enormity.

Jacomo put his hand into a leather bag and brought out an iron key. He opened the narrow door to the darkened shop, and the two of them stepped inside. He closed and locked the door behind them and the noise outside faded.

It was too dark for Lucrezia to see much, and before she had had time to gain more than a brief impression of jar-lined shelves, hanging bunches of herbs and polished floorboards, Jacomo had taken her hand again and was walking her towards a cramped staircase, which rose awkwardly out of the shop: more a ladder, Lucrezia thought, than a flight of steps. He stood back to let her climb first.

'It's a great deal easier in breeches than skirts,' she said, glancing over her shoulder at Jacomo.

'It's a pleasure to watch, too.'

Lucrezia felt once more that hot, slithering thread, sliding down from her throat to hook deep in her belly.

She climbed into the upper room. It was clearly some sort of a storeroom for the apothecary: barrels and baskets and boxes stood ranked and piled, and dozens more bunches of dried herbs hung from the ceiling beams. Three enormous sacks stood along one wall, sagging plumply like a trio of fat old men, and several shelves were lined with glass bottles and jars, indistinct in the half-light from the open casement.

'Alessandro lent me the room,' Jacomo said. Lucrezia was suddenly anxious, but Jacomo smiled and took her face in his hands. 'I didn't tell him who I was bringing here.'

Lucrezia tilted her face upwards within his hands and Jacomo kissed her.

'He told me last week that he sometimes stays here overnight when he's been working late,' he murmured, 'but he has a house elsewhere, where he lives when he isn't working, he says.'

Jacomo led her between the barrels and boxes to a low truckle bed that stood against the furthest wall. A linen sheet covered the straw mattress; several pillows were piled at one end and a jumble of blankets lay untidily across the other.

He turned to face her.

'Are you quite sure you want to do this?' he repeated.

'Oh, Jacomo!' Lucrezia said. 'I think I shall die if I don't.' He smiled at her, his mouth in parenthesis again, and the melting feeling in her belly intensified.

'Well, let's get those old things off you, then,' he said quietly. He held her gaze as he unfastened the brownish-grey jerkin. Lucrezia reached forward, between his arms, and her fingers began exploring the knot in the lacing of his shabby deerskin doublet, working by feel; she was reluctant to take her eyes from his face.

Jacomo's clothes were easier to unfasten than her own, she discovered. She removed his doublet and shirt with ease, but as she and Jacomo soon discovered, Catelina had, in her agitation, tied all the unfamiliar laces very tightly; it took Jacomo several moments of delicate knot-picking to release a visibly quivering Lucrezia from her borrowed garments. But at last she was free of them, and before long, she and Jacomo were facing each other in the torch-light, skin to skin.

Lucrezia moved to tuck a wisp of hair behind her ear – and

realized she was still wearing the scarlet cap. She raised her hands to her head, but Jacomo laughed and held her wrists.

'No – leave it on,' he said. 'It's beautiful. *Piccolo ragazzo.*'

Still clasping her wrists, he held his hands out, sideways and down, holding Lucrezia's arms away from her body; he crouched before her so that his mouth was on a level with her breasts. For a moment, she closed her eyes, and her breath came in shallow, shivering gasps as he kissed her there.

Then he stood up, both her hands now held inside his own. 'Ready?' he said.

Lucrezia looked at his long, lean, brown body, and then at his face, her limbs taut and trembling with longing. Eyes fixed on Jacomo's, wearing nothing but a boy's woollen hat, she nodded, and scrambled backwards towards the pile of pillows on the untidy bed. He followed, pausing only to shift a pile of baskets that were blocking the window; a shaft of light fell fitfully across the bed.

'I want to be able to see you,' he said. 'All of you. I've been imagining you for weeks – and drawing what I imagined – but now I want to see as much of the reality as I can.'

'Did you ever imagine me in a hat like this one?'

Jacomo laughed. 'It has tended to be what I imagined you *without* rather than *with*.' He kissed her again.

For a time they did not speak, had no need for words as they began to search and learn each other's bodies – as they explored and discovered every cleft and crease with eager fingers and hungry mouths. Lucrezia found herself brim-full of an unprecedented energy; Alfonso's attentions had always paralysed her, she realised – left her each time as little more than a passive puppet – but now the touch of Jacomo's hands was freeing her, creating in her a vibrancy she had not known she possessed.

After a time, Jacomo laid the length of his body along hers; he gently kissed her mouth, leaning his weight upon his elbows. Then, nudging her legs outwards with his own, he slid on top of her. Lucrezia wrapped her legs around him, lacing her fingers through his hair and pushing her breasts up against his chest. She held her breath, feeling a sudden fierce rush of unexpected gratitude for all the months of humiliation she had had to endure, because, she realised, it meant that now, even after two long, difficult years of marriage, it would be Jacomo who would be the one to take her maidenhood from her. A gift, she thought, that would be most willingly given.

Jacomo said, 'Ready?'

Lucrezia nodded.

He waited for the briefest moment. There was one stab of hot pain, which made her wince, and then a melting sweetness. She was surrounded by him; filled with him; consumed by him. Every sense was glutted with him.

Jacomo saw Lucrezia flinch, and heard a little indrawn breath. He stopped. 'Did I hurt you?'

'Please don't stop.' She wrapped her legs more tightly around his waist and tilted her face to his. He kissed her again.

'I want this. I want to do this,' she said indistinctly through the kiss, 'I want you inside me.'

Her words sent a shudder of longing right through him. Sliding one arm around her back, he reached for her breast with the other hand: she squirmed with pleasure.

It was, he thought, as though he were being offered a feast to sate starvation, water to quench a raging thirst. He could not get enough of her. This need for her that had been growing and swelling for days was now all-consuming; nothing had ever invaded him like this – nothing – not even the wildest, most explosive moments of his creative inspiration. He was drowning in her, she was all he could see and hear, the taste and smell of her were intoxicating and her skin beneath his fingers entranced him.

'Let me roll over!' Lucrezia said then, into his thinking, and he smiled at her, and rolled with her, their bodies still joined, until he lay on his back and she sat above him. She dipped her head down and ran the tip of her tongue around and around each nipple. Jacomo closed his eyes and the corners of his mouth crooked up in sybaritic abandonment.

They played together for what seemed like hours, breathlessly delighted, combining their bodies in every way they could devise: sprawled amid the rumpled bedding; standing pressed against the back wall of Alessandro's storeroom; at times they faced each other, at others Jacomo felt his breath warm on the nape of Lucrezia's neck as he pressed up against her back – until at last they sank in exhausted repletion under the thin and scratchy woollen blankets, as content as though sumptuously wrapped in imperial luxury.

They lay side by side. Jacomo let out a long breath and stretched. He felt something bunched under his knees and pulled out the scarlet woollen cap, crumpled and squashed. Smiling, he held it out above Lucrezia and laid it on her chest. Her eyes were closed. She fingered it with one hand, exploring it; then, feeling its rough woollen texture, opened her eyes and picked it up. She said nothing, just held the hat in both hands, then laid her cheek on his chest and, to his astonishment, he felt the hot dampness of tears.

He sat up. 'What is it? What's the matter, *cara*?'

She curled against him. A little sob escaped her.

Jacomo put his arms around her. 'Oh, *cara* – what on earth is wrong? Why are you crying?'

Lucrezia wiped her eyes. 'Nothing – it's nothing. It's just . . . just – oh, Jacomo! This is the happiest I've ever been – ever! – and it's shown me how horrible everything has been, for so long, and . . . I can't bear to go back to it and—'

'Oh, *cara*.' He held her close; she tilted her face up to him and he kissed her, wiping away the wetness on her face with the ball of his thumb. The kiss was tear-salted, slow and soft. *This is the happiest I've ever been.* He stroked her hair, and her mouth was tender and sweet beneath his own; then he pulled himself up onto his elbows and leaned over her. Running a hand around her breast, he felt the kiss ignite again, flames licking at a soft-blown ember. Once more they clung together, hungry and searching all over again, once more they fed upon each other until sated, once more lay back, entwined in each other's arms.

Jacomo pulled one of the blankets up and over them both, and closed his eyes.

Lucrezia awoke in a drowsy tangle of warm limbs and untidy hair. Alfonso had never held her like this, she thought. This was the first time in her life that she had lain so, relaxed and content in the embrace of a lover. Cradled in Jacomo's arms, she lay with her head against his chest, listening to the soft bellows-pull of his breath.

Jacomo stirred and smoothed her hair away from her face, tucking it behind her ear. 'Are you all right now?'

Lucrezia nodded.

'Can I draw you?' he asked, still lying back on the pillows. 'Now?'

He made a rumbling noise of assent in his chest, against which Lucrezia's ear was still pressed.

'If you'd like to,' she said.

Jacomo was fiddling with her hair now, winding strands of it into ringlets around his fingers. Lucrezia reached for his hand, pulled it away from her hair and began examining it. It was strong and square, blunt-fingered, ingrained with coloured flecks of paint. A hand gifted in many more ways than painting, though, she thought, another hot little pulse of wanting sliding down through her belly. She drew a circle on his palm with the tip of her tongue, then slowly sucked each finger. He tasted of paint, and woodsmoke, and brine, she thought, as he grunted softly with pleasure and pulled her in more tightly to him.

She released his hand, and he cupped it around her face. 'I left my bag downstairs, with my paper and charcoal,' he said. 'I'll get it, and see if I can find a couple of candles.' He kissed her, pulled his arm out from underneath her; then she gasped softly as he bent over her and ran his tongue around one of her nipples. 'Don't move,' he said. 'I won't be a moment.'

Lucrezia watched him walk to the stairs, his buttocks round and tight as a couple of apricots. He went down into the shop below and a moment or two later, a yellow glow preceded his reappearance. He climbed slowly, carrying two lit candles in a wax-encrusted candlestick. Slung over one shoulder, bumping against his bare leg, was a scuffed leather bag. The candle flames dipped and bobbed as he walked, sending frantic, dancing black shadows around the low walls of the storeroom.

'Can you see to draw in this light?'

'It's not ideal, but I expect I'll manage.' Jacomo put the candlestick on a table, opened the bag and took out a roll of paper and a small wooden tube plugged with a wad of cloth. Unplugging the tube, he shook out a handful of thin sticks of charcoal. He beckoned to Lucrezia to sit nearer the foot of the bed, and knelt next to her on the mattress. She smiled up at him as he moved her limbs into the position he wanted, but then he stopped. Lucrezia was startled to see him looking suddenly concerned and serious. He reached towards her and gently ran the fingers of one hand down the inside of her thigh. She looked down to see what he was doing, and saw a long smear of dark red.

'Is it your time to bleed, Lucrezia?'

She shook her head and ran her own fingers along it – it was dry. 'I might have bled because . . . because that was my first time, Jacomo,' she said.

He stared at her. 'I don't understand.'

Lucrezia said nothing.

'You've been married nearly two years.'

'Alfonso . . .' Lucrezia paused, drew in a long breath and let it out again. 'Alfonso has . . . difficulties. Our marriage . . . has yet to be consummated. But,' she said fiercely, 'I don't want even to think of him, Jacomo. Forget him – just forget him. Please, do your drawing.'

'But, Lucrezia,' he said anxiously, 'if you should have a child now, after tonight . . .'

Lucrezia did not know what to say – she had not even thought of this. But the fear that she knew it should have inspired in her was in fact quite smothered by a warm rush of delight at the prospect.

'Don't think about it now – just do your drawing.' She tried to resume the pose Jacomo had begun to create.

The crease between his brows disappeared as he began again to arrange her arms and legs to his satisfaction. The twist he wanted in the pose was tiring to hold, and at first, because she was concentrating more upon watching Jacomo than on what she was doing, Lucrezia realised that she was being a poor model. Three times Jacomo had to lean towards her and replace her limbs from where she had allowed them to move from their position, but at last he seemed satisfied. 'Now – don't move again!' he said firmly.

Jacomo drew for about an hour, stopping and moving Lucrezia into new positions from time to time. Some were quick sketches, taking only seconds to achieve, while two were more careful drawings, meticulously observed. It struck Lucrezia as curious that her husband's appraising gaze should so often leave her feeling like a lifeless work of art, while this painter's intense scrutiny as he *created* from her a work of art should kindle her to such a vibrant sense of energy.

At last he laid down his charcoal. Lucrezia stretched and yawned, hunched and rolled her shoulders, then rubbed her feet, which had chilled as she had sat motionless. She said, 'May I see what you've done?'

Jacomo nodded. Lucrezia stood up, then walked behind him and looked over his shoulder. What she saw took her breath away.

There could be no doubt.

'Oh, Jacomo, they are . . . they are *your* drawings!'

'Obviously.'

'No! Not these – the fresco! All those pictures, of Jason and Medea and the ship, and – *you* did them, didn't you?' She stared again at the drawings on Jacomo's lap. There was no mistaking the style – the hand was one and the same.

'Ah.'

'But *why*?' Lucrezia said. 'Why let Fra Pandolf tell everyone that they are *his* work?'

19

Jacomo picked up another blanket and draped it around Lucrezia's bare shoulders. Hutching another around his own, he sat down on the end of the bed, his face dramatically underlit by the wobbling candle flames. He took Lucrezia's hand.

'Pandolf is a great painter – well, he *was*,' Jacomo said, 'before his sight started to fail. He's taught me a great deal.'

'But—'

'It's not as simple as it seems. I'll try to explain. I was apprenticed to Pandolf three years ago by my father. I think Papa was ambitious for me, but he had no money to pay for a formal apprenticeship – he's just a fisherman. It had taken him a long time to get over his disappointment that I was never going to follow in the family tradition – God! – we had any number of terrible arguments about it – but in the end, he gave in. I'm not sure why. Perhaps it started to dawn on him that if I made a name for myself as an artist, it might actually mean some money coming into the family, potentially far, far more than he and the rest of them could ever make with the nets.'

Jacomo saw a crease pucker between Lucrezia's brows.

He said, 'I think he chose Pandolf partly because of his reputation, but also because of the fact that he was a friar. Pandolf waived the normal apprenticeship fees, out of some sort of charitable instinct, perhaps, and took me on, on the understanding that I'd stay with him, for nothing, for as long as he thought I could be useful to him. He'd feed me, clothe me, teach me, provide me with materials, but no more than that. Papa was worried about the stories he had heard about artists, as well – their reputation for licentiousness and debauchery.' Jacomo laid a heavy emphasis on the last three words, and his mouth twisted into a wry smile. 'I think he hoped that being in the care of a religious order would keep me under some sort of control, stop me learning bad habits and behaving badly.'

He leaned towards Lucrezia and kissed her mouth. 'That part of it hasn't quite worked, really, has it?'

She smiled at him, and he said, 'The original plan was for me to learn with Pandolf until he and I both felt I was capable of undertaking major commissions myself, at which point, we agreed, I'd move on and begin work as an artist in my own right. Pandolf suggested I might like to contribute some of my first earnings to the friary, a sort of charitable donation if you like. I was quite happy with this idea, and we were both set to work towards it – but then it all went wrong because of Pandolf's eyes.'

'What do you mean?' Lucrezia said. She pulled the blanket more snugly over her shoulders, tucking it around her legs.

Jacomo paused, choosing his words carefully. 'It seems that, despite his appearance of Franciscan humility, the reverend brother has a distinctly worldly streak of pride in him. I don't think he has ever confessed it, either.' He felt the familiar bite of resentment tensing along his jaw.

'I don't understand.'

'A couple of years ago, Pandolf began to complain about his sight. Said it was starting to be like seeing everything through a mist.'

'How horrible!'

'It's worsened over the months, and it's reached a point now where I don't think he can see much in detail beyond the stretch of his arm. Painting anything delicate is now almost impossible for him.'

'So how is it that he is still accepting commissions like this one?'

Jacomo hesitated, then said, 'I do all the work.'

There was a long pause.

'And he takes all the praise?'

'Something like that.'

'Those were your sketches, weren't they, that day you both came to the Castello a year or so ago?'

Jacomo nodded.

'Is that why you seemed so angry when Alfonso was telling the reverend brother how much he liked the pictures?'

'You *did* notice, then. I thought you had.' He went on, 'I knew I might have difficulty in establishing myself—'

'But why? Your work is wonderful.'

Jacomo raised his fingers to his cheek. 'This,' he said, patting the crimson stain. 'There are any number of potential patrons who don't wish to have their costly commission undertaken by someone with the Devil's fingerprints on his face.'

'Surely nobody is that stupid.'

Jacomo huffed a small laugh. 'In our *enlightened times*,' he said drily, 'you would perhaps have thought it impossible. But though people don't tend to come out and say such things directly to your face, it's obvious from the muttered comments and the furtive glances . . .'

Lucrezia reached out and stroked the red blotches tenderly.

Jacomo closed his eyes, then laid his hand over hers, pressing it against his face. 'So, as I say, I knew it would be hard, but I'd planned everything. I was ready to leave, eager to go and prove myself.'

'Then why did you not do it?'

'Pandolf pressured me. "*Just this commission, Jacomo, please. Help me with this one – I cannot turn down an opportunity like this.*" I'd say to myself – very well, I'll do this last one with him and then go, but then I'd see his terror at the thought of his incapacity being discovered, and I'd weaken, yet again. It's been like that for months. But this is definitely the last one. I've told him, quite categorically, that I won't do another commission with him.'

'What will you do?'

'I knew exactly what I was going to do until yesterday.'

'What?' she said, in little more than a whisper.

'Finish this fresco, then go to Rome. I've enough put aside to live for a month or two with no work, in case I need it; I thought I'd start by painting uncommissioned portraits and trying to sell them. See what happened.'

'And now?' Her eyes were dark in the candlelight.

'And now I have no idea what to do.' Jacomo laid his drawings on the floor and gestured towards the pillows. Lucrezia shuffled back up the bed. She was still wrapped in her blanket but looked, Jacomo thought with a stab of longing, like a nymph from one of Buonarotti's ceilings. He sat next to her on the mattress, put his arm around her shoulders and pulled another blanket around them both.

'Why don't I come with you?' Lucrezia said.

Jacomo froze. He said nothing.

'We could leave now. Not go back to the Castello, just go from here to Rome, like you said.'

There was a tremor in her voice. Jacomo watched the flickering shadows on the ceiling for a moment before he answered. 'I wish it were that easy,' he said, picking up one of Lucrezia's hands and holding it to his mouth. He lipped around her fingers and fiddled her thumbnail between his teeth.

'Why? Why can't it be that easy? No one knows we're here. We'd be long gone before anyone even suspected.'

His longing to do as she suggested was so acute that it began to hurt deep in his chest as he imagined it: the two of them, hand in hand, arriving in Rome, searching for lodgings.

He said, 'No one would know tonight, that's sure enough. But we can't do it, Lucrezia. Think of tomorrow, when it's discovered that you are not to be found anywhere in the Castello—'

'Well, it would be too late then.'

'And when I fail to turn up to work on the fresco, how long do you think it would take them to work out what had happened?'

'What would it matter if they did? We'd be miles away.'

'Yes. And what about your little waiting-woman, left behind in the Castello? I'd wager that before the day was out, she'd have been accused of collusion, and would be languishing in one of the dungeons.'

'Oh, dear God, do you think so?'

'I'm sure of it. I doubt the duke is the sort of man to endure such a humiliation without exacting some form of retribution on whoever happened to be nearest to hand.'

Lucrezia looked stricken.

'Do you really think he would just let you go?' Jacomo said quietly.

There was a long pause. Jacomo said, 'And Pandolf. There's Pandolf to consider.'

'What do you mean? You said you wanted to leave him.'

'Yes, I know I did, but I can't leave him in the middle of a commission. I owe him a great deal, Lucrezia. He's taught me everything I know – far more than just the painting. I've learned Latin and Greek, history, poetry, philosophy – *so* much. I can't just abandon him – he simply couldn't finish what I've started here. It's beyond him now. He'd have to admit to the deceit, which would destroy him, or he'd try to complete the fresco and ruin it, but that's not the point. Either way he would be forced to face the duke's displeasure. Which I doubt would be easy for him. Your husband—' The word caught in his throat as he uttered it. 'Well . . . I don't think he would be very happy, shall we say. He's set quite some store by this commission, I think.'

'Yes, he has,' Lucrezia said.

'Too many people would be hurt too badly if we were to do this.'

Lucrezia sat up. He saw that her eyes were wide and scared now. She said, in a voice pitched high with fear, 'But, Jacomo, I shall die if I can't be with you! You can't go from the Castello and leave me there!'

She was trembling. She looked frightened and vulnerable and younger than ever. Putting his arms around her, Jacomo kissed her and said, 'I won't leave you. I can't.' He paused. 'But we cannot go now, like this.'

'What shall we do, then?'

Jacomo considered. 'We have to go back to the castle before daybreak. That's for certain. I must finish the fresco – that's about two more weeks. And then . . .'

'And then?'

'When the fresco's finished and Pandolf, Tomaso and I can leave the Castello, you'll have to make sure that your waiting-woman finds a believable excuse to be absent. Is there ever a time when you leave the castle without attendants?'

Lucrezia shook her head. 'No. Well, I suppose I could say I want to take Violetta out – my mule. I don't normally go far on her – but I do ride alone sometimes.'

'That's it, then.'

A fine drizzle was falling as Jacomo and Lucrezia walked along the last few deserted streets and neared the Castello. Droplets of rain clung like tiny diamonds to the wisps of Lucrezia's hair that stuck out of the ridiculous red hat, and a smell of wet dust rose from the cobbles as they went.

The Castello loomed ahead of them, huge and square, as they walked through the archway and found the basket still hidden in the shadows of the poplars. Jacomo took out the rolled-up dress and shift, which were a little damp, and began to unpick the twine, as Lucrezia pulled off the cap and unfastened the grey doublet.

He saw her glance around to ensure they were alone, and then she wriggled out of the doublet and hose. She pulled the undershirt off over her head and Jacomo's insides lurched with longing as he held out the shift. Lucrezia pushed her arms up and into its sleeves and let it fall down around her nakedness. Jacomo held out her dress. She stepped into it and he pulled the laces tight. She shook out her hair, wound it into a knot, then slid her feet back into her shoes.

He smiled. 'There you are,' he said. 'No one who sees you now could possibly connect you with the grubby little red-capped urchin who went down into the town with me last night.'

He kissed her.

'Jacomo,' she said, as he stopped for breath.

'What?'

'Finish the fresco soon.'

He held her tightly to his body.

'Alfonso will be back before long,' she said, into the stuff of his doublet. 'If he suspects, I think he might kill us both.'

'When I was a little boy,' Jacomo said, his cheek resting on Lucrezia's hair, 'my friends used to mock me because of the marks on my face. They were worse then, the marks – a darker red, much more noticeable. The boys didn't mean much by it, I don't think – it was largely in fun, but it upset me, just the same. I used to try to impress them – wanted to make them forget about my cheek – so I'd climb the most difficult trees, scramble up sheer rocks, jump into deep water. Anything to prove myself to them. My mother used to call me her *piccolo spericolato* – her little daredevil – she was forever bandaging up my cuts and bruises, mending all the clothes I'd ripped. I broke my leg a couple of times too and cracked a rib once, but I never minded the danger. It got me what I wanted – I ended up as the leader of my little gang of friends.'

He put a hand on either side of Lucrezia's face and tipped it up towards his own. 'I've not changed. I'll do what I have to do. I won't leave you here.'

They clung together, not speaking, for a long moment. Then Jacomo said, 'We have to get going – it's past dawn. Go on, get back inside. I'll take these things back to Tomaso.'

'Those are Tomaso's clothes? Did he not mind?'

'He doesn't know.'

She smiled. 'What will he think?'

'I shan't tell him. He won't notice. But if he does, I think he'll be jealous – he's told me he thinks you're very beautiful.'

Even in the grey half-light, Jacomo saw her blush. He hugged her. 'Go on – I'll wait here till I can see you're inside.'

'I have to see you again later.'

'Not today. Too dangerous. I'll be working on the fresco till the light goes, and it's courting disaster to meet again after dark, so soon. Come up to the gallery tomorrow. Don't come today.'

Lucrezia picked up the now empty basket and walked backwards for the first few steps, her eyes fixed upon his; then she blew him a kiss, turned and ran. He watched until she had rounded the corner and crossed onto the main drawbridge, then began walking the other way, scuffing the damp stones on the path with the toe of his boot.

The marriage was unconsummated. The duke had never bedded her. The thought bugled in his head: an unconsummated marriage could be dissolved. It was possible. He felt his hands ball into fists and pushed them down into the pockets of his breeches.

20

As Lucrezia crossed the drawbridge, several men she did not recognize, but who she realised obviously recognized her, were crossing in the opposite direction – away from the Castello.

'Signora.' One of them swept his woollen cap from his head and touched a hand to his forehead. The others followed suit. Lucrezia nodded in acknowledgement, hoping desperately that she did not look guilty. She lifted a hand to her hair; the hasty knot she had fingered into place only moments before was already loosening and several long wisps were falling around her face. She tucked them behind her ears. There were frankly inquisitive expressions on all their faces, but Lucrezia felt sure they would not think to question their duchess.

She hoped their curiosity was no more than momentary.

Feeling exposed and vulnerable as she passed them – as if, Lucrezia thought, she had not only no clothes but no skin either – she forced herself to walk calmly up through the Castello. She realised that she was shivering; it might not be purely the excitement of the night, she thought – her dress and shift were both damp – and by the time she reached her chambers she felt chilled through.

Catelina was already up and dressed, and was busy mending the hem of one of Lucrezia's night shifts. She lifted her head from her work as Lucrezia banged open the door to the little studio, her eyes asking the questions she was evidently restraining herself from uttering.

'Good morning, Lina,' Lucrezia said.

The eloquent curiosity in Catelina's gaze did not falter. She tucked the needle carefully into the lawn of the shift and laid it on her lap.

There was a moment of silence.

Then Lucrezia felt her face pull itself outwards into a smile, a smile that became a breathy little laugh, perilously close to being a sob. She put her hands over her mouth.

'Oh, Signora!' Catelina crossed to her and put her arms around her. A moment later she stood back, frowning. 'But, my lady, those clothes are wet. Let me help you out of them right away.'

The sun had passed its midday height. Franco Guarniero held the door open as Lucrezia walked into the small reception chamber behind the chapel. She flicked her heavy skirts to one side and sat down in an ornately carved, cross-framed chair.

'I am so sorry to inconvenience you, my lady,' Guarniero said. His black eyes were anxious, and he ran long fingers through the shock of white hair that was now standing up like a bird's crest. He said, 'Were my lord not absent, I should not have dreamed of bothering you, but . . .' He tailed off, both hands held up in apology. 'The gentleman arrived unexpectedly, and he has particularly requested a moment's audience with the Signore. My lord is not yet returned, and I have had no word from him as to a date for his arrival . . .'

'Don't worry, Franco,' Lucrezia said, struggling to maintain an impassive expression. Her features seemed possessed of an animation quite separate from her own intentions; she was fighting her mouth's wish to keep stretching itself into a smile, and she wondered if the strange sensation around her eyes was a physical manifestation of the fact that they might be 'sparkling'. Having had little more than an hour's sleep, she knew she must be tired, but rather than the expected heaviness of fatigue, she felt instead light-headed and uncomfortably restless. 'Do you know what he wishes to talk about?' she said.

'I am afraid not, my lady. The gentleman is a priest, though.'

'Well, we will soon discover what he wants. Show him in, Franco.'

Guarniero disappeared, and returned some moments later, accompanied by a thin young man in a black cassock. Lucrezia rose to her feet and held out her hand. Guarniero bowed and retreated, closing the door behind him.

'I am so sorry to inconvenience you, Signora,' the young man said, in a thin voice, taking the proffered hand and lowering a rather wet mouth to her knuckles, 'but I was asked particularly to speak with the Signore, and told most specifically not to deposit a letter or to leave a message with a servant. But as my lord is not here . . .'

'Please, do not distress yourself. It is no trouble,' Lucrezia said. Beneath what she hoped was a semblance of outward composure, her mind was on Jacomo. She eyed the young man before her, and began listing comparisons. This man was bony, where Jacomo was lean; he had thin, pale, nervous fingers, where Jacomo's hands were strong and square and brown – her nipples contracted at the thought; this man's colourless hair was neatly limp, in poor contrast, she thought, to the untidy tangles through which she had laced her fingers last night. And he was a priest! What could he know of the joyous world she had discovered a few hours before, the extraordinary wild country to which she had been taken in company with her painter?

'. . . and I have been sent here straight away with the news, Signora,' the young priest was saying.

Lucrezia started out of her daydream. 'I'm so sorry, would you explain that again? I want to make quite sure I understand the message properly.'

He seemed a little surprised, but smiled and said, 'As I told you, Archbishop Verdi has managed to secure the audience with His Holiness requested by the duke, and he wanted the message relayed to the Signore as quickly as possible. If the Signore would care to present himself in Rome during the first week of September – perhaps just after the feast of Saint Gregory,' the young man said, 'His Holiness will be anticipating his arrival, and, I am told, looks forward to discussing the issue raised by the Signore when he met Archbishop Verdi in Firenze two weeks ago.'

Lucrezia's thoughts raced. Issue? What issue? Alfonso had, as usual, said nothing of his reasons for travelling to Firenze. Was he in search of an annulment? Was this what lay behind the increasingly frequent trips away from Ferrara? Until this moment she had thoughtlessly presumed him to be in search of something . . . well, something rather more physical. Her heart skipped a beat and she took in a long, steadying breath. 'Thank you for coming so quickly to pass on so important a message, Father,' she said. 'And I can quite understand His Grace's wish for confidentiality.'

The young man rose to his feet and bobbed a nervous bow. 'My lady, I should not wish to detain you any longer than I must. Thank you for your gracious attention.'

He stopped abruptly, his bony back still bent, as Franco

Guarniero appeared. Franco, Lucrezia thought fleetingly, must habitually listen at doors, as he always seemed to appear exactly when needed. The young priest straightened, patted his limp hair still flatter, and smoothed the creases from the front of his cassock.

'*Mio padre*, if you are ready to leave, perhaps you would care to accompany me,' Guarniero said.

The thin, black-clad figure nodded self-consciously and, with another brief bow to Lucrezia, followed the steward from the room.

Lucrezia began to pace the floor like a caged animal. Alfonso was seeking an audience with the Holy Father. What other reason could there be but a request for an annulment? Might this be what she so longed for? Was she to be legitimately released from purgatory? She stood still for a moment, as her thoughts tumbled over each other, then she crossed the room in a couple of strides and began to run, past the chapel towards the North Hall. Within sight of the closed door to the hall, though, she stopped. Jacomo had said to stay away today; he was not expecting her until tomorrow. She had no idea who was in the hall – if she surprised Jacomo and he was not alone, he might unwittingly, she thought now, react in such a way as might arouse suspicion. She stared at the closed door for a moment, then turned back, and made her way up through the castle to her chambers, walking slowly now, her thoughts frantic.

Catelina was nowhere to be seen when she arrived. She crossed to her bed and lay down upon it, pulling a blanket over herself. Fatigue swept over her as she curled up on her side; her legs were leaden and immovable and her eyes dry. A tangled mess of feelings – of euphoria, of exhaustion, of chaotic curiosity and a vertiginous sense of precariousness – swirled around her like water around a breached dam. She could grasp none of it. It began to slip away from her and she slid into dreamless sleep.

'My lady?'

Lucrezia opened her eyes. Closed them again.

'My lady?'

Catelina was crouched on her heels beside the bed, one hand stroking the hair away from Lucrezia's forehead. 'You've been asleep for hours, my lady. I was beginning to worry about you – I thought you might have caught a chill from that damp dress. But you're not hot. I don't think you have a fever.'

Lucrezia sat up.

'I brought you a bit of food, my lady. I thought you might prefer not to have to venture downstairs after everything that has happened.'

Lucrezia took her hand and squeezed it. 'Oh, Catelina, I bless the day you tripped in that kitchen! You can help me eat this, and I'll tell you everything that happened last night. Franco interrupted us this morning before I had had a chance to tell you much at all. Well . . .' She stopped, remembering a number of things that she might perhaps *not* share with her waiting-woman.

Catelina laughed. 'You just tell me what you would like to tell me, Signora.'

They walked through into the studio and Lucrezia leaned into the deep window recess. She took out the candles that stood ready to be lit as the light faded, and opened the casement. The sun was reddening. 'Come up here with me, Lina,' she said.

Catelina waited while Lucrezia climbed into the recess, then passed up the platter of sliced meat, dried figs, ricotta cheese and grapes. Lucrezia held the plate while Catelina scrambled up to join her. They sat with their arms around their knees, heads together, gazing out at the slowly dropping sun. And, only now realizing how very hungry she was, Lucrezia ate a few mouthfuls and then began to tell Catelina *almost* everything.

There was a muffled commotion audible somewhere below in the Castello, but Lucrezia was so involved in her story that she took little notice of it. Voices were raised, feet rushed hither and thither, dogs barked and doors banged. The door to the little studio opened and Lucrezia looked around. Perhaps it was because she had been discussing Jacomo that she half-expected it to be him in the doorway. Certainly she was smiling warmly, and her cheeks were glowing as she turned to see who had come in.

But, of course, it was not Jacomo.

Jacomo never wore black.

It was Alfonso.

Returned from Firenze at last.

He was clearly not pleased to see her. He seemed, she thought, taller than ever. His eyes were huge and black and they glittered in the low yellow light from the window. His face had been coolly expectant, but had darkened menacingly when he saw what she was unable to prevent: the fading of her smile.

21

Alfonso looked at his wife. A sweet spot of colour had risen in her
cheeks and her hair was disordered, as though she had been asleep.
Sleeping in the daytime? He wondered briefly if she were unwell.
That would solve everything, he thought, imagining her untimely
demise and his consequent – counterfeit – grief. Would it be counterfeit, though? Would he mourn her?

The entrancing smile that had so prettily lifted the corners of
Lucrezia's mouth and shone in her eyes as she had turned towards
him had vanished as she recognized him, and the pictures in his
mind disappeared with it, pushed from his head by the surge of a
black anger that tasted of blood. He looked from his wife to the
little Cafaggiolo slut who sat beside her, hunched with anxious
embarrassment, her eyes wide and wary. Jerking his head towards
the door, he said to the girl, in barely more than a hiss, 'Get out!
Wait in the other room!'

He watched as she scrambled untidily from the window-ledge
and disappeared into the bedchamber.

Lucrezia jumped down to stand with her back pressed against the wall.

'Exactly what do you think you are doing?' Alfonso said.

She tried to smile again. 'I was watching the sunset,' she said.

'With a *servant*?'

'Yes. When did you arrive? Have you been back long? Are you—'

Alfonso cut through her questions. 'Have you no sense of propriety at all?' he shouted. He saw her flinch, knew he had never raised his voice to her before. His eyes stung – it was as though he had forgotten how to blink.

'Does the antiquity of the name of Este mean absolutely *nothing* to you, Lucrezia, despite having been a part of it for nearly two years?'

She said nothing.

'I have lost count of the number of times I have told you that fraternizing with the menials who are paid merely to keep us in bodily comfort is . . . is . . . *inexcusable*!' Alfonso could hear his voice growing in volume. His face felt as though it were swelling. 'Whether it is the head cook, the stewards, the courtiers or your uneducated whore of a waiting-woman.' He paced the room, feeling the iron studs in the soles of his boots catch on the floorboards, then stopped, facing away from her, one hand gripping the back of a chair. 'I cannot tolerate a liaison such as I have just witnessed. She will go.'

'No!' There was panic in Lucrezia's voice now. 'No – you cannot—'

He turned slowly to face her and she fell silent. 'Oh, I think you will find that I can, madam,' he whispered. The colour drained from her face. Her breathing was shallow and rapid – almost panting. He watched the upper curve of her breasts rise and fall for a moment, and then she said, her voice cracking, 'Please, Alfonso, don't do this. Please – let her stay.'

He ignored her. 'The first time I laid eyes on her I saw that she did not know her place – I was astounded that your parents had allowed you to bring a raw, inexperienced *kitchen girl* as a waiting-woman – and this merely confirms that neither she nor you have any sense of what is and what is not acceptable.' Alfonso glared at Lucrezia, a muscle in his jaw twitching. 'Not only has she always been an utterly unsuitable attendant for the mistress of the House of Este, it seems now that you see this vulgar little slut as a more intimate confidante than you do myself. It cannot continue. She goes tonight.'

Lucrezia's eyes were big and dark. She stared at him, not speaking, stifling jerky little sobs and biting her lip. After a moment's silence, he heard her say in an almost soundless whisper, 'Please, Alfonso, please let her stay.'

'A replacement will be found. For tonight, at least, you shall have no one. Except myself.' He paused, and then, remembering a snatched conversation with Guarniero some moments before, he said, 'Franco tells me you received a visitor earlier today. What did he want?'

Lucrezia did not answer.

'Who was he and what did he want, Lucrezia?'

He saw her mouth open and close, as though she were trying to speak. At last she said, in a small voice, 'He was a priest. I don't remember his name. He brought a message for you from someone called Verdi. Archbishop Verdi.'

Alfonso's scalp contracted. 'What . . . what was the message?' The words pushed out through a throat suddenly tight.

'He said that – that this Archbishop Verdi has managed to secure the audience with His Holiness you had requested. He will see you in Rome during the first week of September.'

'What else did he say?' Alfonso's face was stiff and cold. How specific had this message-bearer been? Did she now know everything? His mind raced – Lucrezia and the little whore on the window-ledge, laughing together about his incapacity, about how she now knew she had the power to bring down the duchy.

It was not to be borne.

He saw her open her mouth to complete her answer, but knew he could not endure to hear it. He strode from the room before she could speak.

The kitchen slut was standing by the bedchamber door, shivering, her face swollen with tears. For a moment he imagined the humiliating revelations that Lucrezia had been sharing with her with such obvious delight just now – pictured the images of his impotent self that must, even now, be in the forefront of this girl's mind as she stared at him – and then, sickened by a wave of shame and a gut-churning anger, he said, 'Take your belongings and be gone from the Castello before nightfall, if you value your continued existence.'

His skin crawled as he saw the fear in her eyes, and he turned away from her. He wrenched open the door, and saw Folletto, standing in the corridor outside, ears drooping, tail between his legs. Not even pausing to speak to the dog, Alfonso grabbed the scruff of his neck and, with a snarl, pulled him back and out of his way, kicking out behind him. The wolfhound yelped and cowered as Alfonso's boot thudded into his side.

Alfonso strode away to the staircase, and stood irresolute in the hallway. The blood surged in his ears; he could hear little else. What would best serve to quiet this tumult? Perhaps if he were to go down to the dungeons . . .

No. It would not do. Not tonight. He had to see Francesca.

He ran down to the stable block and, ignoring the head groom's offers of help, saddled Farfalla himself. He swung up onto her back with such haste that the mare shied, ears flat to her head, her hoofs skidding and slipping on the cobbles. Alfonso reined her in tightly, pulled her head round and kicked her into an untidy trot. Still with no word to any of the stablemen, he and the mare left the yard.

Francesca Felizzi stood in her doorway, looking up at Alfonso on his horse.

He said, 'Come down to the *villetta* as soon as you can.'

'When did you get back from Firenze?'

'About an hour ago. I'll go to the house straight away. Be there.' He did not wait for a response, but wheeled the horse around and disappeared at a taut canter. Francesca drew a long breath and held it as she watched him leave. Then, puffing it out again, she went back into her front room.

As she neared the little house, she pinched colour into her cheeks, and worried her lower lip between her teeth to redden it. Wriggling one hand down inside her bodice, she repositioned her breasts, pulling each one upwards, then tightened the front-fastening laces to hold everything in place.

She paused for a moment on the threshold of the *villetta*. Alfonso's expression had been dark and closed, and Francesca was in little doubt that he would not be in a particularly good humour. She might, she thought, be in for a rough time. It had, after all, happened before. One hand on the latch, she hesitated, then opened the door.

Alfonso was standing by the fireplace. He had lit a fire and was staring moodily at the flames, hands clasped behind his back. The latch clattered as the door closed, but he made no sign that he had heard it.

Francesca took off her coat and laid it over the chest that stood at the end of the bed. She raised her hands to the laces of her bodice and, eyes fixed upon Alfonso, began to undo the knot.

'You took your time,' he said at last.

'I came as soon as I could. I don't have a horse.'

Alfonso made a noise in his nose, but otherwise offered no comment.

'Did you have a successful trip?' Francesca said, flipping the laces out through their eyelets.

There was a long silence. Then Alfonso reached up to the shelf above the fire, picked up a small glass pot, containing a handful of wilted wild flowers, and flung it at the opposite wall, where it shattered. The flowers flew in all directions across the room and droplets of water glittered in the firelight as they fell with them.

'With a servant!' he shouted. 'With a damned *servant*! I am away from the Castello for a mere matter of *weeks* and she *dares* . . . she . . .' He stuttered to silence, visibly shaking, quite incoherent with a rage Francesca had never even glimpsed before. His face was bloodless, his eyes black pits. If she had been asked, at that moment, she would have said that she thought he looked quite mad and, for the first time ever, she was afraid of him. Deciding that she would probably do well to begin as soon as possible, she moved to stand in front of him and reached for the fastening of his doublet.

Alfonso stepped back from her, and turned away. Francesca wondered if he might have decided to leave – to forgo his pleasures and return to whatever was happening at the Castello – when he wheeled back round without warning and lashed out with a backhanded swipe, with the full force of his arm. It caught Francesca across the side of her head. She staggered and fell to her knees.

Staring at him, she held her burning cheek with one hand, rigid with shock. He might have raised a hand to her many times, slapped her, laid stripes across her buttocks with a belt, but it had always been in play, always in the pursuit of pleasure. He had never hit her in anger before. In fact, she realised, she had never seen him lose control before.

'Why? Why hit *me*? What have I done?' she muttered.

For an instant, Francesca saw a blankness in Alfonso's face, as though he really did not know why he had hit her, but then he spoke. 'Your immediate reliance upon the physical mocks me, Francesca. Ever the harlot – you still think you can attempt to solve my problems just by baring your breasts and opening your damned legs. But, I tell you, your wanton lubricity will no longer suffice. *She*,' he hissed the word, 'has taken from me now any pleasure I ever took in uncomplicated carnality.'

His voice was not much more than a whisper, but the hairs on the back of Francesca's neck stood up. He caught her by the arm, pulled her towards him and snatched up her other wrist. Gasping, she looked into his eyes and was shocked by the black emptiness she saw there. The glittering, pleasure-seeking lasciviousness she would normally have expected to see had gone.

She was suddenly truly afraid. 'Let go, Alfonso,' she said, trying to sound calm, and trying to pull her wrists from his grasp. He did not reply and did not let go. Then, with a stream of oaths, his anger burst over her. Despite her struggles, he walked her backwards to the big bed with ease, and, holding both her wrists in one hand, he pushed her skirts up to her waist and tugged at his laces with the other.

Never before, even at his wildest, had Alfonso overwhelmed her like this. Every time she gasped in a breath, every effort she made to ease her discomfort from under his unthinking, thrusting weight, he hit her. And he was hitting to hurt. Her gasps became incoherent sobs; she struggled for a while longer, but in the end she stopped fighting him and numbly waited for it all to finish.

She had no idea how long it lasted. A minute, an hour – she did not know. But finally, as a guttural cry escaped him, Alfonso was gripped for a moment by what seemed to Francesca to be close to a convulsion. His weight upon her became unbearable – she could not breathe. Fighting again – this time for air – she pushed at his shoulders, arched her back upwards, twisted her hips in frantic panic.

And then it was over.

In one movement, it seemed, he pulled away from her and got to his feet. Released from the suffocating weight of him, Francesca rolled onto her side, bent her knees up to her chest and started to cough, dragging air back into her lungs in ragged sobs. Alfonso stood by the fire, refastening his laces and adjusting the disarranged sleeves of his doublet. He pushed a hand into a pocket in his breeches and brought out a small bag, saying, 'Be here tomorrow at noon, Francesca. I will need to see you.'

He dropped the bag onto the chest. It clinked as it landed.

Francesca closed her eyes and turned her head away from him. She heard the door-latch clatter, the scrape of hoofs on the cobbles outside, and then silence.

A log in the fire shifted, crumbled and fell.

She sat up, touched her cheek with the tips of her fingers and winced. Running her tongue along her lip, she tasted blood. Then, feeling giddy and disoriented, as though she had a fever, she rose from the bed, went to the chest and picked up the little bag of coins. She held it for a moment, then with a wordless, yowling cry, she flung it across the room. The contents scattered over the floor.

*

'Have you been crying?'

'Your dress is torn, Mamma.'

'What did you do to your eye?'

Francesca bit the inside of her lip to quell the tears that threatened again, and found a smile from somewhere to reassure her little girls.

'It's nothing – I tripped and banged my face. Has it left a bruise?'

Little fingers gently probed and stroked, and four small arms encircled what parts of their mother they could reach. Francesca felt inexpressibly comforted.

They lit candles, scrambled a fire together and cooked pasta and beans. Food, warmth and the mindless chatter of her daughters finally began to banish the hovering tears, and as the girls played and bickered happily in front of the fire, Francesca reflected on what had happened. She knew that her relationship with Alfonso had irrevocably changed.

She thought back, rather sadly, to the day they had first met.

She had been in Ferrara for some six months, scratching a living. Since the day she had retched in the mud beside the cathedral, her life had been an exhausting continuum of bruised breasts, aching thighs and the drunken breath of men in seemingly constant need of satiation, unvarying and demanding, until the day she had entered into a conversation with the baker in the Via Frizzi.

'Rushed off my feet, I've been, these last few days!' he says grumpily, as Francesca waits for him to wrap two small loaves.

'Why's that, Alberto?'

'Banquet!' He rolls his eyes, in irritation.

'What banquet?'

'Over in the Castello – day after tomorrow.' Alberto jerks his head

towards the ducal palace. 'Not had an order this big in years and, of course, it has to come just when my wife is as big as a house with child and that great lump of a lad who's supposed to be my apprentice has broken his wrist punching one of the miller's boys. He tries that again, I'll break the other one for him . . .'

He grumbles on and Francesca looks up at the great red fortress. An idea forms in her mind.

Two days later, in a pale grey silk dress she has quite shamelessly stolen from a seamstress's workshop, Francesca steps into the long banqueting hall in the Castello *Estense and stares about her, trying not to laugh at her own audacity.*

She has, by means of copious lies and wheedling offers of future sexual favours, gained entry through the servants' quarters into this glittering, sumptuous celebration, and she is determined not to waste a second of it.

She largely keeps to herself as the evening progresses. She watches and listens more than she attempts to speak, but when pressed, she tries to imitate the accents and phrases of the exalted guests and she invents family and background, history and circumstances, which seem, for a time, to be plausible enough to delude her companions.

Perhaps, she thought now, it was just that they had been too caught up in the excitement of the occasion to pay close attention to individual parts of the whole. Or perhaps she had been more adept at deceiving than she had imagined she could be.

Francesca thought of herself as she was now. She had learned much from Alfonso, she knew: she realised now that she had unwittingly taken on his accent, adopted much of his vocabulary. Maybe she was more of a mimic than she had thought. She no longer sounded like the Crespino slut she had once been, that was for certain. Whatever the truth of it, though, until the host himself approached her that evening, Francesca did not think she had been suspected by anybody; although she had never actually asked him, she thought Alfonso had probably seen through her before he even spoke to her.

He has been watching her for some moments. She thinks him attractive and interesting, and wonders briefly how likely it is that she will find her way into his bed tonight. With no more than a brief raise of an eyebrow and a hint of a deliberately arch smile, she acknowledges the glances he has been casting her way, but makes no other response than this.

Some moments later, he takes the bait and, walking away from a finely dressed, furious-looking woman who, until now, has been hanging on his every word, he crosses the room to where she stands. 'Signora, forgive me, I do not remember having had the pleasure of speaking to you before,' he says, as he reaches her.

Francesca drops into a deep curtsy. 'No, Signore.'

'Remind me — forgive my forgetfulness — exactly who you are, madam. I do not immediately recall . . .'

'The Countess of Crespino,' Francesca says glibly.

'Ah. Not a name I recall on the list of my invited guests. No doubt — what an abominable oversight — it has just slipped my mind, Signora.'

He is playing along with her, she is sure. She says nothing, but smiles up at him and waits to see what will happen. He speaks with her for some moments and she answers as best she can, but at last, it seems, he can no longer endure teasing the situation out. He is like a fisherman, she thinks, with an enticing catch upon the line, finally knowing that the moment to haul in has arrived.

'Perhaps you would enlighten me, Signora — I should be extremely interested . . .' he drops his voice to a conspiratorial whisper '. . . to

know your real name. I may be mistaken – and will have to make quite humiliating reparations should this be the case – but it occurs to me, firstly, that you are no countess and, secondly, that you have gained ingress into my banquet under preposterously false pretences.'

Francesca knows instinctively that he will respond best to the truth. She says, 'You are quite correct, Signore.'

'Who, then, are you?'

A pause. She resumes her usual accent. 'A street harlot from the Via Pozzo.'

There is not even a flicker of a smile. His face remains impassive and serious. He says, 'How, then, do you come to be at my party?'

'I lied and bribed my way in, Signore,' Francesca says serenely. Her heart, though, is racing and she is wondering whether she is now only minutes away from being thrown either out onto the streets or down into one of the palace dungeons.

'Indeed,' he says. 'Why?'

'Curiosity and a sense of adventure, Signore.'

The rest of the guests continue their braying, chattering, laughing enjoyment of the evening, but something seems to be separating her and the duke from the bustle of the banquet.

He leans towards her and whispers in her ear, 'How much, then, harlot, do you normally charge for a night spent in your company?'

She doubles her usual fee.

'I have a house – a little villetta, just beyond the city walls,' he says. He describes how to find it. 'I shall be there an hour after the end of the banquet. Do not plan any other work for a week.'

The week becomes a month, and then the month stretches out indefinitely.

At first, this man's wild, extravagant brutality takes Francesca by surprise. Despite her whore's apprenticeship, she has not come across anyone who demands quite as much from her as he does, but from the *first she fights back with vigour and unexpectedly finds that she and Alfonso enjoy each other immensely. From the very beginning he demands her total exclusivity and, certainly at the start, she complies.*

As their relationship develops and matures, Francesca realizes that only with her is Alfonso ever truly himself. The dignified persona that everyone else thinks they know falls away during the hours he spends in her bed. From what he has always said, she believes that none but she ever sees the raw, uncovered seed of degeneracy he can never entirely suppress, and though he is unable to express any warmth or affection towards her, she soon comes to see that beneath his cool detachment lies much more than desire.

He needs her.

As she sat in front of her fireplace and fingered her swollen eye, feeling the pain of the bruised graze on her cheek, Francesca feared that the rage which Alfonso kept suppressed and chained at all times had finally broken its bounds. Its new unpredictability now truly frightened her. Their relationship, such as it had ever been, was irreparably shattered.

Until now, even in her most disaffected moments, she had never seriously thought of leaving him: she had borne him two children, and his continuing patronage was their best chance of future security. She had always planned – when the time was right – to pressure him into finding their daughters either husbands or employment, had always hoped that his natural fastidiousness would recoil at the prospect of his own flesh and blood, albeit a couple of bastards, whoring on the streets of his city.

But now . . .

She held her hands up in front of her; they were still shaking. Curling them into loose fists and pressing them into her lap to stop the trembling, she looked over to the children, who, heads together, were proudly comparing the little green knots of pearl-embroidered ribbon that they had been given by the duchess.

The duchess.

Oh, dear God, she thought, that poor girl. Francesca had been touched by her kindness to the twins that day. She had, she had thought, seemed sweet and vulnerable, and an unlikely match for Alfonso's precarious volatility. Francesca touched the graze on her cheek, and a cold worm of fear writhed in her guts as she imagined Alfonso's return to the Castello.

22

Alfonso stopped in the candlelit hallway to admire the bronze of Hephaistos. Of all the objects that had accompanied Lucrezia from Mugello, this, he thought, was the piece that gave him the greatest pleasure. He ran a hand over the muscled forearm, its dark patina smooth and gleaming. The lights from the candelabra caught it at wrist, knuckle and elbow as the hand of the great lame blacksmith gripped the hammer. His sinews were stretched, his gaze focused upon the shield – Achilles' shield – which his left hand held firm across the anvil. The bearded face was contorted with the effort of swinging the hammer up, over and down; the downward swing had just begun. The piece, Alfonso thought, had a tremendous sense of motion.

His own hand was dwarfed by the huge bronze arm, and he could see a thin dark cut across the knuckles where it had caught on Francesca's earring. Putting his hand to his mouth, the blood tasted thinly metallic. He thought briefly of Francesca: hers was a body with which he knew he frequently took many liberties. Tonight had perhaps been one liberty too many, he thought, though, of course, Francesca's predilections were such that she was no stranger to violence. The red clouds that had blotted out reason in Lucrezia's bedchamber had had to find vent in some direction, though – and Francesca had often been happy to aid him in the banishment of his dark demons.

Lucrezia was wayward, he thought. She was unthinking, indiscriminate, promiscuous, lacking in respect for him or for the duchy. The thought of its imminent destruction seemed actually to amuse her.

He had brought from Mugello an impressionable child, whose vivid animation and beauty had unexpectedly captivated him. And, much to his chagrin, it still did. The tantalizing glimpses of the vitality and passion he had first seen in her had been offered frequently enough to make him believe they were exclusively meant for him, but, he thought now, he had been deceived. Indiscriminate. She was indiscriminate – she continually shamed him by acting like a whore, smiling and laughing and making eyes at anyone, with no regard for the position she had espoused, caring nothing for the fact that the shameful failures in their marriage bed would inevitably lead to the end of the nine-hundred-year line. Alfonso pressed a hand to his forehead as humiliating words pushed through into his thoughts and sneered at him. *Eunuch; she has married a eunuch; you won't sire an heir with a gelding; thought you should be made aware of the gravity of the situation; no legitimate issue; the end of the might of the Estes* . . . Lucrezia was little better than a common doxy. She bestowed warmth and affection like profligate largesse upon – it seemed – anyone she passed, regardless of position, rank or entitlement. Except himself – the current last link in the nine-hundred-year-old chain. If Lucrezia had her way, the final link.

Alfonso stood at the foot of the great staircase. He had told

Lucrezia he would return, and he intended to keep his word. The vigour released in him after his encounter with his whore still surged in his blood and it gave him to believe that at last, tonight, he might be able to escape his usual humiliations. He would end it all tonight – they would consummate this marriage, conceive the heir, and he could thus force his wife into conformity. Once with child, she would have no choice.

He made his way up to her bedchamber, the great black-brindled wolfhound padding behind him, and opened the door. It was dark, and the light from his candle bobbed and swagged as he turned to close the door behind him, leaving Folletto in the corridor.

Lucrezia was no more than a hunched shape under the bed-covers; she made no sign that she had heard his entrance.

He turned the key in the lock.

Unlacing and pulling off his doublet, Alfonso walked to the ebony table that stood by the side of the bed and picked up the carved rosewood box. Opening it, he drew out the string of garnets; he let them run through his fingers with a soft clicking sound, like cold, angular pebbles.

As he fingered the stones, he thought of his mother, their original owner, and remembered, from when he was a very small child, the excitement he used to feel when she allowed him to open this same box, and bring out the Red Rope.

He does not understand why, but there is something secretively visceral about the sinuous redness of the stones, an illicit something that squirms in his belly, dries his mouth and quickens his pulse. Sometimes – the most special times – when his father is away from home and he is not afraid to go to his mother's chambers, she lets him climb upon her (at other times forbidden) lap, to wind the garnets about her neck. 'Make me beautiful, chéri.' His fingers are too small to manage the clasp, so he kneels up against her gem-embroidered chest, his face close to hers, breathing in her faint, peppery scent, and she fastens the Red Rope herself. He holds her wrists, feeling them twist under his fingers as her hands move behind her head. She sings softly in her native French, songs he does not understand, but whose very strangeness renders them entrancing to him.

But that, of course, he thought, with a stab of remembered pain, had been before his mother had been sent away from court by his father, for a misdemeanour he was not fully to understand until he had reached adulthood. She had taken the garnets with her when she left, and it had been years before Alfonso saw them, or his mother, again, by which time he had come to understand how very much greater would be the allure of the Red Rope if it were seen against unclothed skin.

Lucrezia sat up as Alfonso fiddled with the garnets. She propped herself on one arm and pushed her hair from her face with the other hand. 'Go away,' she said, and Alfonso heard a hard anger in her voice. She had never spoken to him like that before and he was shocked.

'I wish to be on my own,' she said. Her eyes flashed with a fury he had never even glimpsed in her, and colour rose in her cheeks. 'I wish to be on my own,' she said again, her voice trembling. 'Put the garnets away, Alfonso, and leave me alone. I don't want—'

He dropped the garnets. They rattled as they fell onto the wooden floor.

She fought him with more strength than he would have expected from a creature so small and slight, but he soon found that her frantic resistance aroused him quite as much as Francesca's well-rehearsed – and often-repeated – pretence of the same, and an anticipation of imminent ingress swelled in his head, pulsing in his ears and pushing up like hot fingers behind his eyeballs.

He had her on her back. Crouching on all fours, gripping her hips between his knees, he held her wrists and pressed them onto the pillows on either side of her head, feeling them twist within his fingers, small as a child's.

And then—

'Kiss me,' Lucrezia heard him say, his words indistinct, as though he spoke through the sound of running water. She turned her head away from him and tried to pull her wrists from his grasp. As his fingers tightened, and his knees dug into her, a flash of a memory – of heat and laughter and chirring crickets, and the pungent smell of crushed thyme – flickered into her mind, vanishing as fast as it had come.

'Kiss me, Lucrezia,' he said again, and this time there was a neediness in his voice. Almost a plea. She shook her head. He let go of one of her hands and clutched at her face with hard fingers, beneath her chin, tipping it towards his own. His mouth covered hers, filled it; his cheek was against her nose, blocking her breath – for too long. Pinpricks of light flashed. She clutched and tugged at his wrist. The water ran louder and faster, deafening her.

Almost too late, he let go and knelt up, and she sucked in a cold slab of air that hurt her throat. She wiped the wetness away from her mouth with her palm, her chest heaving.

Feeling sick now, she saw Alfonso fumbling with his laces, tugging at a knot in the fastening of his breeches, pulling them open, muttering, still with his knees vice-tight around her hips.

'No . . . no, no,' he was muttering through clenched teeth, his hand over the opening in his breeches. 'No. Too many times. Not tonight . . . it can't happen again. I won't let it. *Merda!* You won't ridicule me again, Lucrezia. We'll do this tonight and then never again will you have the audacity to sit there with the whores and the servants and the hirelings, spilling out secrets and laughing at my inadequacies. There'll be no more of it. I won't – *won't* – lose it all because of *you*! Get up!'

Alfonso snatched up her hand, held it by the wrist, pushed her fingers in through the opening in his breeches, where he pressed them onto a soft little mound of hot, clammy flesh that twitched at her touch. She tried to pull back, but he curled her fingers round beneath his own, his breathing quick and urgent. As his other hand reached for her breasts, she froze.

He could feel himself stiffening beneath her fingers – but not enough. Not enough. A cold wire of anxiety pricked in his throat. It was not going to work. She was no Francesca. He would need her mouth.

'Here,' he said. 'Come here. We'll try another way.'

He swung his legs over so that he sat on the edge of the bed, then took Lucrezia's hand and pulled her round to stand between his knees. His hands on her shoulders, he pushed downwards until she was kneeling in front of him.

He saw her eyes widen, and she shook her head again.

'No,' she said, and her eyes begged. 'This has never worked before . . .'

'Maybe so. But we have all night, do we not? We are going to succeed, Lucrezia, whatever it takes.' Alfonso took her chin between finger and thumb and turned her face up towards his again. 'We need an heir. It has to happen. I will not have you ridiculing me and the duchy any longer.'

'But . . . what do you mean? Alfonso, I haven't—'

'If you were *not* regaling your little slut of a waiting-woman with the sordid details of the fiasco of your marriage bed, then perhaps you would be good enough to tell me what you *were* discussing,' he said, gripping one of her shoulders and loosening his laces still further with his other hand.

He saw a dull flush colour her cheeks. She said nothing, just stared at him, breathing quickly. Fury, fear and an ugly greed for her writhed in his belly like a tangle of snakes.

Lucrezia tried to pull away from him, but Alfonso grabbed a handful of her hair.

'I think you know what to do,' he said, pulling her head in towards him. 'I've shown you enough times – you should have learned something by now. After all, it's a task even the cheapest whore manages without thinking too hard about it.'

Her knees pressed painfully onto the wood of the floor, the roots of her hair burned as Alfonso's grip tightened, and the stuff of his breeches scraped against her arms.

'Please, Alfonso – please don't make me do this – ' she began, but her words just breathed back hot against her face and he seemed not to hear her. She pushed her hands between her mouth and Alfonso's body; he grabbed one and jerked it out of the way, pushing his own hand in to take its place. Ineffectually straining her head backwards against his grip on her hair, Lucrezia felt Alfonso's fingers opening her mouth, and then she was fighting for breath, her protests now no more than inarticulate noises.

'We'll do whatever it takes, Lucrezia,' she dimly heard him say through the panicked sounds she could not prevent. 'We must have an heir.'

She felt his knees grip her body and knew she could not move.

When Alfonso snatched up his doublet and left the chamber as the first greyish light of the morning filtered into the room, Folletto was not lying across the doorway, as he would have expected. He was surprised to see the dog on its feet, blocking the way out, hackles raised and eyes white-rimmed.

'Get out of the way!' he said, but the dog did not move. Alfonso said it again. Folletto growled. Alfonso cuffed him hard across the muzzle with a hollow smack, infuriated that in every respect, every one of his dependants seemed determined to thwart him that night. Folletto snarled at him, blocking the doorway, showing teeth fully an inch in length, but Alfonso stood his ground. 'Will you move, you miserable, misbegotten black hellhound? Just get out my way and let me pass!'

The dog stood square and the rumbling snarl continued.

A red mist clouded Alfonso's vision. He pulled a pair of hunting gloves from where they were folded through his belt and swiped them, back-handed, across the dog's head. The snarling stopped.

Alfonso strode past, deliberately ignoring the almost soundless sob that came from the room behind him. Pulling a candle from a wall-bracket, he ran down and down through the levels of the Castello, hutched his way awkwardly along the short, low-ceilinged corridor and stepped down into the windowless cell.

Pushing the heavy door to, he leaned against it, his forehead and hands pressed against the blood-smelling iron. Nausea swirled through him. He screwed shut his eyes and held his breath, begging wordlessly for stillness – but the clotted silence was punctured now with bleating whimpers, and jeers and the soft voice of the Archbishop, and he could find no peace.

The early morning light was flooding through into the North Hall and the day's *giornata* was ready to accept its paint. Jacomo ran a hand over the smooth, warm surface of the plaster and thought of Lucrezia's skin. He closed his eyes and saw her – creamy pale and huge-eyed, nose and cheeks freckled like a robin's egg. Clothed, she had seemed delicately small and rather vulnerable, but naked he had found her possessed of a quick, taut energy that had entirely delighted him. All those layers of lawn and silk had hidden the truth most effectively.

Even as he thought this, Jacomo's eyes snapped open. He held his breath as his mind made an almost muscular movement: an idea for a change in the fresco's design pushed its way into his consciousness. His breathing quickened and he jumped down from the trestle upon which he had been standing.

'Brother,' he said, his voice a little husky, 'I've just had an idea.'

The friar looked up from his paintpot. 'What is it, child? Come on, Jacomo, tell me. I've seen that smile on your face too many times before. This looks like a good one.'

And Jacomo explained. He scrambled back up onto the trestle and roughed out the new design with his hands, his fingers tracing onto the plaster all that he could see in his mind's eye as clearly as though it were already complete. 'And it's the height of aristocratic artistic taste at the moment, is it not, Brother?' he said, turning back to the friar. 'Hopefully we can fool him completely, and then he can enjoy confusing – no, more than that – *bewildering* – anyone who sees the painting!'

There was one element to the subterfuge, however, that Jacomo avoided sharing with the reverend brother.

Fra Pandolf frowned, lower lip jutting as he considered what he had heard. Then the frown cleared and a boyish smile took its place. 'Oh, yes, Jacomo. It certainly *is* a good one – I wish I had thought of it myself! Of course . . . I am not sure that I'll be able to . . .' He tailed off, hesitating.

'I'll do it all.'

'Yes, yes,' said Pandolf, more enthusiastic by the moment. 'Judging by the *sinopia*, I would say that we have three more *giornate* to complete before the new section. Would you agree?'

Jacomo nodded.

'How many days will the new section take, Jacomo?'

'Another four or five, perhaps.'

'A little more than a week, then, for the work to be completed.'

A little more than a week, Jacomo thought. He would count it in hours.

Tomaso appeared then, yawning, rubbing his eyes and hitching up his breeches. Jacomo's heart lurched. Yesterday, he thought, those breeches had clothed a very different body.

They set to work and rapidly progressed with the day's *giornata*, Jacomo tackling the more complex sections – the great bronze Talos, creaking to terrifying life, the fear in the faces of the Argonauts and Jason's wild flight from the scene. Fra Pandolf was busy with sky, sea and sand.

They had been intensely busy for some two hours when the sound of footsteps coming up the spiral staircase interrupted their almost silent progress.

Jacomo's heart skipped a beat and his face felt suddenly cold as the duke appeared, gazing intently at the painting.

He had Lucrezia by the hand.

She was ashen-faced, and bruise-coloured shadows stood out under her eyes. Looking up at Jacomo, her gaze was eloquent. The duke, without releasing his hold upon Lucrezia, turned from her, as, in conversation with the reverend brother, he stretched with his other arm to point out some feature of the fresco that had caught his attention.

Lucrezia, her eyes still fixed upon Jacomo's, turned her head as far from her husband's eye as she dared and mouthed silently, 'I love you.'

Facing directly towards the duke, he did not dare answer, but he risked the smallest twitch of a smile. Lucrezia's mouth opened a fraction and its corners lifted infinitesimally.

'What think you, Fra Pandolf?' the duke asked.

Jacomo started.

'A charming idea, Signore, and one I shall be delighted to undertake forthwith. Jacomo?'

The plump friar's words were cheerful and confident, but his expression, Jacomo thought, was tainted with suppressed panic. He had no idea what they were discussing, but Pandolf prattled on, covering his incriminating ignorance.

'A portrait of the fair Signora! A lovely idea! As a fresco, Signore?' He threw Jacomo another frightened glance.

'I think so,' said the duke. 'The Signora will then become a permanence within the Castello Estense, for many generations to admire.'

Jacomo saw him turn to Lucrezia, who met his gaze briefly, then looked at the floor.

'I suggest we place the portrait at the southern end of the landing that leads to the stairs from the Entrance Hall. The light from the double window falls there for much of each day. Perhaps you will come with me now, Fra Pandolf, and reassure me that this is a suitable location in terms of light, of visibility – of viability.'

'Yes, yes, Signore, straight away.'

'Lucrezia!'

It was, Jacomo thought, more of an order than a request, but she did not move.

'I should like to stay a while longer and look further at the progress of the Argonauts, Alfonso.' Her voice was cool and firm.

The duke stared at her for a moment, then turned on his heel and descended the spiral steps, closely followed by the flapping brown robes of the reverend brother.

Tomaso's gaze moved from Lucrezia to Jacomo. The tension that hung between them was almost palpable, and Tomaso's whole body radiated curiosity. Jacomo widened his eyes at him and jerked his head towards the stairs. 'Just give us a few minutes, Tomaso, please . . .' he said.

Tomaso grinned, shrugged and shambled off towards the staircase.

Jacomo dared not hold her; his hands were covered with paint. Lucrezia was trembling visibly, but she smiled and reached forward. She touched one of his hands. Then, as she had before, looked at the coloured smear on her fingers and folded them into a fist; she touched the fist to her lips and then turned back to the painting.

Jacomo watched her.

Her voice was low and fast as she said, 'He says he has to meet someone at noon, I don't know who, and then he wishes to go hawking. That will give us about four hours. Meet me—'

Jacomo interrupted. 'I know just where to meet,' he said. 'I found it the other day before I went to get the boat. Go to the bottom of the steps to the Torre San Paolo just after noon – as soon as he's left – and we'll climb to the roof.'

'I'll be there,' Lucrezia breathed, still apparently scrutinizing the fresco.

'Has he hurt you?'

'He did not strike me,' she said, without expression.

Jacomo saw her pallor and the deep violet smudges beneath her eyes, and a heavy feeling of foreboding swelled in his chest. He ached to put his arms around her, but before he could take even a step towards her, Tomaso's untidy head appeared at the end of the gallery.

'They're in the Long Corridor, on their way back, Jacomo.'

Lucrezia's eyes widened as she turned first to Tomaso and then to Jacomo. Her unspoken question was easy to answer.

'I trust him,' Jacomo said softly, as the ringing footsteps of the duke preceded their owner into the hall; Fra Pandolf's aged sandals softly scuffed the stone floor behind him. Both men climbed to the gallery.

'I should like you to begin work immediately upon finishing this piece, Pandolf. Can you estimate how long the portrait will take?'

Jacomo saw the friar's eyes snap to him.

'Well . . .' Pandolf said '. . . young Tomaso can prepare the wall while we finish work on this painting, Signore, which will save a great deal of time. Then perhaps a day, maybe two, to complete initial sketches and studies. I . . . er . . . I should like Jacomo here to sketch too, as it will be . . . er . . . excellent practice for him – and then, given the size of the area to be covered, I think perhaps a week after that, Signore.'

The duke nodded and reached once more for Lucrezia's hand. She did not raise her arm, Jacomo saw, but allowed him to lift her hand from where it hung loosely at her side. She did not look up at him once. They left together.

Jacomo's teeth clenched; he pushed fisted hands down into his pockets. Scuffing the toe of his boot against one of the big earthenware paint jars, he imagined himself hurling it over the balustrade, heard it shattering on the floor below.

The reverend brother sank down onto the wooden trestle and put his hands over his face. His shoulders were shaking.

'What is it, Brother?'

The friar dropped his hands and burst out, 'Oh, Jacomo, this portrait. What shall I do? You said *this* would be your last commission with me, absolutely the last – what am I going to do? How can I do a portrait alone? I can hardly see further than the end of my sleeve. And all in front of *him*! He'll be watching the sketching, seeing what I do. He'll know, Jacomo: there'll be no hiding it.' He buried his face in his hands again.

Jacomo crouched next to him and laid an arm over the plump shoulders. 'Stop, Brother! Stop this! I'll – listen, I'll do this portrait.'

'But you said—'

'I know what I said. But I'll do it.'

There was a long silence, during which the friar appeared to be struggling with himself. After several moments, he said, 'I'll tell the duke that *you* are going to do the portrait. I'll make sure that you finally have the recognition you've deserved for years. I have been proud, Jacomo – no, more than that, worse than that. I have been *conceited* – but now I am deeply ashamed of myself. *Santo cielo*, I am a member of the order of Saint Francis, one of the most humble men in Christendom, and I am not worthy of this habit. I shall not paint again after this.'

There were tears in his eyes. Jacomo pulled a paint rag from his pocket and handed it to him.

As Pandolf blew his nose and wiped his face, streaking it with paint, Jacomo imagined the duke's reaction to being told that it would be his commissioned artist's apprentice who would paint his wife rather than the master; imagined the suspicion, the scrutiny, the watchful eye upon them during every day the picture took to complete.

'I don't want you to tell him,' he said.

Pandolf put down the damp rag. 'What?'

'We'll do it as we usually do. You can leave here with your reputation intact and then announce your retirement.'

'Jacomo, I—'

'It's best this way.'

Pandolf nodded. Then, as though a thought had just struck him, he said, 'But what about the sketches, Jacomo? The duke will see my work, and—'

'He won't have to. Sit up close to her, work slowly and tell him you are focusing on detail. He will soon tire of watching.'

'Will you do the face and the hands and—'

'I will do it all, Brother. I could do it from memory.' That slipped out before Jacomo could stop it. He saw the reverend brother's eyes widen and held his breath. But it seemed that Pandolf's smothering anxiety and guilt were all-consuming and he showed no more than a moment's flicker of interest in his apprentice's inappropriate familiarity with the duchess.

They returned to work. Jacomo's desire for Lucrezia was now tangled painfully with a sharp fear for her safety. But the knowledge that their release from this purgatory could only come with the completion of the fresco – and now, it seemed, a portrait – focused his energy on what he had to do, and he found himself painting with a speed and dexterity he would not have thought possible.

Some time later, he glanced out of the window and saw that the sun was almost at its height. It was nearly noon.

'I'll be back soon, Brother. There's something I must do,' Jacomo said, washing his brush and wiping it on his shirt. He rinsed his hands, then soaked a cloth and washed the worst of the paint from his face. Pandolf, still swaddled in his anxiety over the coming portrait sittings, did not appear to grasp what Jacomo was saying. Muttering vaguely to himself, he turned back to the wall, and raised his brush.

23

Dust danced across the thick stripe of yellow sunlight that cut the little room in two. Catelina put down her basket and looked around her: it was clean enough, and quite homely, but sparsely furnished and without, she saw, even a speck of decoration. A small, scrubbed wooden table stood in the middle of the room, along with three mismatched chairs. Over the backs of two of the chairs were an assortment of bridles, leather straps and a roughly folded brown blanket, matted with hair. A row of hooks on the far wall held several heavy coats, a grubby doublet, a long stick like a shepherd's crook and a woollen hat. A pile of boots lay on the floor beneath them. All four walls were bare, but on a rough shelf along one side stood – in no decorative order – three plates, two bowls and four pewter goblets. The fireplace was empty, though ash and the unburned ends of branches spoke of a recent blaze.

'There's another two rooms upstairs,' Giorgio said. 'Would you like to see?'

Catelina nodded.

She went up the narrow staircase before him, and peered into each of the two rooms which lay up under the eaves. In each was a bed: around each bed were heavy woollen curtains that had been roughly nailed to the ceiling beams. A low stool stood under the window in the larger of the two rooms, and a huge wooden chest took up much of the floor space in the smaller. The walls, again, were bare.

Catelina crossed to the window of the larger room. Behind the other dwellings that clustered near to this one, she could see outbuildings in varying states of dilapidation, stacks of wood, rows of barrels, a patchwork of vegetables and flowers. A hairy black pig rootled in the earth in the cramped little square of land next door.

'It's not much,' Giorgio said, sounding apologetic, as they went back down the stairs. 'What do you think?'

Catelina's eyes filled with tears.

'Oh, Lina.' Giorgio put big arms around her. He held her head against his chest and pulled her close. Catelina pressed her face against his horse-smelling jerkin and felt the tears hot on her cheeks.

'It's sooner than I had expected,' Giorgio began, 'but I had already decided to ask you anyway.'

'Had you?'

Giorgio's face cracked in a broad smile. 'Yes. I had. So – what do you say? Will you?'

Catelina felt entirely certain. 'Yes, Giorgio,' she said, 'I will.'

Giorgio lowered his face to hers and kissed her with enthusiasm, then straightened. 'I have to go up to the Castello now,' he said, 'I'm expected back any moment. I'll be here by sunset. Will you manage on your own?'

'Well,' Catelina said, 'if we are . . . to be married, Giorgio, I shall have to get used to managing, shan't I?' She felt the colour rise in her cheeks.

'Do you have any money?'

Catelina shook her head.

'Here.' Giorgio pushed one of his big hands down into a pocket and pulled out a few coins. 'Could you find us something to eat? I've nothing in the house at all.'

Catelina nodded. Giorgio kissed her again, then opened the front door. A bulky silhouette in the doorway, blocking the light, he paused for a moment, then came back in and kissed her once more.

She pulled away from him, laughing. 'Go on! I'll see you this evening.'

Catelina spent an hour or so arranging Giorgio's rooms to her satisfaction. She ordered the table and the chairs; she laid the plates and bowls out on the shelf in a more deliberate pattern; she straightened the hanging coats, and separated the boots into pairs, standing them neatly against the wall under the hooks. Finding a broom in a lightless corner behind the curve of the stairs, she swept the floor.

She climbed to the upper rooms, taking the broom with her. At the head of the bed in the larger room, two cords were nailed to the wall, one on each side; Catelina pulled back the bed-hangings and secured them with the cords, flapped out and straightened the blankets, then plumped up the rather uncomfortable-looking pillows.

The covers on the – obviously unused – bed in the smaller room were folded in a pile at the foot. Catelina refolded them and laid them back where they had been.

She opened the wooden trunk. In it she found several linen shirts, a couple of pairs of breeches, a woollen doublet and a tangle of limp and lifeless hose. She smiled, lifted out one of the shirts, held it to her face, then replaced it tenderly back in the trunk.

She swept the floor of each room, then went back downstairs and sat at the table. It was very quiet.

She sighed.

Yesterday already seemed unreal and distant. Her life at the Castello had ended so abruptly, snuffed out like a smoking candle.

Everything had happened so quickly.

The expression on the duke's face as he had burst into the Signora's chamber – Catelina shuddered. She had quite genuinely thought he might be about to kill them both. He had seemed – she struggled to find the words to describe it – as though he were *possessed*, haunted by something. Those great dark eyes of his had been stretched wide and he had been trembling so that Catelina had been able to see it from the other side of the room.

She stands shivering in the antechamber, listening to him shout at her poor mistress, then he bangs out of the room, stops in front of her and tells her to leave the Castello this very night. If she values her continued existence, he says. She does not think she will ever forget the look on his face as he says those words. Then he kicks the dog out of the way and whirls off in a flurry of flapping coat and clinking metal. The poor thing just stands with its tail between its legs, ears drooping like wilted cabbage leaves.

When she peers back into the bedchamber, the Signora is standing there, chalk-white, staring at nothing. A tear is trickling down her cheek; she does not brush it away, but leaves it to fall. It catches at the corner of her mouth and clings there. 'I'm so sorry, Lina,' she says. 'Where will you go?'

Catelina bites her lip. 'I don't know, my lady. Back to Mugello, perhaps, to my mother.'

Her mistress holds out her arms and they hug each other close. Catelina is crying too, by this time, but she thinks she hears the Signora say, 'You'll be safely away, Lina. We'll be able to go, after all.' Her voice is muffled with tears though, so Catelina wonders if she is mistaken.

It does not take her long to pack her things: her two spare dresses, a couple of shifts, a pair of shoes, a few trinkets she has collected over the months she has been at the Castello. It all fits comfortably in the basket the Signora took into the town with Jacomo.

They stand back from the packing. Catelina feels suddenly awkward. She says, 'I'll go to Giorgio, my lady. He'll ride with me to Mugello, if he is allowed the time away.'

'Lina . . .'

'No, my lady – I'll just go. Don't come down with me. It will make it worse.' She pauses then, her words catching in her throat, and then blurts out, 'Be safe, my lady. Don't let him hurt you.'

And after one more fierce hug, she grabs the basket and runs from the room, down through the castle and up to the stable block, where she finds Giorgio sitting on a mounting block, cleaning a harness with a horsehair scrubbing-pad.

'Lina! What is it? Why are you crying?' he says.

There is no point in pretending. She tells him.

'Dismissed?' He stands up, scrubbing-pad dripping in one hand. 'But I don't understand. You . . . but why? What could you have done to—'

She tries to explain.

'What will you do, Lina? Where will you go?'

She shrugs.

'Don't go anywhere,' he says then, dropping the scrubbing-pad and the piece of harness and hugging her. 'Stay here, with me. I have rooms in town.'

Now Catelina sat in Giorgio's cramped downstairs room and

thought how shocked she had been at the impropriety of his suggestion. 'But, Giorgio, how can I?' she had said. 'We're not married!'

'That can be arranged,' he had said, very seriously.

Catelina picked up the basket containing her few belongings and carried it upstairs. She hesitated, unsure in which of the two rooms she should leave her things. Deciding upon the smaller, unused room as less presumptuous, she took out her dresses, shifts, shoes and trinkets, and put them all neatly on the bed.

She took the basket back downstairs, picked up the coins Giorgio had given her, and, swinging her cloak over her shoulders, she set out for the centre of the city in search of food.

She bought a rabbit at the little butcher's in the Via delle Volte, some vegetables, salad leaves, a large bunch of grapes and a head of garlic from a stall in the Corso, and a flagon of ale from a small shop in the next street. That last purchase took her to within sight of the Castello; she stared at its heavy red-brick bulk, wondering what was happening within those walls, not knowing quite what she should be thinking.

Her basket was bulging and heavy as she made her way back to the little house in the Via Vecchie, pleased with her purchases. It had taken her some moments to reach the street – she had made two wrong turns before she recognized the brightly painted armourer's shop at the end of the road – and by the time she turned the corner and could see Giorgio's front door, she was tired and longing to sit down.

She had gone some two or three steps down the street when she heard a sound like an animal in distress. A low, guttural moaning. She looked about her but could see nothing. It came again, a little louder. Catelina moved towards where the sound had come from, and her scalp contracted in shock. A girl, filthy and dishevelled, eyes tightly closed, was slumped in an untidy heap in a dark alcove between two houses.

Catelina put down her basket, stepped forward and crouched in front of her. 'Can you hear me?' she said softly.

There was no response. She reached forward with trembling fingers and stroked the girl's hair back from her face. 'Signorina, can you hear me?' she said again, and this time the girl opened her eyes. She moved position, and Catelina saw that her belly was hugely distended: the strings holding her filthy bodice together were loosened to their utmost.

'Here, let me help you to stand,' Catelina said.

The girl lifted her arm and Catelina took her hand. As she steadied herself to take the girl's weight, she heard her suck in a ragged breath. The girl gripped Catelina's fingers so tightly she feared they might break, and then the guttural moaning came again. For maybe a minute, the girl sat hunched over her belly, clinging to Catelina's hand, and then her hold relaxed. 'I'm sorry,' she said, hoarsely, panting as though she had been running.

'Come on, try to stand. I'll not let you fall.'

She pulled the girl to her feet. Her dress was filthy, her face streaked with dirt and tears; the great belly protruded incongruously. Catelina wiped the girl's face with the edge of her sleeve, and tried to sweep some of the dirt from her clothes. Turning her around, intending to brush down her shoulders, she saw that the back of the creased and crumpled skirt was sodden, encrusted with the dust in which she had been sitting.

'Is this – oh, God, has it started?' Catelina said, appalled.

'I . . . I think so.'

'Well,' she said, 'you had better come with me, hadn't you? You need to lie down.'

She picked up the basket, took the girl's arm and together, step by faltering step, they walked the last few yards to Giorgio's house.

24

The little peregrine snapped her dark wings open and flapped them irritably; underneath, the feathers were the same soft, freckled cream as the plumage on her breast. Alfonso felt the yellow talons grip the thumb of his gauntlet as he fastened the thin red straps of the jesses to the metal ring at the end of the leash; he wound the leash around the fourth and fifth fingers of his gloved hand. The falcon ducked and dipped her head in an effort to avoid the hood he now held out – her wings flapped open again and she bated. But, fastened as she was to his hand, she could do little to avoid it, and in an instant she was blind-folded and calmed, and sat suddenly quiet in her enforced darkness, the terrible pale beak curving out from under the scar-let kid of the hood. Alfonso drew the strings close around her head, pulling one with his right hand and holding the other taut with his teeth. His face came within inches of the dagger-sharp beak, but the peregrine sat still now, in blind dignity, and took no notice.

Alfonso stretched his left arm towards the falcon's tall wooden block. Tilting his fist, he encouraged her to stand down, off his hand and onto the block so that, hawking glove held by its tassel between his teeth, he could use both hands to fasten the little hunting bells onto her legs. He had always found these tiny straps too delicate to tie successfully one-handed.

'Are you nearly ready with that peregrine, Este?'

Francesco Panizato sounded amused, Alfonso thought. He knew that his friend took little care over these preparations, preferring to leave them to his – or Alfonso's own – falconer. For himself, though, Alfonso found that much of the pleasure he took in hawking came from the time he spent with his birds, preparing for work. This one, Strega – the witch – had always been his favourite. Wild-caught, she had been an instinctive bird since she was in the down, and now she could wait-on higher than any other falcon he had come across; she regularly brought back more game than he felt he had the right to expect from any bird. He was looking forward to seeing her fly that afternoon.

'You know perfectly well that you cannot hurry a bird, Francesco,' Alfonso said, leaving the falconry at last. 'It will not serve you well if it resents your haste.'

He held his free arm up and across his eyes as the June sun dazzled after the gloom of the almost windowless stone shed. Strega sensed the light, even through the hood, and turned her head away from the glare.

Panizato was mounted; his pale, hooded goshawk bobbed her head angrily and shifted her grip on his glove. 'Like women, eh, Este?' He laughed. 'If you ask me, you spend more time attending to that bird's needs than you do your wife's.'

Suppressing a shudder, Alfonso thought of the previous night and made no reply.

'Am I to understand by your scowl, sir, that I scored a valid touch there with the very tip of my rapier?' Panizato persisted. 'Perhaps you should employ some of your falconer's techniques with your duchess, Alfonso, teach her not to bate—'

'You go too far, Panizato.'

Alfonso saw the laughter die in his friend's eyes; Panizato had the grace to look abashed. *Teach her not to bate*. Alfonso heard the words again in his head and was gripped by an arresting image. It was not of Lucrezia that he thought, though, but of Francesca: wild, vicious and very like his Strega.

Francesca had been angry with him today, he knew, and their noontide assignation had been wordless, humourless and physical. But as he looked with pride now at his peregrine, who, though daily given a sky in which to roam, would always return to him, he knew that he held his whore, too, in bonds stronger than jesses, leash and lure. It seemed to Alfonso at that moment that Francesca might, perhaps, be all that stood between him and madness.

He forced a smile. 'Perhaps you are right, Francesco,' he said. 'Perhaps the falconer's skills might be gainfully employed in the bedchamber, though I think it – *perhaps* – beyond the remit of our friendship for you to suggest it to me quite so disrespectfully.'

'I stand chided, Alfonso.' Panizato held up his free hand in apology.

Alfonso took Farfalla's reins from the horseman and handed him the peregrine as he mounted. The horseman lifted the falcon back onto his hand, and Alfonso and Panizato left the yard, their two dogs trotting at their heels, heading for the hunting ground that lay outside the main walls of the old city, where it had stood since Alfonso's great-grandfather Ercole had planned it, ordered its construction and enjoyed it until his dying day. Alfonso had frequently had occasion to bless the old man's energy and enthusiasm and often wished he had known him.

They jogged in silence for some moments, and Alfonso found his mind filled again with Lucrezia. When they had first met in Mugello, he reflected, he had seen his future duchess as a perfect image in a flawless mirror. Since their marriage, though, each forcible reminder of her failure to live up to the exquisite reflection he so longed to possess had damaged the mirror's surface: cracked it, chipped and distorted it until ultimately he found himself wholly unable even to glimpse the reflection he had seen at the start.

He had been so sure of success last night. So determined. But now that he was certain Lucrezia knew about His Holiness's intentions, now that he knew she stood before him as a potential agent of the destruction of all he held so dear, she was not only more unreachable than ever, but dangerous. It was not so much that he could no longer see her in the glass, it was more that the cracks and distortions were now twisting the image until it resembled nothing so much as a laughing, tormenting little fiend.

To his shame, though, he knew that he still wanted her as much as ever. As a man bent upon self-slaughter might gaze at the jewelled dagger with which he means to stop his own heart, and, in a last moment of unexpected stillness, find its craftsmanship irresistibly beautiful, Alfonso knew he still longed to possess Lucrezia. He had to have her. He had thought last night that if he reinvented the image – tried to force himself to see his duchess as nothing more than a whore – he might somehow break down the inexplicable barriers that still stood so resolutely between them. But – humiliatingly – his plan had been entirely unsuccessful.

It had been exhausting, undignified, ugly – and a complete failure.

The hunting party reached open ground, and Alfonso and Panizato both broke into a fast canter. After a while they stopped, tethered the horses in the shade of some trees, and walked away from the cover onto higher ground. Both dogs – Folletto and Panizato's hound, Lontra – raced away from them across the heath.

There was a strong breeze. Alfonso was pleased: he knew Strega liked to feel the wind beneath her – it seemed to give her courage, entice her higher into the air. At times, he thought, his little falcon seemed to be waiting-on in the very clouds themselves.

Over in the tops of the nearby trees were the ragged twig-ends of a number of rook nests. If he was lucky today, he might get Strega to pull a couple of rooks. There would be no game on the heath at this time of year, so he had brought a lure in his hawking bag and would at least be able to let Strega stretch her wings and lose some weight – no bird has much of an appetite for hunting without an edge of hunger.

He and Panizato took the hoods off their birds. Both the peregrine and the goshawk blinked in the light and looked around them, sizing up the terrain they now saw. Panizato's bird, Foschia, was, Alfonso thought, a moody, difficult creature, and he doubted that his friend would succeed with her that day. A creature like Foschia needed endless time and the patient repetition of instructions if she were ever to become more reliable. Francesco's excitable, energetic nature was too exuberant for hawking, Alfonso thought.

He released the jesses from the leash and Strega immediately pushed down with her feet and soared from his arm, spiralling up and up, until she was no more than a motionless speck in the vivid blue. Foschia, too, took off, but flew in sweeping arcs some few feet from the tussocky grass. Panizato appeared unconcerned at her lack of height, however – he turned to Alfonso and spoke. 'Has your cousin returned from France yet?'

'No, not until August.'

'Does he know of the – er – situation, with regard to the titles?'

'Not yet. It is not the sort of information I feel I should trust to a letter.'

'No. I can see that. Rather delicate. And no – er – progress?'

Alfonso knew he was referring to Lucrezia's potential fecundity and could not trust himself to do more than shake his head. *The lack of issue is not yet a catastrophe.* But how long would it be before it was? The future stretched ahead: a desolate, endless road filled with a thousand unseen potholes.

There was a long and awkward silence. Then Francesco spoke again, rather obviously making an effort to change the subject. 'I need to know when the land committee will be meeting again, Alfonso.'

'Not before the end of the month. Why?'

'I have several testimonials to prepare, and I find I shall have to be away from Ferrara for a week or so,' he said, 'so I shall have to make sure everything is completed before I go.'

'Away?' Alfonso was surprised.

'My mother has been ailing, and . . . I received a letter from her this morning, asking me to come and see her. I believe from what she tells me that she is on her way back to health, but she rarely asks for me, and I think I should go.'

'Yes, of course you should.'

'I plan to take her something to ease her sleep. She is far too proud to ask, but she admits in her letter that she is wakeful at night, and I think she is troubled by disturbing dreams when she does manage to sleep.'

A problem, Alfonso thought, with which he was all too familiar. 'Is there anything you wish me to do, Francesco?' he said.

'Yes, actually. Recommend me a decent apothecary. That scoundrel Corelei, in the Via Fondobanchetto, is as like to sell me a fatal hemlock brew as to aid me in easing my mother's restless nights. He seems a veritable villain.'

'Alessandro Giglio serves the Castello and has always seemed to me both capable and honest. I will speak to him for you.' Alfonso gave his friend the answer he sought, and Panizato saw nothing unusual, but Alfonso's mind was suddenly reeling and he felt close to falling. The words he had spoken echoed in his head as though his ears were blocked, and colour began to drain from what he saw before him.

Francesco had unwittingly handed him the key to the silent door at the end of the shadowed corridor in his mind's maze. The door through which he knew he should never allow himself to go. Now, though, with the key in his hand, he would find it all but impossible to resist.

He knew all too well what lay within that room. In contemplating it, he felt winded and the seconds that followed hung frozen, as he imagined the unthinkable.

It would bring an end to it all.

But, afraid of letting his discomfiture show, he pulled himself back to Panizato and the heath. The two dogs were loping back towards him. Folletto had a rabbit in his jaws; there was blood around his mouth.

Alfonso pulled the lure from the bag. Looping the long tether across his hand, over and over, he swung the rook-winged bundle.

Strega dived.

He watched her streak down, slicing through the air in search of the lure – which he then swung wide to tempt her off her straight course. His little witch held fast to her aim and caught the lure in her talons in an instant. She hit the ground some few yards from where he and Panizato stood, and he threw her a dead pigeon by way of reward.

25

Lucrezia sat in the dark a dozen steps up from the bottom of the Torre San Paolo, wrinkling her nose at the musty smell. Her heart beat fast in her throat. She waited what seemed an age and then heard footsteps approaching. She stood up. Jacomo was running by the time he reached the first step and knocked right into her as she hurried down to meet him. He caught her in his arms to stop her falling and then, with a soft noise of longing, he kissed her mouth.

Lucrezia pulled back. 'No! Not here – quick, let's go to the roof, like you said.'

It was a long, long way up. Lucrezia's heart was thudding against her ribs by the time they reached the dim little room at the top of the tower.

'Where now?' she said, her chest heaving.

'Up there,' Jacomo said, pointing to another flight of some half-dozen wooden steps. Lucrezia climbed them and turned the big iron handle of the door at the top. It would not move. Jacomo edged past and shoved the door with the full force of his shoulder.

It gave, and he stumbled forward as it swung open. He scrambled back onto his feet and stood back to let Lucrezia through first, followed her, then pushed the door to behind him.

Pulling her into his arms, he began to kiss her again. It seemed to Lucrezia as though they sought to unify their bodies into one single being – as though by kissing they gave to each other their life's breath. They moved, in their tight, awkward, wordless embrace, across the room – Lucrezia was walking backwards – until she felt the chill of the wall behind her.

Jacomo put his hands under her arms and lifted her, and it took only seconds to pull her heavy skirts out of the way so that she could wrap her legs around his waist. With one arm encircling her, and pressing her against the wall to hold her up, he snatched at his own clothes with his free hand.

It was rough and frantic, and the unplastered wall caught against Lucrezia's back and head, but she hardly noticed the discomfort. No more than a few moments later, she gripped Jacomo's shirt and turned her face into his hair to muffle a cry she could not prevent, as what felt like a great fist clenched itself inside her. Jacomo let out a long, slow, shivering breath and stood still, holding her more tightly, supporting her weight between his body and the wall.

They stayed like this for several long moments. That first time, Lucrezia thought, their loving had been carefree and joyful; they had relished taking their time to explore and discover each other in every way they could. Today was different. They had between them created a need for each other that was now consuming them, overwhelming them, blotting out everything around them. Quenching that raging thirst would take more than a few moments' desperate embrace in the face of danger – but it was now no longer a matter of choice. Desire had become necessity.

She stood down on the floor once more and put her arms

around Jacomo, breathing hard and resting her face against his shoulder. He stroked her hair and kissed the top of her head. A few moments later they sat down on the rough-hewn wooden boards of the tower room, pressed close to each other, Jacomo's arm lying warm and heavy around Lucrezia's shoulders.

Neither spoke for several minutes.

Then Jacomo said, 'So he wants a portrait now, does he?'

'I think he sees it as a way to control me. But I don't care any more. In fact, I am beginning to think it's a perfect idea. Listen!'

She moved out from under Jacomo's arm and sat on her heels, her dress rumpled and rucked around her. Holding both his hands in hers, she said, 'Paint him a portrait of me, Jacomo. Make it beautiful – make it a portrait of a woman made beautiful by love. Give him a beautiful, lifeless work of art – that's all he's ever wanted me to be – an image of beauty confined and controlled by him. And then, once you've given him what he has wanted all this time, you can take from him the person he has never understood and never really wanted at all. And *I* will know what *he* will never understand: that I was in fact made beautiful in my portrait by love of *you* – not him.'

All the bitterness and anger that had seethed in her since Alfonso had dismissed Catelina and subjected her to such indignities rose like bile. Jacomo's gaze flicked from one of her eyes to the other. He frowned. 'What happened last night? Were you telling me the truth? Did he hurt you?'

'I told you – he did not strike me,' Lucrezia repeated dully.

'Lucrezia . . .'

She shook her head. She did not want to speak of Alfonso – not after the fierce joy of what she and Jacomo had just shared.

But he persisted. 'Something happened last night, didn't it? What did he do?'

Lucrezia turned away from him, unwilling to describe the terrible night she had spent. She hung her head, inexplicably ashamed. 'I don't know how to tell you,' she whispered. 'It was horrible. I did try to stop him, Jacomo. I didn't want him to touch me.' She wiped her eyes. 'He didn't actually manage to . . . but . . . but he . . .'

She could not finish her sentence.

Jacomo looked stricken for a second, then pulled Lucrezia towards him. She felt his hand cup the back of her head, holding it against his shoulder; with the other arm he drew her in close to his chest. A rush of love for him, beyond anything she had yet felt, swept through her and she clung to him, as she remembered clinging to her mother as a tiny child. The tears she had held back began to fall, and she found herself sobbing. Her voice distorted with crying, she told him everything: the loss of Catelina, her fear at Alfonso's wild anger, her terror and shame at what had happened after his return to the Castello the previous night.

Jacomo's arms were warm around her. He held her without speaking until she had cried herself to silence.

Jacomo thought quickly. Whatever the rights and wrongs of this impossible situation, he knew for certain now that he would have to take Lucrezia with him when he left the Castello. His troubled conscience cleared. Married or not, he could not leave her here with that man – it was now unthinkable. The waiting-woman had already left the Castello and the fresco was only days from completion. But how long could they dare risk staying? How could he even contemplate another painting? What else, he thought, his stomach flipping uncomfortably, might that bastard do before they were safely away?

'Lucrezia,' he said, 'after last night – we should go as soon as the fresco is finished. Forget the portrait.'

'No!'

He was surprised at how definite she sounded. 'But—'

Lucrezia sniffed. 'All those things we talked about before. There's the reverend brother – Alfonso will be sure to blame him if we run away before the portrait is done. You said yourself that he might. And—'

'I know what I said, but—'

She interrupted him: 'And I don't think Alfonso will come near me again for a while.'

Jacomo was unconvinced.

'He usually stays away from me for days after an embarrassing ordeal like last night's.' Tears glistened again in Lucrezia's eyes. 'I'm almost certain he won't try anything for at least a week.'

Jacomo made a disbelieving noise in his nose. He reached for Lucrezia's cheek and stroked it with his thumb. 'I meant to tell you,' he said. 'I had an idea for a change to the fresco – I'd almost forgotten.'

And he began to tell her about his plan. She sat staring at him as he spoke, nodding from time to time, the ghost of a smile flickering across her tear-blotched face. 'It's so clever. It's a wonderful idea, Jacomo,' she said, as he finished. 'I love it. Will you need any more drawings?'

'No. The image I want is fixed in my head.'

'And the portrait?' she said. 'You have to do the portrait. I want it to be here after we leave. I want him to have to see it every day so that he won't be able to forget.'

As she spoke, Jacomo suddenly knew, with an exhilarating rush of inspiration, just how his portrait would be. 'I'll paint you as Persephone,' he said, smiling.

'What do you mean?'

'You'll see – you'll have to wait.' He stood up, and held out a hand to help Lucrezia to her feet. She unfolded her legs and stood awkwardly, stiff from having sat so long in the same position. 'Come on, *cara*,' he said. 'We should go.'

Lucrezia said, 'I shall have to see you often or I think I shall die.'

Jacomo wrapped his arms right around her again.

'I'll come to the gallery when I can,' Lucrezia said. 'If I can arrange to see you, I'll try and find a way of telling you when and where.'

He smoothed her hair behind her ears. 'Come at first light tomorrow – you'll be able to see the sketch before it disappears.'

'I'll try, I promise,' she said.

He led her to the top of the stairs. They went down the many steps, pausing before they reached the bottom.

'Stay there a moment,' Jacomo said quietly. He crept down the last few steps and peered out into the corridor. It was deserted. 'Come on,' he said.

She followed quickly and, with one last kiss, she hurried away towards the Roof Garden, while Jacomo ran back to the North Hall.

The following morning, Jacomo reached the gallery a little after dawn. Fra Pandolf was still sleeping and Tomaso had been no more than an angular, hunched lump under his blankets when Jacomo had left the room. He had to get this drawing done, and cover it with the day's *intonaco* before the reverend brother came down to begin work. These sections would be the last of the great fresco, and, Jacomo thought, his silent gesture of defiance had to be made and hidden before it was too late.

He struggled up the spiral staircase with a heavy folding screen in his arms.

The *sinopia* had been cured and ready for some time and the many tiny marks made by the pounce charcoal were easily visible. But that morning Jacomo took a cloth, dipped it into a bucket of clean water and began to scrub them off the smooth surface. He wanted the plaster unmarked this morning.

While he waited for the water to dry, he mixed the day's *intonaco* in a big bucket and readied his pallet and trowel. He put the folding screen up behind him. It would give him, he thought, a little more privacy, but there was no time to waste and he wanted to be able to cover his subversive statement as soon as he could. It was not to be seen – only he and Lucrezia would ever know it was there, unless future inhabitants of the Castello ever decided to redo the fresco and take back the top layers of plaster, and then it would be uncovered and their secret defiance laid bare. Literally. Imagining the expressions on the faces of those unknown future castle decorators, Jacomo smiled to himself.

The image was clear in his mind as he mixed up a small pot of grey paint. He took a largish *riga* brush, wet it, sucked the bristles to a fine point and began to paint.

The identity of the two figures whose intimate and passionate embrace he now depicted on the wall was clear: the years he had spent before his apprenticeship, capturing likenesses in streets and taverns had served him well, he thought. Had the Signore approached him unawares at that moment, he would have been presented with such unequivocal evidence of his wife's infidelity that both Jacomo's and Lucrezia's lives would quite certainly have been instantly forfeit.

He finished his sketch and looked with longing at the image he had produced.

There was a sound of footsteps.

He froze.

If this were not Lucrezia, he had no chance of hiding the painting in time.

'Jacomo?'

He closed his eyes and let out the strangled breath he had gasped in. 'Here – in here, quick!'

She appeared around the end of the screen and stopped. 'Oh. Oh, Jacomo! It is – it is . . . oh, I'm so glad I was able to see it in time . . .'

'So am I.' He kissed her. Then, his mouth still on hers, he reached across and touched the paint with the tip of his finger. It was almost dry already: the *intonaco* could be laid on. He drew back from her.

'Can I help you? It will be quicker with two.'

'No – if you get dirty, we're finished. Stand back.'

He saw frustrated disappointment on her face, but she stood away from him as he scooped the plaster from the bucket onto the big square pallet.

'Wait,' Lucrezia murmured, as he raised his trowel to slice on the first arc of plaster. He waited, and she reached forward and gently laid her small hand flat on the painting, as if, Jacomo thought, in solemn benison.

Then she stood back and he began to layer on the *intonaco*. Within minutes, the painting had gone and a gleaming layer of pristine plaster glistened in the early sunlight.

This beautiful, triumphant, insolent depiction of covert infidelity was now – like the reality – hidden from all but the two of them.

Jacomo saw, too, with a frisson of pleasure, that the shadow of the folding screen was falling exactly where he wanted the new addition to the fresco to be placed – and that the effect was precisely as he had hoped it would be.

'I had better go before anyone sees me up here,' Lucrezia said then. Kissing him once more, she slipped behind the screen and left the gallery. Jacomo's whole body ached for her, but well aware that he needed to finish at least half of the new addition to the fresco that day, he told himself sternly that he had better stop daydreaming and concentrate on the task ahead of him.

26

Catelina leaned against the wall of the smaller of Giorgio's two upstairs rooms and looked down at the two sleeping faces. The girl's cheeks were still tear-streaked and dirty; and the baby boy, whose head now lay in the crook of her thin arm, was small and blotched, his straggly black hair plastered flat to his skull, like wet feathers.

'Well done,' said a soft voice.

Catelina smiled at the fourth occupant of the room. What an extraordinarily beautiful woman she was, Catelina thought. Even like this, all dishevelled and tired and grubby. She did not think she had ever been this close to someone so lovely. There was something hard and pinched around her eyes, though. And one of those eyes was bruised.

'Thank you for helping, Signora,' Catelina said.

'Francesca,' said the woman.

'Francesca,' repeated Catelina. 'I'm so very grateful. I don't know what I should have done if you hadn't been there . . .'

'Having seen you at work, I'm certain you would have managed perfectly well without me. But I'm glad you thought to knock. I'm proud to have helped.'

'I'm still very grateful. Whatever you say, I didn't know what best to do. I was close to panicking. We're all very lucky that Giorgio has such a capable neighbour.'

Francesca smiled. 'Don't think of it.' She took Catelina's hand and squeezed her fingers, then turned and made for the stairs. Catelina heard the front door open and close. She looked back at the girl and her baby. What in heaven's name would Giorgio say when he arrived home? It had been a momentous day. Giorgio had asked her to marry him; he'd left her to make herself at home in his house. He had given her some of his precious money and sent her out to buy the wherewithal to make a meal, and what had she done? She had brought back a homeless waif and delivered a baby without his knowing anything about it.

The little boy snuffled in his sleep.

Poor mite'll need a crib, she thought.

She sat down on the lid of the wooden chest, then stood up again, lifted the lid, and took out of it Giorgio's shirts, breeches and hose, which she carried into the larger room and laid on the end of the bed.

'The chest will do very nicely,' she said to herself.

The latch on the front door clacked and Giorgio's voice called up the stairs. 'Lina?'

She hesitated and then said, 'I'm just coming down.'

27

The evening sun was no more than a sliver of rich yellow above the distant line of the mountains. The light was low and a deep pinkish-gold, and the shadows it cast over the statues in Cosimo de' Medici's *loggia* were a rich slate blue. The sky was clear above the big house of Cafaggiolo, but far to the north a dark mass of cloud was gathering and a rumbling growl presaged a storm.

Cosimo de' Medici's face, too, was thunderous.

'There is simply no point in looking like that, Cosimo,' Eleanora de' Medici said, a muscle in her cheek twitching. 'I know what you're thinking.'

'I very much doubt that.'

'It's not difficult. You're angry that we have yet to go to Ferrara, even after nearly two years.'

Cosimo's scowl deepened, but he said nothing.

'But I don't care how long it has been, you are not going. The apothecary says it would be madness. You – and I – will have to stay here. We will see Lucrezia in August when she comes down here to Mugello. It's all arranged – we will stay here and Giovanni will go to Ferrara.'

'There's nothing wrong with me now and I fail to see why—'

'Oh, for heaven's *sake*!' Eleanora stood up, one hand on a hip, the other fisted against her forehead. 'Do you not think I miss Lucrezia easily as much as you do? Can you not imagine how I *long* to see my daughter? But we have to be realistic! You've been ill again. And it's the third time it's happened. At any significant exertion, you struggle to breathe. You have had pains in your chest that – in an aberrant moment – you told me felt like knife cuts, and you are *dramatically* thinner than you were a matter of months ago. You are *not* travelling to Ferrara.'

'But the fresco is finished and I—'

'That fresco has been carefully crafted and, unlike you, is likely to last at least two hundred years. The fact that you might have to wait a few more months before you are recovered enough to travel to see it will make not the slightest difference to the painting. *Not* waiting might make a *great* deal of difference to *you*.'

Cosimo de' Medici glared at his wife, his jaw jutting mulishly. She held his gaze.

Giovanni sat in the shadow of a large bust of Lorenzo the Magnificent, listening to his aunt and uncle's bickering quarrel and thinking hard about the letter he held in his hand. He turned it over and over in his fingers, imagining Lucrezia writing it, and wondered why his cousin's invitation had made him so uneasy. There was, he thought, flapping the small sheet of paper open again and re-reading it for the twentieth time, nothing specific he could put his finger on – it was just a *feeling*. Something about the tone of this letter was making him think that she was . . . not unhappy, Giovanni thought, but *agitated*. That was it. Something, he thought, was not right.

His uncle's voice grew louder and more insistent. 'It's not just the painting, Eleanora, I want to see Lucrezia. Before August. After Alfonso's news about the Holy Father's *unaccountable* intentions to . . .' He frowned, apparently searching for a word which would adequately sum up his sense of outrage. '. . . to *sack* the duchy and completely *ignore* the fact that Alfonso has made entirely *legitimate* arrangements to—'

'Calm down, Cosimo – you will make yourself ill yet again!' Eleanora said firmly.

'Why has she not conceived in two years?' Cosimo jabbed an accusatory index finger in his wife's direction.

Giovanni saw his aunt bite her lip. 'It happens, Cosimo. You know that.'

'Not in this family! There must be some problem, something they're not telling us. We need to see her.'

'I'll talk to her, Uncle Cosimo,' Giovanni said.

His uncle started. 'Eh? What?' he said.

'I'll talk to her. When I see her. Find out what's happening.'

'Don't be ridiculous, boy – she is unlikely to want to share any intimate confidences with a . . . with a child.'

A mouthful of angry profanity pushed up into the back of Giovanni's throat like rising bile. He was on the point of retorting when he was interrupted.

'Cosimo!' Eleanora sounded angry now. 'Giovanni is nearly eighteen. He is no longer a child. You were not much older than that when I first met you.' Eleanora flashed an apologetic smile at Giovanni. 'But if it makes you happy, why not let Giulietta go to Ferrara with him. If there are any . . . intimacies to be shared, Lucrezia will surely be as happy to confide in her as she would in you or me. Possibly more so.'

A knot of irritation tightened in Giovanni's chest at this and his jaw tensed. He had been looking forward to travelling alone, the sole representative of the family, and was longing to see Lucrezia again. Of all the people he could have chosen to travel with, one of the last would have been the implacable, nit-picking, unquenchably righteous Giulietta, who would, he was quite certain, dominate the days they spent at the Castello and make it almost impossible for him to spend any time alone with his cousin.

But his uncle was nodding. 'Yes . . . yes, Eleanora, I do believe that would be the next best thing to her having her parents there. We will send Giulietta.'

'We must be nearly there, Giovanni,' Giulietta said, peering out of the window of the little carriage.

Giovanni reined in his horse and slowed until he was level with her. 'Yes,' he said. 'Can you see there?' He pointed, and Giulietta stretched to see where he was indicating. Her fingers gripped the edge of the window, the knobbed knuckles bone-white. 'That's the Porta Paula. The edge of the city. We'll be there soon.' She was tired, he thought. The three-day journey must have taken its toll on her, and there were shadows under her pouchy old eyes that he had not seen before. Compassion fought with exasperation as he watched her pull herself stiffly back inside the carriage. He kicked his mare into a faster trot and nodded to the carriage driver in an invitation to keep pace, eager now to reach their destination. With a quick flick of the whip, the carriage horses, too, picked up speed, and it was not much more than a half-hour later that the little party drew to a crunching halt in the great central courtyard of the Castello.

Lucrezia was waiting for them. Arms folded in front of her, shoulders hunched, she stepped out of the shadows of an archway as Giovanni stretched and dismounted. He was shocked: she was drawn and pale, the freckles on her nose darker than usual, her eyes red-rimmed and over-bright. She said nothing to him by way of greeting, but walked up to him, put her arms around him and clung to him as though she were drowning. He hugged her and could feel her trembling, her breath shallow and ragged.

'Crezzi, what is it? Is something wrong?'

'Where are Papa and Mamma?' she said, into his doublet.

'They didn't come. Uncle Cosimo is still ailing – Aunt Eleanora says he is in no danger but she was afraid the journey would be too much for him. Giulietta's here, though—'

'Giulietta!'

Lucrezia pulled back from him and Giovanni saw a flicker of what looked like panic cross her face. Then he glanced across to the carriage. The door opened and Giulietta appeared, crumpled and sunken with fatigue.

'Lucrezia! *Cara!*'

'Oh, Giulietta!' Lucrezia ran to help the old lady down onto the cobbles.

They stood close-clasped for a moment, and then, holding Lucrezia's shoulders, the old woman drew away from her and frowned. '*Cara* – you're so pale. Are you ill?'

Giovanni was unconvinced by the levity of his cousin's answer as she swiftly sidestepped a response. 'I might say the same about you, Giulietta,' she said. 'You look quite exhausted. Was the journey *very* tiring?'

Several castle servants appeared, as Giulietta began to describe the voyage, and, as they fussed around the carriage, reaching for the luggage, Lucrezia caught Giovanni's eye. She said to Giulietta, 'Why don't you go in and change your clothes? The ladies will show you to your apartment and fetch you some hot water so that you can wash. I'll . . . I'll just go across to the stables with Vanni, and then I'll be with you. Alfonso is somewhere about the castle – he'll join us later, I'm sure. We'd love to hear about your journey, and you must tell us all the news from Cafaggiolo.'

She spoke quietly to one of the servants, who held out an arm to Giulietta. Doubt and suspicion were etched across the old lady's creased-parchment forehead, but she nonetheless gripped the proffered arm and began to walk with the young man towards the castle's main entrance.

Giovanni lifted his mare's reins over her head and held them in one hand up under her muzzle. She tossed her head and snorted, jerking his arm upwards, but he held fast and scratched her between the eyes with his free hand, soothing her disquiet. 'What the hell is wrong, Crezzi?' he said quietly.

'I can't tell you here. Let's go to the stables.'

They walked together, the mare now droop-headed beside them, and as they walked, Lucrezia looked about her warily, and then began to speak.

Giovanni listened, his gaze on the ground. Several times he opened his mouth to say something and each time he closed it again, unable to find the words he sought.

They reached the stables and were shown to an empty stall. Giovanni led the mare in; Lucrezia followed and sat on a bundle of hay in a corner. Giovanni unfastened the mare's bridle, and a heavy silence stretched between him and his cousin as he worked. The only sounds in the cramped stall were the tiny clinkings of the harness buckles, and the scuffing hoofs and soft snorts from the mare as she tore hay from her manger.

Several minutes passed before Lucrezia spoke again. She said, very quietly, 'I love him, Giovanni. I will die if I cannot be with him.'

She was not exaggerating – Giovanni could see that this was a simple statement of fact. He could think of nothing to say.

She said, 'Come and see the fresco with me, Vanni, and you'll meet him. He won't know that I've spoken to you. We have to be very careful.'

She was so small and fierce and determined, he thought, and he really did love her. He knew her so well – if this was what she wanted so very badly, then, however shocking he might find it, he wanted it for her. How could he want anything else? How could he even think of judging her?

'When did this happen?' he said. 'How long ago?'

'A couple of weeks.'

'Is that . . . is that enough time to be so sure?'

He expected angry protestations, accusations of unreasonable suspicion and lack of understanding, but Lucrezia just nodded. 'I knew that first day.'

'What will you do?'

'When the paintings are finished and they leave the castle, I shall go too.'

'But—'

She interrupted him. 'I've made up my mind.'

There seemed to be nothing more to say.

Giovanni finished unsaddling his mare, gave her a final pat, then he and Lucrezia walked slowly back up to the castle.

'How did it happen that Giulietta came with you?' Lucrezia said, as they crossed the central courtyard. 'I'm surprised she wanted to travel so far.'

'Aunt Eleanora suggested it. Uncle Cosimo's worried about you – they both are – because of what *Il Duca* said when he stayed a few weeks ago.'

'Alfonso went to Cafaggiolo?' Lucrezia stopped abruptly, clearly alarmed. 'When? Why? What was it – what did he say?'

'Did he not tell you? He came for a couple of days – on his way back from Firenze, he said – with that curly-haired friend of his. He was all fired up about what the Holy Father had said . . .' Giovanni was expecting to see her expression clear, but Lucrezia's eyes widened.

'The Holy Father? What did—'

'Don't you know?'

'Don't I know *what*?'

This Giovanni had not expected. He had presumed she knew. But, he thought, Lucrezia had just confided in him her most intimate and treasured secret: he felt he owed it to her to be honest. 'I was not in the room with Uncle Cosimo and *Il Duca* when they discussed it, I admit,' he said, 'but from what my aunt and uncle have said to each other since, I think . . . that the Vatican has said it means to reclaim the rights to Ferrara if there's no heir and—'

'Oh, dear God!' Lucrezia cut across him. 'Then it wasn't an annulment. *This* is why he hates me so much.'

Giovanni stared at her. 'Hates you?'

There was a long pause. Then Lucrezia said quietly, 'There are times when I think that even the sight of me is almost more than my husband can endure.'

Giovanni thought back to that moment in Cafaggiolo when he and Lucrezia had gone down to the *loggia*, and she had curtsied to the duke, her hair gilded with the evening sun, and he had smiled at her. Giovanni had been overwhelmed by a wash of antipathy so strong it had made him feel sick, he remembered. He looked at his cousin now, nauseous again with anxiety. 'Has he done anything to hurt you, Crezzi?'

She smiled. 'That's what Jacomo asked.'

'*And?* Has he?'

'I can only say to you what I said to Jacomo. He hasn't struck me.'

'God, Crezzi, what are you not saying?'

'None of it matters now. I'm leaving, aren't I?'

'But what if—'

'Stop it, Vanni!' Lucrezia leaned forward and kissed his cheek. 'Come and meet Jacomo, and then we must find Giulietta.'

Giovanni saw on his cousin's face a familiar look of determined implacability and knew better than to continue questioning her. He stopped talking, and followed her up through the castle to the North Hall.

At the far end of the hall was a balustraded wooden gallery, reached by a delicate spiral staircase. Across part of this gallery a makeshift folding screen had been carefully placed to conceal one end of the painting, but the bulk of the fresco was already visible. It was, Giovanni thought, his eyes moving from scene to scene, truly astonishing.

He felt a small hand slide into his palm.

'There he is, Vanni.'

Giovanni turned to where Lucrezia was pointing. Someone had walked out from behind the screen: tall, dark, with untidy hair, a faint shadow across his chin and a vivid splash of crimson over his nose and cheek. Even from where he stood, Giovanni saw the tremor that shook Jacomo as he caught sight of Lucrezia, and for a second he fancied he could feel the great pulse of heat, or whatever it was, that swooped between them. He knew at once that *this* – this wild intensity of emotion – was something to which he had never even come close. It was so much *bigger* than anything he had yet experienced. He was touched by a moment's keen jealousy.

From his vantage-point in the gallery, Jacomo saw that Lucrezia was clasping the hand of a dark-skinned boy in a mud-stained green doublet. As she let go of the boy's fingers and smiled up at him, the now familiar hot slither of longing slid down into his belly.

The two figures crossed the hall and climbed up the spiral staircase.

'Reverend Brother, Jacomo, Tomaso, this is my cousin, Giovanni de' Medici,' Lucrezia said. 'He's just arrived from Cafaggiolo. Vanni, this is Fra Pandolf,' Giovanni bowed briefly, 'Tomaso de Luca,' another little bow, 'and this,' Lucrezia said, 'this is Jacomo. Jacomo Pennetti.'

Jacomo met Giovanni's gaze. He knows, Jacomo thought – Lucrezia must have told him. The boy's stare was steady, appraising, searching: warily protective of his cousin, Jacomo thought with approval. They eyed each other for a few long seconds, then Fra Pandolf bustled forward to place himself deliberately between Lucrezia and the folding screen, one plump hand splayed on his hip like a fat starfish. He wagged a finger at her, saying, 'Now, you are not going to see behind the screen, Signora, not until the day after tomorrow. The final section of the fresco must remain a mystery to all except the painters until it is completely finished – eh, Jacomo?'

Jacomo raised an eyebrow and, catching Lucrezia's eye, smiled more broadly by way of agreement. Looking back at Pandolf, he saw that Lucrezia's cousin was still watching him closely.

'We unwrap our masterpiece on Saturday morning, Signora, and not a moment before,' Pandolf added.

'It's been long in the making, Brother,' Lucrezia said.

'Indeed it has, Signora, and I have enjoyed every moment.'

'Oh, so have I, Brother,' Lucrezia said softly. 'I am so very glad you came to the Castello.'

Four viol players, an oboist with a bald head, two lutes and a small boy with the voice of an angel: *Il Duca*, Giovanni thought, obviously wanted to mark the unveiling of the masterpiece with a flourish. 'It's quite something, all this, isn't it, Giulietta?' he said.

The old woman seemed overawed. 'I'm sorry that your aunt and uncle are not here to see it,' she said. 'They would have been so pleased and proud.'

Giovanni took her hand and pressed her fingers.

'Has Lucrezia spoken to you at all?' she muttered.

Giovanni hesitated. 'About what?'

'About whatever it is that has made her so tired and drawn – and so very much reduced since she left the countryside. I know she is avoiding talking to me, and I wondered if she had spoken to you.'

'No. Nothing,' Giovanni lied.

'And where is that kitchen girl? I haven't seen her since we have been here. Who is attending Lucrezia?'

'I've no idea,' Giovanni said, truthfully, this time.

By the time the midday bell had tolled, quite a crowd had gathered to see the spectacle. Some fifty or so people, adorned in their most impressive finery, stood in groups in the North Hall. Up in the gallery, a shimmering green curtain had been hung right across the length of the fresco, concealing it from all in the main hall.

The music began, and the duke appeared, dressed, as always, in black, holding Lucrezia by the hand. He greeted his guests warmly, clearly delighted to be at the centre of this new artistic spectacle. Lucrezia, though, seemed ill-at-ease and uncomfortable. The contrast between this tight-lipped anxiety and the obvious delight Giovanni had seen in her face when she had looked up at her painter the other day could not have been more marked. But as she greeted the guests, he could see she was making an effort.

She spotted him and Giulietta, and slipped her hand from her husband's. 'I'm so glad you're both here,' she said, kissing

Giulietta's cheek. 'I'll come and find you after the painting has been unveiled, and we can sit together at dinner. I'll see you a little later.'

She hurried back to where the duke stood, but Giovanni saw her turn to Jacomo, who was standing with Pandolf by one of the windows. Perhaps it was no more than fancy, but it seemed to Giovanni that, as their eyes met, everything else in the room seemed somehow to lose colour, to drain of sound. His cousin and her painter were at least thirty feet apart, and dozens of unwitting individuals stood between them, but it was as though Lucrezia and Jacomo were quite alone, entwined into an intimate embrace.

The music rose in volume. After a moment or two, the duke held up his hands for quiet. The musicians stopped and he began to speak. 'My honoured friends, it is a great pleasure to see you here at the Castello Estense today to witness the unveiling of an artistic treasure, created here for me by a rare and – to my mind – unrivalled talent. I have been fortunate indeed that the father house in Assisi has been prepared to lend me its most extraordinary son so willingly and for so long.'

Giovanni saw the friar turn a muffled shade of crimson, while Jacomo stared moodily at the floor.

'The generosity of the brothers has resulted in what I am sure you will soon agree is an image of almost miraculous ingenuity – I cannot in all conscience conceal it from you a moment longer.'

He strode to the foot of the stairs and gestured with a flourish for everyone to move back across the hall, the better to see the painting when it was revealed.

Giovanni, Giulietta and the others waited expectantly. The music swelled once more and the little angel's voice hung above the instruments with a sweetness that cut to the heart.

The duke reached forwards and pulled a cord, which released

the green curtain. It fell to the floor and the guests let out a gasp of astonishment. The picture was vibrant – almost ecstatic, Giovanni thought: the figures of Jason, Talos, the great ship and the Argonauts almost leaped from the wall as they moved from one scene effortlessly and fluidly into the next. His heart jumped as he recognized the face of the wild-haired woman at the far end. And just beyond this beautiful echo of Lucrezia, he saw that the end of the fresco was still hidden by yet another hanging. The tip of a curled golden horn and the end of a twisted branch were just visible beneath it. Giovanni found himself impatient to see the final section, and then one of the guests voiced his own curiosity.

'Pull back that last curtain then, Este – let's see the rest.'

Smiling, and nodding to the man who had called out, the duke reached behind him towards the shining silk curtain, creased with deep fold-marks that caught the light.

His fingers touched nothing but chill plaster.

His head snapped around to stare at the painting.

Giovanni's mouth fell open.

The curtain was no more than a painted image. It had fooled them all.

There was a moment's shocked silence, and then a ripple of murmurs began. Giovanni looked quickly from the duke, who seemed bewildered, to Lucrezia, who was watching Jacomo. As Jacomo's gaze met hers, Giovanni saw that they each wore a covert smile of pleased collusion.

Lucrezia felt a surge of fierce pride as the fresco was finally revealed. Even though she was prepared for it, she was astounded by the cleverness of Jacomo's depiction of the silk curtain. Watching Alfonso's fingers touch the surface of the plaster, his hand less than an inch from the hidden picture of her and Jacomo's brazen infidelity, she was rocked by a thrill of suppressed delight. She pictured the image that she and Jacomo alone knew truly lay behind the concealing paint and plaster, and a savage sense of redress – retaliation – for the loathsome things Alfonso had made her do ten days before fizzed through her. When she risked a glance in his direction, she saw that Jacomo's eyes were shining and she could not suppress a smile.

The fatigue she had been suffering for days had left her. Here, in the face of this astounding proof of Jacomo's prodigious skill, she felt exhilarated and joyful, bursting with new-found energy. Her face, which for days had been stiff with tension, seemed possessed again of its own animation. Her smile was an animal released from a cage.

Lucrezia heard Alfonso clear his throat, and looked up to where he stood on the gallery, in front of the painted silk curtain, his fingers tracing its folds and creases. His expression was difficult to read. After a moment's contemplation of his fresco, he walked the length of the gallery, descended the spiral staircase and stood, one hand on the end of the banister rail, looking at the reverend brother.

'Signore,' Fra Pandolf began, 'I am delighted and deeply honoured that our simple deception has proved so successful. Jason's great prize, for which he has searched for so long, remains tantalizingly obscured and we can only guess now at the image the curtain conceals. The eye is truly deceived—' He broke off and reddened, suddenly anxious. He had noticed the expression on Alfonso's face.

Lucrezia imagined the group of dignitaries actually being confronted with *the image the curtain concealed*, pictured their prurient outrage, and smothered a laugh.

Fra Pandolf said, his voice less sure – even conciliatory, 'No doubt you are aware of the rise in popularity of this style of work . . .'

There was another pause, as the friar appeared to be trying to gauge Alfonso's reaction. The duke seemed lost for words, but before Pandolf could speak again, a tall, heavy man in a dark red doublet said, 'Wonderful, Este – quite extraordinary! Heard about this sort of thing only recently . . . never seen it until now. Would not have thought it possible if I had not seen it with my own eyes. Remarkable, Este, remarkable!'

A murmur of agreement trickled around the hall.

Alfonso straightened, smiled broadly and blinked slowly and deliberately at his guests. 'As I said,' he began, 'this piece shows a truly miraculous ingenuity . . . more so than even I thought possible. Fra Pandolf, I believe we owe you a substantial round of applause.'

A rumble of muttered consensus preceded a sustained bout of clapping. Lucrezia's eyes were fixed upon Jacomo's as she joined in with enthusiasm.

After a moment, Fra Pandolf raised plump hands for quiet. 'Thank you, gracious ladies and honoured gentlemen. I am humbled by your appreciation of our latest achievement and would remind you that I did not create it alone. Please remember in your acknowledgement of what you see today, the others who have helped in its execution: young Tomaso de Luca, here, who so willingly shoulders much of the heavy preparation work, and of course my valued assistant, Jacomo Pennetti, a talented artist in his own right . . .' Fra Pandolf turned to Jacomo. Lucrezia saw Jacomo widen his eyes and shake his head almost imperceptibly. Pandolf laid a hand on his sleeve, and finished his sentence. '. . . a talented young artist, without whose help I know I really should not manage at all.'

28

Giulietta was shivering. She laid a hand on Lucrezia's arm. '*Cara*, could you have someone fetch me a wrap? It is rather colder out here than I had foreseen . . .'

'Of course.' Lucrezia beckoned to one of the servants. 'Run up to my apartments, could you, and fetch the fur-lined wrap – the embroidered one – from the painted chest?'

A wordless nod and immediate action.

'That should be warm enough, Giulietta,' Lucrezia said. 'Dining out here in the *cortile* is lovely but, it must be said, it's never as warm here as it is in Mugello.'

Giulietta looked around the great yew-wood table. The huge central courtyard of the Castello Estense had been brightly lit to celebrate the unveiling of the fresco: many little braziers around its edges burned cheerfully, and some two dozen candles illuminated the table, lighting it brightly enough so that their fuzzy yellow glow effectively hid the guests on the far side. The plates, silverware and glass sparkled in the flame light and it seemed to

Giulietta that the excitable chatter of the thirty or so guests was that glitter made audible.

Above them the sky was a star-pricked, velvet black.

Lucrezia sat on one side of her, and Giovanni on the other. The duke, on Lucrezia's right, had begun his celebratory meal in an ebulliently animated mood, Giulietta felt, but it had been somewhat brittle, and, as the evening had progressed, he had become increasingly taciturn, and now was doing little more than watching his guests converse, with an expression of brooding suspicion clouding his features.

Lucrezia, though, was positively sparkling.

Giulietta did not know what to think. She had been shocked at the sight of the girl on their arrival in Ferrara – Lucrezia had been ashen, and had visibly lost weight since she had last seen her. Giulietta was quite sure that her former charge was avoiding talking to her – oh, she had been genuinely pleased to see her, that much she could tell, but instead of, as Giulietta had expected, kissing her and clutching her arm and walking with her up to her rooms, regaling her with her usual over-embroidered tales, Lucrezia had clung instead to Giovanni in what had seemed to be silent desperation, and then had disappeared with him to the stables.

Giulietta had been quite alarmed.

Earlier today, as they had gathered in the great North Hall for the unveiling, the child had seemed just as drawn and anxious and tired and, knowing that her fertility – or lack of it – was causing concern back in Cafaggiolo, Giulietta had begun to fear for Lucrezia's health. But as the unveiling ceremony had progressed, and she had watched Lucrezia's face light up, and had seen the direction of the girl's gaze, her fears had dramatically changed course. And intensified.

She was not stupid.

Or blind.

The servant reappeared, carrying a dark red, embroidered wrap lined with rabbit fur. Lucrezia smiled her thanks, and took it from him. 'Lean forward, Giulietta,' she said, and, as her former nurse complied, Lucrezia laid the wrap across the old woman's bony shoulders. 'There,' she said, kissing Giulietta on the cheek, 'that should warm you a little.'

Lucrezia could hardly see Jacomo where he was sitting with the reverend brother on the far side of the table: the glow from the candles was too bright, the table too wide and heavily laden. Any conversation with him was impossible. But its very impossibility was probably fortuitous, she thought. They were too close to the culmination of their plans to risk discovery. It was enough just to know he was there. The fresco was finished. The portrait, he had said, would not take long – Tomaso had already nearly finished the preparations – and the day of their departure drew ever closer.

The more she thought about the intoxicating excitement of flight, the more it seemed to her as though all her senses were ready to explode. She felt as she had as a child after one of Giulietta's punitive baths – after a sound scrubbing with a rough wash-cloth, she remembered laughing at the sight of herself, hot and rose-pink; remembered tingling all over for more than an hour on numerous occasions.

The thought of the hidden image beneath the painted curtain continued to disturb Alfonso as the meal progressed. The moment at which his fingers had touched the plaster and the deception had – so humiliatingly – been made public, was repeating itself in his mind. He had been smiling at that idiot Rovigo – *Pull back that last curtain then, Este – let's see the rest.* How fatuous and ill-informed they must all have thought him! *Jason's great prize, for which he has searched for so long, remains tantalizingly obscured.* How could he not have seen? Why had he not turned back to the wall before reaching for the curtain? Had he done so, he must surely have realized the trick. It was clever – dear God, it was damnably clever. The depiction of that silk was minutely brilliant. He had not thought Pandolf so skilled, even given his reputation. Even close up, it was all but impossible not to believe what the eye imagined it saw.

But what lay beneath? *We can all only guess now at the image the curtain conceals . . . It remains tantalizingly obscured . . .*

Why had Pandolf covered the last image?

Was something being kept from him deliberately? Was it symbolic? Had Lucrezia told the painters, too, about the potential fate of the duchy, and did this image of the curtain – which had never been discussed with or agreed by him – symbolize their amusement at his ignorance of their scorn? *We can all only guess now at the image the curtain conceals.* He pictured her up on the gallery, her eyes glittering as she related the sordid details; imagined the painters' pruriently shocked reactions. But perhaps he was mistaken: his guests, after all, appeared to have been equally deceived and had ended by gasping their incredulity and admiration for the skill of the execution. Whatever the origin of this change in the design, it might in fact, he thought, attempting to console himself, be a piece that would truly rank amongst the memorable works of the century.

Further down the table, a chair was pushed back, scraping on the cobbles. Alfonso leaned back to see who had stood up. Signor della Pretura – small-brained, large-bellied, grey-haired, with lardy, pendulous jowls. Why had he got up from the table? Without comment, Alfonso watched him walk past the visitors from Cafaggiolo, then past Lucrezia and himself, and saw that his guest's eyes were fixed upon the duchess. Lucrezia opened her mouth to speak, but Pretura held up a fat forefinger and inclined his head towards her. She remained silent, smiling. Several of the other diners had suspended their conversations and were watching him. Alfonso stared in disbelief as his corpulent guest stepped across to a potted cherry tree and – without so much as a by-your-leave – broke off a small branch, which he then brandished like a trophy, as he swaggered back towards Lucrezia, who was watching him over her shoulder.

With an exaggerated flourish, Signor della Pretura bowed deeply and presented her with the wilting branch. 'My lady, beauty such as yours deserves recognition. Humble my gift may be, and – ' he cleared his throat and nodded to Alfonso, 'and – I must confess – *purloined* from my noble host's *bounteous* castle flora, but let it stand here as a symbol of the beauty of the lady of the house.'

Other guests pattered fitful applause, and someone on the opposite side of the table laughed.

Alfonso's gaze moved from a contemplation of the bulbous and quivering cheeks of one of – in his personal opinion – Ferrara's least intelligent magistrates, to the face of his wife. Lucrezia's eyes were shining. Then, to Alfonso's chagrin, that exquisite spot of joy glowed again in her cheeks, and the corners of her mouth crooked wide. But not for a moment did she include her husband in her enjoyment of the pleasantry. Not for a moment. Instead she favoured that fat, talentless, officious fool with a smile so radiant that he fairly melted before it. It seemed to Alfonso that his wife was now taking pleasure in bestowing her affections with pointed extravagance – and choosing to do so in her husband's presence whenever she could, presumably that she might enjoy rubbing the salt of her profligacy into the wounds of his humiliation.

Alfonso heard a roaring in his ears, which drowned the noise of the party. He turned away from Lucrezia, battling to maintain an impassive expression, and, as he looked up at the stars, he thought of his peregrine, waiting-on so patiently, so high she was all but invisible. Thoughts of Strega reminded him of Panizato's unwittingly offered key. The unthinkable key that would bring him peace. He had only to wait for the best moment. It would not be long now.

He looked back at Lucrezia, his heart racing, and his skin crawled.

Every feeling was heightened: Lucrezia sat still and allowed it all to wash over her. All the colours around her were brighter, the music sweeter, the food tasted more intense and the evening air was heady in her nostrils.

Even the gauche attentions of one of Alfonso's tedious guests seemed delightful to her in its unsophisticated artlessness as she contemplated the nearness of her departure with Jacomo. As the stout and red-faced gentleman – she did not know his name – bowed and presented her with a drooping spray of leaves, as impressively as though it had been a cluster of diamonds, Lucrezia found his foolish simplicity charming, so different was it from Alfonso's black, difficult depths. She heard Jacomo laugh from the other side of the table as a few people clapped, but he was still hidden by the glow of the candles.

29

Two days after the unveiling of the fresco, Alfonso entered Lucrezia's little studio and announced that he had a trip to make to Bologna. He seemed agitated and reluctant to go; she wondered at his repeated assurances that he would only be away for a few days.

'The first sitting for your portrait will be tomorrow,' he said, 'and they will be hard at work on the painting itself by Tuesday. I do not wish to let the piece progress too far without being certain that I am satisfied with it.'

'You must arrange it as you wish, Alfonso,' Lucrezia said coolly, not daring to meet his eye in case he detected the swelling bubble of excitement that threatened to escape her at the thought of his imminent absence.

'Shall you be happy to have this portrait painted, Lucrezia?' he asked.

'Oh, yes!' she said. Startled by the question, her enthusiasm spilled over and she saw Alfonso's surprise at her unexpected response. There was a long pause before he spoke again.

'I . . . er . . .' He hesitated, sounding uncharacteristically nervous.

'What?'

'I . . . wondered if you would care to wear the garnets in your portrait.'

Lucrezia stifled a shudder. She would prefer to hang live coals around her neck. Those garnets had come to symbolize everything about her incomprehensible relationship with Alfonso that now bewildered, chilled and ultimately appalled her. She hated them. She weighed her words carefully before replying. 'Perhaps,' she said, 'they are something too . . . intimate to expose so openly to public view.'

Alfonso blinked slowly, a frown like a knife-cut between his brows. 'Perhaps you are right. I shall wait until I see the sketches on Wednesday.'

As he spoke, there was an unfamiliar expression on his face that Lucrezia could not fathom. It seemed, more than anything else, like guilt.

Alfonso clattered away from the Castello just before noon. Lucrezia stood in the silk-hung antechamber overlooking the central *cortile* and watched him leave. There would be three days before his return, he had said, and, as she left the room and hurried down towards the entrance hall, her heart began thumping up under her ribs.

'Lucrezia, *cara*?'

She turned sharply as a door opened and Giulietta stepped out into the corridor from the little painted chapel; Lucrezia fought to keep her frustration from showing in her face. She tried to smile.

'You seem rushed, *cara* . . .' Giulietta said. 'Is anything wrong?'

'No, nothing at all. Should anything be wrong?'

Giulietta did not answer, but Lucrezia saw the old woman raise an eyebrow, and she felt her face burn.

Oh, dear God, was it to be Giulietta who would wreck their plans, after so many days without detection and so close to their departure? The old woman had guessed that something was amiss: Lucrezia could see the suspicion etched across her face and she dreaded what might happen if they began to talk. Since babyhood, Giulietta had always been able to get from Lucrezia any information she sought, and she had been terrified of allowing a conversation to develop that might run away from her and prove catastrophic. It would be the end of everything, she had thought, so she had tried simply to avoid talking with Giulietta ever since her arrival from Mugello.

But her strategy, it seemed, had not gone unnoticed.

'I've seen so little of you in the days I have been in Ferrara,' Giulietta said. 'We have had almost no chance to talk properly.'

Lucrezia took Giulietta's hand and began to walk with her away from the entrance hall. 'I'm sorry,' she said. 'I do seem to have been busier than usual. And now that Alfonso is away for a few days, and I have the portrait sittings to keep me busy, I fear that my unavoidable preoccupation is unlikely to change.'

There was a long silence, during which all Lucrezia heard was the soft rustle of the stuff of their two skirts as they walked: Giulietta's stiff black linen and her own russet damask.

Giulietta drew in a short breath, as though about to speak, but she said nothing. Lucrezia imagined her nurse's suspicions. Even if – God forbid! – she had deduced the truth, Lucrezia hoped desperately that – old-fashioned, upright, moral, implacably virtuous – she would find it all but impossible to broach the subject, so suffocating would surely be her sense of embarrassment.

How could she have guessed, though? They had been so careful. Lucrezia did not think she and Jacomo had exchanged even a sentence in Giulietta's presence.

The silence was oppressive. She had to open some sort of conversation. Hoping her voice sounded more natural than it felt, she said, 'Are your chambers comfortable enough, Giulietta?'

The old woman threw her a sharp look, which Lucrezia met with a smile.

'Yes, child,' Giulietta said. 'Very comfortable. Perhaps a little chilly at night, though.'

'Oh, I'm sorry – I'll have someone bring you more blankets, and they can build up the fire for you.'

Lucrezia could feel Giulietta's gaze tugging at her, urging her to look around, but she feigned a sudden itch on the side of her wrist and stared instead at her hand. They walked on, up a long flight of steps, and neared Giulietta's apartment.

'Lucrezia . . .'

There was pain in Giulietta's voice, and rejection. 'Please, *cara*, what is wrong?' Giulietta said. 'I know there is something. I know you are not telling me something important.'

This was how she had always done it, Lucrezia realised: this subtle, carefully timed concoction of intimacy and guilt. Giulietta was an expert. Determined to resist, she smiled and said, 'Truly, Giulietta, there is nothing. I've not been sleeping very well, though, and I am a little tired. Perhaps that's what is worrying you. Perhaps I look tired.'

'Your parents are anxious,' Giulietta said.

Lucrezia bit the inside of her cheek. A sudden, vivid image of her parents' reaction to the news of her defection from the Castello pulsed through her mind. She imagined her mother's face, tear-swollen and blotched, her father angrily pacing his bedchamber. She pictured Giulietta returned to them from Ferrara, her wrinkled old face in her hands, weeping out to them the sorry details of their beloved daughter's adulterous elopement with a vagabond painter. To do as she and Jacomo planned would devastate them both. At that moment, Lucrezia truly believed it would hurt them less were they to hear of her death. She loved them both very much and the thought of the pain she would cause them was terrible. But she knew she would do it. She could not give Jacomo up. It was impossible even to think of staying at the Castello after he left.

'They need not be worried,' Lucrezia said, opening the door to Giulietta's bedchamber and standing back to let the old lady through. 'When you go home, you can tell them I am quite well.'

Giulietta cleared her throat. 'They are concerned that . . . that you have not yet conceived. When the duke your husband came to Cafaggiolo, he . . .'

Lucrezia stiffened. She moved across the room to the window, and said, with her back to Giulietta, 'There is no hurrying such an event. What will happen will happen when God deems it appropriate.' She turned back into the room and smiled. 'And now I must go and ascertain from Fra Pandolf exactly when he wishes me to sit for my portrait.' She kissed Giulietta's soft-wrinkled cheek and left the room before the old lady had time to reply.

Jacomo ran his hands over the newly firm plaster. The surface was cool and silken. 'Well done, Tomaso, that's perfect. It'll be ready for us to start as soon as the sketches are done. I've roughed out the cartoon already, in fact – I might pounce it up this afternoon. I'm only going to need sketches for the details.'

'Working from memory, then, are you?'

Jacomo saw a smirk lifting the corners of his friend's mouth. He frowned quizzically. Tomaso grinned and said, 'I can't quite make up my mind.'

'What do you mean?'

'Well – I can't decide: is it just that you're tired of being alive, Jacomo, or have you have lost your reason completely?'

'What are you talking about?' Jacomo tried to look puzzled, but his heart was in his throat.

Tomaso leaned towards him and lowered his voice. 'The duchess,' he mouthed.

'What about her?'

Tomaso opened his mouth to reply, but a flurry of footsteps startled him and he stopped. Jacomo turned. Lucrezia was at the door to the entrance hall, bright-eyed and flushed as though she had been running. She saw Tomaso and checked, slowed her pace and began to walk towards the stairs.

Tomaso raised an eyebrow. Jacomo ran his tongue over his lip. He held Tomaso's gaze, then said, 'Just give us a moment, will you? Please?'

Tomaso shook his head, as though in disbelief. He shrugged and set off down the stairs, passing Lucrezia some two steps up from the bottom, his ill-fitting shoes flapping against the flagstoned floor.

Lucrezia watched him go, then turned to Jacomo. 'Does he know?' she said.

'He has his opinions, no more than that.'

'But—'

'Don't worry. He wouldn't say anything to anyone, even if he did know.'

Lucrezia eyed the door through which Tomaso had just disappeared. After a moment she said, 'Alfonso's just left the Castello. He'll be in Bologna for three days.'

'Are you all right, Lucrezia? Has he—'

'He has not been to my chambers since that night.'

Jacomo laced his fingers through hers.

'I want to see you,' Lucrezia said. 'Tonight.'

Jacomo nodded. It was well over a week since he had spent any more than a few seconds in Lucrezia's company and his desire for her – no, his need of her – was becoming a physical ache. 'That tower room,' he said.

'It will have to be well after dark.'

'Midnight. I'll go up before – I'll take blankets and candles, perhaps a bit of food. It might be cold.'

'I expect we'll find a way to keep warm.'

Jacomo moved a little closer to her, and ran his fingers around the curve of her breast. 'I'm sure you're right,' he said.

The moon was at its height and Lucrezia judged that it must be close to midnight. The castle had been still and silent for some time: the only sounds she had heard for at least an hour had been the soft creaks and sighs of the great building settling itself for the night.

Since dark she had sat with Giovanni in her bedchamber, almost exploding with anticipation. Cross-legged on her bed, endlessly pleating one of its hangings between her fingers, she had talked with him for hours, telling him in ever greater detail about everything that had happened over the past few weeks – everything except tonight's immediate plans – until Giovanni had yawned and stretched and told her that if she was even half as tired as he was, after his long afternoon's riding, she ought to go to sleep. 'But I'm going out again tomorrow. Would you like to come with me?' he had said.

'I have my first portrait sitting.'

'All day?' he had said, rubbing his eyes with the heel of his hand.

The familiar gesture had sent a surge of panic through Lucrezia. She had scrambled across her bed to where he was sitting and hugged him fiercely, gripping as tightly as she could until he had laughed and, holding her upper arms, had prised her from him. He had said, 'What is it? What's happened, Crezzi?'

'I promise I'll make sure you know where we are.'

'What?'

'After we leave here. I promise I'll make sure you know how to find us. Wherever we are.'

The laughter had died in Giovanni's face. 'You'd better,' he said softly.

'I couldn't bear it if I lost you.'

'You won't.' There was a long pause. 'That won't ever happen.'

Not having dared to carry a candle, Lucrezia, in her night shift and a wrap, climbed to the top of the Torre San Paolo in total darkness. Heart leaping, she paused at the top of the stairs to catch her breath. The door to the lobby opened, sending a yellow stripe of fluttering candlelight out across the dirty floor.

Jacomo ran down the short flight of wooden steps and, wordlessly, started to kiss her. With a little squeak of longing, she reached up and cupped her hands around his head and then, her mouth on his, she turned and led him up the wooden steps into the tower room.

Jacomo kicked the door shut behind him, then leaned against it, pulling Lucrezia close to him.

After a moment, she broke away and said, 'Oh, God, I've missed you so much.'

'And I've missed you – missed *this*.' He kissed her again. 'Come and see – I've brought some things up here for us.'

In a corner of the room some half-dozen candles were burning. A few tawny blankets had been laid out, one on top of another on the wooden floor, giving the room, Lucrezia thought, a strangely exotic, foreign air, like a painting she had once seen of the inside of a Bedouin tent. On the blankets were a bottle of red wine, a small basket – in which there appeared to be fruit, cheese and bread – a single pewter goblet and Jacomo's leather bag. 'How lovely,' she said.

'I could only find one cup. We'll have to share.'

'Where did all this come from?'

'The blankets are from my bed, and one of the girls in the kitchen found everything else for me.'

At the look on Lucrezia's face, Jacomo laughed. 'Don't worry – despite all my best efforts, I've only managed to seduce just this one of the ladies of the Castello so far . . .' He reached for the bottle, pulled out the cork and filled the goblet, then handed it to Lucrezia. 'There you are,' he said.

Lucrezia felt the dryness of the wine suck against the back of her teeth. 'Thank you,' she said.

'You're in your night clothes,' Jacomo said. He took the glass from her and drank.

'Yes.' She hesitated, hoping he would not think her foolish. 'I – I thought I might be able to pretend to be sleepwalking if anyone were to find me on my way here or going back to my rooms.'

Jacomo laughed again. 'Sleepwalking all the way to the top of the Torre San Paolo? Come here!' He put the goblet down behind him, and placed the bottle and basket next to it. Shrugging off his doublet, he rolled it into a bundle and laid it at one end of the blankets, as a pillow. He began to kiss Lucrezia again, saying between kisses, 'A sensible thought . . . very sensible . . . to say nothing of the fact . . . that . . . night clothes are considerably easier . . . to take off . . .'

310

Aware this that was the other – predominant – reason she had chosen to wear them, Lucrezia's face glowed warm.

Lucrezia opened her eyes. She must, she realised, have fallen asleep, despite the discomfort of the inhospitable tower room. For a brief, sleep-sodden instant, she was bewildered to find she could not move, and then she realized that Jacomo had curled himself up behind her: his body was pressed against her back, and his legs were crooked up under her own. A sleep-heavy arm was draped across both of hers, pressing them to her chest; she could feel his breath on her neck through her hair.

The candles had burned out and the silent room was in near darkness, lit only by the soft grey light of the moon. Lucrezia lay still for a moment, luxuriating in her lover's embrace. Now she was awake, though, the wooden floor felt horribly hard; the blankets did little to cushion the uneven boards, and her shoulder and hip felt bruised and stiff. As she did not want to wake Jacomo, she tried to shift as surreptitiously as she could. Her efforts were in vain: almost at once a drowsy voice murmured, 'Stop wriggling – I was asleep . . .'

Lucrezia rolled over within Jacomo's encircling arm and his eyes opened – a gleam of moonlight reflected in the whites. He smiled, held her more tightly and kissed her mouth.

'Mmm . . .' Lucrezia said, detaching herself from the kiss. 'I'm hungry now. Can we eat?'

Jacomo sat up and reached for his leather bag, pulling from it a rather battered tinderbox. He opened this, and picked out a few scraps of baked linen, which he laid in the lid; then he sliced at the little flint with the steel. A sputter of sparks showered red in the darkness; he bent over it and blew gently; the linen smouldered, glowed and ignited. He added a few wisps of feathered wood-shavings picked from the box, then, still blowing, felt behind him for a candle. He lit this and sat up, and the tower room walls wobbled in the yellow flame-light. Taking up another two candles and lighting them from the first flame, Jacomo dripped a little wax onto the floor and set them all upright.

Lucrezia was wrapping one of the blankets around her bare shoulders. The candlelight threw her face and the fuzz of her tangled hair into deep-shadowed relief and the folds of the blanket stood out like thick, black brushstrokes. Jacomo pictured the image as a *chiaroscuro* woodcut, and wished he had thought to bring charcoal and paper with him this time. 'Hungry now, are you?' he said, smiling at her. 'Well . . . there's some bread.' He held up a round flat loaf. 'Grapes. A couple of peaches. And a piece of cheese.' Picking each item out of the basket as he spoke, he laid everything on the blanket between them.

'Can you tear me off a piece of bread?' Lucrezia said.

Jacomo tore the loaf in two and held out half. A small hand appeared from within the blanket and took it from him.

'Are you cold?'

She shook her head, her mouth now too full to answer. Reaching out again, she put down the rest of the bread and picked up a peach. For a few moments, neither spoke. They ate and drank, eyes fixed upon each other rather than upon their food. Jacomo remembered giving Lucrezia his bread that day in the North Hall – *What about you, Signora? Are you hungry?* – remembered the unprecedented, unexpected longing that had filled him as they had watched each across the gallery, and his growing certainty that his feelings were reciprocated.

He picked a grape from the bunch and held it to Lucrezia's mouth. She took it from him, lipping the tips of his fingers. He offered her another, and this one she held between her teeth. She leaned in towards him, bringing her face close to his; as they touched, she bit through the skin and pushed the grape into his mouth with her tongue. For a second they both tasted the same sweet-sharp juice, and it seemed to Jacomo that this was as intimate as any more obvious moment of their couplings had been so far.

A candle guttered. He looked up at the window. It was noticeably lighter. 'Nearly dawn,' he said. 'We should go.'

'Not yet.'

'The portrait will be finished a week tomorrow. We'll leave the next day. It's so soon. We can't afford to risk discovery now.'

'You're right, but surely—'

'We have to go,' Jacomo said, moving forward onto hands and knees. Lucrezia was still huddled in her blanket: this he now unwrapped. Holding her bare shoulders, he laid her back down and bent over her, elbows splayed wide. She squirmed and gasped, laughing as he ran the tip of his tongue from below her navel, up between her breasts, under her chin and round onto her mouth. One more swift kiss and then he was on his feet, scrambling into his clothes.

'That's all – come on! Get dressed!'

Lucrezia crawled across the blankets to retrieve her shift, which she pulled on over her head. She picked up the wrap and draped it around her shoulders as Jacomo put the remains of the food back into the basket and drained the last of the wine straight from the bottle. This he also put into the basket. He shook out and folded the blankets, then, pinching out the candles, he threw them into the basket, which he tucked into a dark corner. 'I'll fetch it all later,' he said, seeing Lucrezia's quizzical look.

They went back down the many steps, slowly this time, hand in hand near the outer wall of the tower where the treads were widest. Jacomo carried his blankets under his free arm. 'It's only a few days,' he said, as they reached the bottom. 'Even if we can't see each other properly until the day we leave, it's not long.'

'No,' Lucrezia said. 'Just as long as nothing happens in the intervening time.'

30

Lucrezia felt stiff, tired and faintly ridiculous. It was off-putting being scrutinized so intently by Fra Pandolf, who squinted as he stared at her, and she was also struggling to ignore Jacomo, who was drawing with a familiar frown of intense concentration.

She had found it most distracting over the previous two days – and it was no better today – to see at such close quarters the man she had come to love so much and not to be allowed to show any of her feelings in her face. It was all conspiring to bubble laughter up through her, like boiling water in a tightly lidded pan. She would not, she thought, have been surprised if wisps of steam had begun escaping from her ears.

At the first sitting, before the reverend brother had arrived, Jacomo had described to her more carefully his plan to paint her as Persephone. She had been bewildered.

'But – but because Persephone eats six of the seeds of the pomegranate, Dis says she has to stay with him for half of each year in the Underworld. In Hades. Oh, Jacomo, I don't know whether—'

He had kissed her, and explained that although he intended to paint her as Persephone, there would be one big difference: she would, he said, be holding the pomegranate in one hand, and the other would be open, palm up and empty. The twelve pomegranate seeds he would paint where they had fallen, lying uneaten on the ground.

'This time,' he had said, 'the painting will show us that Persephone has *not* succumbed to temptation; she'll be able to escape the King of the Underworld and leave Hades intact and safe.'

The symbolism was perhaps a little unsubtle, Jacomo had admitted, but he had said that he was pleased with the idea.

Alfonso went straight up to the landing as soon as he arrived back from Bologna. After the unexpected changes to the design of the great fresco, he was taking no chances with this portrait. If there were any elements of which he disapproved, he wanted to ensure they were changed well before it was too late.

The friar and his assistant were drawing busily – Pandolf had seated himself surprisingly close to where Lucrezia stood. She was undeniably lovely, he thought, in that dress, the deep red one with the gold, which he had given her himself, last Christmas. He was pleased to see her in it: he had thought she did not care for it. He had seldom seen her wear it.

These few days away from her had calmed him, he realised, and, somewhat to his surprise, he found himself able to look at her now without the disquiet of the previous weeks.

Neither of the artists nor Lucrezia appeared to have noticed his arrival, and for some moments Alfonso stood silently in the shadows watching the artists at work. From where he stood, he could see Pandolf's paper. He was, it appeared, making studies of

Lucrezia's hands, though he did not appear to have drawn much, which surprised Alfonso: the painting itself was progressing fast. On the wall behind Lucrezia, the cartoon of the whole design had been drawn across the plaster surface; the painted head and upper body were already complete. The depth and passion in her face were striking, he thought. It was going to be a most beautiful piece.

He wondered why Pandolf had asked Lucrezia to hold a pomegranate. There was little doubt that the colours of the exposed seeds were most attractive, set against the crimson of her dress, though the symbolism of the fruit escaped him. He determined to ask the friar after the sitting had finished.

Fra Pandolf seemed to have lost the rhythm of his drawing. He fiddled with his drawing implements, dropped something, bent with difficulty and picked it from the floor. For a moment, Lucrezia wondered what was wrong with him, and then she saw Alfonso at the far end of the landing. He was still in his riding clothes, his hair dishevelled by the wind. She caught his eye but, in a pretence that she had to sustain her serene expression for the portrait, did not respond to him.

Fra Pandolf was frowning now, obviously trying to regain his concentration, she thought, though the fleeting glances he was giving behind him gave away the unease he clearly felt at the presence of his patron. Suddenly, he got to his feet, drawing board clutched in his thick fingers, and stepped towards her, smiling artificially and saying almost to himself, as he moved the tasselled edge of her wrap away from her right hand, 'Your mantle laps over your wrist too much, my lady. It has slipped down since I began . . .'

Lucrezia tried to catch his eye, hoping to put him more at his ease, for his anxiety was unsettling, but he would not look directly at her. Within moments, he was back in his seat, twitching the folds of his brown habit out of the way of his drawing and adjusting the white, knotted cord that hung at his waist, freeing it from where it had caught on the leg of the chair.

It was then that Lucrezia unexpectedly met Jacomo's eye.

She had been trying to avoid doing so, in fear that she would somehow betray their intimacy. He was now leaning back in his chair, flexing cramped fingers and brushing a lock of hair out of his eyes. Seeing Lucrezia watching him, the crescent-creases deepened in his cheeks; the corners of his mouth lifted in a smile. His eyes danced mischievously and then, suddenly, he ran the tip of his tongue across his top lip. Lucrezia was instantly filled with a melting rush of longing; she thought of his parting gesture in the room at the top of the tower, and a traitorous flush burned its way across her cheeks.

In stunned disbelief, Alfonso saw the colour rise in Lucrezia's face. He had, he thought in fury, returned from Bologna just in time. He had thought himself able to look at his wife without disquiet? A foolish misapprehension. A cataract roar began in his ears, colour seemed to fade from the scene in front of him and a red mist threatened to engulf him where he stood. It was unaccountable. Fra Pandolf had left his seat, crossing to rearrange a fold of Lucrezia's mantle, lingering just a little too long, Alfonso thought, with his hand upon hers. He had watched the friar return to his seat, looking distinctly awkward. He had listened to the man's muttered comments about her mantle and had seen Lucrezia's wide-eyed gaze follow him as he walked back to his place. He had watched Pandolf pick up his charcoal and begin once again to draw. And, in utter disbelief, he had seen Lucrezia – her gaze still in the friar's direction – flushing vividly and quite obviously suppressing a smile.

She had told them! She must have told them! A ribbon of ice twisted through his guts. They must all now be exquisitely aware that the future of the entire nine-hundred-year-old duchy was to be determined solely by a shameful lack of rigidity in his prick.

Perhaps the whole castle knew it.

His humiliation was absolute.

But even as the thought scoured through him, he saw again the spot of colour in Lucrezia's cheeks and was almost felled where he stood by a drench of desire so strong it all but paralysed him.

She sensed his gaze. He saw her eyes widen with – was it fear? Was it indifference? Whatever it was, the look she gave him unequivocally extinguished the desire that had threatened to engulf him; left in its sizzling remains were great jagged lumps of a screaming anger Alfonso could feel was fast becoming more powerful than he was. Closing his eyes tightly for a moment, he stood still, feeling giddy.

His head cleared. With icy clarity he knew what he would do. She had to be silenced. Immediately. It was obvious now. Whether or not she had told the painters – and he felt quite certain that she had – it was imperative to ensure that she tell no one else. He had been given the key – and the moment had arrived to use it. Turning on his heel, he hurried down the steps and out of the main door, Folletto at his heels.

Jacomo felt a cold thrill of shock as the duke strode away. By that one thoughtless gesture, he might have undone them both. His heart raced with fear, and he could see from Lucrezia's face, suddenly white, that she, too, was afraid.

31

Francesca and the girls started as a great pounding shook the front door. Beata and Isabella stood behind the table and held hands as Francesca went to open it.

Alfonso's face was tight and closed. Francesca was shocked to see him – he rarely came to the house. She could not read his expression but, after what had happened before, she was not going to risk saying or doing anything unless she had to. She waited for him to speak.

The silence stretched out so far that it began to seem ridiculous. They were all just standing like statues, staring at each other and saying nothing.

Then Alfonso spoke. 'Put on a cloak. I have a job I should like you to undertake.'

He handed her a piece of paper, folded and sealed. 'Take this to Signor Carolei, the apothecary in the Via Fondobanchetto. Tell him that the substance I require is to be made up as quickly as he can provide it, but do not tell him who sent you. Bring the letter back with you. Whatever you do, don't leave it with him.'

Francesca frowned. 'I will willingly run an errand for you, Alfonso, you know that, but I don't understand why one of your servants cannot—'

'This is not a job I wish to delegate to anyone other than you, Francesca. I will wait for you here.'

'In my house?' Francesca said, surprised.

'It seems preferable to being left in the street,' Alfonso said, with a faint smile. Francesca saw that his eyes were glittering strangely and felt distinctly uneasy.

'I want,' he said, 'to hear the results of your errand straight away.'

'We will be as quick as we can.'

The girls flattened themselves against the wall as they and their mother left the house. Francesca could see they were afraid of the great black dog, which, some inches taller than they were, must, she thought, have seemed a truly formidable monster to them. As they walked away, she turned back, but Alfonso and the wolfhound had already entered the house and the door was closed.

Francesca and the two girls hurried up the street. 'Would you rather go to Catelina's?' she asked them. They nodded. Francesca stopped outside Giorgio's house and knocked on the door.

Some seconds before Catelina appeared, they heard the baby crying.

She opened the door with the child in her arms. It was screaming, red-faced and sweaty, its tiny hands clenched into angry fists. Catelina's exhausted face lifted into an attempt at a smile when she saw her visitors. 'I'm sorry,' she said. 'As you can see, he's a little fractious. Did you want anything?'

'No,' said Francesca, seeing that her request would be unwelcome. 'I was going to ask if I could leave the girls here for an hour, but I can see that . . .' She tailed off.

'Oh, Francesca, I'm sorry—' Catelina said, swaying from side to side in an attempt to soothe the furious baby, '—but . . . oh, God, that poor girl's so sick. It's getting worse. Worse every day. I hope I'm wrong, but I think it's childbed fever.'

'What about the baby?'

'He's not ill, just hungry. That poor little thing's far too sick to feed him. Giorgio's gone searching for a wet-nurse.'

'I'm so sorry. I'm . . . on an errand to an apothecary. I'll ask him if he has anything he can give me that might help her.'

'Thank you. Perhaps he'd come here and see her? We've tried everything, and nothing's working.'

'I'll see what he says,' she said, looking down at the girls, who were both staring huge-eyed at the howling baby.

It took Francesca and the twins a matter of minutes to reach the Via Fondobanchetto: a narrow, dirty street with a scummy ribbon of dank water trickling along its centre, and Francesca found the apothecary's house with little difficulty.

Signor Carolei himself opened the door when she knocked. He was of middling height and softly plump. His skin seemed unnaturally pale – like uncooked pastry – and his bulging eyes were the almost hueless colour of old dust. These eyes regarded Francesca and her children coldly for some moments before the apothecary either moved or spoke.

'Yes?' It was not much more than a whisper. The end of the word stretched into a hiss.

Although the apothecary's substantial bulk all but blocked the doorway, Francesca could see past him into a cramped chamber filled with boxes, crates, jars and bundles; they were stacked in neat piles that reached virtually up to the low, beamed ceiling and only a small narrow space was left clear, leading to a staircase that descended steeply out of sight.

'I have a letter for you,' Francesca said. 'I have been told to let you read it and obtain a response, but to keep the paper myself and return it to its author. He says he wants the substance made up as quickly as you can manage it.'

Signor Carolei nodded and took the letter. He jerked his head to indicate that Francesca and the girls should follow him and led the way across the cramped room towards the stairs, reading as he walked.

His windowless workroom was underground, lit with torches that burned in brackets. It was a spacious chamber: large and low, smelling of an acrid mixture of spices, rotten eggs and a sweet metallic tang, like the smell of blood. A heavy table stood in the centre. Made of a coarse-grained wood, it was pitted and cross-hatched with knife-cuts like a butcher's chopping block, and a variety of different coloured stains spattered its surface. Bunches of leaves of many shapes and textures lay upon it, beside a number of jars of varying sizes. Some were glass and the contents could be seen through the sides – yellow, green, white and a deep brick red – and others were of fired earthenware. The walls were lined with shelves containing dozens – perhaps hundreds – of similar jars. A delicate set of brass scales stood to one side on the table, gleaming in the torchlight. One of its small, flat pans contained a heap of white powder, which had unbalanced the scales so that one side hung lower than the other; the graded weights the apothecary would use to measure his ingredients lay scattered around beneath the mechanism. Francesca presumed it to have been the act of weighing that she had interrupted when she had knocked at the door.

It was hot and airless and she shuddered at the thought of spending long hours in a room like this, away from the light; now she understood Signor Carolei's pallor. Beata and Isabella stood on either side of her, their fingers gripping her skirt. They were still and silent, and Francesca knew they were afraid.

The apothecary read Alfonso's letter again. 'Tell him yes. Tell him it will be ready for collection tomorrow night after sunset. I can see that he already understands the need for . . . discretion. And in answer to the last question in the letter – tell him it works almost instantly. In little more than . . . moments.' The bulging eyes widened as he spoke this last word, and he held out the note, slightly creased now and torn where the seal had been broken.

'Thank you, Signore,' Francesca said, taking it from him. Her fingers touched his hand. His flesh was chill and pale, damp with cold sweat, and she recoiled as though the touch had burned her.

'Are we going home now?' Isabella asked, as they emerged into the street, all three blinking in the brightness. Francesca hardly heard her; she was struggling to control a cold, swelling feeling of panic. Flapping open Alfonso's note, she read it and, with a sickening rush of comprehension, understood all too clearly the import of her 'commission'. Alfonso had had good reason not to entrust it to a servant. He was planning to end a life. And, though he did not identify his intended victim in these lines she read here, Francesca was in no doubt of her identity. Perhaps it was the mad glitter she had seen in Alfonso's eyes as he had handed her the letter – something she had only seen before on the occasions he had spoken to her of his tearing unhappiness with his wife. As she stood in the street outside the apothecary's, she pictured the freckled girl with the sweet smile, sitting so uncertainly on the bay pony. 'Oh, dear God, I won't let him do this,' she said. 'I can't. I have to get word to her.'

'Who, Mamma?'

Francesca was startled to discover that she had spoken aloud, and that the twins had heard her. She answered honestly, but briefly. 'A lady, at the Castello Estense. The kind lady who gave you the ribbons. But I don't know how best to reach her.'

She was so frightened, and so bound up in the horror of Alfonso's intrigue, that she did not hear Beata say, 'Giorgio works at the Castello.'

When she did not respond, Beata said, 'Mamma – he does . . .'

'What? Who are you talking about?'

'Big Giorgio who lives next door. He works with the horses at the Castello. He told me.'

Giorgio. Catelina. That baby. Oh, God, she had completely forgotten about them . . .

She said, 'Giorgio works at the Castello?'

'Yes. And Catelina said she used to work there too. She worked for a lady, she said, but not any more.'

Francesca stopped mid-stride, startling the children. She said, 'When the man who is waiting in our rooms has gone, I want you to stay quietly in the house whilst I go to Catelina. You are not to say anything to the man about this. It's very important. Do you understand?'

They both nodded.

Some moments later, they arrived home and Francesca hesitated on her doorstep, one hand on the wall beside the door, thinking fast.

Alfonso stood immobile as Francesca held out his letter and said, 'It will be ready tomorrow night after sunset. He says he is sure you understand the need for discretion. He says it . . . works in moments.'

Her voice was expressionless, but she was trembling, and Alfonso knew she understood what lay behind the commission she had just undertaken.

'I will collect it for you,' she said. He watched as his beautiful whore seemed to struggle with herself – it took her some seconds to utter the words she then dropped into the silence like pebbles into a well. 'And shall I . . . shall I have you back again . . . as you were, when this is . . . over?'

Unable to speak, Alfonso let all the air out of his lungs in a long, shivering sigh. He nodded. 'I shall spend the night at the *villetta* after . . . after it is over,' he managed to say. His voice sounded hollow and distant, as though he was hearing it from the far end of a tunnel. 'Perhaps you would care to accompany me. I do not plan to return until later the following day.'

Without replying, Francesca nodded slowly.

'Be then outside the main drawbridge from midnight tomorrow, Francesca.'

She crossed the room to where he stood. Tilting her head sideways, she kissed his mouth languorously, sliding her tongue over and around his own. He put his arms around her, but she drew back. Her mouth was wet.

'No,' she said. 'Not with the girls here. You will have to wait until tomorrow night.'

And saying nothing more, she turned from him and padded up the stairs.

Many years before, a friend who had travelled through the lands of the Bedouin had described to Alfonso the night he had once spent in a sandstorm. His vivid description of the howling inexorability of the sand, the demonic wailing of the wind and the fierce, stinging pain of the grains on skin and in eyes seemed to Alfonso at that moment to be the only thing that might come close to describing the turmoil that was fast pushing him to the edge of the precipice. Terror at what he had just set in motion, an aching desire for the voluptuous calm of that shadowed chamber in his mind, a new stab of longing for his whore, and a horrible, dragging weariness at the shaming humiliations of his blighted marriage. He screwed up his eyes and gripped his skull with his fingers, the heels of his hands pressing hard into his eye-sockets as it all raged through his head.

Then it quieted and he saw an exquisite image of the creature he had brought from Cafaggiolo. He still wanted her more than he had ever wanted anything – he had ached with the wanting of her ever since the ignominious failure of the wedding night. She had to be destroyed – he had made the decision. If the duchy were to survive, he had no choice. But he had, too, to get her out of his head. Whatever Lucrezia was, whatever she had done, whatever danger she represented, he knew that if he were ever – ever – to be able fully to exorcize her from his mind, it was imperative that he possess the image completely – just once – before he destroyed it. Now, with the key gripped tightly in his hand, he thought he knew – at last – how he could achieve that possession.

Alfonso crushed his letter into a ball in his fist and threw it into the fireplace. A fat little flame licked around the ball and then ignited it. The paper shifted as it blackened, burned and disintegrated.

32

'Oh, thank goodness you're here!' Catelina stood back and Francesca came inside. Catelina saw her glance up the stairs. 'Giorgio couldn't find a wet-nurse,' she said. 'He's had to go back up to the castle, and I've just given the baby some goat's milk. First time he's stopped crying in hours, poor little thing.' She paused. 'Did the apothecary say he would come?'

Now she looked properly at Francesca and was taken aback by her expression. 'What? What is it? What's wrong, Francesca? What did he say?'

Francesca hesitated. 'I'm so sorry, I didn't ask him because . . . because . . .'

'Please – what is it?'

'The girls . . . they said you used to work up at the Castello . . .'

Catelina frowned at her. 'Does it matter if I did?'

'No, of course not, but— oh, God, I have to know – is it true that you used to work for the duchess?'

'Why do you ask?'

Francesca stared at her for several long seconds before she began to speak. Catelina listened, and every word she heard sent icy threads of terror across her scalp. 'I don't understand,' she said. 'Why you? Why would the Signore ask *you* to deliver his message for him? How does he know you so well, as to trust you with . . . ?'

Francesca flushed.

'Exactly who are you?' Catelina said slowly, realising that she had never thought to wonder before now.

'Isn't it obvious?'

Catelina thought of the twins, and their vague familiarity made sudden sense. 'You . . . and him?'

Francesca nodded.

'Since when?'

'Nearly nine years.'

'And those little girls, are they . . . ?'

Another nod.

'Oh, dear God, my poor lady. But . . .' Catelina was suddenly angry. 'But I don't understand. If you and he have . . . well, why are you telling me this? Why do you care? Surely your loyalties lie with him. What's she to you?'

'Why do I care?' Francesca's voice cracked. 'Oh, God, if you had seen him contemplate this *loathsome* thing with such utter heart-lessness – you wouldn't even think to ask *why*!' She paused, and then said, 'He is no longer the man I have known for so long. I don't know what has happened, but . . . I'm afraid he is losing his reason.'

Catelina saw that there were tears in her eyes, and she believed her.

Francesca said, 'The duchess has to be warned. I cannot go to the Castello myself, but I understand that your Giorgio works there and . . .'

It was obvious. 'Yes. We must tell him. He can get word to Jacomo. Jacomo will get her out.'

There was a sudden keening wail from the baby upstairs.

Francesca glanced up the staircase. 'You need to stay here. The twins can deliver a message. Once they've gone, I'll go and find what help I can for that baby. Do you have paper and a pen?'

'Yes, but you'll have to write the note. I'm afraid I don't know how.'

Giorgio saw the neighbour's two children waving to him from the gateway. He smiled and waved back. One of them flapped a hand, beckoning him over, and Giorgio strode across the yard towards them.

'What a surprise to see you two here,' he said, squatting on his heels in front of them.

'We have a note for you.'

One of the two wriggled a hand inside the neck of her bodice and pulled out a now crumpled piece of paper. She handed it to Giorgio. He took it from her, smiling, and read it, expecting something inconsequential, but what he saw smothered his smile and sent a cold drench of shock down his spine. He felt suddenly nauseous.

'Thank you, girls,' he said, trying not to let his anxiety show. 'Now you'd best get off home quickly. Tell Catelina and your mamma that – that I'll do everything I can. Will you do that?'

They nodded and ran back towards the town, hand in hand once more, glancing over their shoulders and waving at Giorgio as they went.

Giovanni glanced up from where he had been examining Brezza's newly shoeless hoof, and watched the two pretty little girls leave the stableyard. Giorgio's face was blank – almost as though someone had just hit him. Giovanni patted his mare, and walked across the yard. 'What is it, *amico*?'

'I have to go . . . I must find . . .' Giorgio seemed quite distracted and unaware of what he was saying or doing. Whatever had been in that note had shocked him, Giovanni thought, now more alarmed than curious. 'What's happened, Giorgio?' he said.

Giorgio was now visibly shaking. 'Signore, I have to tell you – she's your cousin.' Suddenly Giovanni was no longer alarmed – he was frightened. 'What's wrong? Quick – tell me!' His heart was banging as he looked at Giorgio's white, drawn face. He took the note Giorgio held out to him, and read it. 'Oh, God!' he said. 'I must get her out – now.'

'No. You can't. First of all, she's out with the riding master – I harnessed the horses not an hour since, and I don't know where they went. The Signore said he would meet her back here in an hour or two – and if he suspects that we know anything about *this*, I believe he'll stop at nothing to silence us all.'

A long, loud pause.

'We have to tell Jacomo,' Giovanni said, more to himself than to Giorgio. 'No time to explain, but just believe me, he needs to know.'

'I'll go back to our house,' Giorgio said, and he told Giovanni how to find it. 'Bring this Jacomo there now.'

Giovanni made his way into the Castello, trying not to look as though he was hurrying. He found Jacomo on the landing above the entrance hall, working alone on the portrait. Giovanni only vaguely registered what an astounding likeness he had created in so short a time – the head and much of the body were already complete, and he was crouched in front of the second hand. The first, clutching a partly peeled pomegranate, was also finished.

Jacomo sensed his presence and turned, peering up at him quizzically from where he was half-kneeling on the floor.

'Can I talk with you – urgently?' Giovanni muttered.

Jacomo stood without a word, put down his brush, and followed him.

Giovanni told him everything.

'I'll go and get her now,' Jacomo said. His face was set and pale but his voice was steady.

'No, you can't. She's not here. She's out riding, and *he'll* be there when they get back, Giorgio says. We wouldn't stand a chance of getting her out undetected. Come with me now to Giorgio's and we can try to work out if there is any way to get her away from here without *Il Duca* knowing you've gone.'

As Jacomo and Giovanni went into the little house, a baby was crying. It was a wire-thin, desolate sound, the only sound in the house; it seemed a noise of utter hopelessness, and panicked, flapping wings began to beat inside Jacomo's head.

He looked around him. Giorgio was standing in the shadows against the far wall, shoulders hunched, arms folded, his face stretched and stiff, one leg twitching. Seated at the small table in the centre of the room were three people Jacomo had never seen before: an astonishingly beautiful woman with a greenish bruise under one eye, and, on either side of her, two identical small girls.

Giorgio stepped away from the wall. 'Signori, this is Signora Felizzi,' he said, indicating the woman at the table. Jacomo and Giovanni inclined their heads towards her. The little girls shuffled closer to their mother.

Catelina appeared on the stairs with the now sleeping baby in the crook of her arm. Behind her, much to Jacomo's surprise, stood an elderly man with an almost hairless head and white-fluff eyebrows: Alessandro Giglio, the apothecary. Catelina was exhausted, Jacomo thought, her face pale and tear-stained. Holding the baby close to her chest, she picked her way down the steep steps with care; Signora Felizzi motioned to her children to stand so that Catelina could sit.

Alessandro followed Catelina, shaking his head sadly. Seating himself on the other empty chair, he ran a gnarled finger over the baby's head.

'Francesca,' Giorgio said, and everyone turned to him. 'Francesca, tell the signori what you told me.'

Jacomo watched the beautiful Signora Felizzi nod at Giorgio, then look from Catelina to him and Giovanni. She hesitated a moment, then said, in a low voice, 'The duke has commissioned the apothecary in the Via Fondobanchetto to produce . . . a substance with which I think he means to . . . to rid himself of a problem he can no longer endure.' She took a long, slow breath. 'I have no proof, but I believe he means to poison the duchess. He has ordered a phial of *La Cantarella*. I am . . . to pick it up for him tomorrow evening after sunset.'

Her words took Jacomo's breath away. She was unearthly, he thought, a beautiful sorceress from the realms of the Styx. He had no idea who she was, or why she should be thus errand-running for the duke, but he could see that she spoke with honesty, and he found himself unable to take his eyes from her face.

Giovanni said, 'But what can we do? How can we stop him? We can't just sit here and let it happen.'

A taut silence stretched across the room.

Nobody spoke.

Then Catelina said, glancing at Alessandro, 'There is something we could do. Signor Giglio suggested it just now. He said it ought to work. Tell them, Signore.'

The old apothecary spoke softly into the silence.

'Dear God – we'll all go to hell!' Giorgio said, his voice cracking.

Catelina hugged the baby closer to her and said, 'But now that the poor creature is dead—'

'Lina – that child has been motherless for less than half an hour. The girl's still warm!'

Catelina said, 'I know it sounds terrible, but it's the only chance we'll have to get my lady out without the Signore knowing she's gone. I think it's the only way.'

Francesca, Jacomo, Giovanni and Alessandro Giglio walked quickly and silently through the streets of Ferrara. At the fork in the road where they were to part, they stopped.

'Jacomo, should I tell Crezzi what's going to happen?' Giovanni asked quietly.

'No. She'd be frightened. If the duke sees her fear, that might alert him to what we're intending to do. If we're to succeed and get her away, he has to believe implicitly that his plan has worked.'

Giovanni swore. He looked, Francesca thought, very young and very scared. 'But what if his plan *does* work?' he said.

'I shall do everything I can to make sure that it does not, Signore,' Alessandro said. 'But I must hurry – there is a great deal to prepare.'

Francesca laid a hand on Giovanni's sleeve. 'We must trust Alessandro. He knows his trade better than anyone. And the duchess is safe enough until tomorrow night, in any case.'

Giovanni nodded and wiped his eyes with the heel of his hand, breathing through an open mouth for a moment, as though he had been running. Then he said, his voice thick with anxiety, 'It just has to bloody work,' and, turning towards the Castello, he broke into a run.

The other three began to walk fast towards the river, Alessandro and Francesca almost trotting to keep up with Jacomo's long strides.

Catelina laid the baby gently upon a lambskin rug in the wooden trunk and tucked a blanket around him. Tightly swaddled now, he slept, his tiny belly at least partially filled with the goat's milk she had so painstakingly fed him with her fingers, drop by drop. She watched him for a moment, painfully moved by his minuteness, and then she sighed and her eyes went to the little figure on the bed. The dead girl was small and pale and insubstantial, and looked unbearably fragile, Catelina thought sadly, like a bruised petal fallen from a flower.

'I'm so sorry, Chiara,' she said, sitting on the edge of the bed and stroking the hair back from the waxy-white face. 'You worked so hard to bring your little boy into the world. It's unfair that this should have happened. I'm so terribly sorry that I couldn't help you properly. I did try. And Signor Giglio tried too. If anyone could have saved you, I think he could. You deserved better than this, though. I'll take care of him, I promise you, as well as I can. I'm going to call him Paolo, because it means "small". He's so tiny . . .'

The baby snuffled and whimpered. Catelina bent across him and rested a hand on his belly. 'I hope you're not too shocked by what we've proposed,' she went on. 'I know it does all sound so very dreadful, but . . . but I think it's the only way to save my lady so – please – forgive us.'

33

Lucrezia had been desperate to find Jacomo when she arrived back at the Castello after her ride, even though she knew it would be foolish to do so, but in the event it proved impossible: Alfonso was in the courtyard waiting to meet them. That in itself was unusual, she thought. He rarely chose to spend time with her during the day. There was something more than this, too: something disconcerting about his manner. He had, she thought, been distant and darkly brooding for weeks, and she had grown used to seeing a look of moody melancholy on his face – but now, she realized, there was a new agitation about him: a vivid, restless energy. He smiled up at her as he raised a hand to help her down from the saddle, though she saw no tenderness in that smile; his grey eyes glittered and behind them lurked what seemed like a hunger, a feverish appetite for – for something she could not fathom.

'Did you enjoy your ride, Lucrezia?'

She forced a smile. 'Yes, thank you, though Signor Bracciante will tell you that I am still far from accomplished as a horse-woman.'

The ever-taciturn riding master said nothing, and Alfonso made no attempt to draw him into the conversation. His gaze was fixed upon Lucrezia. Her stomach lurched at the prospect of a resumption of his attentions. She had hoped, after that terrible night, that she would not have to face another encounter with Alfonso before fleeing with Jacomo and, indeed, had found herself counting the hours – almost the minutes – until she and her painter could leave the Castello. As Tuesday came ever closer, and Alfonso had kept his distance from her, she had until this moment thought she would be lucky. But it seemed that the sight of her today had aroused a memory of that night in Alfonso's mind too: with a sick feeling of inevitability, Lucrezia watched his gaze flick from her eyes to her mouth, from there to her breasts and back up to her face.

'Come, Lucrezia,' Alfonso said then, ignoring Signor Bracciante. 'I have a mind to play a game of *dama*.' He reached for Lucrezia's hand and held it fast, turning and walking back into the Castello by the northern courtyard door at such a pace that Lucrezia found herself almost running to keep up. The black wolfhound paced, click-clawed, some feet behind them. 'We have not played for some time, have we?'

'No,' Lucrezia said.

'Do you know what they are calling it in France, now that the rules have changed?' Alfonso said, looking again at her mouth.

'No.'

'*Jeu Force*. Because now, unlike before, if you *can* take out an opponent, then you *must* do so. Much more exciting, would you not agree?'

'Such a rule certainly doesn't allow much space for compassion,' Lucrezia suggested, and Alfonso laughed.

'In this game there is no place for compassion, Lucrezia.

Ruthless determination to rid oneself of what stands in one's way, and the courage to undertake what others might perceive as reckless moves in the pursuit of ultimate success – that is what will win you the game.'

A door banged open some few yards ahead, and Lucrezia's heart turned over.

It was Jacomo.

He was backing blindly out into the corridor, struggling under the weight of the heavy folding screen he had used to hide the final section of the fresco. Alfonso stopped, unable to continue because Jacomo and his burden were blocking the way. Lucrezia stared at her painter. She had not seen him since the portrait-sitting the day before when Alfonso had stormed away, looking so frighteningly angry. She still had no idea whether or not he had seen Jacomo look at her – but could only presume that he had; she had spent the time since then desperate to find Jacomo, but not daring to draw attention to him.

Now, though, she heard again in her mind the words Alfonso had just uttered, and a truly terrifying thought occurred to her. Had her husband seen the indisputable evidence yesterday, drawn his conclusions and decided to 'take out his opponent'? Was this why he was so strangely agitated and unlike his normal self? Oh, dear God! She wanted to warn Jacomo – felt the words ready to burst from her: *stay with the reverend brother at all times. For God's sake, don't go anywhere alone. He wants to hurt you. Stay away from him*! But here, in Alfonso's presence, she could only stand afraid and say nothing.

She saw that Jacomo's eyes, too, were wide with anxiety. He was deathly pale.

'I – I'm sorry, Signore,' he stammered, struggling to move the screen so that they could pass. 'I'll shift it for you straight away.'

'Oh, for God's sake, boy,' Alfonso snapped, 'just get out of the way!'

Jacomo managed to drag the screen to one side of the passageway and Alfonso strode past him. With tears behind her eyes, Lucrezia snatched a glance at him as she moved on up the corridor, her hand still held fast in Alfonso's. It was unbearable. A howl of longing swelled high in her chest and it was all she could do not to pull her fingers from her husband's grasp and run – back to where Jacomo stood staring after them.

'Was that not Pandolf's young assistant?' Alfonso said irritably, as they walked on.

'I believe so,' Lucrezia said.

'It would appear that that great stain on his face indicates a distinct lack of intelligence – the boy's a veritable idiot.'

Lucrezia said nothing.

'Pandolf says he is a gifted painter – a *gifted painter*? I have to say that I struggle to believe him. It strikes me as extremely unlikely that such an inarticulate peasant could have any high-flown aesthetic sensitivities. No doubt Pandolf exaggerates his minion's skill from some misjudged sense of Franciscan charity.'

Lucrezia's face burned. If this was a genuine opinion then her fears were groundless, Alfonso had seen nothing and had no thoughts of harming Jacomo. But, she thought, what if this was his teasing idea of a way to exact as painful a retribution for this newly discovered infidelity as he could devise? Maybe he wished to belittle Jacomo in front of her, to humiliate her for her – in his opinion – poor choice of lover, before he destroyed him. But before she could think any further upon this conundrum, they arrived at the games room and Alfonso was holding the door open for her. Going in, she saw that he had already set up the *dama*. The little round pieces were in place on the red-and-white chequered board and a chair stood at each side of the table.

Lucrezia looked around the games room, her thoughts in turmoil. Behind the *Dama* game, the *biliardo* table had been left ready for play, with several balls scattered untidily across the cloth surface. Two lutes were propped against one wall, a jumble of tennis racquets lay on the floor beneath the window and, on another, larger, table, lay a number of dice, a chess set and a *ʒara* board. The coloured squares, circles and stars lay heaped in an open, carved ivory box. Upon the walls hung a number of tapestries depicting various sports, while several brightly coloured *commedia dell'arte* masks, beribboned and spangled, grinned from wall brackets – brackets which, Lucrezia thought, just then seemed more like gibbets. In the past, she had enjoyed spending time in this room, but today its vivid cheerfulness seemed wilfully to be mocking her anxiety.

Alfonso spoke into her tumbling thoughts. 'Come, Lucrezia, you play white. I shall play red and start the game. Remember that when I *can* take you out, I shall do so – I shall have no choice.' And, placing his forefinger on one of the circular playing pieces, he slid it forward across the diagonal, from one red square to the next.

'Thank you, Alfonso,' Lucrezia said, some time later, when he had, to his delight and her relief, won the game with some ease. 'You play with more skill than I ever shall.'

'Perhaps,' was his only reply.

'I'm tired now. I should like to return to my chambers,' Lucrezia said.

'Well, then, I shall accompany you. We can dine there, too.'

Alfonso, Lucrezia and the ever-present black ghost made their way across the castle to her apartments.

Why? Lucrezia asked herself. Why? Why? Why? Why, after all these weeks and months of avoiding her presence, did Alfonso now wish to act the devoted husband? Something had changed: she knew it. Something had altered within him and it unnerved her. She felt alone and vulnerable. As they neared her chambers, she reached a decision: she had no idea what lay behind this change in Alfonso's demeanour but, whatever the reason, she decided that she would do whatever it transpired he wanted of her – however much it might distress or disgust her. For, she reasoned, keeping Alfonso happy must surely be the best way of keeping Jacomo safe. She had survived the last ordeal, after all. At most, there could only be a few more days of purgatory. She could endure it.

There was a whining voice inside her head, though, to which she could not bring herself to listen. It bored into her soul, sharp and thin as a wire, goading her to distraction: *you do not think he would carry out such a deed himself, do you? Perhaps*, the voice whispered, *he wants you in your chambers, away from Jacomo, so that some minion can carry out his orders and rid him of his 'opponent' even as you lie in his arms. Perhaps . . . while you submit to Alfonso's attentions, sure that in doing so you are keeping Jacomo safe, elsewhere in the castle—*

'Crezzi!'

A voice broke into Lucrezia's reverie, and she heard running footsteps. Alfonso checked his stride and turned with her. Lucrezia nearly cried with relief to see Giovanni.

He ran up, slowing as he reached her side. 'Signore, forgive me.' He bowed to Alfonso and then turned to Lucrezia. 'Crezzi, I've not seen you since the day before yesterday.'

'No. Where have you been?'

'Readying myself to return to Cafaggiolo, apart from anything. I leave in a few days.'

'Oh, Vanni, I had not realized you were going so soon. You should have come riding with me and Signor Bracciante—'

'Tell me, Signore,' Alfonso interrupted, 'have you enjoyed your stay at the Castello, this time? Were you suitably impressed by the unveiling of our fresco?'

'Indeed, sir, I—'

'And the portrait?'

'Of course, it's not yet finished, Signore, but I promise I will tell my aunt and uncle what an extraordinary likeness of Crezzi Fra Pandolf' – Giovanni flicked a glance at Lucrezia – 'has already produced.'

Alfonso seemed gratified. Staring at Lucrezia, he said, 'You can tell them how fortunate it is that your cousin can be thus . . . immortalized . . . as a permanent decoration within the fabric of the Castello . . .'

Giovanni turned to Lucrezia as Alfonso spoke, and she saw, with surprise, that his eyes were wide and dark, and tiny beads of sweat clung to the line of his upper lip. He seemed profoundly ill at ease.

'Are you . . . are you quite well, Vanni?' Lucrezia asked, reaching for his hand. His palm was cold and damp.

He smiled and nodded, but she was not reassured. His discomposure echoed the forbidding atmosphere that seemed to be hanging over the entire castle that day. Lucrezia began to feel as though an anonymous, menacing being was loose in the building – a savage version of Folletto – padding upon soft paws along the corridors of the Castello, a creature that might confront them at any moment, snarling and ready to strike.

'Would you care to dine with us, Vanni?' Lucrezia asked, as they neared her apartments.

'Oh, I am sure your cousin has many things he should be doing,

Lucrezia. Doubtless he will not wish to waste the short time he has remaining here in Ferrara cooped up in your chambers,' Alfonso said, with unnatural geniality, before Giovanni could answer.

But Giovanni said, 'On the contrary, Signore, I should be delighted to spend as much time as I can with Lucrezia before I have to leave.'

Alfonso still had hold of Lucrezia's hand and she felt his fingers stiffen at Giovanni's words, which, even to her ears, sounded impertinent.

'You misunderstand me, sir. I do not care to have to spell it out so obviously, but since you put me in the position where I am forced to do so, I must explain. I wish to dine alone with my duchess.'

Giovanni flushed. 'Forgive me,' he said – but he said it to Lucrezia, rather than to Alfonso. He sketched a rough bow and strode away.

The light had almost gone, and Lucrezia and Alfonso had finished eating. The candles in the brackets on the walls were alight, and a small fire was burning, casting shivering shadows across the rush-strewn floor.

Lucrezia was beginning to feel sick at the thought of what would soon be expected of her, for Alfonso had made it clear all evening that he quite certainly had something in mind. His gaze, Lucrezia thought, had been searching and hungry since the moment he had helped her from her horse some hours before. A clot of dread sat high in her throat as she waited for him to make his first suggestion. She was astonished, therefore, when he rose from his chair and said, 'You seem tired, Lucrezia. I shall retire to my chambers and let you sleep.' He paused. 'I shall, however, look forward to the morrow.'

Doing no more than running his fingers up the length of one of her arms, and gripping her shoulder for a second, Alfonso left her.

She sat staring into the embers, fear for Jacomo's safety pricking at her painfully, but she dared not leave her room. Sleep seemed impossible, and after having retired to bed, she lay awake for hours, gazing at the sky through her uncurtained window.

She must have slept in the end, although she knew she had seen the beginnings of the dawn. It seemed only moments later that her eyes snapped open, as suddenly as though she had been shaken awake. It was bright outside and the sun was high. Hours must have passed. Any sense of repose vanished and the cold weight of dread pressed back upon her again. She could hardly bear to think about what might have happened while she had been sleeping.

She dragged off her night shift and put on the chemise she had worn the day before. Throwing back the lid of a painted chest so that it banged against the wall, she grabbed from it a blue bodice and skirt. Her fingers were shaking so badly that the skirt almost fell from her grasp twice as she tried to fasten it, but she rough-laced the bodice and pushed her arms into the already fastened sleeves, fighting to get it down over her head with hands that felt like empty gloves.

She heard movement in the next room. There was a knock on the door and one of her waiting-women came in. The girl's eyes widened as she saw her mistress's struggles. 'My lady —?'

'I – I . . . er . . .' Lucrezia could think of nothing to say.

'May I help you, Signora?' the young woman said. She was small and dark, and Lucrezia did not think she had seen the girl before. Since Catelina's departure, her waiting-women had seemed inconsequential and uninteresting, and she rarely spoke to them more than basic civility demanded.

'Thank you,' she said now. 'If you could please help me to fasten this.' She turned her back, presenting the badly laced bodice. With quick, capable fingers, the girl straightened and tightened it; as the bodice pulled snugly around her chest, Lucrezia could feel her heartbeat thudding against it, and wondered if the girl would actually be able to see her body shaking.

Trying to keep her voice calm, she said, 'I have slept longer than I meant to. I shall go up to the roof garden, and enjoy the sunshine.' A trip that would take her past the Entrance Hall.

'Yes, my lady.'

Lucrezia could feel the girl's eyes upon her as she left the apartment. Irritated with herself – why had she felt the need to explain her movements? – she walked as slowly as she could along the corridor, but once round the corner, she broke into a scrambling run. Almost falling, her skirts bunched in her fists, she took the stairs two at a time, skidding as she turned a sharp corner into the long passage. Her shoulder banged against the wall and she stumbled. She forced herself to a walk again and went as quickly as she dared towards where she prayed Jacomo would be at work on the portrait.

The sunlight in the Entrance Hall was dazzling as Lucrezia left the gloom of the passage, and for a second she could see nothing. Then, up on the landing, she saw him. Some feet away from the reverend brother, he was crouching on one knee, brows creased in concentration, one paintbrush in his hand and another between his teeth. Lucrezia let out a strangled sob of relief and stepped back into the shadows. She dared not let Jacomo see her – if he smiled at her now, she was quite certain she would cry.

A few moments in the Roof Garden, she thought, would settle her disquiet to the point where she could return to the Entrance Hall without fear of betraying herself in front of Fra Pandolf.

She had to find a way to speak to Jacomo.

They had to leave the Castello today.

The sun was warm on the red brick as she walked out into the Roof Garden. Crossing the enclosed square, she put her hands on the wall and gazed down at the street below through one of the tiny windows. Tears swelled in the corners of her eyes, and through the glaze of salt water, the people she saw appeared to dip and dance surprisingly merrily as they went their way about their unknown business.

Lucrezia stood thus unmoving, her head on her arm, for several minutes, allowing her racing pulse to settle. Then, breathing in slowly, she turned, determining to return to the Entrance Hall and to Jacomo. She had not taken more than a step, however, when she heard feet on the stairs.

Alfonso strode into the sunshine, a hand held up to shade his eyes.

Lucrezia felt a sob puckering in her throat.

'Good!' Alfonso said. 'You are here. Your waiting-woman said you would be. You confessed to a lack of skill in the saddle yesterday, Lucrezia. I shall take you riding this morning.'

He did not appear to be offering her any choice in the matter, and had apparently observed neither her tears nor her agitation. She looked back at him, but said nothing.

Alfonso took her hand and strode back towards the stairs. 'You will need to change your clothes. We can go to your chambers now, and you can ready yourself for riding. Perhaps you should eat before you go, too – we might be some time.'

They returned to Lucrezia's apartment without passing the Entrance Hall.

Lucrezia somehow endured the day. By sunset she was exhausted. Alfonso had stayed at her side since the morning, still strangely energetic and vivid. He seemed, Lucrezia thought, quite consumed with a twitching, febrile vivacity, entirely unlike his usual dignified demeanour.

The hours had passed in a blur of anxiety and tiredness. Lack of sleep had made Lucrezia's eyes gritty and she had no appetite for the meals Alfonso had had prepared for the two of them. She still did not understand. Never in the two years of their marriage had he been solicitous like this – never had he seemed to take such an interest in her everyday well-being. His anger of two days previously seemed to have evaporated entirely. Lucrezia supposed that an onlooker might have said that her husband was behaving impeccably, but she still felt profoundly uneasy.

The day drew to a close; daylight began to drop and all over the Castello candles and torches were lit as the sun set.

'I have a brief visit to make, Lucrezia,' Alfonso said, not long after the great red ball had sunk below the city's roofscape. 'I shall return a little later.'

Lucrezia was unable to speak for the wild thudding of her heart in her throat as Alfonso picked up a candle and left the room. Black fears for Jacomo's safety screeched in her head, though she dared not set out to warn him, not knowing how long Alfonso would be away, terrified that were she wrong in her surmise, she might unwittingly draw his attention to her lover and cause Jacomo's destruction by the very act of trying to keep him safe.

She paced her rooms, walking between bedchamber and studio for the best part of an hour, breathing in jerky, agitated gasps and twining her fingers around each other as though she meant to twist them right off. Despite her terror, though, fatigue at last overwhelmed her, and she decided to undress. Preferring not to call for one of her ladies, she unfastened and removed her jewellery, then managed to unlace her bodice. She eased it off, unhooked her skirt and stepped out of its heavy folds. Then she pulled off her chemise, dragged her night shift over her head, and with trembling fingers, undid the plaits in her hair and shook it loose.

Feeling sick, she sat on the end of her bed, but stood up again almost immediately, hearing footsteps and the clicking of claws.

The door opened with a soft scrape as it caught against the floor and Alfonso appeared.

He was carrying a bottle of wine and two silver cups.

34

The sounds of the street outside pushed their way into the downstairs room as Catelina shifted the baby into the crook of her elbow, opened the front door and stood back. Giorgio hitched Chiara's body more comfortably into his arms. Wrapped in a blanket, she was peaceful and pale, and her head lay on his broad shoulder as though she slept.

'Can you really carry her all that way, Giorgio?'

'She weighs almost nothing, poor little thing.'

'Jacomo and Giovanni will meet you at the back drawbridge, they said.'

Francesca stood up. 'I'll walk with you, Giorgio,' she said. The twins were sitting on stools by the fire, staring at Giorgio and his burden with round-eyed fascination. Between them lay a nanny goat, its legs neatly curled under it, eyes closed against the heat of the embers. 'Bella, Beata, listen,' Francesca said. 'You stay here with Catelina and the baby. I may not be able to come back here until the morning.'

The children nodded.

'Thank you,' Francesca said to Catelina. 'I'll be back as soon as I can.'

Catelina brushed the top of the baby's head with her lips and nodded.

Despite Giorgio's apprehensions, no one paid any attention to the little group as they made their way up towards the Castello. He felt the chill weight of the dead girl in his arms, and shivered at the thought of what lay ahead.

'*Santo cielo* – I cannot believe I am doing this,' he said, more to himself than to Francesca.

Francesca took his arm, and Giorgio looked down at her. 'She's heavier than I expected,' he said, resettling Chiara's body higher up his chest.

'Can you manage?'

'We're nearly there.'

They rounded the front of the cathedral and saw the square bulk of the Castello, black against the darkening sky.

Francesca pointed. 'There they are.'

Two figures moved out of a blot of shadow and began to walk towards them.

35

When Alfonso entered her bedchamber, Lucrezia was clad in her night shift, her hair loose about her shoulders. She was wide-eyed and wary as he approached, but perhaps, he thought, their last nocturnal tryst rendered that particular response somewhat predictable.

He was surprised to find himself quite calm as he contemplated her nervous anxiety, as from the moment he had taken the decision to end the agony of this benighted marriage, he had felt more vividly alive and energetic than at any other time since Lucrezia's arrival at the Castello. Restless and fretful throughout both days, he had been astonished to find himself taking what seemed, after all that had gone before, a perverse enjoyment in his wife's company. She was, conversely, subdued and taciturn, though for some reason this quietude only served to excite his new volatility. Alfonso found, however, that now that the moment had come – now that he actually, physically held in his hands the means to a complete and irrevocable conclusion – his inner tumult was assuaged. He faced his duchess with an unprecedented sense of serenity.

He put the bottle and the cups on the table next to the bed, then leaned against the carved bedpost, watching Lucrezia all the while. She made no comment, but held his gaze.

'I thought we might make another attempt at conceiving the heir to the duchy, Lucrezia,' he said.

Her face twitched, but she still said nothing.

'I had thought about trying again last night.' This was a lie: Alfonso was well aware that he had had absolutely no intention of laying even a finger on Lucrezia until tonight. 'But I could see that you were tired, and I had no wish to distress you. It occurred to me,' he added, 'that having had – I hope – a restful night's sleep, you might be able to approach the prospect with a little more enthusiasm than you did before. Perhaps a fine wine might render the attempt more palatable to you this time.'

Alfonso poured wine into each of the two cups; a prickle of anticipation shivered across his scalp as he saw the spoonful of golden liquid already in the bottom of one of the two. Having filled it, he handed that cup to Lucrezia, who took it from him, frowning.

'I do not normally take wine at this hour, Alfonso,' she said.

Blood pulsed loud in his ears. If she refused . . . He did not care to coerce, he thought – it was offensive to his sense of dignity. She had to choose to drink.

'Perhaps the novelty will prove entertaining,' he said.

Lucrezia did not look convinced, but nonetheless raised the cup to her lips and sipped. Alfonso waited, drinking from his own goblet, and Lucrezia took another mouthful.

There was, he realized, one more element needed to complete the scene. As Lucrezia raised her cup again, he reached for the rosewood box on the bedside table and brought out the string of garnets. She made no comment but gave a soft sigh, and Alfonso saw her shoulders droop, as though in resignation. He handed her the Red Rope. She lifted the stones and wound them around her throat herself, sliding the string each time under the bulk of her hair. Alfonso watched her breasts move beneath the loose shift as her hands worked behind her head; her nipples showed dark against the thin fabric.

He pictured the key that Panizato had unknowingly given him out on the heath – pictured it so clearly that he could almost feel its cold iron in his hand. It turned in the lock and the door to the final shadowed room clicked open. On the far wall in the final room was the mirror. The cracks, distortions and taints on the glass, which had distorted the reflection for so long, were beginning to clear and the perfect image, for which Alfonso knew he still hungered, was re-emerging.

He sat on the bed near Lucrezia and put his own cup on the table. He leaned towards her, hoping this time, rather than dreading, that her desire to repulse him would encourage her to drink. And, indeed, she drew back from him and said, 'In a moment, Alfonso. I should like a little more wine first. It was a sensible idea of yours to bring it.'

Her voice sounded stilted and unnatural, though perhaps, Alfonso surmised, this was already due to the effects of Signor Carolei's concoction. Lucrezia drank deeply from her cup and replaced it, almost empty now, upon the table.

Alfonso found then that he could not look at her. He got up and walked from the bedside to the window. The moon was a few days from the full and seemed to him somehow misshapen and imperfect, flattened along its lower edge. A few hours before, he had seen it hanging near the horizon: huge, flat and a pale pinkish gold. Now risen, shrunk and silvered, it lit the city streets with a brightness not far from that of day, and, as he looked down, he saw that it was reflected too in the oily blackness of the moat. He stared at the wobbling silver disc in the water for several moments until he was startled by a soft 'Oh!' and a whimper of distress from behind him. He could not turn around, but his fingers gripped the window-sill and he closed his eyes, wishing he could as easily stopper his ears.

When at last he found the courage to turn into the room and look at the duchess, she was sprawled untidily across the bed. Her shift had rucked high, exposing her legs and the jut of her hipbone. Her face was pale, the freckles dark below the tangled mass of her hair, and her mouth had opened. A hint of a frown had creased between her brows as though in annoyance, though Alfonso surmised that the cause must in fact have been pain.

He could see no breath. No movement. No life.

It was done. He had silenced her.

He sat back down near her. Pushing his hand beneath the rucked linen of her shift, his fingers touched one small breast: already chill, veined a delicate blue like malleable marble. She was no more than a soft statue. Her cold curves slid comfortably under the warmth of his cupped palm as he ran his hand over her skin, and he wondered at its exquisite unresponsiveness.

Looking down at her now, he saw at last the image for which he had longed for so many months. She was beautiful, he thought. In this breathless silence she was truly beautiful. The perfect reflection had finally been restored and the glass was again quite flawless. He knew that at last he would be able to claim her completely, gain untainted admittance to this creature whose very vitality and spontaneity had in life so diminished and crushed him. It would happen only once, he knew. But that would be enough. Complete possession.

A greed for her now grew within him and he found himself stiffening as he contemplated the accomplishment of an act whose very nature he had scarcely been able to admit, even to himself. He had until this moment locked it away and relished his awareness of its clandestine presence at the fringes of his consciousness; had frequently enjoyed toying with an idea that at once entranced and appalled him.

He imagined his warm flesh contained within her chill stillness and his skin crawled.

He could wait no longer. A terrifying sense of trespass into dangerous territory constricted his breath, but as he unfastened the lacing of his doublet, he knew that it was all still perfect. No fear of the exquisite image being shattered as it had been so many times before.

He wanted to take off her shift. He slid each heavy arm from its sleeve, then pushed his hand around and under her back, intending to lift her and free the linen from beneath her body. He had to bend close to her, but found he could not look at her face as he did so.

A sense of the imminence of the approaching moment of consummation ballooned in his head.

He threw the chemise to the floor as he laid the duchess back on the pillows. Her head drooped slackly to one side and her hair fell away from her face. In this flawless stasis she was entrancing, and at last he looked at her features.

And then he saw it.

A single tear, which must have gathered some moments before in the corner of her eye, spilled over as he watched. It ran slowly down the side of her cheek and slid towards the tangled hair.

Alfonso froze.

In the event, the perfect image did not shatter.

It dissolved.

It dissolved and the dream was destroyed.

Bile rose in Alfonso's throat and he pressed a hand across his mouth. From the start he had known his dream to be profane – *wicked* – but its glamour and terrible beauty had sustained him . . . he had *needed* it . . . he had wrapped himself in its hell-spun folds for months, preening himself in it, ignoring its implications and relishing the comfort it offered him. But staring now at the little figure on the bed, he began to shrivel; the great swollen bubble of his monstrous self-absorption was punctured, and as it deflated, leaking its horrible contents around him, he felt himself dwindling, shrinking, wizening.

He could no longer bear to see her. A blanket. He wanted to cover her. Without touching her. He dropped the blanket over her; she seemed to be sleeping. He should feel reassured, he thought, but at once a whining need to see her wake began insistently inside his head. He wanted to shake her – but no. To do that, he would have to lay hands on her.

Lines from Catullus that he had known since childhood came into his mind, so horribly apt; his mouth formed the words without his seeming to choose them. *Odi et amo: quare id faciam, fortasse requires. Nescio, sed fieri sentio ad excurcior.* I hate and I love: why I do so you may well ask. I do not know, but I feel it happen and am in agony.

Unable to stop himself, Alfonso looked again at Lucrezia's face. That tear still clung to her cheek, its track glistening in a line towards her hair. He straightened, reached forward and, with a finger, wiped away its last trace. He touched the finger to his lips and tasted salt. Nausea wrapped itself around his head, muffling and smothering, and for a moment he thought he would fall. He closed his eyes and steadied himself against the bedpost until the worst of it had passed. He had to get out. The inside of his head was inflating and he began to fear it would crack his skull as it expanded.

He picked up the candlestick – but as soon replaced it next to the bed. He did not want to leave Lucrezia in the dark.

Everything was silent. He backed towards the door, reached behind him, groped for the handle and pulled the door open. The lower edge caught with a scrape against the floor. He took another step backwards and his foot bumped against Folletto's side. With a grunt, the dog started, scrabbled to his feet and nosed Alfonso's hand – cold, wet, insistent. Alfonso stood still: the tremor that had begun at the sight of that tear was now shaking his entire body. He pulled his hand away from the probing muzzle.

Folletto lifted his head and howled. Sitting back on his haunches, nose to the ceiling, he let out a long and unearthly noise.

Alfonso froze.

His heart raced and his breath caught cold in his throat.

'*Stai zitto!* ' he hissed. 'Stop it! Someone will hear you.' He wrapped his hands around Folletto's muzzle, but the wolfhound pulled away from his grasp.

The noise continued.

Howling for the dead.

Alfonso grabbed the animal's head, tried to smother the noise in his doublet, but the cries went on, echoing along the stones of the corridor.

'*Stai zitto!* Someone will hear.'

Hardly aware of what he did, Alfonso put his arm around the dog's head; he pushed down hard with one hand upon its back. Then, Folletto's muzzle in the crook of his other elbow, he jerked upwards and back. There was a cracking sound.

The noise stopped.

For a second, Folletto hung from Alfonso's hands, which were wet with the dog's saliva. Alfonso retched and released his grip. The great black body slumped to the floor and was still.

The door to Lucrezia's chamber was still open, and in the candlelight Alfonso saw her lying unmoving beneath her crimson blanket. He backed away, wiping his palm against the leg of his breeches.

36

Five figures waited silently in the little antechamber, though only four of them breathed.

Giovanni stood tall against the furthest wall, by the door – Jacomo could see little of him in the deeper shadow. Coaxed into helping less than an hour before, Tomaso was sitting on a low stool with his back against a wall, his hands clasped loosely between splayed knees. Giorgio was a silhouette against the window, and a small silent figure sat in a high-backed chair, wrapped in a blanket, sagging at an unnatural angle against the wood.

The pictures that Jacomo's mind conjured up as they waited were horrible. To have Lucrezia so close, going through so unthinkable an experience and to be just *standing* there, letting it happen . . . it was almost unbearable. But Catelina's extraordinary suggestion had to be the best – possibly the *only* – way to prevent the duke discovering the deception, Jacomo kept telling himself. If he knew himself to have been duped, Jacomo was sure the duke would stop at nothing to exact his revenge for the humiliation he would feel at such a betrayal. The immediate reality of what they were doing, though, was far, far worse than he had imagined when Catelina had suggested how they might try to accomplish the rescue.

He looked at the little figure in the chair and swallowed.

The moon was high now and lit the antechamber with a pewter-grey light. They had no candle – the door had to be left ajar. Giovanni was listening for any sounds from the corridor beyond.

Seconds were minutes; minutes, hours.

Then into the silence came a click.

The iron handle shifted and the door opened.

Jacomo jumped to his feet, his heartbeat wild, as a figure came in, carrying a candle. Distorted shadows leaped up the walls. Giulietta sucked in a shocked breath at the sight of them all, but Giovanni stepped up behind her and put his hand over her mouth before she could do or say anything. She swung the candle wide and the flame went out but, to Jacomo's breathless relief, she did not drop it.

Giovanni stood behind Giulietta, his hand still over her mouth, his cheek against hers. 'If you make even a sound, Giulietta,' he whispered into her ear, 'Crezzi will probably pay with her life.' He paused. 'If I let go of you, do you promise to keep silent?'

Jacomo saw the old woman nod behind Giovanni's fingers.

Giovanni loosened his grip and stood back.

'*Santo cielo!* What in heaven . . . ?' Giuletta mouthed.

Holding her by both upper arms, still whispering, Giovanni told her as much as he dared.

Mouth open, Giulietta's gaze moved from him to Jacomo, from Jacomo to Tomaso and Giorgio, then to the crumpled creature in the chair. 'It is not possible . . .' she breathed.

'Believe it, Giulietta,' Giovanni said. He stopped abruptly, and stood very still, obviously listening. Flapping a hand at Jacomo, he jerked his head towards the door. Lucrezia's chamber door clicked open, and they heard soft footsteps and a scrabbling of claws. They readied themselves to move.

And then the wolfhound began to howl.

It was a terrible sound, echoing against the stone walls. Everyone stood motionless. It seemed, Jacomo thought, a lament for the dead and the hair on the back of his neck stood up.

The howling stopped. Footsteps passed the door and died away.

Waiting until he was certain the duke had left the corridor, Giovanni peered out of the antechamber, then beckoned. Jacomo, Tomaso, Giorgio and Giulietta left the room and walked silently the few yards to Lucrezia's chamber.

Jacomo held his breath.

The duke's dog lay dark and still on the floor of the corridor. Jacomo tentatively pushed its side with his foot, but it did not move. He squatted before the creature and stroked its head; its eye was open and the tongue lolled. Though still warm, there was no doubt that it was dead.

They stepped across the big black body into Lucrezia's chamber.

After having been so reluctant to allow himself to conjure a picture of what they might find in that room, Jacomo was startled to see what appeared to be Lucrezia asleep, tucked under a dark red blanket, a candle burning on the table next to her pillow. The scene was too peaceful, too ordinary, somehow; Jacomo did not know what to think.

He crossed the room and bent over her.

In the wide-windowed apothecary's shop the night before, Alessandro had described in meticulous detail the effects of his terrifying mixture of laudanum, mandrake and valerian as he had deftly prepared and bottled his ingredients. Jacomo knew that he would detect no breath, no sign of life at all. He knew she would be cold to the touch, that her breathing would be imperceptible, and that it would be some hours before she would wake; he had thought himself prepared. But when he saw her face, so slack and vacant, he was nonetheless almost overwhelmed by a cold, hissing panic.

Pulling the blanket back from her then, he saw that she was naked. Her shift lay discarded on the floor next to her bed, and wrapped around and around her neck was a long string of dark red, glittering stones.

'Bastard,' Jacomo whispered, hardly able to believe the appalling thought that had come into his mind. 'You . . . you bastard!'

He picked Lucrezia up in his arms and held her close. She was limp and heavy, and her head hung back across his arm. A moment later, trembling, he placed her back down on the pillow.

'Jacomo?' Giovanni was at his side and, though Jacomo quickly pulled the blanket over Lucrezia, he heard a soft little indrawn breath, and knew that Giovanni had seen what he had seen, had deduced what he had deduced.

'But – he believed her truly dead . . .' Giovanni sounded sickened.

'We have to get her out of here. Take Giorgio and get Chiara.'

Giovanni and Giorgio peered around the door to check that the corridor was still deserted, then left the room.

Jacomo unfastened the string of red stones and took them from Lucrezia's throat. They would have to be put around the unfortunate Chiara's neck, if the substitution were to be credible.

Giulietta laid a hand on Jacomo's arm. Her eyes were big with tears. 'Oh, dear God – look at her! How could he do this? How?'

'Please – help me to dress her,' Jacomo said.

He pulled Tomaso's hose and breeches from his bag and, with difficulty, fitted them onto Lucrezia's lifeless legs. Giulietta shook out the shirt, doublet and cap with visibly trembling hands and passed them to him. Within moments, an inanimate echo of the shining-eyed creature he had held in his arms above Alessandro's shop lay silently before him, and it only remained to hide her hair before he carried her from the castle.

He tried hard. Standing behind her that night in Alessandro's storeroom, he had enjoyed winding Lucrezia's hair around his hand, had managed to pull it into a rope and tuck it away into Tomaso's hat, but now, try as he might, with Lucrezia seemingly lifeless and so utterly unresponsive, it refused to comply with his still inexperienced efforts. In the end, frantic to leave, he whispered to Giulietta, 'Can you find me some scissors?'

'Oh, no, you cannot—' Giulietta began, but she passed him nevertheless a long-bladed pair from a bag of sewing under the window. Jacomo bunched and twisted the hair and then took the scissors in his free hand. With a slow scrunch, the blades sliced together, the long hank of hair fell away and the cut ends curled and wisped forward around Lucrezia's face. Jacomo picked up Tomaso's red hat and pulled it onto her head with ease, then laid her gently back onto the pillow. Giulietta reached for the already unwinding rope and took it from him.

It was done, Jacomo thought. Time to go.

Giulietta was staring at Lucrezia, tears spilling unchecked onto the front of her dress, blotching the cloth. 'Oh, God! This is too – I cannot bear to think I will never see her again. And that poor, poor child in there . . .'

Tears came to Jacomo's eyes too as a rush of guilt pushed its way up into his throat. Here was this old lady, weeping in anticipation of a loss she could hardly contemplate; back in Mugello,

Lucrezia's unwitting parents were still entirely ignorant of the news they would receive in a few days' time, and within minutes he would be leaving it all behind, carrying Crezzi away, for them to begin a joyful future together. The injustice seemed unbearable. But he could see no alternative. He took Giulietta's hand. 'I will always take care of her.'

'I know, child.'

'I . . . I love her, Signora.'

Giulietta's face was inscrutable. She said softly, 'Go on – take her now.' She laid the long rope of hair down on the table by the bed, picked out a thick strand and wrapped it around her fingers, then slid the little bundle off and rolled it into a piece of linen pulled from the bag that had contained the scissors. She held it out to Jacomo.

Jacomo smiled his thanks and tucked it into a pocket in his breeches. 'Thank you, Signora. We must go now. Giorgio and Giovanni will stay with you – it's not safe for you to be alone. They'll do . . . well – they'll do what must be done.'

Giovanni and Giorgio appeared, Giorgio carrying Chiara, her blanket-wrapped body no bigger than a child's in his big arms. Tomaso edged past them and crossed to Jacomo.

'Am I coming with you, Jacomo?'

A nod. 'I need you to come as far as the drawbridge. And, please, will you give this to the reverend brother in the morning?' He held out the long letter he had written – a mixture of apologies, heartfelt thanks and detailed instructions. And a plea for a blessing. In the knowledge of his mentor's distress at the slow failing of his skills, Jacomo had found his letter all but impossible to write. Tomaso tucked the paper inside his doublet.

Jacomo bent forward, slid one arm under Lucrezia's knees and pushed the other behind her shoulders. Her head sagged into the crook of his elbow and his fingers gripped beneath her armpit. With an effort, he stood upright and shifted her weight so that she lay more comfortably in his arms. Her head was heavy on his shoulder and the newly cut hair wisped across his cheek.

Giorgio laid Chiara in Lucrezia's place.

Giovanni crossed to Jacomo, bent and kissed his cousin's forehead tenderly. 'Look after her,' he said.

It was, Jacomo knew, an order as much as a plea.

He said, 'I promise. We'll write. Tell you where to find us.'

Giovanni wiped his eyes and nose with the heel of his hand. 'I'll come straight away. Tell her.' His voice shook.

Jacomo looked from Giovanni to Giorgio. 'Will you manage . . . manage the rest of this?'

They nodded. Jacomo told them briefly about the string of red stones.

'Wait!' Giulietta leaned towards Lucrezia, held the lifeless face in both her hands and kissed her. Then Giovanni put his arm around her shoulders. Giulietta turned to him. He held her close, then looked at Jacomo and jerked his head towards the door. Jacomo nodded. Giorgio opened it and peered out into the corridor. Then, with Lucrezia in his arms, Jacomo stepped over the lifeless body of the dog in the doorway. With Tomaso at his side, he began to make his way – for the last time – through the lightless Castello.

Giulietta picked a tiny carved box from a shelf, opened it and drew out a rosary. Giovanni recognized the coral beads and silver chain – it had been Aunt Eleanora's and she had given it to Crezzi when she had left for Ferrara. Giulietta wound the rosary around the dead girl's thin fingers, tucking the silver cross so that it was held firmly between her two thumbs. 'What will happen tomorrow,' she said, 'when the Signore sees that Lucrezia has gone and this child is here in her place?'

Giovanni swallowed and said, 'He won't know. He'll never know. Giorgio and I will make sure of it. You're not going to like it, Giulietta, but we must do it if *Il Duca* is to believe Crezzi dead when he returns.'

'What do you mean, child?'

Giovanni glanced at Giorgio, and drew in an uncomfortable breath. He explained their plan.

Giulietta gasped. 'Oh no! Giovanni, no – the poor child . . .'

'Look, Giulietta, this girl – Chiara – is already dead. We can harm her no further. If we don't do this, Crezzi's life will always be vulnerable. She'll be waiting for him to catch up with her – always looking over her shoulder, never knowing. Please, go and wait in the studio for now. You won't want to watch what we're doing.'

He turned to Giorgio. 'Ready?'

His face ashen, Giorgio nodded. He pulled a waxed-cloth bag from where it was tied to the belt around his waist and followed Giovanni back towards Lucrezia's bed. Giovanni drew back the covers, then stopped at the sight of the little body in its white shift. He and Giorgio exchanged glances, then Giovanni crossed himself and silently begged forgiveness for what they were about to do; Giorgio pulled his cap from his head and closed his eyes.

Giovanni picked up the long string of red stones and wound them around Chiara's thin neck. The great mass of red looked like a slit throat, and Giovanni wondered why Lucrezia had been wearing it: he could not imagine her liking such ostentatious jewellery. They had to have been *his* choice, he thought with a surge of loathing. He tucked the blanket back around the body, and rewrapped the rosary around one hand, folding the thin fingers around the crucifix and the jumble of dark pink and silver beads.

Now Giorgio took from his bag a large lump of glistening white fat, badly wrapped in greasy sacking.

'Bring it here!' Giovanni hissed, pointing to the pillows. Giorgio held the lump in both hands; he placed it on the bedside table and pulled a knife from his belt. Holding the block firm with one hand, he began to chip nut-sized pieces from it, handing them to Giovanni. Giovanni placed them carefully around the stark hair, across the girl's collar-bones, neck and chest, and along the length of her arm. There was a faint smell of roast sheep. Giovanni lifted his fingers to his nose.

'Mutton tallow,' Giorgio said. 'It was all I could find in the kitchens. I hope there'll be enough.'

Giovanni crossed to the studio. 'Are there any spare candles, Giulietta?'

Wordlessly, she opened a long box on a window-ledge and brought out two new, yellow beeswax tapers. Giovanni took them from her and returned to his task. Breaking the largest into three pieces, and sliding them off the wick, he handed the fragments to Giorgio, who placed them gently up against Chiara's yellow-white face. The second candle, also broken into fragments, Giovanni laid in the crook of Chiara's other arm, which he had positioned to lie across the pillow. Giorgio took the greasy piece of sacking, shook the remaining crumbs of tallow over the bed and flattened the cloth across Chiara's body. Then, crossing the room, he opened one of the windows wide. The breeze lifted the bed-hangings, which billowed softly in towards the bed.

They stood back and stared at what they had arranged. Turning to Giorgio, Giovanni saw that he was shaking.

'Oh, God,' Giorgio said, 'what are we doing? We'll all go to hell . . .'

Giovanni said nothing. Giulietta had to leave the studio, he thought. Fire is unpredictable. He went back to her and took her hand. 'Giulietta, you must come out of here. It's time to make sure Crezzi is safe from that bastard for good.'

Shivering, Giulietta followed him back into the bedchamber, looking open-mouthed at the figure sprawled on the wide bed, the little lumps of white tallow tucked around her face and body. 'Oh, dear God, Giovanni . . .'

'Just think, Giulietta,' Giovanni said, to convince himself as much as the old lady, 'she'll have more than a Christian burial in the end. This little homeless waif, instead of ending her days in lime-spattered sacking, dumped into an anonymous mass grave, will leave this world with all the pomp of a sumptuous state funeral.' He paused, and then added, 'The state funeral that would have been Crezzi's.'

Giulietta smothered a sob.

'Giorgio . . .' Giovanni said.

Giorgio picked up the candlestick from the table next to the bed and placed it nearer to where the dark bed hanging was moving in the draught from the open window. Then he put his fingers under the base of the candlestick and lifted, as though the candle was being tipped by a billowing fold of the curtain.

At that moment Giovanni saw that the duke had unwittingly left them the finishing touch to their set piece: an almost empty wine bottle and two silver cups. *Il Duca* had provided them with a perfect excuse for why their 'duchess' had failed to wake when the wind had knocked her candle into her bedding.

The candlestick tipped sideways. The candle rolled from it and fell onto the pillow; the flame touched one of the lumps of tallow that lay around Chiara's head. For a moment, flame licked from lump to lump, around the upper edge of her head and it seemed to their horrified eyes as though a bright halo had just glowed. Then suddenly, the tallow was blazing and Giulietta turned her head away with a whimper. Giorgio put his hands over his mouth and Giovanni felt as though he were suffocating.

Chiara's hair caught then and burned with a fizzling flare, just as a flicker of flame ran along the length of her outstretched arm, across the pillow and over to one of the bed-hangings, which ignited almost immediately. As the material scorched, flamed and began to drop in blackened fragments down onto the already burning rushes on the floor, Giovanni looked back at the supine figure and saw that, as Catelina had imagined, the flames were now licking around the thin face, already rendering it quite unrecognizable.

It was almost time to leave, he thought, and for Giulietta to raise the alarm, as though she had just discovered this horrible scene – too late to save the person they wanted all to believe to be Lucrezia.

The room was hellish as Giovanni turned at the doorway. The bed-hangings were ablaze and flames were now cradling Chiara's body. Her face and hands had blackened and her fingers had contracted, as though in supplication.

37

Even as Alfonso crossed the central courtyard of the Castello, he heard a howling scream from somewhere inside the castle, begging for assistance. His heart raced, and for an instant he stood torn, his thoughts fragmenting, unable to leave, but unwilling to return to face whatever was happening within.

Then Francesca was beside him. 'Is it over?' she said.

Alfonso found that he could not answer, but he nodded once.

Francesca stood in front of him. Her mouth should have been irresistible, he thought. Its ripeness was unchanged, and its latent invitation obvious. But an unprecedented weight and weariness were seeping through him and, with a shock, Alfonso found himself for the first time contemplating his whore without stiffening. The fear-sodden torpidity that had suffused him as he had gazed at the body of the duchess still hung around him like a wet cloak. He could see, though, that Francesca sought a kiss and he bent his head to hers, but he found with distress that he had no sensation in his lips. He could not feel his mouth upon hers at all.

'Don't go back in, Alfonso,' Francesca said. 'It is better if you are not seen until tomorrow. Come with me.' Taking his hand in hers, she led him away from the Castello and the unfolding catastrophe.

It is as well, Francesca thought, as they walked, that a whore's training allows her to look with believable desire upon someone whose very proximity makes her want to vomit. To look up into Alfonso's eyes that night and offer to kiss him, knowing what he had intended to do, knowing what he would have done had they not prevented it, knowing what he believed himself to have achieved . . . it had been, she thought with a shudder, very nearly beyond her.

When they arrived at the *villetta*, after a silent walk through the streets of Ferrara, Alfonso seated himself in the elmwood chair under the window by the bed. Francesca lit the fire and opened one of the many bottles of wine. Pouring a generous glassful, she handed it to him and he took it from her without a word. He seemed hardly aware of her presence, and she saw, when she looked closely at him, that what she had at first taken to be the effect of the flickering firelight, was in fact a slow tremor right through his body.

'Come to bed, Alfonso,' she said. She had told them she would hold him here for the night, and she intended to keep her word.

He looked up at her with blank eyes, as though uncertain what he should do next. Francesca took his coat from him, then unfastened doublet, breeches, boots and hose. He submitted to her ministrations without response. For the first time since she had known him, he made no attempt to touch her. She had to undress herself.

Even given her new antipathy to her former lover, Francesca was shocked, in the event, to see the disintegration in Alfonso.

After caressing him and attempting to engage his attention for some moments, she saw him at last focus upon her face. He seemed to register her presence, and even attempted to kiss her, but then, as his hand closed upon her breast, he stopped, shivering and motionless. He seemed utterly consumed by what appeared to be panic, Francesca thought, like a child who suddenly realizes that, after running and playing thoughtlessly in an unfamiliar place, he is entirely lost; and with a soft noise as of despair, he clung to her. Though she could hardly bear to offer him any semblance of comfort, she felt, as she put unwilling arms around his shaking shoulders, a kind of bitter satisfaction in the contemplation of this unprecedented, helpless distress.

They stayed in the little house throughout the following morning. Alfonso was silent and tense, and sat before the fire, clasping a glass of wine in both hands and staring into the flames.

At around noon, he professed himself tired, and Francesca suggested that he sleep. A distracted nod was the only sign he gave that he agreed with her suggestion, and, putting down the now empty glass, he crossed the room, lay on the bed and closed his eyes. He slept almost immediately.

Francesca waited and watched him for a while, and then, as soon as she was certain he was truly unaware of her presence, she covered him with a blanket, collected her belongings and left the house.

She walked quickly, wanting to get back to the twins and take them away from Ferrara as soon as possible. Before Alfonso woke and came after her. She was certain that her life – and theirs – would now be vulnerable, were he ever to learn of her duplicity. She had little doubt of his reaction should he ever discover the truth of her visit to Alessandro's workshop with Jacomo: how they had waited while the apothecary created a means of saving the life of the duchess. She and Jacomo had talked of an antidote – something they could administer once she had removed Alfonso from the scene – but Alessandro's substitute had been better, Francesca thought now. Safer.

She would go to Napoli, she thought, as she crossed a bustling piazza. She would take the girls to Napoli. That would be far enough away from Ferrara. They would set out that afternoon.

Alfonso woke with a start as a frantic knocking shook the door of the *villetta*. He reached for Francesca but, to his surprise, she was not there. His heart pounding, he lay still. The knocking came again, louder now. He pulled on shirt and breeches and went to open the door.

He was astonished to see the shock of white hair and the bird-black eyes of Franco Guarniero. It was not difficult, he thought, to guess the import of Guarniero's visit, but until this moment Alfonso had been unaware that his steward even knew of the *villetta*'s existence.

'Oh, Signore!' Guarniero's voice was higher-pitched than usual, and Alfonso watched him struggling visibly as he sought for a way to tell his master the untellable. 'I am so sorry to come here, Signore. So dreadfully sorry – it is quite inexcusable! An unwarranted intrusion . . . I would never normally . . . But I did not know what to do. The du— the duchess!'

Alfonso feigned disquiet. 'What, Franco? What about her? Is she ill? You seem – tell me! What is it?' Even as he spoke, Alfonso felt a warm slither of pride at the authenticity of his counterfeit consternation.

'A – a fire, Signore.' Guarniero stared at him, wide-eyed with remembrance of recent horror, and now the disbelief in Alfonso's gaze was genuine. A *fire*? he thought, bewildered. What fire? He did not understand.

'Oh, my lord, the duchess is dead.'

The words hung in the air between the two men like the reverberation of a tolling bell after the sound has ceased to sing.

Neither man spoke for several long seconds.

Then Alfonso said tonelessly, 'How did you know where to find me?'

Guarniero reddened and did not reply. Alfonso was shocked that his private business seemed to have become public property within the Castello. He said, 'Where is the duchess now?'

Guarniero's voice was shaking. 'Still in her poor burned chamber, my lord. We did not know what we should do . . . We wanted to wait for your arrival, Signore. We – we couldn't find you . . . thought you might be here, and . . . oh, Signore – your dog.'

The steward was almost gibbering in his distress – Alfonso had never seen him so discomposed.

Someone had moved Folletto. Alfonso felt chilled and rather sick as he passed the untidy black body, which lay like an abandoned puppet against the wall of the corridor. He stared at the dog for a moment, then turned, a few steps ahead of Guarniero, and pushed open the door to Lucrezia's bedchamber.

The acrid smell of scorched wood, burned feathers and charred flesh hit him like a fist in the face, and he flinched. He looked around the room in breath-held disbelief at what remained of the wooden wall-panels, the cracked window-panes and the black ceiling.

And then he saw her.

Some images, he had thought many times before, can sear themselves instantly into the mind at first sight – white hot, scarring the memory indelibly, exquisitely ineradicable. The twisted, blackened body on the ruined bed, its stick arms bent in grotesque entreaty, was like an image from a Bosch nightmare and Alfonso knew that what he saw now would never leave him.

In fact, he thought, were it not for the portrait, he might have lost her entirely. Thank God for the portrait! She would have been quite lost to him! The scene in front of him was even now chasing his remembered image of Lucrezia's loveliness from his mind. He should never have left the candle burning.

Turning away without comment, Alfonso pushed past Guarniero and the other half-dozen servants who had accompanied them into the chamber, and strode out into the corridor. Averting his eyes from Folletto's body, he drew in several deep breaths, then walked swiftly down through the Castello to the Entrance Hall.

She gazed out at him from the wall.

He sat on the stairs, a few steps up from the bottom of the upper flight, and looked at her for a long time. He had been right, he thought. There was nothing else he could have done. Too many elements had conspired for too long to push him to the edge of Dante's '*lamentable vale, that dread abyss that joins a thunderous sound of plaints innumerable*'. One thing or another he could perhaps have endured, but not all combined. The displays of affection she had so frequently bestowed upon all as unmeasured largesse; the eviscerating power she had had to reduce him to the status of a eunuch in her bed – this would surely have been enough in itself, without the appalling new knowledge of the fate of the duchy should he be unable to produce an heir. *His Holiness thought you should be made aware of the gravity of the situation.* No, he thought, avoiding Lucrezia's gaze now: for *that* he would never forgive her.

He would have to make enquiries about other potential consorts. To retain Ferrara was of paramount importance.

It seemed to Eduardo Rossi that the whole of the duchy must have flocked to Ferrara to see the spectacle. The streets were lined five or six deep along the route that the funeral cortège would take. They were not taking the duchess straight from castle to cathedral, they had said that morning – the distance was no more than a few hundred yards. The procession would wind around a looping maze of streets: a longer route, he had been told, to exalt the occasion and to give the people time to honour the passing of their duke's tragically young wife.

Tragically young. Not much older than his Chiara. Even as he thought this, Eduardo felt tears sting behind his eyes again. He pushed his lime-pitted hand up against one eye and the side of his nose, and held his breath, willing himself not to sob. Barnabeo gripped his arm, while Antonio and another two of the guildsmen grunted in awkward sympathy.

The procession filed past and the crowd's soft murmurings died to silence.

Some thirty clergymen led the way, behind a dozen caparisoned horses: the archbishop of Ferrara, a dozen or so priests and a drab brown huddle of Franciscan friars, one of whom – plump and elderly – appeared to be weeping. The bier, draped and canopied in a purple so deep it was near to black, was carried by six young men. The little body on the bier was uncoffined, wrapped in a lighter purple silk. So small, Eduardo thought, his tears spilling unchecked now. Poor little thing – for all her privileges.

As he stared at the close-wrapped figure, he found himself swallowing down a now horribly familiar bloated throatful of guilt, and the cold weight of his ignorance of Chiara's fate dropped once more into his belly like a block of lead.

Behind the bier walked the relatives. The duke, upright and expressionless, then at least twenty men of varying ages – one he imagined must be the girl's father, given the tragic bleakness of the poor man's expression. The youngest, tall, thin, dark-skinned, could be no more than seventeen, Eduardo thought, dressed in his finest, his face set and closed, holding the older man's arm. Torch-bearers, men holding banners, a group of musicians, more horses. As they passed, the crowds bowed their heads, made fervent signs of the cross; some fell to their knees. Eduardo imagined the women, back at the Castello, left to bear their grief in private.

He took a step back, and knocked against a tall, round-faced young man, who had his arm around the shoulders of a dark-haired girl. She was dressed in yellow and was carrying a baby. Eduardo saw that the back of one of the girl's wrists was red and puckered – not unlike a lime burn, he thought inconsequentially. Apologising for his clumsiness, he looked at the baby and the emptiness of his loss yawned wider. The young woman smiled at him, mutely accepting the apology, then turned back to watch the procession.

Epilogue

August 1562
Ardea: a short distance
south of Rome

The cicadas chirred in the heavy evening heat. The sun was sinking visibly; its lower edge seemed to bleed out beyond the circular rim as it touched the horizon. Deep purple shadows were lengthening and thickening as the light faded, and the encroaching evening began to take on a warm, soporific lassitude.

A young woman was sitting on a wooden bench against the outside wall of a small cottage. A heavily laden vine grew up and over the uneven stone at the back of the house and branched out across a rough trellis under which the young woman had seated herself. She was suckling a tiny baby; her head bent and tilted as she watched the child with an expression of rapt fondness. Dappled blotches of blue shadow fell across her face and the baby's head through the tangle of vine stems and leaves above them.

The child appeared to be asleep. The young woman slipped the tip of her little finger into the corner of his mouth to detach his grip on her nipple, but at her touch, he batted a small hand, which had been resting on the slope of her breast and began to suck again. His ear, a pink curl of pale ham, moved back and forth as he sucked. His mother smiled at the renewed enthusiasm of her little son and looked up to share her pleasure with her companion. He was perched on a low wall, which ran at right angles from the side of the main house, out and round, forming a small enclosed yard; on seeing the young woman look up at him, he lowered the board on which he had been resting a sheet of paper and tucked a stick of charcoal behind his ear. 'Can you keep still?' he said.

'Will you be long?'

He shook his head, lifted the board once more and began again to draw. A lock of black hair fell across his eyes and he blew upwards to get it out of the way. When this failed, he pushed it back off his face with an impatient hand, leaving a smear of charcoal across the crimson stain that coloured his left cheek. He frowned in concentration as he lifted his eyes from the sketch to the woman and the baby.

Some moments later, he appeared satisfied, for he laid the board on the wall, put the charcoal next to it, walked across the yard to the bench and sat down. He draped an arm around the woman's shoulders, stretched long legs out before him and smiled. Closing his eyes, he tilted his face up towards the vines that hung in tangled clumps above him. The young woman laid her head against his shoulder and twisted herself around so that she could lean her weight more comfortably against his body than against the hard back of the bench.

The baby stopped sucking again. This time his head drooped sideways and he slipped off the nipple. A slow line of milk trickled from the corner of his soft, curled-petal mouth as he lay in satiated ecstasy in the crook of his mother's arm. The young man stroked the little head gently with the fingers of the hand that hung loosely across the woman's shoulders. They sat in silent contentment for some moments. Then the girl spoke. 'Will you be going out with Cristoforo on the boat again tomorrow?'

'Mmm, I'll have to. Can't say I want to, but it was such a good catch today; he asked if I'd help him again.' He sounded sleepy and reluctant to think about the activity to come.

'What about Signor de Lavallo, though? When will you have to go back into the city for his next sitting?'

Eyes closed, the young man murmured, 'He's away until next Friday, he said. I'll go after that. We can all go, if you'd like – the three of us.'

The girl tilted her head up towards his face, and he smiled at her fondly and kissed her, cupping her face in his free hand. Then he tipped his head back towards the vines.

'I should make us something to eat,' the girl said. 'Are you hungry?'

The young man nodded again, eyes still shut.

'Will you take him?'

He smiled assent.

The girl tucked the bodice of her dress back around her breast, one-handed, and pulled the laces loosely back into place again. Then sitting forward, she slid her free arm up and under the baby's body. Scooping her son up in both hands, she held him out to his father, who smiled again, and took the baby from her. He laid the child along the length of his chest, so that the little head was tucked in under his chin; he held the baby in place with one brown hand.

The girl refastened her hair, which was too short to stay comfortably in place, and before moving into the cool of the interior of the house, bent to kiss the back of her sleeping son's downy head. As she straightened, the young man lifted his free hand and caught her wrist. Pulling her back towards him, he kissed her mouth with an unhurried thoroughness.

After a moment's compliance, she laughed into the kiss and drew back from him. 'Enough. If you want to eat before it is completely dark, I should go in and begin.'

The young man raised her hand to his lips. 'What will you make?' he said indistinctly, over her knuckles.

'What would you like?'

'I don't know.' He paused. 'Anything but fish.'

She laughed again, and looking with love at her son and his father, she turned and went inside.

The candle sputtered: the wick was drowning. The duke picked up another and lit it from the guttering flame, then set it upright in a soft little pile of dripped wax upon the stone floor. The ceiling of the cell was covered in writing: big, untidy, scrawling lines of black words, painted in candle-smoke over the low, curving vault – the final thoughts of countless past occupants. Perhaps, he thought, as he had so often before, some of these words had been penned by whoever had howled down here in such agonized despair that day when he was ten. He wondered, too – he wondered this every day now – what the duchess's final thoughts had been. She, of course, unlike all those incarcerated down here across the years, would not have recognized her final thoughts for what they had been; she had been unaware of the imminence of her demise. Her last words had been distinctly mundane: '*It was a sensible idea of yours to bring it.*' She had been mistaken, though, the duke thought now: it had not been sensible – it had been *essential*. He had had no choice. He had only done what he had had to do.

A charred, stick-armed figure, its claw-like hands held out in entreaty, dragged itself into his mind and he shuddered, muttering to it to go – to leave him alone. Even down here now, he saw it. This had been the last place he had been able to escape it, but it had found him out. Followed him. Now there was nowhere. He bent forward, put his head between his knees and pressed it between his hands, trying to force out the unwanted image, but it stayed where it was and then, as it always did, it opened its eyes. He knew that they would be shining with tears in its blackened face.

He stood up.

He would go and look at the portrait.

It was an astonishing likeness. Everyone who had known the duchess said as much. A work of astounding skill. Although he had not spoken a word to Pandolf after the day of the fire, the castle servants had told the duke that the old man had been devastated by the events of that night and had struggled to complete the painting. Alfonso supposed it was fortunate that in the event the portrait had almost reached completion before the loss of the sitter.

Gently detaching the candle from its little wax pedestal, he opened the iron door and stepped out of the cell. The bobbing flame threw untidy black shadows over the low ceiling of the passageway, distorted and twisted like burned limbs.

She was smiling at him as he pulled back the red curtain and sat down, a few steps from the bottom of the upper flight in the Entrance Hall, and in the face of that smile, the black-limbed creature crept away. He could see in her countenance now the look with which she had favoured him when first they met. A look of flushed delight, like a woman warmly nourishing fond memories of euphoric coition, she bestowed upon him again, unable to tear her painted eyes from his fixed gaze. This was how it should always have been, he thought, her profligate and consummate promiscuity controlled and silenced. She was held in silence now, within the very fabric of the walls of the Castello itself, and that spot of joy in her cheek, so faithfully reproduced here, burned now at last for him alone.

It had finally been contained.

He loved to see her smile for him.

Even when some other person looked along with him, he thought, it was her husband alone upon whom her eyes remained.

Others could see her only when he chose to allow them, of course. It had been the clever deception with the great fresco that had given him the idea of the curtain, and now none put by the damask he had hung before the portrait but he. He found himself drawn here increasingly frequently, but most often, as at this moment, it was when he was alone.

He preferred to keep her to himself.

He stared at the portrait. He had never asked the painters the significance of the pomegranate, he realized. Scattered on the floor before the duchess, below where her other hand was held, palm up and empty, lay a trail of scattered crimson seeds, which looked for all the world, he thought, as though she had just let fall the Red Rope to lie snake-like at her feet.

The young emissary from the count of Tyrol was tall, thin, very nervous of his new position, but extremely proud of having successfully – he hoped – completed his first official assignment. Some of what he had seen and heard during his short stay in Ferrara, however, had quite discomposed him.

He knew he had followed his instructions to the letter.

'Present the duke with these tokens of my estimation, Udo,' the count had said, handing him two objects. Udo had, upon arrival in Ferrara, duly handed over, with trembling anticipation, a calf-bound folder containing a watercolour by Albrecht Altdorfer, and a plain wooden box, in which lay a tiny masterpiece: a maquette, in gleaming elmwood, by none other than the great Veit Stoss. He had been told much of the duke's reputation as a patron of the arts, and had looked forward with pride and some trepidation to presenting him with these gifts.

They had been well received.

Udo had been impressed with the duke's command of German, which he had employed almost effortlessly.

'I must write and thank the count, your master. His known munificence is amply illustrated by such generous gifts – though his fair daughter's self is to be, of course, the greatest gift of all.'

Something about the duke's dispassionate anticipation of the imminent acquisition of a new bride raised the hairs on the back of Udo's thin and rather pimply neck. He brushed aside his momentary discomposure, though, as the duke suggested a tour of the works of art he already had in place in the Castello. Udo was anxious to please, for his master had been most insistent upon stressing the importance of such an alliance between the House of Tyrol and the Duchy of Ferrara. Udo did not want to be the cause of a change of heart on the part of the prospective bridegroom. His master's young daughter was a charming and sweet-natured girl, he had always thought, and it would break her heart if her newly betrothed were to retract his proposal.

So he duly exclaimed and admired, and absorbed his host's prodigious explanations of his works of art, with very little understanding but much appreciation.

After some time, they stopped at the top of a flight of steps and stood before a floor-length crimson damask curtain. The duke reached forward and pulled back the hanging to reveal a painting of a woman, dressed in deep red, with a pomegranate in her hand.

This time Udo was truly moved, for the woman was beautiful and seemed to look at him – only him – with desire in her shining eyes.

He forgot his companion and gazed, entranced, upon the image painted into the plaster on the wall. As he stared, however, he became aware – as if in his peripheral vision – of a change in his host's demeanour. There was a catch in the duke's voice as he spoke again, and Udo pulled his gaze away from the painting to look at his companion. For a brief moment, the duke looked quite distracted and Udo began once again to listen more intently.

'That's my last duchess,' said the duke, blinking slowly, 'painted on the wall, looking as if she were alive . . .'

MY LAST DUCHESS

Robert Browning

Ferrara

That's my last Duchess painted on the wall,
Looking as if she were alive. I call
That piece a wonder, now; Fra Pandolf's hands
Worked busily a day, and there she stands.
Will't please you sit and look at her? I said
'Fra Pandolf' by design, for never read
Strangers like you that pictured countenance,
The depth and passion of its earnest glance,
But to myself they turned (since none puts by
The curtain I have drawn for you but I)
And seemed as they would ask me, if they durst,
How such a glance came there; so, not the first
Are you to turn and ask thus. Sir, 'twas not
Her husband's presence only, called that spot
Of joy in to the Duchess' cheek: perhaps
Fra Pandolf chanced to say, 'Her mantle laps
Over my lady's wrist too much,' or 'Paint

Must never hope to reproduce the faint
Half-flush that dies along her throat: such stuff
Was courtesy, she thought, and cause enough
For calling up that spot of joy. She had
A heart – how shall I say – too soon made glad,
Too easily impressed; she liked whate'er
She looked on, and her looks went everywhere.
Sir, 'twas all one! My favour at her breast,
The dropping of the daylight in the West,
The bough of cherries some officious fool
Broke in the orchard for her, the white mule
She rode with round the terrace – all and each
Would draw from her alike the approving speech,
Or blush at least. She thanked men – good! but thanked
Somehow – I know not how – as if she ranked
My gift of a nine-hundred-years-old name
With anybody's gift. Who'd stoop to blame
This sort of trifling? Even had you skill
In speech – (which I have not) – to make your will
Quite clear to such an one, and say, 'Just this
Or that in you disgusts me; here you miss,
Or there exceed the mark' – and if she let
Herself be lessoned so, nor plainly set
Her wits to yours, forsooth and made excuse,
– E'en then would be some stooping; and I choose
Never to stoop. Oh sir, she smiled, no doubt,
Whene'er I passed her; but who passed without
Much the same smile? This grew; I gave commands;
Then all smiles stopped together. There she stands
As if alive. Will't please you rise: we'll meet
The company below, then. I repeat,

The Count your master's known munificence
Is ample warrant that no just pretence
Of mine for dowry will be disallowed;
Though his fair daughter's self, as I avowed
At starting, is my object. Nay, we'll go
Together down, sir. Notice Neptune, though,
Taming a sea-horse, thought a rarity,
Which Claus of Innsbruck cast in bronze for me!

Author's Note:

This novel was originally inspired by Robert Browning's monologue *My Last Duchess*, rather than by historical events. It was only after beginning to explore the poem in greater depth, as I began to rough out the initial outline of my book, that I discovered – much to my surprise – that Browning's eponymous characters had really existed.

While I have taken every care to research my novel meticulously, and while the social history is as accurate as I can possibly make it, this remains at heart a work of fiction, and where I have needed to tweak historical facts or rejig geographical locations to allow the smooth passage of my plot, I have taken the liberty of so doing.

The actual facts pertinent to the story are these.

Alfonso d'Este (Alfonso II) was the fifth Duke of Ferrara and in 1559 he married the Medici heiress, Lucrezia. Three years later, she disappeared from the records. The various sources I have explored have differing opinions on the matter: some suspect foul play, some believe she died from natural causes. Browning himself said that while he had toyed with the idea that Alfonso had had Lucrezia committed to a convent, he preferred to think that the duke had ordered her demise.

Alfonso married twice more after Lucrezia: Barbara of Austria, and Margherita Gonzaga, Barbara's niece.

Alfonso spent much of his childhood in Ferrara without his mother, Renée, a Calvinist Frenchwoman, who was banished from court by her husband over a matter of blasphemy. As I understand the accounts, she stood in defence of one of her French servants, who had been accused of blaspheming before the Blessed Sacrament in the duchess's chapel and because of this she was sent away from court for many years.

It is also a matter of historical fact that the Vatican reclaimed the rights to the Duchy of Ferrara, because of Alfonso's lack of legitimate issue. The Este family retained rights to Modena and Reggio, and – as in the novel Alfonso fears will happen – their importance as a dynasty was drastically reduced.

Acknowledgements

There are just so many people to thank! First of all, of course, thank you to my family: to Steve, to my lovely daughters Katy and Beattie, and to Ricky. Thank you to my sisters: Vicky Kimm, Buffy Kimm and Fiona Kimm; to my very special friends Cathy Mosely, Sahra Gott and Becky Paton; to Kate Goodhart, to Annie Thomson, to Chloe White and to Professor Michael Irwin – all of whom in their different ways and at different times have offered their opinions and their time honestly, generously and without ever pulling their punches. A big, big thank you to Rebecca Saunders, my editor at Little, Brown, and to Judith Murray, my agent. And thanks and love to my dedicatees – my parents.

I am very grateful too, to those who have generously offered practical knowledge, expertise and assistance: the remarkable Tod Todeschini, my Renaissance SOCO; Mark Wade Stone, an expert on the dangerous business of lime-slaking; Dr Jono Prosser, psychiatrist; Susan North of the V & A; Roy Figgis, who advised on period lighting; my sister-in-law, Mary Rowlands-Pritchard, for peace and solitude in Calmynsy. Thank you to all of those who offered help with early drafts of the book – even if your input didn't make the final cut, it was all of enormous help. And to Stephanie Norgate and all the tutors on the MA in Creative Writing at the University of Chichester – thank you so much, all of you! My debt to you all is considerable.

Several books were of great value: *Daily Life in Renaissance Italy* by Elizabeth Cohen and Thomas Cohen; *The Cardinal's Hat* by Mary Hollingsworth; *The Story of Art* by E H Gombrich; *Practical Falconry* by (the late and utterly delightful) Gage Earl Freeman; *Gender and Society in Renaissance Italy* by Judith Brown and Robert Davis; *Il* Castello *di Ferrara* by Marco Borella; *Cafaggiolo, La Villa de' Medici nel Mugello* by Mattia Tiraboschi; and *Inside the Renaissance House* by Elizabeth Currie. For advice on the painting of frescos, I spent many hours poring over the invaluable information provided on the Internet by the estate of the late Lucia Wiley. Any historical or technical errors in the novel will quite certainly be mine, and not those of any of the above authors.

If you enjoyed *His Last Duchess*, read on to find out more about how Gabrielle Kimm was inspired to write this wonderful novel, a list of discussion points and an exclusive author interview.

Exclusive Q&A with Gabrielle Kimm

How much research did you have to do for *His Last Duchess*?

A simple answer would be – a massive amount! After I had got over the initial excitement of hatching the idea for *His Last Duchess*, I remember sitting back and wondering what on earth I had started. I knew next to nothing about the Renaissance and not a lot more about Italy – there was going to have to be a monumental amount of research done if the book was going to be in any way credible. So I read and read for months before starting to write, learning about fresco-painting, sixteenth-century food, clothes, architecture, the politics and geography of the country . . . the list goes on, and the research didn't stop when I began the narrative: it has continued right the way through the writing of the book. New plot ideas continually throw up new areas of ignorance, and then new research can in turn inspire alternative plot developments. I also did a fair amount of hands-on research: I spent a day flying falcons, for instance, and passed a fascinating evening with a psychiatrist friend, analysing Alfonso. I struck up email correspondences with costume curators at the Victoria and Albert Museum; I was introduced to a historical forensics wizard who helped me set up my 'scene of crime' at the end of the book, and, perhaps best of all, I made a magical visit to Ferrara and to Cafaggiolo, which was truly inspirational for me – to be in the place where the real people had once lived, even as I was dreaming up my own version of their lives.

What made you focus on the story of Lucrezia and Alfonso in particular?

Browning's poem. I first met Browning's 'My Last Duchess' as an undergraduate, and loved it. I was fascinated by the character of the duke and found him irresistibly sinister. He seems to revere this painting of his wife, describing the '*depth and passion*' of her '*earnest glance*' with enthusiasm – but then, within a few lines of these compliments, he admits to having loathed her enough to have had her permanently silenced. The complex psychology behind these contradictory stances fascinated me; I wondered whether the duke's description of his wife's thoughtless and promiscuous flirtatiousness could possibly be trustworthy. Could I believe anything said by such an apparently amoral character? What had the duchess *actually* been like? Were her husband's accusations justified, or were they merely the misperceptions of a damaged mind?

I don't know exactly what it was that gave me the idea of turning these musings into a novel – all I remember is that I was listening to something entirely unconnected on the radio a few years ago, and then it was like one of those moments in cartoons where a character has a light bulb appear over their head – I just suddenly knew that turning it into a novel was what I had to do. In that instant, the basic plot and who my characters were and what the outcome of the story would be came to me. One minute the idea for the novel didn't exist and the next minute it did. It was a wonderfully exhilarating moment. The book has been through seven or eight major re-drafts since then, but the germ of that initial inspiration has remained intact throughout.

What would you most like your readers to get out of this novel?

Oh, that's a difficult question. Although *His Last Duchess* is, technically, a 'historical novel', I have always seen it as being much more character- and plot-driven than history-driven. In the end, it's a story about people who just happen to live where and when they do. So I suppose I would most like readers to empathize with my characters and to feel fully involved in their story and their world for the duration of the novel – and I hope very much that they'll enjoy what they learn about sixteenth-century Italy along the way.

Were there any things you found particularly difficult to write?
Probably some of Alfonso's scenes. Right from the start, I found it fairly oppressive spending any significant amount of time with the Duke of Ferrara. Although I found him challenging and fascinating to write, he is such a difficult, damaged man, and some of the things he thinks and says are so unpleasant and misogynistic. I frequently found that on occasions when I had spent hours intimately cooped up with him, as it were, I ended up feeling quite tense and tetchy, and on one occasion, trying to commit to paper one of his more appalling utterances, I sat with a pen in my hand for literally twenty minutes, physically unable to write what I wanted him to say.

Which authors of historical fiction do you admire?
I grew up with Rosemary Sutcliff's wonderful historical children's novels, of which my favourites were *The Queen Elizabeth Story* and *The Armourer's House*. They are charming and atmospheric and beautifully written, and have truly stood the test of time (I re-read them a few years ago with my own children and enjoyed them all over again). In terms of modern historical fiction – difficult to pick favourites, but I particularly like Rose Tremain, Sarah Waters and Sarah Dunant.

Can you tell us something about your next novel?

When I came to the end of *His Last Duchess*, I felt that I had dis-covered all I wanted to know about almost all of the characters – except Francesca Felizzi, Alfonso's long-suffering mistress. Francesca continued to intrigue me, and I began to feel that I really ought to give her some more space to develop. At the end of this book, she runs away from Alfonso and from potential trouble, and sets off for Napoli, ready to face whatever life throws at her. As I imagined her there, the idea for the second book began to burgeon. I would, I decided, set the scene some three years after the end of *His Last Duchess*; and Francesca would be forging a new career . . . as a courtesan. But fiction being what it is, of course, this was always going to be a career fraught with problems.

So is it a sequel to *His Last Duchess*?

No, not really. I suppose you could describe it more as a spin-off. Anyone who has read this book will be familiar with Francesca and her children – the twins play a much more significant part in the next book than they did in the first – and there are one or two pass-ing references to events in *His Last Duchess*, but the story does definitely stand alone.

How is it different to *His Last Duchess*?

I suppose the flippant answer would be . . . further south, and more sex! But seriously, the two books are very different in tone. The new one centres around the character of Francesca and how she experiences the complicated psychological burden of the life of a courtesan. She has had a horribly difficult past, which colours everything she thinks and does; the book begins at the point at which a chance encounter forces her to question absolutely every-thing in her life, leaving her uncertain and vulnerable. There's also a difference in that I have moved away from the noble court into the lives of working people. The cast of characters includes not just the courtesan but (among others) a university professor, a castrato soprano, a scurrilously immoral entrepreneur and a privateer.

I've divided the narrative in this book in two – Francesca narrates her own chapters, while the rest is told in the third person. This first-person narrative strand has allowed me – and will hopefully allow the reader – to experience Francesca's emotions particularly intensely. She has some difficult choices to make in the book, and allowing her to make those choices has been a very liberating experience for me as a writer.

Reading group questions

Is Alfonso beyond redemption? Or is it possible to forgive him in the light of his damaged character?

Discuss the Castello Estense as a 'character' in the book. To what extent do you think its imposing physical presence impacts on the people who live in it?

What is it about Lucrezia that renders Alfonso impotent, when he so clearly has such a vigorous sexual appetite elsewhere? Discuss his relationships with the various women in the book – Lucrezia, Francesca and Agnese de Rovigo. What do you think the liaison between Alfonso and Agnese was like while it lasted?

Why do you think Lucrezia and Jacomo were so quickly drawn to each other? How do you imagine their life unfolding beyond the end of the book? Will they be good for each other?

If you could pick just three words to describe Alfonso's character, what would they be and why?

And Lucrezia – which three words would best sum up the last duchess, do you think?

To what extent in the novel can you see the influence of the Robert Browning poem that originally inspired it?